Sweet Wattle Creek

KAYE DOBBIE

OTHER BOOKS BY AUTHOR

THE BOND
THE DARK DREAM
WHEN SHADOWS FALL
WHISPERS FROM THE PAST
FOOTSTEPS IN AN EMPTY ROOM
COLOURS OF GOLD
SWEET WATTLE CREEK
MACKENZIE CROSSING
WILLOW TREE BEND
THE ROAD TO IRONBARK

**Also books previously written as
Deborah Miles**

A PASSING FANCY
SWEET MARRY ANNE
JEALOUS HEARTS

*For my mother, thank you
for sharing your memories.*

CHAPTER I

SOPHIE

Sweet Wattle Creek, 1986

A RECTANGULAR BROWN CARDBOARD box was sitting on the top step of the *Herald* offices when I arrived at work. I picked it up awkwardly—it was about a metre long—and unlocked the door, and I was immediately caught up in the overwhelming smells of oil and ink that were emanating from the old press.

The *Herald* was Sweet Wattle Creek's one and only newspaper and it came out once a week. Tim's grandfather, the famous Bill Shaw (that was how everyone in town spoke about Bill Shaw, always with 'famous' at the front), had started it in the late nineteenth century, and sometimes I wondered how Tim kept it going. I knew he saw it as a legacy. So many other small newspapers had had to close down or amalgamate and yet the *Herald* remained. The townspeople were supportive of their rag—there was always something of local interest that everyone wanted to read. Tim occasionally had a rant about world politics, but mostly what he had to say in the newspaper was relevant to the nine hundred and sixty-two people who lived in the town, and the roughly two thousand and five hundred people who lived in the surrounding district.

Sweet Wattle Creek was situated in the flat and dry country of northern Victoria, before you hit the Murray River. The majority of farmers were running sheep or cropping, or keeping dairy cows. Some of the families had been here forever, although there were incomers, too, moving into the new housing on the edges of the town. Interest rates were high and the lower prices in Sweet Wattle Creek had brought in a few new residents from Riverton as well as further afield. But even so, the town was still small enough that you couldn't walk down the main street—which funnily enough is called Main Street—without coming to a stop every few moments for a chat with familiar faces.

I wasn't exactly a 'local'. Me and my son, Dillon had been here in Sweet Wattle Creek for almost a year—we'd chosen it from a map of Victoria, a state we felt was far enough away from Brisbane to be out of harm's way. I suppose I liked the name, it had a welcoming ring, and the fact that it was small. It was slowly beginning to feel like home. I felt calmer, I really did, and Dillon was settling in at the region's high school, which was in Riverton, about thirty miles away—forty-eight kilometres that is, but even after all these years using the metric system was slow to take off in the country. So far all was good.

We were safe and well and we were getting our lives back on track.

I walked past the ancient printing press, its metal workings silent. Brad, Tim's apprentice, was fiddling with something. The machinery was a constant source of frustration to him.. 'Do you think he'll ever get something more modern?' he muttered gloomily. I gave him a sympathetic pat on the head. Ellie, our ad sales person and general dogsbody, hadn't come in yet. I noted her small bottles of nail varnish, neatly lined up on her desk from black to metallic blue, as I exited through the door into my small office. Placing the cardboard box onto the desk, I tried to ignore the mess that I seemed to have created and never had time to tidy.

My wall calendar had a big black circle around tomorrow—Tim and Brad would run the press tonight and the newspaper would be ready to go out in the morning. I needed to have everything prepared before Tim went to print. The press wouldn't be quiet then. Sometimes the whole building shook and the rattle and rumble of it could be heard all the way down Main Street.

My gaze rested once more on the cardboard box. I'd learned to be suspicious of mysterious packages and I wasn't expecting a delivery. The cardboard looked old and faded, with a tear on one corner. At least there were no kittens mewling in it. That had happened once. Someone had dumped them at the door, and I'd had to find homes for them. Of course there had been one left—wasn't there always?—and Dillon had taken one look and insisted we keep it. BC, short for Black Cat, was now huge, more lion than cat, and he could wrap Dillon around his big paw with just one plaintive meow.

With a growing sense of trepidation I lifted the lid.

Tissue paper and a faint scent of lavender. I rustled my way through and found cloth that smelt musty and appeared fragile. A garment—a dress. There was faded satin and lace and velvet. Sewn onto the cloth were diamantes and pearls. There was also a very long, matted train. An evening dress? Or might it be a wedding dress? It looked ivory rather than white, but perhaps that was simply because of the age of the garment.

Carefully, I lifted it out of the paper and held it up.

There was a lot of it. The train tangled around me, getting in the way. It seemed to be made of metres and metres of velvet trimmed with tulle, now discoloured and moth-eaten. The dress itself consisted of two tunics, satin underneath and lace in a flowery pattern on top, both of them old and frail. When I held the dress against myself I could see that the hem was scalloped, the silk hanging down beneath the lace, and looked to be around mid-calf or ankle-length—depending on how tall the wearer was of course. There was a velvet band to define the waist. At a guess the dress size was about my own, a modern twelve, perhaps even a ten, and actually it would fit me quite well.

Diamantes stuck to my clothing. Some of the pearls sewn onto the bodice fell off and clattered to the floor. The threads must be rotten. I cursed under my breath, and laying the dress back on my desk, knelt down to find the pearls. They seemed to be everywhere and I was crawling beneath the desk to capture a couple of escapees when Tim knocked and stuck his head around my door.

'What are you doing down there?'

'Someone left this on the front steps.'

I stood up, cautiously placing the runaway pearls into the box. Tim came over and peered down at the dress with a frown. He looked tired, the dark circles under his eyes clearly visible. Tim and his wife, Maureen, had a new baby, a surprise addition to what they had imagined to be their already complete family, and I suspected he wasn't entirely happy about it. A late baby could be a wonderful thing, but with the added worry of the running and viability of his newspaper, Tim was feeling overworked and overloaded. The fact they hadn't named the baby yet might be a clue, too.

'I think it's a wedding dress,' I said helpfully. 'An old one. It's really beautiful, isn't it?'

Tim looked dubious. 'It's probably meant for the guy across the road. He's working out of the library. For the Centenary Exhibition, you know? In five weeks' time, Soph.'

I twigged. The Centenary was a big thing for our little town: 1886 to 1986, A Hundred Years in Sweet Wattle Creek. The Centenary committee had hired some expert curator from Melbourne who was going to set up an exhibition in the RSL Memorial Hall, and he'd been sending out requests for items that might be of interest.

Significant and tangible memories from a hundred

years of history in Sweet Wattle Creek. That had been the wording of the request he'd asked Tim to run in the paper. I had seen him about but had yet to meet him. He sounded rather daunting, if the truth be known, the sort of man I would normally keep well away from. And he wore a suit. It was the end of January, for God's sake, and in a few days it would be February, usually the hottest month of the summer here. Everyone else was in shorts and t-shirts and Centenary man was wearing a suit.

'Why didn't they give the dress to him then? Why put it on our front step?' I asked, smoothing the satin cloth with my finger as if it was alive. I was oddly reluctant to part with it.

'I've had a few bits and bobs lately. Maybe people are in a hurry and they get confused between us and the library. I think a lot of it's junk. They're having a clean-out and think, Hey, let's get rid of Great Aunt Such-And-Such's doilies by giving them to the Centenary committee!'

'I suppose that might be it.'

He half smiled. 'Why don't you take the dress over to him? Get his comments on it? Might make a nice little paragraph for tomorrow's paper. I was going to do a proper interview with him at some point, maybe put it in the special Centenary edition, but if you want you can do it now. Give our readers a short version and then work it up for a longer piece.'

'I guess I could.' I knew I'd have to meet him eventually and it was silly to avoid the man. He was probably lovely and I was being ridiculous.

Just because he looked like Walter from a distance didn't mean he was anything at all like Walter.

'You'll be fine. He's a little odd, but I hear some of the ladies have given him a ten.'

I couldn't help but smile—Tim had that effect. 'Give me a minute to get my thoughts together. Do you want a coffee?'

'Thanks but no. Haven't got time. Is that Ellie?' He glanced over his shoulder. 'You're late.'

Ellie's voice drifted from the other room. 'One minute late and that was because I had to deliver some quotes for you!' Unfazed, she came and stood in the doorway. She was only twenty but already more sure of herself than I'd ever be. Today she was wearing a black skirt and a yellow blouse with a wide black belt around her slim waist. 'Wow, that looks awesome,' she said, seeing the dress. 'Is it yours, Soph?' Her eyeshadow was a blend of gold and pink, and her red hair was fashionably dishevelled.

'It was on the front step. Tim thinks it was meant for the Centenary.'

'Yeah. The other day someone left a box of old jam jars.'

'Work, everybody,' Tim cut our conversation short. Ellie rolled her eyes and headed for her desk, and Tim gave me a wink and followed.

Tim had been good to me and Dillon. When we arrived, probably looking pretty shell-shocked and bedraggled, he'd offered me a job writing for the *Herald*. We'd rented his house—he had a couple of properties he rented out—and he'd come around and we got talking. I said in the past I'd

written some articles for legal journals and was
hoping to write a book about my experiences
as a private detective. It was a cover story Dillon
and I had worked on, with enough truth in it to
sound plausible. My reason for leaving? A new
start after my husband's death. If said in just the
right tone of voice and with a downward glance,
it stopped any further questions cold. Tim was
convinced. He had just lost a journalist to a city
daily and was looking for a replacement, and so
far none of the applications had been suitable. He
said he was run off his feet. So I put up my hand,
expecting him to go away and try to check out
my story, which would have been tricky, or at
least think about it. But he hadn't. He'd offered
me the job on the spot and the next thing I knew
I was a reporter. He said his grandfather had liked
to give new people a chance, but the truth was
Bill was fond of strays. Maybe Tim thought I was
a stray, and maybe he'd be right. Not that I was
going to tell him that.

I made myself a tepid coffee—that was all the
old kettle would run to—and sipped it as I set
about sorting through some paperwork and
returning a phone call. My eyes kept going to the
box, though, and the wedding dress inside it, as if
it was some sort of magnet.

Eventually I gave in.

The flowery lace attached to the dress was torn
in several places, as well as coming away from the
stitching that held it to the satin beneath. The
velvet was an unusual touch, and yet I thought it
must have been beautiful. It *was* beautiful. There

was even a veil—I hadn't noticed it before. That clinched the wedding dress theory then. I reached inside the box, but I could see at once the netting was completely decayed. Falling to pieces. With a grimace I let it be.

I arranged the dress into its tissue-paper bed and closed the top. That was when I noticed there was faded writing on the lid. A name. I'd missed it in my hurry to remove it and rummage around inside. Now I saw there were in fact two names. Possibly the groom and bride.

'Charlie and Belle.'

I don't know why I spoke the names out loud, but when I did the room went very quiet, as if— and I am not usually a dramatic person—but it really was as if the past was holding its breath in anticipation.

CHAPTER 2

MARTHA

Melbourne, 1904

*M*Y *DEAREST LOVE,*
It's four o'clock on a winter's afternoon and already getting dark. Spencer Street Station is dingy and Rory isn't waiting as he promised. I haven't seen him in fifteen years and I'd forgotten that about him, how he can never be on time.

Martha was composing the letter in her head, the words she would send to her lover.

She tightened her grip on her daughter's hand in its colourful woollen mitten. Small fingers returned the pressure and big blue eyes lifted upwards, as if trying to read her thoughts. Martha smiled and was glad to see Belle smile back. At four years old her child had gone from a happy little girl to a quiet and serious one. Her smiles had become few, but when she did smile her face lit up the world around her.

Unfortunately, that world had become an uncertain place. Dangerous. Although Martha had once believed that to be impossible in Sweet Wattle Creek. Yes, there were storm clouds on the horizon and Martha knew that no matter how difficult, she must honour her promise to Belle's father. The child must go away, just for a little while, until matters calmed down.

A pigeon landed on the grimy platform and began to peck on a morsel of food someone had thrown down. Belle pointed at it and asked, in a doubtful voice, 'Nellie? Is that Nellie, Mama?'

There wasn't much in common between Nellie, their beautiful snowy-white sulphur-crested cockatoo, and this mangy creature, but Martha supposed they were both birds.

'Nellie's at home with Mr and Mrs Maxwell. Remember? And Michael.'

Belle smiled, her face lighting up again.

Michael was good with Belle. Despite the four years' age difference between them, he was always kind to her and willing to join in her little-girl games. And the Maxwells were upright people, even if they were too strict with the boy. But for that very reason she couldn't tell them the truth. They would turn their backs on her.

Anxiously she looked about. Trolleys of luggage rumbled along the station platform, and the steam train hissed impatiently. Everybody seemed to know where they were going and were looking forward to getting there. She watched a woman draped in furs strut past, her small dog cradled in her arms, her entourage following. Martha settled her own fox fur about her throat, telling herself she was just as good as anyone here. That's what they told you in Australia, that there was no one better than anyone else.

It was a lie, of course. Australia, and Sweet Wattle Creek, had its social hierarchies and social mores. Her family, the Bartholomews, had been pillars of the community, and Martha herself was a respectable married woman. But married women didn't have children to men who weren't their husbands.

It's only for a short while, she reminded herself, repeating the words, as if repetition would make them true. *Belle will be home again soon.*

'Mama?' The husky little voice interrupted her thoughts and her hand was tugged. 'Mama!' Martha followed the direction of her daughter's gaze and saw a tall man approaching, his dark hair the same shade as her own.

She knew it was Rory and yet, just for a moment, she found herself looking at him as if they were strangers. A handsome man of middle height but solid, and with the famous Bartholomew soulful black eyes. He was smiling at her as if he also was glad to see her, and in that instant she realised how very much she had missed her older brother since he'd shaken the dust of their small town off his shoes.

No handshakes or cool cheek kisses for Rory. It was either all or nothing for him, he hadn't changed in that, and now he caught her in his arms and hugged her tight. Martha pressed her nose into the wool of his coat and breathed in his cologne and hugged him back. It was only when he released her that she noticed the changes in his thirty-four-year-old face. The signs of maturity. And grief.

She squeezed his hand. 'I'm so sorry about

Poppy.'

He nodded, all the light leaving his dark eyes, and then he looked down at her daughter. Belle stared up at him, her head so far back that her hat slipped off. The scar on her smooth forehead was still raised and pink, although thankfully the cut, while deep, was healing.

Rory touched it gently, raising his eyebrows at Martha.

'The witch did that,' Belle said confidingly.

'The witch, was it?' Rory smiled.

Belle smiled back. With those icy fair curls and blue eyes, she was as unlike her mother and uncle as any child could possibly be.

Doubts swamped me, my love. I thought I could still change my mind despite my promise. I could still take Belle home. That was when Rory bent down and swung her up into his arms. He held her at eye level and she was dazzled, just as he's dazzled every other female who crossed his path.

'I believe you've come to stay, Belle,' my brother said, and he gave me a look that held a question in it. 'I just know you'll like Melbourne so much that you'll never want to leave again. That's what happened to me.'

I found myself nodding and smiling back at him, but my mouth felt stretched and wobbly, and my eyes were so full of tears I couldn't see. It's for the best, I told myself, it really is for the best. But oh, my dear, my heart was breaking.

CHAPTER 3

BELLE

New Year's Eve 1930–31,
St Kilda, Melbourne

BELLE BARTHOLOMEW PAUSED outside the door of the downstairs salon. Inside, the party was well under way. The musicians she had hired for the evening had been a great success, and even Henry, her father's usually staid solicitor and business partner, was dancing his own awkward version of the charleston.

Henry Collier was also Belle's fiancé, a comfortable agreement of longstanding. Sometimes Belle thought that to Henry, nearly fifteen years her senior, the idea of a wife was a pleasant daydream rather than something he felt inclined to progress to the next stage. She was just as bad, always telling herself there was no hurry to walk down the aisle.

The canapés and champagne probably contributed to the good cheer—loud voices were drowning out 'Puttin' on the Ritz'—but there was a sort of desperation in the air tonight.

She'd seen the same thing when the war had ended, people wild to put the turmoil of the past behind them. This time it was the aftermath from the stock-market crash in New York and the world sliding inexorably into a financial depression. She'd recently seen the queues—the one outside the soup kitchen stretched for blocks—and heard whispered stories of businesses drowning in a tide of bad debts.

Not that they talked about such things in the circles the Bartholomews moved in, where most of them barely felt a ripple, but Belle couldn't help noticing that St Kilda was getting seedier by the day. Those with the money to do so left for the new outer suburbs, and those without money moved in, seeking cheaper accommodation. Large houses like her own were being turned into lodgings, street by street, and the inevitable seemed to be creeping closer. But still her father refused to join the exodus. Why, he demanded, should he go to Glen Iris when he had a perfectly good house here?

Belle wondered if that was entirely the truth. Rory was a clever man, and recently he'd become adept at keeping his worst fears to himself. Belle, who'd never had to worry about anything money-wise, found herself lying awake at night, consumed by this new and faceless terror.

Her anxious gaze searched the room and found her father, as usual smiling and chatting as if he hadn't a care in the world.

Rory Bartholomew was the sort of man others were drawn to. He had a glow about him, a charm, a charisma. Looking at him now you would think he was completely unaware of the state of the world, or at least if he was then his boundless optimism would be enough to overcome any obstacles in his path.

Belle knew that wasn't true. The certainty she'd always felt about her father and her life had recently begun to shift and shake. It was as if she was having difficulty keeping her balance.

A few weeks ago she'd come upon him standing in the garden, staring at nothing, a cigarette turning to unsmoked ash in his fingers. He'd seemed pensive and sad. Belle had asked him what was wrong.

'A blue day,' he'd said with a shrug. 'I seem to have the megrims, Belle. You know what I'm like when I'm in one of my moods. I need cheering up.'

She hated her father's melancholy states. When she was a child she could remember her mother, Iris, whispering to her that they must not make any loud noises to upset him. Well Iris was gone and Belle was no longer a child.

'I can't cheer you up if you won't tell me what's worrying you, Father. I read the newspapers. Is it the business? Is Bart Homes in trouble?'

He'd looked at the cigarette in his hand as if he didn't remember lighting it, and then he'd tossed it aside. 'People aren't buying new houses,' he'd said. 'In particular, they aren't buying Bart Homes. That new development we put up? Most of the houses are still sitting there empty. People are scared. They think they might lose their jobs, or find they can't pay for what they already have. It's up to me to persuade them to think differently. I don't want us caught up in this circus.'

He hadn't sounded his loud, confident self—a persona he wore like a coat even when privately he was down in the dumps—and in that moment she'd understood why. He was worried about the business.

'You don't think —' she'd begun tentatively, hardly knowing how to frame the next question. He wouldn't let her finish.

'It'll turn around. I've seen this before. In the last depression everyone was full of doom and gloom, and we came through it. We'll get through it this time. People will have to buy houses, they have to live somewhere, Belle. I don't intend to go back to inhabiting a cave like my ancestors and I doubt anyone else will, either.' He'd smiled as he'd said it but he'd avoided meeting her eyes.

'You will tell me if things get worse?' she'd said, refusing this time to be comforted. 'You mustn't keep it to yourself.'

'We might lose the cottage at Sorrento.' He'd blurted out the words, as if he couldn't hold them back.

She'd been so shocked that she'd almost been unable to hide it from him. Their little place by the sea! Iris had chosen the furnishings and decorated it with such love. Whenever she went there to stay Belle felt close to Iris, who'd died tragically five years ago. The week after the funeral, Belle had built a little memorial in the garden, silly really, but it had made her feel better.

'I'm sorry, Belle,' he'd said, 'I know how much the cottage means to you.'

She'd shaken her head. 'No. That is, yes, of course it means something to me, but the cottage isn't as important as our home, is it? And I've read some people are losing everything. If the cottage has to go, then of course it must.'

He'd smiled—that wide Bartholomew smile her mother used to say made her fall instantly in love with him and want to marry him, despite her family's objections. Her parents had still been alive then and they'd called him 'the boy from the bush', and said he wasn't good enough for the only child of a Melbourne middle-class family with aspirations—there had been twin boys who had died at birth in London, before they emigrated. But Iris had been determined and they'd married and managed twenty-seven years of happiness before she died.

'Should we cancel the New Year's Eve party?' Belle had asked hesitantly.

He'd cried out in mock dismay. 'What? After you've worked so hard?' And then his face had softened in a smile. 'Not at all, my dear. We'll go ahead and enjoy ourselves, and who knows, perhaps by then I'll have some good news to share.'

'Will you come inside?' she'd asked, reaching out her hand. Although he'd taken her fingers in his and squeezed them, he'd said he would stay a while longer. She'd left him there by the roses.

Now here he was, their party in full swing, dancing a foxtrot as if he hadn't a care in the world. He hadn't said any more about the business and Belle hadn't asked. Perhaps in her heart she was afraid to. All last week Henry was coming and going, and they'd been closeted together in the office, but he hadn't told her what they were discussing. To be honest, she hadn't wanted to know. After the party, she'd promised herself. I'll deal with the bad news after the party.

'Belle, come and dance!' Her father had seen her in the doorway and was making his way through the crowd towards her.

'I have two left feet,' Belle retorted. 'And someone has to make sure there's enough food to feed everyone.'

She couldn't help but think how smart he looked in his dark suit, his bow tie not quite as neatly tied as it had been, his dark hair rumpled. Bartholomew hair, he called it. The dark, almost black colour, that Belle hadn't inherited.

He reached her and grabbed a champagne cocktail from a passing tray, handing it to her. 'Enjoy yourself, Belle. Come on. I want you to.'

He was flushed, his dark eyes bright and glittering. She made herself smile back. 'I am. I will.' She was no party girl, and never had been. Belle was the practical one, the organised one, the one people came to when they needed sensible advice. People relied on Belle and if sometimes it was a burden mostly it gave her a reason to be.

Her father was talking. A rambling sort of conversation.

'I don't know if you know quite how much I appreciate you, Belle. After your mother died . . . well, I couldn't have managed without you. The house . . . you took on everything like the trooper you are. Never complained.'

Belle had been the obvious choice to fill her mother's shoes—she'd been running things for years, really, ever since she was eighteen. Her sweet, gentle mother was not the most effective housekeeper. Brought up in a wealthy mercantile family, she'd been prepared to be decorative rather than sensible. In their early marriage Rory hadn't had the finances to pay for any help, nor would he take it from his in-laws, and although they had servants off and on in the later years, recently he'd taken to employing them only when they were throwing a party or entertaining guests. It didn't matter to Belle; she managed perfectly well on her own.

If at any time Rory had shown an interest in marrying again, Belle might have been able to spread her wings—after all, she was twenty-five when her mother died—and since the war there were plenty of women to spare. Rory had always been the sort of man women were drawn to, and although Belle suspected he might have had a fling or two, he'd never shown any intention of replacing Iris.

'I've been selfish.' The sound of his voice tugged her back to the party. He took a gulp of his champagne. He'd had too much to drink and—Belle breathed a sigh of relief—he was having one of his highs. Of course, that was it. He was tiddly and the blue mood had given way to a giddy one.

'How have you been selfish?'

He looked almost guilty. 'I didn't give you the chance to make a life of your own. I know there was Charlie, and afterwards, well . . . You're such an oasis of calm, Belle. After Iris died, when everything seemed so impossibly insane and . . . broken, you were the only one able to fix it. Good old commonsense Belle. Honestly don't know what I would've done without you.'

'It was my choice,' she reminded him. After Charlie went to war and didn't come home, she'd been like an injured animal, and dedicating herself to running the home for her parents had been the perfect way to hide and lick her wounds. And they'd been so flatteringly grateful, which was very seductive. It gave her a reason not to step outdoors and face the world. Then Henry had asked her to marry him and it had seemed a perfect solution for both of them, and as they were in no hurry to book the church, she'd stayed on with her father.

'Belle? Will you promise me that you'll be happy?'

His words were spoken in a dreamy way that startled her. She frowned. 'Daddy, I don't understand what you're asking me to do,' she said, the childhood name slipping out without her realising it. 'Of course I'll be happy. Henry and I will marry and we'll be happy.'

'I know Henry is a good chap but . . . You don't smile like you used to, Belle. Do you really love him? As much as I loved Iris? As you loved Charlie?'

Deliberately she laughed. To love someone as much as she'd loved Charlie was not something she'd been looking for when she'd agreed to marry Henry. 'You're a fine one to talk. I didn't see you rushing down the aisle after Mother passed away. And Henry is exactly what I want at my time of life.'

'Your time of life? Oh, Belle, you're young!'

'Thirty is *not* young. And women are different now. The war changed us. We don't need to marry to feel as if we're completing our lives. Henry and I will be a partnership.'

It sounded cold and organised, and she didn't mean it to. Belle was genuinely fond of Henry, but for reasons she didn't want to explore her father was making her feel frustrated and worried and even a little trapped.

'I wish I'd taken you to visit Martha.' He spoke again in that odd dreamy way. 'I know she said it wasn't safe but —'

'Martha?' She must have looked blank.

'At The Grand. At Sweet Wattle Creek. Martha, my sister.' His dark eyes were hard and intent.

'I didn't know you had a sister!' She felt shocked and hurt that he'd never mentioned Martha. In fact, he never spoke of any of his family, or if he did it was in a general way, and she'd assumed they were all dead. Part of the reason for his reticence was Iris's posh background—Rory was rather a snob, and he was uncomfortable with his own inferior circumstances. Had she been wrong? Was there something else at the heart of her father's reserve?

'I told you I was selfish,' he murmured, and to her dismay she saw tears in his eyes, before he blinked and they vanished. She touched his arm, and, as if he understood then that he'd frightened her, his face slipped back into his customary smile and he said, 'No need to worry about it now.'

'But you just said . . .'

'Too much champagne.' He laughed. 'Don't mind me, Belle.'

And then he turned and was gone.

'Belle!'

Belle was debating whether to go after her father. His words and his strangeness had stirred up doubts inside her, but although she was worried she wasn't sure what she was going to say to him if she did manage to extract him from the wildly dancing crowd. Later, she told herself, as she turned to smile at Charlie's mother. She would deal with Rory after everyone had gone home.

Mrs Nicholson was a striking woman. Not petite and feminine, but tall and angular and eye-catching. She made the most of her appearance, having her hair cut in a way that shortened her long face, her eyebrows impeccably plucked and her lips painted. Unless you stood close and looked hard, you'd never know she was nearly sixty.

'The dress fits perfectly,' she told Belle, her gaze sweeping over the cream tulle cocktail gown. 'I like the rose,' she added.

Belle reached up to touch the red silk rose in her fair hair. 'You don't think it's a bit much?'

'Not at all. A little flair is always a good thing,

Belle. I like your hair cut short like that. The colour is so pale . . . it's almost silver.'

'Father said the cocktail dress was from your latest collection.' Rory had also said it was a well-deserved gift for all the work she'd put into the party. Belle expected it had been horridly expensive because most of Mrs Nicholson's exclusive creations were. Suddenly, she was worried about spending too much money, something that would never have occurred to her before.

Mrs Nicholson pulled a face. 'It may be my *last* collection. Times are tough, Belle. The Collins Street shop doesn't get nearly as many customers as it used to. Even my rich and feckless clients are cutting back on their spending. *Very* inconsiderate of them.'

Seeing Belle's serious expression, Mrs Nicholson rallied a smile. 'Nothing I can do but wait and see, I suppose.'

Someone bumped into them and the champagne cocktail Belle was holding sloshed over the side of the glass, almost onto her new frock. The woman, one of Iris's old friends and decidedly tipsy, settled her fur wrap more securely around her shoulders, sending up a gust of Arpege, and ventured back into the fray.

'We have quite a crowd,' Belle said, raising her voice above the noise.

Mrs Nicholson sipped her cocktail and idly perused the room. 'I feel a tad guilty enjoying myself. The line at the soup kitchen gets longer every day. Rather confronting to see so many desperates.'

'Yes.' Belle knew Mrs Nicholson to be a compassionate woman.

'I do wonder how Rory's business is holding up, but he won't talk to me about it.'

'He won't talk to me either,' Belle admitted reluctantly. It wasn't a subject she could discuss without feeling disloyal, not before she'd spoken with her father. 'Will you stay and watch the fireworks? There'll be dancing on the lawn afterwards.'

'Will you and Henry dance?' Charlie's mother asked with a keen look.

Belle shook her head. 'Henry doesn't dance. Well, not usually,' she added, with a doubtful glance at the crowd in the smoky salon. Did Mrs Nicholson want the same thing as Rory? For her to be wildly in love? Because that was the sort of love they both believed in. Except to fall in love like that one needed a heart that was intact and now, at thirty, Belle's wasn't. She didn't look at things in the same way she had when she was seventeen and anything seemed possible. She wasn't even sure she believed in love anymore, not that sort of love anyway.

'Perhaps I'll dance when the clock strikes midnight.' Belle quickly shrugged away the doubt in Mrs Nicholson's eyes, and then excused herself, saying she had things to do.

And she did have things to do, but irritatingly her thoughts began to turn back. Mrs Nicholson had struck a chord and now it reverberated down the years. She remembered dancing with Charlie in 1917, shortly before she'd seen him off on the boat that was to take him away from her. It had been a waltz called 'Destiny', the hit of the day. She remembered the feel of him in her arms, young and strong and full of life. They'd come home that night flushed and happy and certain that everything would be all right. For how could it not be? Belle was only seventeen and Charlie not much older. He'd promised her he would come back and marry her. He'd sworn to her that nothing and no one would keep them apart.

Her steps slowed as the noise from the party waxed and waned. She had intended to go to the kitchen, to see how the champagne was holding out, but now she wanted to be alone. With a guilty backward look, Belle made a right turn up the stairs, her steps quickening as if she was running away from something.

George Lambert's portrait of her mother hung in the recess at the top of the landing. In typical Edwardian fashion, Iris Bartholomew was seated on a chaise lounge with her glossy brown hair coiled at her nape, a fingertip beneath her chin and an enigmatic smile on her lips. Forever elegantly beautiful.

It was a silly way to die, really. Iris, in a daydream as usual, crossing the road and being knocked down by a man in a brand-new Ford motor car.

She had lived long enough for them to reach the hospital. Belle had held her hand. 'Poppy?' she'd said, peering up, waxy-faced. 'Is that you, my dearest child? But you're dead, you've been dead for years and years, and Belle is here now.'

'She's delirious.' Rory had looked so distraught

that although Belle had wanted to ask who Poppy was she hadn't felt able to.

When she was a child Belle had believed her father capable of all things wonderful. He was exuberant, always ready for a laugh and a game, and she loved him. If he had his other side, the melancholy side, then it was just accepted as part of the whole. Since Iris had died, though, he seemed more inclined to the blues. When was the last time she had seen him happy, truly happy, rather than playing a part?

Upstairs, Belle could still hear the music and the loud voices of their guests. Soon she must give the order for the fireworks, to bring in 1931 with a bang, and then the party would go on outside, and the guests would dance and drink until they'd had enough and decided to go home. Not that she was holding her breath. Parties at the Bartholomews' tended to go on until dawn.

Her room was like a sanctuary. She stood a moment, leaning back against the closed door, and breathed out a huge sigh of relief. Her head was spinning from her one glass of champagne and she knew she should have eaten something, but she'd wanted the new dress to fit her properly. The shoes she was wearing were new as well, cream to match the dress, with a nice heel, and for colour there was the red silk rose in her hair.

She touched it now. Rory was so dark and Iris had had soft brown locks and tea-brown eyes. Mrs Nicholson had said Belle's hair was silver, and she was often told it was the colour women aimed for when they peroxided their locks. Except that

Belle's shade was natural and strikingly different from her parents'.

Perhaps her father's sister, Martha, was fair-haired and blue-eyed and practical like Belle? Why on earth hadn't she known about her aunt? Was it really because her father was ashamed of his background? Or was there more to it—a mystery that wanted solving? Belle supposed that if anyone could solve it then she could.

There was plenty of time. She would talk to him tomorrow and insist on hearing the whole story, not just the bits he wanted to tell her.

Charlie's photograph no longer sat on the table by her bed. She'd put it away in the drawer when she and Henry had got engaged. Now something—perhaps the conversation with Mrs Nicholson—prompted her to fetch it. She looked at his young—too young—serious face that seemed on the verge of a smile. The flop of brown hair across his brow and his long fingers clasping his new gloves. Charlie as she'd known him. But that Charlie, the Charlie she had kissed goodbye as he went off to war, was gone forever.

Mrs Nicholson had said she'd felt as if something inside her had stopped when Charlie didn't come home. Belle had felt the same thing herself, like a clock unwinding and slowing down, and then only empty silence. Charlie's death had taken away all her joy in life and she had never really regained it.

Or was that overly dramatic? With her father's pendulum-like moods and her mother with her head in the clouds most of the time, someone had had to be the capable one. Belle had no time for dramatics.

She walked to the wardrobe and opened the doors and took out the box. Inside, carefully stored amongst tissue paper and lavender bags for the moths, was a dress. A wedding dress. *Her* wedding dress.

'You don't want to rush things,' she remembered Mrs Nicholson saying. 'You can have a proper wedding if you wait, and I'll make you a dress that'll be the envy of every other bride.'

Belle didn't need to take out the dress to remember what it looked like. Other wartime brides had worn day suits or hand-me-downs, but Belle's dress had been the height of fashion, just as Mrs Nicholson had promised. Satin with exquisitely patterned machine-made lace over the top. The train was velvet, a blush pink, to match the waistband, and the dress itself was ivory. Diamantes sparkled and pearls glowed, and Belle knew she would have worn it like a princess with Charlie, her prince, at her side.

But it was not to be.

When she became engaged to Henry she had made up her mind that she would not wear this dress. Not because it was dated, she didn't care about that, but it would not have felt right. No, she'd wear something else when she married Henry.

Deliberately, Belle shook off her sad thoughts. She slid Charlie's photograph back into the drawer and returned the dress to its shelf in the wardrobe and closed the doors with a snap.

There! She'd allowed herself her little journey into the past. Now it was time to return to the party and be level-headed, sensible Belle again. She was sure no one had thought to refill the glasses or set out more food or even offer the musicians something to keep them going.

There was a loud noise downstairs. Fireworks? They weren't due to start yet. Irritably, still feeling out of sorts, Belle wondered if anyone could get anything right without her. A brief glimpse at the mirror, checking to see her face was still presentable and her hair in its style, reminded her again of the family mysteries.

She touched the small scar on her forehead, barely visible but she could always feel the faintly raised line of it. Rory couldn't remember how it happened, he'd told her. Her nose was too big. Why couldn't she have inherited her mother's neat little nose? It was a Bartholomew nose, her father informed her whenever she complained, just like his. Was it Martha's nose? She really must find out tomorrow.

Belle closed her door and started back along the corridor. She realised she could no longer hear the music, and the voices from the guests were much louder. That was strange. Then, just as she reached the stairs, somebody screamed, before the sound was quickly muffled.

Belle began to run, following the sounds as they grew louder and more erratic. Afterwards she didn't remember pushing through the well-dressed crowd in the doorway to her father's study. All the familiar faces, now strangers to her.

Someone tried to catch her arm, their fingers tearing a flounce on her new dress as she pulled away. She was inside the room now and her gaze slid over the same old English hunting prints on the wall—they'd hung there ever since she could remember, brought to Melbourne from London by Iris's parents—and the smell of the leather armchairs and cigar smoke, mingled with the woody scent of Rory's cologne.

There was another smell, metallic and nasty.

Henry was standing in front of her. He was blocking her view of the desk, and she stepped to the side and around him, so that she could see what everyone was looking at.

It was Rory. He was slumped over his desk, the pistol he'd had since the war lying loosely in his hand, and bright-red blood pooling around his dark hair. Her first thought was that the blood was all over his papers and how would he ever get it out? Her second . . . that no one could survive such an injury. Because now she could see there was so much blood, so much.

Belle didn't hear herself cry out, only knew that Henry was clutching at her, pressing her face against his chest so that all she could smell now was musty wool, and then she was stumbling blind as he bundled her outside the room.

She pulled away from him, gasping, dizzy. 'Henry?'

'He's killed himself,' someone said, one of those business associates, and the voice was familiar although Belle seemed unable to put a name to it. Her mind was fragmenting, everything coming at her in quick bright flashes, like scenes from a silent movie.

She wanted someone to reassure her that everything was all right. That her father wasn't really dead from his own hand and life would go on as usual. But it wouldn't. It couldn't.

Through the cotton wool in her head she heard whispers of 'Bankrupt', 'Things in a bad way' and 'Bank foreclosing'. A warm arm slid about her waist.

'Belle, my dear.' Mrs Nicholson's face was pale beneath her makeup, her hazel eyes—they were Charlie's eyes—reflecting Belle's pain. 'I can hardly believe it. I'm so sorry.' Her voice trembled but her arm remained steady, and she led Belle into the salon where moments before their party had been in full swing. Where were the musicians? And the staff she'd hired for the occasion. And all the food yet to be eaten, and the fireworks she'd wanted to be perfect . . .

Belle choked on a sob.

'Oh my poor dear,' murmured Charlie's mother, and held her close.

Belle hung on tightly, but a large part of her felt as if she was somewhere else, as if life had stopped, just as the tram at the end of Annat Street did every half hour. Sitting there, waiting, before it lurched forward again. In a moment of clarity Belle knew that although her life would move forward again, it would never be the same.

The unexpected explosion of fireworks and the chiming of bells filled the air. Bewildered, she asked what it meant.

'The new year is in,' Mrs Nicholson said, her voice husky with tears. 'Oh, Belle, it's 1931.'

CHAPTER 4

SOPHIE

Sweet Wattle Creek, 1986

THE LIBRARY WAS small and crowded. I stood for a while, trying to decide whether to march up to the counter and interrupt Nola and the formidable woman she was serving, or go in search of the man himself. Alternatively, I could turn around and go back across the road and let Tim handle it.

I tightened my grip on the cardboard box, telling myself not to be such a coward, just as Nola looked up and caught my eye. No escape now. I went over to the counter, smiling in a placating way at the frowning book-borrower.

Nola was head librarian, in fact the only librarian, although she did make use of some of the unemployed youth from time to time, training them in book stamping and tidying the shelves. She was very community-minded, always thinking up new ways of bringing people together. She'd tried to interest me in her Tuesday evening poetry classes but so far I'd managed to find excuses. I wasn't against poetry, far from it, but I'd found it was better not to get too comfortable with my surroundings.

'Hi, Nola. I was looking for Mr, eh, the curator from Melbourne.'

'McKinnon. Ian,' Nola said helpfully, with a slight pink tinge to her plump cheeks. 'He's over at the RSL Memorial Hall.'

I thanked her and turned on my heel, wondering if Nola was one of the local ladies who gave Ian McKinnon a mark of ten.

The RSL Hall was on the far side of a little park and it was a nice day to take a stroll. The grass was green and an enormous pepper tree offered shade, where one of Nola's recruits was taking a break, sitting on a bench, smoking. The solemn statue of a First World War soldier oversaw my progress across the sprinkler-damp grass, the plinth he stood on carved with the names of all the Sweet Wattle Creek boys who had died in two world wars.

The door to the hall was propped open and I could hear someone moving about inside. I climbed the broad steps. There wasn't a great deal of light from the high windows and the electrical bulbs were obviously low wattage. I could see Ian McKinnon halfway up a ladder attaching a large board to the wall. The board itself was covered in what appeared to be maps.

'Hello?'

He turned his head. The ladder wobbled and he caught hold of the rung to steady himself. Luckily, the board was already secured on the wall. 'Yes?'

Did he sound like Walter? Not really. I took a

couple of steps inside.

They *were* maps. I could see now that the first one was of the district of Sweet Wattle Creek before settlement and then there was a plan of the town, with parcels of land named for the settlers who had bought them, and then the progression went on to the final map, the present-day town that I knew.

'Is that for me?'

I'd been staring so intently at the maps I hadn't noticed him climbing down. He was looking at the box, still clasped in my arms, and for some reason I held it a little tighter.

Ian McKinnon wasn't quite what I was expecting. He was probably in his early to mid-thirties, and today he'd taken off his suit jacket and rolled up his shirtsleeves. He was still wearing a tie, but his tawny hair was untidy and a little long, and he was tall and on the thin side.

He didn't look like Walter after all. Walter was shorter, more compact, his hair a smooth, dark cap, and Ian McKinnon's eyes might be brown but there was none of the judgemental stare I had learned to dread from my ex-husband. Instead, he was beginning to appear concerned.

'Are you all right?'

My mouth lifted in a half-smile. 'Sorry. This is for you. Tim thinks someone put it on our steps at the *Herald* by accident. Must be a donation for the Centenary.'

He reached for the box. I let go and he nearly dropped it, juggling with it for a moment before he had it secure. He turned around and nearly ran into the ladder, side-stepping just in time. None of this seemed to faze him, as if he was used to it. I watched him carry the box over to a long trestle table against the far wall and set it down.

'I think it's a wedding dress,' I added belatedly.

He glanced at me over his shoulder, and then turned back to the box. I saw him begin to remove the lid and then stop to read the writing on top. He was certainly more observant than me.

'Come and look,' he said.

I shouldn't, I knew I shouldn't, and yet I found myself moving over to the table and standing at his side. Suddenly I was aware of the smell of his cologne, which was subtle compared to Tim's Old Spice. He must be over six foot tall and I reached his shoulder. I'd always liked tall men.

'Hmm.' He was humming as he held aside the tissue paper, taking in the fabric and the state of it. Unlike me he didn't pounce on the contents and lift them out.

'I was thinking it could be a wedding dress,' I offered for the second time. 'An old one.'

'Might be from the 1920s.'

I looked at him with respect. 'You can tell that already?'

His eyes met mine. He was amused. 'I could be wrong. I won't take it out until I get back to the library. I'm worried about those pearls. They look as if they might fall off.'

I leaned forward, pretending to examine where his finger was pointing, and hoping he wouldn't sense my guilty conscience.

'Do you know who left it?' he said, and put

the lid back on again. His hands were big but his fingers were long and oddly delicate.

'No, I don't. But maybe "Charlie and Belle" is a clue?'

'Could be.'

We looked at each other. I thought I might say something more, make a silly joke, and perhaps he was thinking the same, but in the end the silence went on for too long.

'Well. I'll leave you to it, then.' I made a vague gesture at his ladder. I had almost reached the door when he spoke again.

'Do you want a coffee? Sorry, I should know your name. Tim's mentioned you.'

I wasn't insulted—I hadn't remembered his name either—but I did wonder what Tim had said. The coffee I should refuse. It was deadline day and I had things to do, but Tim had wanted me to speak to this man and here was a chance to get a bit of background and a decent coffee at the same time.

'Sophie Matheson.' The name no longer sounded strange. 'And I'd like a coffee, thanks. As long as you don't mind an impromptu interview. Tim wants me to do a paragraph on you for tomorrow's paper. And we'll do a special article for the magazine Tim's putting out for the Centenary day edition. For collectors.' At least, that was what Tim hoped would happen.

Ian pushed down his sleeves and straightened his cuffs, clearly uneasy with the thought of so much attention. Once again it made him human and not Walter.

Once outside he locked the door to the RSL Hall while I waited. The committee had put up posters around the town, reminding everyone—as if they could forget—that the Centenary celebrations would take place in five weeks' time. There was one on the door, showing a cheerful-looking sulphur-crested cockatoo sitting on a sprig of Sweet Wattle, and giving times and events. The program seemed ambitious, but Nola, who was on the committee, had told me it was all going nicely to plan.

Ian cleared his throat and I stared up at him from the bottom step. 'Actually, there was also a box left for me this morning.'

'Another wedding dress?'

It was a joke but he just looked confused. 'No, a bundle of letters written during the First World War.'

'So you think they'll be useful?'

'Very. I can use extracts to make up a display, or print some of them in full if they're appealing enough. You never know what people have tucked away until something like this comes up and they dig it out.'

We walked back across the park, and Ian flicked me a sideways look. He had pulled on his suit jacket and now he smoothed some creases. He must be cooking, but I thought I knew why he was wearing it. Not because he was a professional from Melbourne, but because he was shy and his suit was his armour. I recognised the affliction. I'd done enough interviews to have learned the signs of the sort of people whose every word had to be dragged painfully from them. Unless they had an interest. A hobby. Something that fired them up. I was hoping that would be Ian McKinnon.

'You're from Melbourne?' I started off.

'Yes. I was driving back and forth but now I have a place to stay.'

'So you're living here?'

'Yes. For now anyway. After the Centenary I'll be gone again.'

Well, that wasn't too difficult.

'The Centenary's a big thing for Sweet Wattle Creek,' I said.

The town itself was surveyed in 1886, a few years after the surrounding district was opened up for selection. It was around this time that most of the settlers arrived. Of course there had been people living here before 1886—the original Aboriginal owners of the land, the squatters who were here as far back as the 1840s, and a few other early residents who blew in around the time of the gold rush. But the actual town was gazetted in 1886, a hundred years ago. Hence the Centenary.

'Tim said you were a new arrival,' Ian spoke, giving me another sideways glance. He shooed a fly away from his face. 'It might be good to have a display on newcomers as well as the families of original settlers. Get your thoughts on the place? As long as they're approved by the committee, of course.'

'Of course.'

We'd reached the cafe by now. *Keep your answers simple and change the subject.* That was what I usually did and I tried to stick to my own advice. Sometimes it was tricky not allowing people to get too close, sometimes it felt lonely, but it was much, much safer.

'My son, Dillon, wasn't doing so well in the city. He's a lot happier now. I moved for him, really.'

'And your husband?'

'He's dead.'

'I'm sorry.'

I made a non-committal sound in my throat.

He followed me inside the busy cafe. Locals were here meeting up for an early lunch and several farmers' wives were in for a gossip. Sweet Wattle Creek was the service centre for the area and places like this did very well. Although times were changing. Recently, I'd seen several new houses going up beyond the town boundaries, as farmers sold off their land to be subdivided. The general store did okay, but most people went off to Riverton once a week to do their main shop. In many ways Sweet Wattle Creek was still a small town.

Men at Work played on the radio behind the counter, and I waved at Maureen. The mirrored shelves where the glasses were stacked showed my face, thinner, more delicate, and disconcertingly unfamiliar. I'd been a plump girl and a chubby teenager, but living with Walter had made me gaunt. I'd regained some of my lost weight since the move south, but not my innocence and it showed in my wary blue eyes. After ordering, I zigzagged through the crowded room to find us a table against the wall. Ian squeezed in beside me, apologising when he bumped against someone, but there was a twinkle in his eye, as if he was enjoying himself rather than feeling uncomfortable.

Shy and a little clumsy but not antisocial, I updated my mental checklist.

People recognised us and there were some nods and smiles, but most of the cafe customers were more concerned with their food and drink. Maureen soon brought our coffees.

'How's the baby?' I asked as she set them down.

She rolled her eyes. 'I've forgotten what sleep feels like. Have you seen the bags under Tim's eyes?'

'Suitcases not bags.' The joke was an old one but she smiled. 'Have you thought of a name yet?'

'Chaos, Tim says.'

She was gone before I could respond, too busy to chat. I sipped my coffee and it was so hot and strong I might have purred. No comparison to the pathetic efforts I concocted in my office. When I looked up it was just as Ian did the same. His eyes weren't completely brown after all, they had flecks of green and gold in them.

'The gap between heaven and earth.'

I tried to follow what he was saying but the context eluded me. He noticed my confusion and his ears turned a faint pink.

'Chaos. It's Greek. It means the gap between heaven and earth.'

'Oh.' I smiled. We sipped our coffee. 'So,' I said in my best reporter voice. 'Tell me about your work. You're based in Melbourne?'

'Ah,' he set down his cup, 'is this the interview? Well, I work for a small company, just two permanent employees. Freelance. We do everything from advising government departments on keeping their archives mould-free to conserving and repairing costume collections to running exhibitions. My partner . . . her real passion is vintage clothing.'

I shouldn't have been surprised he had a partner. I *wasn't* surprised, and refused to admit to any disappointment whatsoever. He seemed rather nice to be on his own. And what was I thinking anyway, that we would have a whirlwind affair? That wasn't going to happen. Never, ever. Dillon was my number-one priority these days and it was going to stay that way.

'Ergo the wedding dress,' I said with a smile, to show just how indifferent I was to his private life. 'Will you get her to take a look at it?'

'I'll take a look myself first. It may be nothing special. But then again you never know. Places like this, out of the way, forgotten, can be a hiding place for real treasures.'

Is that how he saw Sweet Wattle Creek? Out of the way? Forgotten? I felt myself bristle on the town's behalf before I remembered that that was exactly why I was here.

'Do you want to sit in while I examine the dress?'

He took me by surprise. Did I? I knew that I did. Something about the dress had tweaked my curiosity, or perhaps it was just the two names on the cover of the box. It might make a good story. Wedding dress. I mean, come on, it had to be a romance. Perhaps even a story of love gone wrong.

'Okay. Thank you. When were you planning to examine it?'

'I have a few things on first. Tonight? I'm allowed to stay in the library as late as I like. Nola has been very good.'

I wondered if Ian read poetry.

'Say eight?'

Dillon would be home and fed by then, and I could drop him over at Tim and Maureen's. If he'd let me. My fourteen-year-old was fond of telling me that he wasn't a kid anymore.

'Okay. Eight. Can I take some photos for the newspaper?'

'I suppose. But maybe you should wait to publish them until we know more about the dress, in case the owner takes exception.'

We parted, he going back to the RSL Hall, and I returning to the *Herald* offices. I watched him walk briskly away. I had discovered some things about Ian McKinnon, and I could ask more questions tonight when I'd be sure to take notes. But I told myself it was the dress I was drawn to, not Ian.

He tripped on an uneven section of footpath, turning to give it an accusing glare, before he crossed Main Street and regained the park with a long, loping stride. When I realised I was smiling, I forced my mouth into a hard, straight line and looked away.

CHAPTER 5

BELLE

New Year's Day, St Kilda, 1931

THE DOCTOR HAD come and then the police. Henry dealt with all of them, taking charge, his normally amiable face appearing grey and sombre. A long time afterwards it occurred to Belle that the guests were all gone. She could remember Mrs Nicholson asking if Belle wanted to come home with her, but somehow it had seemed wrong to leave the house. To leave her father.

The questions went around and around in her head. Why hadn't she known what he planned to do? She should have sensed it when they had that strange conversation in the garden. His face, his eyes, the expression in them making him seem so lost and alone. She remembered how uneasy she'd been, and yet she'd let it pass. She'd walked away. And then earlier tonight, when he'd spoken about his sister, Martha . . . Now she replayed it back to herself, once, twice, going over every word, every nuance, until her head began to ache.

A shiver ran through her and she hugged herself, and it was only when her fingers brushed soft wool that she realised someone had placed a blanket about her shoulders. There was a glass of neat brandy beside her. She could taste it on her lips, in her throat, but she didn't remember drinking it. Brandy always made her feel queasy and it did now. She stumbled to her feet, almost falling. A strong hand gripped her arm, holding her upright, and when she had regained her balance she looked up and saw that it was Henry.

His familiar face seemed full of creases, new lines she hadn't noticed before, and his steel-grey hair was standing up where he'd run his hands through it.

'I'm so sorry, Belle,' he said in a tired, gravelly voice. 'If I'd known what he meant to do I would've tried to talk him out of it. We could've cobbled together some sort of deal with the banks and . . .' He waved a hand and cleared his throat.

Her uncomprehending stare must have warned him.

'He didn't tell you. Oh, Belle.'

'I don't understand. He said things were difficult but he was sure it wouldn't be for long. We were going to lose the cottage, I understood that. I—he said everyone needed somewhere to live and Bart Homes would have to start selling soon.'

Henry shook his head as if he couldn't bear to hear it. 'When he was optimistic he spoke like that but . . . I don't think even he could pretend much longer. In his heart Rory knew. The business was insolvent. You're right, he was still building houses, but no one was buying. They hadn't been for quite a while. The bank had given him limited time to get himself out of trouble and that time was up. They foreclosed. Last week he rang me to say it was over. He sounded beaten. You know Rory, he has his ups and downs, but I'd never heard him like that before.'

'Why didn't he tell me?'

Henry shook his head again, but she guessed the answer anyway.

'He was trying to protect me.' Despite what was a comfortably cushioned life, Belle read the newspapers. She knew people everywhere were losing their jobs, their homes. The country was in a depression the likes of which none of them had ever seen before, but for some reason she'd thought they would escape. Her father seemed invincible. He could fix anything, make miracles happen, she'd always believed that. Perhaps as well as protecting her, he hadn't wished to destroy her belief in him.

Henry was watching her expectantly and she had to ask him to repeat himself. 'Rory left you a note. Do you want me to read it?'

Belle glanced down to the folded paper in his hand and could see that someone already had.

'The police,' he explained apologetically.

She took the paper from him and slowly, carefully, she opened it out. Her father's sprawling, untidy writing greeted her.

Darling Belle.

Her eyes blurred, but she blinked hard and forced herself to read on.

Darling Belle. The bank is foreclosing and the stock market has been bloody. Lost everything I'm afraid, but at least the house is safe. I tried to keep everyone work-ing, kept hoping it would turn around, but it hasn't and now we're finished. So many men out of work. I think that's what I feel the most, the thought of them without anything to look forward to in these dark days ahead. I'm sorry to spoil your party, you worked so hard. I wasn't planning to be selfish. I thought that at least if I did it here you wouldn't be the one to walk in and find me, and good old Henry would be around to take charge.

The megrims won't seem to go away this time and every day is darker than the last. For a while now I've known I can't go on. I hope that one day you'll find it in your heart to forgive me.

Remember you have your life ahead of you, don't waste it feeling sad about me. I'll be with Iris.

Belle closed her eyes. She felt as if she was float-ing. Drifting further and further into the dark night. Her father was gone and she was alone.

'Belle?'

But of course she wasn't alone. There was Henry. Belle opened her eyes and saw that he was hovering anxiously over her. She cleared her throat.

'What about your share of the business? Will you lose everything, too?'

He grimaced. 'I sold it back to him. I didn't like the look of things. I know Rory used to laugh at me and call me a fuddy-duddy, but I'm naturally cautious. He was always so confident he could push through. He thought he was indestructible. I'm not like that, and when he made me an offer I took it. Belle, he knew I would've helped him in any way I could, but everywhere you look there are people going under. No one has the capital to rescue a failing business and the banks aren't lending. I know he tried to find some way out. He tried everything.'

'So you're all right.' She didn't mean it to sound like an accusation, but somehow it did.

'I'm walking a fine line.' He said it stiffly.

What was happening to the world? She didn't recognise it. Suddenly she was frightened.

'I must see to-to things.' There would be tasks to perform, lists to make, anything to keep her mind off what had happened.

He put out his hand to stop her as she passed him and reluctantly she paused. 'Belle, I'm so sorry.'

Her throat was tight and all she could manage was a nod, before she hurried from the room.

When she was seventeen Belle had wanted to marry Charlie, and then she'd had to cope with his loss. She'd withdrawn into herself, taken sanctuary. It was fair to say she hadn't ventured very far since.

I've been spoiled, Belle thought bleakly. *I've been pampered and kept safe. I hid myself away after Charlie died. And now I have to face the world again.*

She tried to stir her mind into thinking in ways she'd never had to before. Henry always said they would move into this house when they married. If worst came to worst, she supposed they might have to find somewhere smaller, less expensive.

Their engagement had been a long one, so long that her father used to tease, wondering aloud if

they'd ever tie the knot. Well they'd have to now.
With a fierce determination that seemed to have
risen to the occasion, Belle told herself that it
would be all right.

She would make it all right.

All Saints' Church was almost empty. Belle's
eyes were aching but mercifully dry as she stared
ahead at the lectern. Seated behind her were
some of the people who had known her parents,
and one or two of the older employees from Bart
Homes. But so many had stayed away. It was as
if Rory's business failure and tragic death were
somehow catching.

Beside her on one side of the pew was Henry,
head bowed, and on the other was Mrs Nicholson. Dressed in a black silk dress that looked
rather like Chanel, she was wearing a hat with
black netting that turned her face into a pale blur.
If what she had said at the party was true, then
Eileen's establishment was also in dire straits.

Belle couldn't think about that, not yet. After
the funeral Henry had said he would formally
read the will to her, and then they were to discuss
what was going to happen with the house and
what she was going to survive on now that Bart
Homes belonged to the bank and their creditors.

Belle had the feeling that she was expected to
bow her head and gratefully agree to whatever
Henry decided for her. He was more than capable, but the idea irritated her, and frightened her,

and she didn't completely understand why. There were unfamiliar feelings stirring inside her, feelings she'd kept locked away for over ten years.

She'd stood back and let events wash over her, and she'd done that for so long that now she wasn't exactly sure how to regain control of her life. Perhaps it was too late. Perhaps she would slip back into the shadows and let others take care of her. It was certainly tempting.

The sound of the church organ brought her back to the solemn occasion. The instrument was huge, and so was the church, and it seemed a shame that it was so empty. She should have chosen a smaller place to say goodbye to her father, somewhere more intimate, and yet she'd thought there would be lots of people.

Tears stung her eyes as they rose to sing a hymn—'O God Our Help in Ages Past'— one of Rory's favourites. Belle was not one to believe in a rosy heaven where everything was sweetness and light. The war had shattered any illusions she might have had that endings were inevitably happy. Nor had she followed the road of so many grieving parents and partners, searching for meaning in the murky arms of mediums and séances. Belle knew herself to be too clear-headed to believe in anything but the here and now. And yet there was comfort in the thought of her parents lying together in St Kilda cemetery, never again to be parted.

After the burial, Belle offered refreshments to those who came to express their sympathy, but barely anyone took her up. The few who came back to the house stood rigidly, with their cups and saucers balanced in one hand and pocket sandwiches in the other. Henry had found himself a glass of brandy and every now and then he would give Belle an urgent glance, as if he was keen to speak to her about the will. Surely, she thought, there was no hurry? There could be no surprises left. Could there?

When the door closed on the last of them, and the room was empty apart from herself and Henry, she breathed a sigh of relief. However, a glimpse of his serious face made her muscles tense again. There was definitely something brewing, and she knew she wasn't going to like it.

'Let's go into the sitting room,' she said, forcing a smile. 'I'll light the fire.' The day had started out sunny, but a cold front had swept in from the south-west, and now clouds covered the sky and a bitter wind rattled the window panes.

When they'd made themselves comfortable, Henry produced his briefcase and took out a sheaf of official-looking papers. Belle smoothed the skirt of her black crepe dress and eased her feet in the tight shoes—she'd worn the same outfit when her mother had died. It had seemed reckless to buy a new one in the circumstances, and Rory would have understood. She'd arranged her pale hair in finger waves, but now it felt tight and she ran her fingers through the curls, massaging her aching temples.

Belle was tired and when she looked at Henry she could see he was, too. When she had offered him a coffee and something to eat before they began, he'd refused. He'd said he wanted to get on with it and Belle couldn't help but notice how he'd discarded the role of her fiancé, as easily as taking off his coat, and slipped into that of her solicitor.

She tried not to feel hurt. Officialdom had always been easier for Henry in a crisis—a barrier to hide behind. It didn't mean he wasn't fond of her.

His voice broke the silence. 'Rory hoped the house was safe.'

Belle felt her heart stutter under the impact of his words and tried to calm herself. 'But the house *is* safe. Isn't it?'

'I thought the debts might be cleared through the sale of the business. I know that was what Rory believed. But prices have fallen sharply and Bart Homes still aren't selling quickly enough. The creditors can't wait any longer, and neither can the bank. I'm sorry, Belle. This house will have to be sold and the bank will take the proceeds.'

She looked about her, at the room with all its familiar furnishings and objects. The comfortable sofa and the armchair that had belonged to Iris's father, the trio of Dresden Shepherdesses on the mantel, the leather-bound books in the glass-fronted case and the heavy velvet curtains on the windows. Even the rug at her feet had memories and meaning, and she stared at the swirling pattern until her vision cleared again.

'Will anyone be able to afford the house? If it's to sit empty then surely it would be better for us to live here, Henry?'

'Property developers are snapping up places like this,' Henry said with another grimace to show what he thought of the breed. 'Everyone's looking for lodging rooms and a big house like this can be turned into accommodation for several families. You've seen what's happening around you, Belle. St Kilda is changing.'

Belle clenched her fists. 'I hate it. I hate what's happening. It isn't fair.'

'No, it isn't, but we have to deal with the reality of the situation.'

Belle shot him a look of actual dislike, and immediately felt guilty. Henry was doing his best, he always did, and really she was grateful. It was just . . . she felt so alone and he seemed to have stepped away. Not exactly abandoned her, of course not, he wouldn't do that, but she sensed a distinct chill in the air.

'There's something else.'

'There's more?' she whispered.

Henry was searching among his papers and now he held up an envelope. 'I found this amongst Rory's things. I must say I was surprised. I'd have thought he would've drawn my attention to it at the time.'

'What is it, Henry?'

'It's a letter from a solicitor. Rory's sister, Martha, died six months ago.' He was watching her face. 'You didn't know either?'

'Martha's dead?' She tried to gather her thoughts but she was struggling to absorb so many blows in quick succession. 'No, I didn't know. Why would he keep that from me? He spoke about her . . . at the party. Before he . . . Henry, that was the first time I'd heard her name.'

'Well, according to her solicitor, Martha left you the Bartholomew family home. In Sweet Wattle Creek.'

'Sweet Wattle Creek?' she repeated blankly. 'My father spoke of it, as well. Where on earth *is* Sweet Wattle Creek?'

'About a hundred and fifty miles north east, I'm afraid. I wish it were closer to Melbourne. But at least you now have some property that you can dispose of, hopefully for a decent amount of money, and —'

Again Belle shook her head. 'Why didn't he sell this place in Sweet Wattle Creek himself? It might've helped him pay some of his debts or the bank or —'

'He couldn't. It was left to you not Rory.'

'But I didn't even know Martha existed!'

'Neither did I. Rory rarely spoke of his background. I hunted out your father's old files and gleaned a little from them. Rory's parents were originally from Adelaide, and if there were other relatives then they stayed behind when the family settled in Sweet Wattle Creek. His father died in 1890 and his mother in 1896. All of their property went to Martha—there were only the two children. He did not endear himself to his parents by leaving home and failing to return. I had the impression that—forgive me—those times were not happy ones for him.'

Belle knew she was close to tears once again.

'I haven't finished yet. I'm sorry.'

He looked apologetic, and embarrassed. As if he was about to lead her down a road he'd have preferred not to.

'What else can there be, Henry?'

'This.'

It took her a few seconds to see that he was holding something in his hand and he had the oddest expression on his face. She looked down. It was a document, long and rectangular with creases where it had been folded in three. Reluctantly, Belle took it from him. She'd already had some dreadful shocks this evening, but the fact that Henry had saved this until last . . . Belle knew it was going to be the worst of all.

The ink was thick and official-looking, and she saw at once that it was a birth certificate. *Her* birth certificate. There was her name, Belle, and her date of birth and . . . Belle's eyes widened.

'This says that I was born in Sweet Wattle Creek.'

'Yes.'

'And my father . . .'

The section reserved for her father had been scratched out in heavy black ink. The pen responsible had torn into the paper in a couple of places. Whatever had been written there was no longer legible. The violence in the act made her feel queasy.

Her eyes skittered to the next section, to the name of her mother.

'Martha Bartholomew,' she whispered.

Belle dropped the certificate and stood up. She

had to escape. Without warning, she found she couldn't breathe and black spots were dancing in front of her eyes. Henry was looking up at her as if he didn't know what to say or do, and she didn't blame him. He was engaged to marry a woman who did not exist, and for someone who liked order as much as Henry, it must feel very disturbing.

'Excuse me,' she said in a voice which was polite and bizarrely normal, and then she walked from the room.

Her feet took her outside and into the garden, to the same spot where she had spoken to her father only a few weeks ago. The roses were valiantly holding up their heads, and the sight lifted her heart briefly, and then let it fall again, because she knew she would not be able to enjoy this for much longer. Someone else would be living here, someone else would stand here in the dusk and listen to the trams along St Kilda Road, and watch the gulls flying overhead to the waters of the bay.

This was the house she had lived in all her life as Belle, daughter of Rory and Iris Bartholomew. She was still Belle, yes, but everything else had changed. Her mother was Martha. Her father . . . someone had made it impossible for her to read his name. Someone who clearly hated him. Or Martha. Or her.

Could Rory have done that? But Belle did not think so. It was not in Rory's nature to transfer his feelings to a piece of paper. He preferred to sort out his grudges face to face. Who had given him the birth certificate? Was it Martha? Belle didn't understand why Martha had given up her daughter to her brother. To Rory, the only father she'd ever known, and her mother, dear sweet Iris.

The swelling of grief in her heart grew too much to bear and tears slid freely down her cheeks. It didn't last for long. Belle's rational streak reasserted itself and she mopped her face with her handkerchief and blew her nose. There were things that needed doing, things she needed to discuss with Henry, and she couldn't allow herself to be self-indulgent.

When she walked back into the sitting room Henry eyed her uneasily, as if he was afraid she might erupt into the sort of emotional outburst he loathed—they both loathed, Belle reminded herself. Restrained emotion, keeping oneself in check, these were things they had in common. With a sense of unease she realised she'd almost forgotten what it was like to be passionate about anything, and now there were all these unfamiliar emotions inside her.

As if she was beginning to unravel.

'Belle, I'm so dreadfully sorry,' Henry said, and she could see he meant it.

'You didn't do anything. I'm grateful for your help, Henry.' Belle rested her hands on the back of a chair, digging her fingers into the antimacassar. 'This has been a shock. It must be a shock to you as well.'

But he was shuffling about again in his brief-case. 'I got this the other day, when I saw ... It's a copy of course.' He handed the certificate to her, and when Belle recognised that it was a replica of her birth certificate, she scanned it eagerly for the name that had been scratched out on the original.

'Nathan Ambrose. And there's a marriage date. They were married two years before I was born.' Belle looked at him in bewilderment. 'I don't understand. She was married. I wasn't illegitimate. Why did she give me away to her brother?'

Henry shrugged. 'I don't know. And does it matter, Belle? As far as everyone is aware, you are the daughter of Rory and Iris. I think we should leave it at that. Forget this nonsense. It means nothing, not really.'

The 'nonsense' comment stung, but she forced herself to consider his words without bias. Henry wouldn't want to open a can of worms, not when he had his clients to think of, and his practice, and the current financial situation. Although there was nothing scandalous about the revelation of her birth, Belle couldn't imagine their circle of friends and acquaintances being anything but horrified if she told them. Henry wanted her to pretend she'd never seen the document. Pretend none of this had ever happened.

Once again the idea was comforting. Forget it all, step back into the shadows. But she knew she couldn't do it. Not even to please Henry. And if she did then she would regret it.

Sweet Wattle Creek. That was where she was born, where her beginnings were. There was a swift, urgent need to go there and see it for herself, and Belle grasped hold of it.

She sat down beside Henry, bracing for an argument. 'I want to go and see this property in Sweet Wattle Creek. The Bartholomew family home.'

'I don't think that's a good idea, Belle.' Henry spoke quickly, worried eyes searching hers. 'For a start the building has been empty for six months. It could be in a dreadful state.' He reached for her hand and this time she allowed him to hold it. 'Let me sell the place for you and then you can decide what to do with the proceeds. You never know, it might be enough for you to buy another cottage in Sorrento. I know how much you love it there. And in the meantime you'll camp with friends until we get married.'

Friends? Their friends seemed to be rather thin on the ground since Bart Homes had gone under. But Belle let him say what he had to, knowing it would make no difference to her. She'd made up her mind. She was going to Sweet Wattle Creek to see Martha's house. It seemed important, in fact, it was the only sensible thing to do.

'Belle?' Henry was saying her name, squeezing her fingers, clearly believing her deranged.

'Is there anything else you have to tell me?' she said in a voice that strove to be light and instead sounded overwrought. 'Martha's property in Sweet Wattle Creek. Do you know anything more about it?'

Henry gathered his thoughts, reaching for the letter she'd seen earlier, and removing it from its envelope. 'Yes . . . Here we are. The property is called The Grand. It was a hotel, Belle, and was run by Martha and her husband.'

Belle gave a laugh. It sounded wild. 'A hotel

called The Grand. I think I must see it now.'

'Then I'll come with you. I won't let you face this alone.' He started to pack up his paperwork, almost as if they were about to set out immediately.

Belle knew she'd be glad of his company. She wasn't quite brave enough to say no to him.

'In the meantime, I'll see what contents can be sold from this house and then we'll set about putting it up for sale,' Henry was saying. 'This is no time for sentimentality.'

Belle wished he would insist she keep all the furnishings and the paintings and anything else she wanted to keep. But that wasn't Henry's way. She reminded herself that he was logical, like her, which was why they'd always been so well suited.

They would get through this and out the other side and everything would be just as it should be. She and Henry would marry and set up house together and life would settle back into the routines she had craved since Charlie had died. They'd stroll along the Esplanade on Sundays, and have dinner parties and welcome in the new year.

That was her future.

Then why, suddenly, did all of that seem like such a flimsy and insubstantial dream?

CHAPTER 6

SOPHIE

Sweet Wattle Creek, 1986

I SLAMMED MY FRONT door, sank down on the sofa and kicked off my sandals. It was Friday night and when I was young Friday night meant getting dressed up and going out with my friends for a good time. That was when the sixties were in full swing. Of course there were the sixties and the *sixties*. The first were more or less a carry-on of the 1950s, with their strict social rules, although with a little more freedom. And then there were the other sixties, for girls like me, who were prepared to push boundaries. Oh yes, plenty of good times to be had. Not that I didn't pay the consequences, because I did, but I still liked to look back fondly on my wild youth.

Even after Dillon was born and I was a parent and a nine-to-five employee, Friday nights were good. Pizza and video nights, with Dillon cuddled up beside me, or later on, with some of his school mates giggling in their sleeping bags. It was when Walter came along that Friday nights changed. A series of jerky images flickered through my brain: waiting for the sound of his key in the door. Heart thudding as I considered what mood he would be in. Hands fisted as I ran through my strategies if he should be angry. And with Walter you could be sure that anger was never far below the surface.

'Tim rang and said you'd arranged for me to go over to his place later.' Dillon was in the doorway, frowning beneath his dark eyebrows and dark fringe. He seemed to grow taller by the minute.

'That's right. Work. I have to interview the man who's running the Centenary Exhibition.'

He considered this. He was still in his school uniform and I could see that he was going to outgrow it by the end of the term. He was as tall as his father, the boy I'd fallen pregnant to when I was sixteen. My parents had been horrified, and then I'd married Walter, and he'd seen to it that the wedge between us was widened until we rarely saw them. And after a while it just seemed easier, and safer, not to. Now Dillon and I had even more reason not to contact anyone from the past. I'd always hoped that one day we might knock on their door and . . . well, that day was yet to come.

'Tim asked if I wanted to come to tea and I said yeah. He's coming to pick me up in a minute.'

'Oh. Okay. You'd better change, then.'

He nodded, still watching me. I waited, but whatever it was he wanted to say he seemed to have changed his mind and now he was heading towards his room. I waited another beat but he didn't come back.

With grim determination I got to my feet. Seeing I didn't have to get tea for Dillon, I could make do with a sandwich and go for a jog first. I knew I was better for the exercise—if I stayed home I tended to agonise about the past and it wasn't as if I could do anything about it, was it? Dillon and I were in a good place at the moment, but I couldn't seem to relax and enjoy it—I was always looking over my shoulder.

I'd just pulled on my jogging gear and was fastening back my blonde hair with a bright-pink scrunchy—I like to keep it short and straight, but it had begun to grow out and I hadn't had time to get the darker colour retouched—when there was a knock on the door.

Tim stood there, his latest family member clasped in his arms, their matching eyes wide and sleep-deprived. 'Is Dillon ready?'

I smiled at the baby. 'He's coming. I believe you tempted him with Maureen's cooking?'

'Yep. He's promised to mind this one for an hour while we go out for a drink at the pub. Is that okay? I'll set my watch. One hour precisely.'

'If it's okay with him, it's fine with me. But . . . he's only fourteen you know.'

'Christy will be there, too.'

Christy was their other daughter, in the same class as Dillon. She seemed a nice enough girl, although a little dippy at times. But then I could hardly take the high moral ground. One thing I was going to make damned sure of: Dillon would not make my mistakes.

'Dillon!' I turned to call over my shoulder and realised he was standing right there.

Tim laughed and the baby gave a hiccup. 'So you're seeing Ian tonight?'

Dillon's eyes narrowed on me.

'I told you,' I calmly reassured him. 'The Centenary man.' I looked back at Tim as if I didn't feel my son like a thundercloud at my shoulder. 'That box I found on the steps? It *was* an old wedding dress. He's going to examine it and let me watch.'

Tim rolled his eyes at Dillon. 'Sounds exciting.'

They set off towards the car, Dillon giving me a half-smile and Tim waving a hand. I could hear the baby begin to howl as they drove away.

I was relieved Dillon hadn't quizzed me further in front of Tim, and at the same time I was upset that he should still feel so insecure where his mother and men were concerned. Walter had cast a long shadow. I could only hope that time would eventually heal the wounds.

Plugging in my walkman, I set off at a steady trot along the side of the road, the Eurythmics keeping me company.

My thoughts turned to the wedding dress. Maybe it was a family heirloom? Someone had been having a tidy-up and found it in the back of their wardrobe and said, *Why don't you take this down to the Centenary bloke?* The owner must be someone who lived in the district, perhaps even someone I knew. There was a good story here somewhere, I could feel it.

I crossed the road and headed towards the edge of town. At this time of year—summer—and this time of day—evening—it was still bright but it was also quiet. The shops I passed were closed, apart from the pub and the Chinese restaurant, and as I reached the end of town I headed out over bare ground. This was my favourite direction to run, out to the cluster of buildings that were set apart from the main town.

There'd been a glitch in the town planning in the old days. The original town of Sweet Wattle Creek was supposed to be out here—there'd been a hotel on this spot for years before the planners had moved in. But the new mayor decided he wanted Sweet Wattle Creek to be five miles—or eight kilometres in modern measurement—to the east, where it now stood. To emphasise the point, he'd constructed his own house in that spot. The heavy weights of the town clustered loyally around him, and the older settlement was left on the outer. Not that being isolated had stopped The Grand doing a roaring trade. It had been there a lot longer than the new pub in town, and it was closer to the railway, and people enjoyed thumbing their noses at the hierarchy. They attended The Grand in droves and a few even moved out to live nearby, although despite best intentions it had only ever been a bit of a shantytown on the fringes.

Now Sweet Wattle Creek was edging closer and closer to its rival, until there was only a mile between them, a fifth of the distance that there used to be. The Grand would one day be swallowed up with new houses and shops.

It was a pity, really, about the fire.

I reached what had once been The Grand

and looked up. The burnt-out shell sat forlornly amongst a jumble of falling-down buildings, blackened spars reaching for the sky, and crumbling brick walls looking increasingly fragile. There was a section that must have been a window, and the dark square seemed to stare down at me. It must have been as grand as its name once, but now it was just a broken ruin. And rather creepy, especially at night.

I wasn't sure when the fire had started. Sometime in the thirties, I think. It was surprising the building hadn't been flattened and the site built on, but perhaps the family still owned it. Had it been caught up in some intestate nightmare? Further out, beyond the old hotel and its satellites, was a new housing estate, but here nothing had changed for decades.

A wasp buzzed by and some parrots screeched overhead. A lizard, disturbed by my passing, rustled through fallen bark. I turned down the narrow laneway that ran behind The Grand. An intact, high brick wall rose between me and the burnt wreck of the hotel. The gate that once opened onto the stable yard had been boarded up and nailed shut. On my other side was a rather nicely restored cottage and a red bottlebrush humming with bees. The last tenants had moved out a month ago and since then it had stood empty, which seemed a shame, but I could understand why they might not like a view of a charred old place. I gave it the once-over as I ran by and almost fell over my feet when I saw that one of the cottage's sash windows was pushed up and the curtain was flapping in the breeze.

Someone had taken up residence. I hadn't heard any talk about anyone moving in, but perhaps that was because no one thought to tell me. According to Tim, I needed to have lived here at least twenty years before I could be considered a local and even then I wouldn't be a 'real' local.

Time to turn back. I quickened my pace, with Annie Lennox's 'Would I lie to you?' accompanying me, leaving The Grand behind. I felt my muscles stretching, and it was a good feeling. At least, I told myself, if Walter found us I could outrun him.

As I reached the outskirts of town I slowed to a jog, down Main Street, crossing the road to avoid the working pub, where a rowdy group was drinking outside. I saw Ellie in her leather miniskirt, standing beside her boyfriend, and waved. She called out something but I didn't hear her and wasn't about to stop and chat. My days of hanging out at hotels and bars were long past. Another shortcut down a side street, and now I was heading home.

My leg muscles ached and my breath caught in my chest, burning my lungs, but I felt better. Stronger. I felt as if I could handle anything life threw at me. This was good. It had taken me quite a while to get into this frame of mind and there had been times when I'd wondered whether I'd ever get myself together.

I knew that was why Dillon had given me that look when he heard about Ian McKinnon. He worried about me just as I worried about him.

We only had each other. But I had no intention of ever taking him into the sort of evil place my marriage to Walter had taken him, not ever again.

The lights were on in the library although they didn't need to be—despite it being eight o'clock it was still daylight outside. There was a warm breeze blowing my freshly washed hair and drying out my skin. I'd be a prune in a few years' time, assuming I was still here in Sweet Wattle Creek.

I pushed at the door but it was locked, so I knocked on the glass panel. After a moment I saw Ian appear from somewhere and he came to open up and let me in.

'I had to lock it. People kept bringing in books,' he complained.

'Well, it is a library.'

His gaze slid over me in a way I wasn't sure I liked. I crossed my arms over my usual uniform—a baggy t-shirt I'd pulled on over my jeans. My days of short skirts were well and truly over. Not because I couldn't wear them—I could. I still had the curves, although not as abundantly as once upon a time. But these days I preferred androgynous.

Ian led the way through the quiet library and into a back room. I almost expected Nola to pop out from behind a shelf, but there was no one else here.

Ian had laid out the wedding dress on a long

table, as if he was about to do a post-mortem on it. I was keen to get started, but I was being distracted by the rich smell of coffee. He didn't offer me a cup, missing my hopeful looks in the direction of the pot, and going straight to the garment.

He was in his shirtsleeves this evening, his jacket folded carefully over a chair back. He looked a little rumpled, his hair, too, and he had a five-o'clock shadow on his manly jaw. Clearly it had been a long day at the office.

I ventured closer to the table. My eye wasn't trained as his obviously was, but there was something about the dress that made me think this wasn't an item someone's mother had run up on their Singer in an afternoon.

I could see the scalloped hem, the satin tunic and then the lace on top of it. The velvet waistband matched the train, which was spread out at the side, and was certainly worse for wear. In the fluorescent light the diamantes and pearls glowed, rivalling each other for beauty. The neckline was a V, and the sleeves were around elbow length.

'Wow.'

Ian was watching me expectantly and now he smiled. 'Wow indeed. You remember I said that sometimes in these little out-of-the-way places you come across treasure? Well this, Sophie Matheson, is most definitely a treasure.'

I looked again as he continued to tell me why, pointing out the cut of the cloth, the fine stitching, the avant-garde touches with the velvet, and the quality of the lace.

'I'd say this is First World War, not 1920s after all.

It really is the height of fashion and that tricked me. This is the sort of wedding dress that other people would be copying years later.'

'Ahead of its time, then?'

'Very much so. You have to remember that unlike today, wedding dresses then were likely to be hand-me-downs or just day dresses. Especially during the First World War. If you had a bit more money or status then you wore an evening dress as a wedding dress. Your dress, Sophie, is made especially for the occasion, and I'm pretty sure there's named couture involved.'

My dress. I liked that. 'So . . . who made it?'

He gave me that little smile, as if he was about to share a secret. He reached for the garment and I saw there was a tiny hand-stitched tag on the inside facing of the bodice. It was shaped like a heart with two letters embroidered in the centre. *E.N.*

'Eileen Nicholson,' he said, touching the heart with his fingertip as if it was made of fragile glass, and the satisfaction on his face grew smug. 'I can't wait to tell Miriam.'

'Miriam?' I darted him a sideways glance. For some reason I was disappointed, but I didn't want to go there.

'Miriam Carroll's my partner. She's an Eileen Nicholson groupie.'

The word sounded strange on his lips, but perhaps that was because I'd been thinking of him as a serious professional. He couldn't be serious all the time, of course not, and probably Miriam brought out the more frivolous Ian.

He was giving me a lecture and I tried to concentrate. 'Miriam is an expert on the small fashion houses of the early twentieth century. Eileen Nicholson was a local, based in St Kilda. Melbourne,' he added, as if he thought I was such a hick I might not know that St Kilda was one of the older inner suburbs.

'If I'm right and this really is an Eileen Nicholson then it's a rare find. Most of her couture garments are in private hands. After she died she was all but forgotten—a footnote in history—until an Australian film star discovered her and began wearing her creations. Of course that brought Eileen Nicholson back into prominence and now there isn't a garment made by her that can be had for love or money. So if this is the genuine article . . .'

'It's worth a lot of love *and* money.'

'It's something precious. It'll certainly bring more people to the Centenary Exhibition than the Sweet Wattle Creek committee expected in their wildest dreams.'

'You mean our little town will be famous?' I joked.

He didn't smile back. 'Very. Let me explain.' He leaned against the table's edge and crossed his arms, thinking, gathering his words, while I fumbled my notebook and pencil out of my bag and prepared to take notes.

'Even accounting for the late Eileen Nicholson's recent fame—our friend the movie star buying up her stuff—there weren't that many of her creations left in the world. She began her couture house in the Edwardian period, before the First World War, and she never had more than a select group of devoted followers. Mrs Nicholson was the owner and designer, and very much her own woman. She was one of the few Edwardian fashion designers who made the transition into the 1920s, and then on into the 1930s—Coco Chanel was a famous one, and Madeleine Vionnet. As the Depression cut deep, and her clientele drifted off, she sold her shop in Collins Street and worked from a room in her house in Annat Street, St Kilda. If memory serves, her final garment was made in 1939, not long before she died.'

I scribbled it down as quickly as I could. This was fascinating and I could feel my inner reporter prick up her ears. Here was a story far from the usual round of sheep stealing or crop damage or the mayor's daughter getting married.

'So, let me get this right, if this *is* an Eileen Nicholson, where did it come from? Where has it been all these years? And why has it turned up in Sweet Wattle Creek in time for the Centenary?'

'I wish I knew,' he answered with a grimace. 'No one has called me to say they left it. What about you?'

'No. Not as far as I know. I'll ask Tim when I pick up Dillon. My son,' I added, in case he didn't know.

Of course he knew. This was a small town. He nodded, turning back to the dress on the table. I followed the direction of his pointing finger, pencil poised over paper like an obedient secretary.

'Mould on the hem. Looks as if it's been there for a while, which means the spores have probably eaten into the cloth fibres. Even if Miriam manages to remove the mould, she'll need to do some structural work. The lace is torn and there are some stains, here and here. They've marked the satin.'

I peered closer. 'Ah, yes. Is it white or ivory? The dress, I mean.'

'Ivory. Not unusual in those times. White weddings weren't as fashionable then as they became later on, and with wartime restrictions women had to make do. But this certainly isn't someone else's cast-off. This is unique, an Eileen Nicholson, an exclusive.'

The man was on a roll, and if I hadn't seen him being shy and awkward I could believe he was always this self-assured.

'You know a lot,' I said admiringly, when I'd done some more scribbling.

Did he flush? Perhaps it was just warm in here with the air conditioning off. 'I've listened to Miriam often enough. She's the textile expert, and as I said, she has a passion for Eileen Nicholson. Hmm, I also looked up a book on the subject.' He grinned. 'It's quite handy being here in the library.'

The grin was rather endearing, not to say attractive, but I did my best to ignore it. 'So you'll send the dress to Miriam?'

'Yes. When we find out who it belongs to. I'll need their consent first. And the committee will need to know.'

'Right.' The committee would be chuffed. There'd be more cheerful cockatoo posters for Tim to print, if they could find enough surfaces to stick them on.

Ian was over by the bookshelf, stooping down to check the titles, and after a moment he pulled out a heavy-looking volume. Flipping through the pages, he found what he was looking for and carried it back to me, not paying attention to where he was going and tripping over a box on the floor. He only just saved himself, but he didn't seem too concerned. It must happen to him a lot.

'Here we are.'

I found myself staring at photographs of posh women in the sort of elegant 1930s dresses which seemed to cling to every dip and curve. He turned back a few pages and we were in the 1920s with the dropped waists, and then he turned more pages and we were in the early years of the twentieth century.

'You see?' He was pointing again. His fingers really were long and narrow—artist's fingers, or perhaps he played the piano, or strummed a guitar.

'Sophie?'

'Oh, sorry. You were saying?'

'Looking at the cut of our dress and considering it's an Eileen Nicholson and the height of fashion, I'd place it around 1916 or 1917. Not yet the radical shift of waistline that you see in the 1920s. The hem looks around ankle-length and the bride would've worn white stockings and cloth-covered or calf shoes, depending on her finances.'

'But we're assuming her finances were pretty good, if she could afford an Eileen Nicholson?'

'We are.'

'Okay.' More scribbling, but I couldn't help feeling pleased he'd said 'our' wedding dress. We'd come from 'my' to 'our' in the space of a few minutes. It gave me a warm fuzzy feeling, which self-preservation immediately shut down.

'What about the veil?'

'Even Miriam can't save that. It's a man made fibre or maybe lace stiffened with a mixture of sugar and water. It rots over time and now it's beyond help. Don't worry, Miriam can make up a copy to put on display. She's done it before.'

'Good.' I smiled and closed my notebook. I had enough for a few really nice columns, and with the photographs it might fill out to a full page. *The photographs* . . . 'Oh no!'

He raised an eyebrow at my wail.

'I forgot the camera. I'll have to take the photographs tomorrow. If that's all right?'

'Well, as I said, we need to find out who it belongs to, but I'm sure the committee would like photographs. As much publicity as possible would be good.'

'Money in the till?' I asked.

'Exactly.'

'So we need to find Charlie and Belle?' The thought of being in on the hunt gave me a little tingle of pleasure. I knew I was good at tracking people down, mainly because I'd had to learn how to cover my own tracks. I knew all about finding someone, even if they didn't want to be found.

'Will we reconvene here tomorrow?' he asked, and it was only half a question. 'Here or the RSL Hall. I'm not sure where I'll be.'

'I'll find you. See you then.'

I realised we were smiling at each other and put a stop to it by turning away. This was business, purely business, and I wasn't going to forget it. Besides, there was the brilliant Miriam in the background. I was glad he had someone like Miriam, then if I did feel any attraction to him— even the tiniest bit—I could remind myself he was already taken.

CHAPTER 7

BELLE

Sweet Wattle Creek, 1931

THE RAILWAY STATION was tiny, a stop on the way to nowhere. When Belle got off and stood on the platform, it felt as if the whole world was stretched out before her, flat and brown, and she was alone in it.

Henry hadn't accompanied her after all. One of his clients had demanded his attention, and because the man was important, and Henry was worried about his practice, he'd felt he couldn't say no. Belle understood that, and if she admitted the truth to herself then she was actually relieved. Henry had begun fussing over her, and looking at her when he thought she wasn't aware, as if her secret had changed something between them.

'I'll manage perfectly well,' she'd told him with what she hoped was a reassuring smile.

But you'd have thought she was going to the other side of the world. 'You don't have to stay more than a night, Belle. That's quite long enough.'

'I want to talk to Mr Thomas.' And anyone else who might have known her aunt. Her *mother.*

And then there was her father, Nathan Ambrose, whose name had been scratched out so aggressively on her birth certificate. No one needed to know why she was asking questions, she'd be discreet, but she had a powerful urge to discover what she could.

On the way north the train engine had broken down and then there had been an altercation when a young man was caught riding in the freight carriage without paying. He'd jumped down while the train was still moving, and run away. She heard one of her fellow passengers muttering. *Riding the rattler,* he called it. Hitching a ride without paying from one town to the next was evidently quite a common event.

As well as that there had been numerous stops— it seemed that every dot on the map had a station where mail or other urgent provisions must be unloaded before they could travel onwards. The rocking motion had made her sleepy and she'd watched through half-closed eyes, trying not to think of her home being auctioned behind her, as the scenery went by. Sometimes groups of people walking beside the track would stare up at her, and if they had children, then they'd all wave so that she felt obliged to wave back. Occasionally they had horses or sulkies to ride, but more often than not they were on foot, carrying or pushing their belongings along with the help of a variety of apparatus. One woman had a wheelbarrow. She supposed these were some of the unemployed she'd read about in the newspapers, who'd taken to the roads in search of work.

She couldn't decide whether it was a brave thing to do, or foolhardy.

Belle couldn't imagine herself or Henry taking to the roads—or the track, as it seemed to be known. But perhaps—although she struggled to imagine it—there were people in the world so desperate they had no choice but to set out into the unknown and hope for the best.

By the time she'd arrived at Sweet Wattle Creek the train was hours later than scheduled and she was tired. The engine had paused, while the usual crates and boxes and bags of mail were unloaded, and then moved off. Leaving her at the edge of nowhere.

This certainly wasn't how she'd imagined her destination, and she had a slight panic, wondering if she'd been foolhardy herself to set out alone in search of her mysterious past. True, it was a distraction from her grief and the tragedy that had befallen her, but there was more to it than that. An empty hollow sensation had formed inside her, which she was beginning to think only the truth could fill. She wanted answers, and surely this was the place to find them?

Belle tightened her grip on her small weekend suitcase—at least it was light. The air was breathlessly hot, despite it being nearly eight o'clock in the evening, and the sun—a ball of brilliant yellow that made her eyes ache—was still casting long shadows. She had a vision of the house in Annat Street in the evening, with the trams rumbling along the Esplanade, and the sanctuary of the garden, with blackbirds settling and the soft colours of the English flowers Iris had planted. There was nothing soft about this place.

Belle rounded the corner of the small brick building and discovered a man in an official-looking jacket. He was stooping over a tub of plants with a watering can. They looked like geraniums, bright-scarlet flowers and large green leaves.

'Excuse me?'

He looked up at her curiously, and then set the can down. He seemed mesmerised by her travelling outfit of tight, mid-calf-length grey skirt and snug-fitting jacket fastened over her white blouse—certainly no longer as crisp as when she had started out. Her hat was unadorned and drooped down to shade her face and was the only item of clothing she was wearing that made any concession to the heat.

He grinned. 'You'll be Miss Bartholomew, then.'

He knows me? Belle thought, startled, before she realised that of course he would. Henry had written to Martha's solicitor, Mr Thomas, and no doubt he would have informed the rest of Sweet Wattle Creek. Her visit would not be made incognito and she'd been naive to think it could be.

'They were waiting for you but when the train was so late coming in . . . They weren't sure you'd turn up.'

'They?' Belle asked.

'Mr Thomas and his sister. They were planning to drive you to The Grand.'

Of course. Henry had said something about

making arrangements, but Belle had thought he was being unnecessarily cautious. Now, looking at the empty landscape, she contemplated whether she hadn't been cautious enough.

'Is there a taxi-cab for hire?'

He couldn't hide his amusement. 'Can't say there's much call for taxi-cabs in Sweet Wattle Creek.' And then he looked past her and his humour gave way to relief. 'There's Mr Davies. Frank! Would you come here a minute? Miss Bartholomew has arrived after all. She needs a lift to The Grand.'

Belle turned as she heard the crunch of booted feet approaching on the gravel path. From the hint of respect in the railwayman's voice she expected someone older, but Frank Davies was young, probably a few years younger than her. Dark hair, a tanned complexion, and grey eyes which he was presently narrowing against the setting sun. He looked like a railway navvy in his old, dusty clothes, but his air of authority caused her to reassess that opinion.

He took the cigarette out of his mouth and dropped it onto the platform, then ground it out with the toe of his worn boot. His hair was flopping over his eyes and he pushed it back with his fingers. Something in the way he did that reminded her of Charlie and the memory was sharp and painful, but she didn't have time to consider it further as he reached out his hand. She gave him hers, and he took it in a brief, hard grip.

'Isn't Aneas Thomas here?'

His eyes were on her, but he was speaking to the station master. It seemed that her arrival had caused a ripple of disquiet.

'Perhaps if it isn't far I can walk?' she suggested. She had only the one light piece of luggage, enough for the night or, at a pinch, two. There'd seemed no point in bringing more.

The two men exchanged glances. No one seemed to be in a hurry. Belle, used to getting things done quickly, felt impatience dancing along her skin. Finally, Frank Davies spoke again, a drawl in his voice.

'I'll take you to The Grand. The place was a mess, but from the moment you let Aneas know you were coming, my mother's been over there, busy trying to make it fit for you.'

'Oh.' She'd put people out. It made her feel uncomfortable. 'I didn't realise. That's very kind of your mother. Was it such a mess?'

He considered his words before speaking, which made her think it was. 'We've had a few vagrants sleeping rough and they found their way inside. Constable Nash moved them on. We don't like travellers here in Sweet Wattle Creek.'

Belle supposed it was meant to sound reassuring, but instead the words had a sinister quality.

'Travellers?' she repeated, thinking of the people she'd seen from the train. The people who in their desperation had taken to the roads.

Frank thought she was asking for clarification. His mouth tightened. 'Travellers, that's what we call them. Or swaggies, transients, sundowners. They leave the cities and take to the track looking for work. They carry their swags with them—their belongings—and set up house wherever they can. Doesn't matter if it's someone else's land or they have to steal to feed themselves.'

'They're trouble,' agreed the station master.

Travellers had been living in Martha's house. Belle wondered just how dilapidated it was. Perhaps she may not be able to stay even one night. Henry had warned her she was acting impulsively—behaviour that had surprised them both—but she'd been determined. Would she now have to return home with her tail between her legs? But no, she didn't want to do that. She wouldn't give up so easily. There were hurdles to be overcome, yes, but Belle told herself she was more than capable of doing so. And she'd prove it to him.

Frank Davies was watching her. He seemed to find her face of great interest. His staring was making her uncomfortable, and she opened her mouth to ask him if there was soot on her nose from the train, just as he bent down and reached for her suitcase. 'Come on,' he said gruffly. 'It'll be dark before we get there.'

Belle let him have it, her fingers nerveless, and he turned and strode off around the corner. The station master misread her hesitation.

'The Davies are one of the most respectable families in the district,' he declared. 'You'll be right with Frank.'

She found the respectable Mr Davies busy loading some substantial-looking boxes that had come off the train into a horse-drawn cart. He was tall and lean but he seemed to have no trouble heaving them about. When he was finished he carefully set Belle's suitcase at the back, so it wouldn't get crushed.

'If I'd known you'd be here I'd have brought the car,' he said.

'I don't mind. Thank you.' Belle tried to sound enthusiastic but it had been a long day.

Frank almost smiled as he pushed back that truant lock of hair. But she was ready for him this time. Although she could see in the fading light that he was good-looking, there was a hardness to his face that made her wary. He was not like Charlie at all.

Out of nowhere there was a terrible shriek and she jumped. Belle looked up and saw a large white bird fly across the pink-streaked sky, giving several more shrieks as it went. 'Cockatoo,' Frank Davies said laconically. 'Plenty around here.'

Belle knew what a cockatoo was. They occasionally strayed into St Kilda and certainly they were at the cottage in Sorrento, but they were generally considered to be an inland bird. Something was tapping at the back of her mind, not quite a memory, more of a feeling. Before she could grasp it, whatever it was slipped away.

Awkwardly, she climbed up onto the seat, staying away from Frank Davies—the last thing she wanted was her thigh rubbing against his. When she was set he flicked the reins and the horse ambled off along the unmade road, leaving the station behind them.

Shadows were stretching out, and it seemed as if

night was finally drawing in. Paddocks on either side were outlined with post and rail fences, and cattle and sheep stopped what they were doing to stare, while a horse tossed its head and ran off into the fading light. Ahead of them a few winking lights shone through the dusk.

'Is that Sweet Wattle Creek?' she asked, hearing the apprehension in her voice.

'Yes. That's Main Street you can see.'

We're nearly there. But Belle's relief was short-lived because the next moment Frank Davies had turned to the left, heading away from the town. Belle gripped the hard edge of the seat, twisting her head to keep the lights in view. 'Mr Davies, what are you doing?'

Frank shot her a look and this time he did smile, she could hear it in his voice. 'The town was always in two parts, five miles between. The Grand is this way, Miss Bartholomew.'

Ahead of her, in the fading light, all the colours melded together like a soggy painting.

'I don't understand.' The brim of her hat was limper than it should be and there was dust in her mouth. She was hot and uncomfortable and she longed for a bath and a soft bed and sleep. She longed for Annat Street and the sad truth was that when she went back there would be no home. Not the one she remembered anyway.

Frank was explaining. 'When the town first went up there was a difference of opinion as to where it should be built. The Bartholomews already had The Grand and the land around it. They wanted to sell to the developers, but the story is they were asking too much. Whatever reason, the new town was built further along to the east, and Sweet Wattle Creek has been split in two ever since.'

The Bartholomews were pioneers. They were here before the town. Why hadn't she known this, why hadn't Rory told her? She would have thought he'd be proud of his pioneering family and yet he had said nothing.

Frank had turned to her and she could see the shine of his eyes and the trickle of smoke from the new cigarette he'd lit.

'I'm sorry, what did you say?'

He sighed and she thought that perhaps he wasn't a very patient sort of man. Or perhaps he'd had a difficult afternoon and this wasn't how he wanted to end it. 'I said I wasn't exaggerating, Miss Bartholomew. The Grand was in a terrible state. My mother has done her best but you don't have to stay there.'

'I can't make a decision until I see it.' She sounded irritable. It had been a long day or perhaps it was his own manner that made her think politeness could be dispensed with.

Frank said nothing and the silence drew out. The movement of the horse and cart wasn't smooth—if it was it would have sent Belle to sleep, but the rattle and jolt kept shaking her awake. She blinked, and then blinked again. There were lights in the distance.

'Is that it?' she asked and pointed.

'Nah. That's the Beauchamp place. Morwenstow is beyond that—that's the name of our property. Here's The Grand.'

She hadn't realised it was so close. The black shape rose up to her right and seemed to tower over her, solid and silent, before she understood Martha's home must be a two-storey building. When Frank slowed the cart to a stop she sat staring, trying to pick out details, only now it was too dark to see them.

'It looks like there's no one here,' Frank said. 'I can't leave you alone, Miss Bartholomew. You're coming with me to Morwenstow.'

His assumption of being in charge put her back up. This, her first foray into independence, couldn't end like this. She wouldn't let it.

'I want to stay. I want to see the house.'

'You can wait until the morning. The constable cleared out the travellers but they could come back.' He lifted the reins, and prepared to set the horse on its way once more.

Belle wanted him to stop—she had an awful feeling that if he drove on her courage would trickle away and she would turn around and go back to Henry. There were things she needed to know, questions to ask and mysteries to unearth.

Just then some car lamps lit up, shining directly at them. Belle held up a hand, blinded. A female voice called out, 'Frank? Is that Belle? We were just about to leave.'

'Jo!' Frank shouted back and secured the reins before jumping down. As Belle clambered off the seat, struggling in her tight skirt, he appeared at her side and reached up to grasp her by the waist. She didn't have time to refuse his help and the next moment she was airborne, but only briefly, before he placed her feet neatly on the ground.

His voice was close to her cheek, his breath warm and smoky. 'Looks as if you got your wish, Miss Bartholomew. I hope you don't regret it.'

She stepped away, making it clear his help would not be further required, and turned towards the person approaching them. In the light from the headlamps Belle could see it was a slender woman in a skirt and a short-sleeved blouse. She wore a scarf tied over her hair.

'I'm filthy from cleaning,' she explained, wiping her hands on her thighs. 'It's been a big job. I think we have some of the rooms habitable at last. Hello, I'm Frank's sister, Jo Davies.' She held out her hand to clasp Belle's in a warm, friendly grip.

'I'm sorry to hear you had to do all this work for me. I didn't know. I should pay you ...'

Jo glanced at her brother and something passed between them. 'Nonsense,' she spoke easily, her voice trembling as if she was trying not to laugh. 'My mother, Violet, was Martha Ambrose's best friend and she was adamant you couldn't spend a night in The Grand in the state it was in.'

Belle knew her face was flushed. They thought she was a fool, arriving here, totally unprepared.

'Come on,' Jo said. Frank stood back, waiting for her to go first, and there was nothing to do but follow.

The Grand had been built butting directly onto the street, but instead of taking them to the front door, Jo led them around to the back. 'The door at the front is locked and we haven't been able to find the key,' she explained. 'You can't get in that way.' There was a lane, and a little way further along, a gate stood ajar within the arch of a high brick wall.

Pale light threw a pattern on the shadowy desolation of an old stable yard, and Belle could see a lamp inside the window on the ground floor.

'Careful, there are some broken bricks,' warned Jo Davies as they followed in her wake.

'Isn't there a generator?' Frank asked with that hint of impatience.

Jo shot him an amused look. 'Couldn't get it started.'

'Haven't you got school?'

'Summer holidays,' Jo reminded him. She turned to Belle to explain. 'I'm a teacher at the Sweet Wattle Creek school. Well I'm *the* teacher.'

'So there's no electricity?' Belle tried not to feel appalled, and wondered if she could remember how to light a lamp.

'Not this far out of town.' Frank answered her this time. His gaze settled on her face. 'I'll give the generator another try. I might be able to start it.' And he disappeared around a corner into the deeper darkness.

'Why do men always think they can do a better job?' Jo said to no one in particular.

Belle lifted her face to stare up at the windows in the second storey. There was no light there and she imagined Martha standing behind the glass pane, staring back at her.

'It looks haunted.'

As soon as the words were out of her mouth

she wished them back. She wasn't the sort of person to imagine ghosts and ghouls. It just showed how tired and rattled she must be, to have said such a thing.

'I wouldn't be surprised.' Jo shot Belle a guilty sideways glance. 'Sorry, that wasn't a very helpful thing to say, was it?'

Away to the right came the sound of a motor spluttering and then failing. Jo smiled smugly and opened the door in front of them. Inside was what appeared to be a kitchen and Belle saw a woman stooped over the oven with a brush and shovel. The bucket on the floor was already full of ash and bits of charcoal. Something scuttled into the shadows.

'Only mice,' Jo said matter-of-factly. 'Mum?' She went to the woman to help her up, and Belle saw that Violet had white hair and her lined face was gentle and sweet, with an almost elfin quality. She must be about sixty years of age, the same as Rory was. 'Mum, she's here after all. Frank brought her. The train broke down.'

'Oh, she's here after all!' Violet's face lit up. 'Belle?' She came forward, passing the dustpan and brush to Jo, and reached out to take Belle's hands. 'Oh, Belle, my dear. I can't believe you're home. After all these years.'

Home.

The word echoed in her head, the building enclosed her, and Belle couldn't breathe.

CHAPTER 8

SOPHIE

Sweet Wattle Creek, 1986

I PICKED UP DILLON and waved goodbye to Tim and Maureen. It wasn't very late but I was tired and I noticed Dillon yawning. Night had brought relief from the worst of the heat, but there was a warm stillness to the air, and everything crackled from the lack of moisture.

'How was Christy? How was the baby?'

Dillon shrugged a shoulder. 'Okay. Tim had to go in to the office to run the presses and Maureen went to bed. The baby went to sleep and we watched a video. They're thinking of calling it Centenary. Can you believe that? What would it be for short? Cent!'

He and Christy had obviously been discussing it. I wondered if Tim and Maureen were serious. Surely not? The baby was barely three weeks old and they were both back at work, so perhaps they were lightheaded with exhaustion.

Dillon went on when I didn't answer. 'Christy says the man who's doing the exhibition for the Centenary is living out near The Grand.'

'Really?' So that was the new occupant in the house opposite what was left of the hotel. I remembered the curtains flapping in the breeze and reminded myself to tell Ian that Sweet Wattle Creek might be a small town but when it came to open windows it still had its opportunists.

'Didn't he tell you?' Dillon was watching me closely.

'No. Why would he? We were looking at an old wedding dress he's going to use for the exhibition. It was interesting. I want to write a story about it. If Tim will let me.' I laughed but Dillon didn't respond.

I turned the corner into our road and slowed to a halt. He didn't move and neither did I.

'So it wasn't a date or anything?' He spoke as if it didn't matter, but when I looked at him I could see the tension in his face.

'Dillon, I told you it was for work. What made you think it was a date? You shouldn't be listening to Christy. Really, you don't have to worry.'

He stared through the windscreen, refusing to meet my eyes. 'I just want to make sure, Mum.'

'I know you do. It's fine.'

I reached for the door handle, wanting to put this conversation behind me. His voice came out of the darkness, and my fourteen-year-old sounded like he was five.

'Do you think that one day he'll find us?'

I felt the cold sweat break out on my skin. It took all my strength to act as if terror wasn't hammering away frantically at the back of my skull. 'Dillon, how can he? We've done every-

thing right. We're Sophie and Dillon Matheson
of Sweet Wattle Creek now. We're different people. He'll be looking for the old me and you. If
we stick to our plan he can't find us. And how do
we know he's even looking anymore?'

He nodded, but I could see he wasn't finished.
I held my breath and waited, my fingers sweaty
on the handle of the door. When they came his
words were rushed, as if this wasn't something he
wanted to admit and yet he couldn't keep it in
any longer.

'Sometimes . . . I think he's coming for me. I
see him in the street, only it isn't him. I look over
my shoulder, just in case. Some days I really think
he's coming for us, Mum. And if I saw him I don't
know what I'd do. I'm worried I might just stand
there and let him take me.'

Sometimes I felt the same, but I didn't want to
tell him that. It wouldn't be helpful. So I prised
my fingers from the door handle and reached out
to rub his arm, giving it a reassuring squeeze.

'He isn't coming, Dillon. In time those feelings
will fade. But, you know, maybe it's a good thing.'

He stared at me and his face looked green in
the security light from the front door. 'How can
it be a good thing!'

'Well, it keeps you—us—alert. It keeps us sharp.
And that was why we got away, we didn't just
stand there. And I know you wouldn't do that
now, if you saw him. You'd run like hell, Dillon.
But you won't see him. It's over. We have our
new life and everything is going to be all right.'

His shoulders slumped and he seemed to relax

at last. I gave him a hug and he let me. Then he pulled away and nodded. 'Okay,' he said, and this time he managed a smile.

We got out of the car and made our way towards the house. BC was waiting, looking as if he'd been abandoned for a week instead of just a few hours. He wound his way around Dillon's ankles and then ran inside, straight to the cat-food drawer. Dillon grabbed a can and began to open it.

'Christy says the Centenary guy is hot,' he said with a sly look. I considered if he was testing me, or just teasing. Or wanting to show he'd moved on from our conversation in the car and was cool with Ian McKinnon's presence in our lives.

'Well, he's not going to be interested in me then, is he?' I retorted.

He gave me a once-over and grunted non-committedly.

That night I didn't sleep well. Dillon's questions and concerns, the trauma that hadn't really gone away, made me aware of just how damaged we still were. I might tell myself, and him, that everything was all right. And we had come a long way. But in reality healing wasn't going to happen in a year.

I forced my thoughts away, turning them instead to the wedding dress and the excitement I had felt when I listened to what Ian had to say. I felt myself begin to relax. Belle and Charlie were engaging me in a way I hadn't felt for a long time. My old job, before Walter, had been in the legal system.

I was a bailiff for the Magistrates Court. It doesn't sound very sexy—serving notices and tracking people down. But I was born to it. I used to tell Dillon I was like a private detective. I was Maddie from the television series *Moonlighting*, but without David. I was like a bloodhound, and once I got my teeth into something I wouldn't let go until I'd completed it. Yes, I was good at my job—which was one of the reasons I felt sure I had covered our tracks so well that Walter would never find us.

After we left all that behind, after we ran, I didn't expect to ever discover anything comparable. Now I had Charlie and Belle. Suddenly, all the old exhilaration was stirring inside me. The anticipation of the hunt. I was back on the job and I wanted to know who they were.

I wanted to know their story.

The *Herald* was printed and fastened into bundles. Despite a last-minute panic, when the van didn't turn up on time to carry copies off to Riverton, Tim had managed to get yet another issue onto the streets.

Afterwards I felt lethargic. Next week we'd go through the same thing again, but for now Ellie was hitting the phone and Brad was clearing up and Tim was off promoting. The story about the wedding dress hadn't been finished in time for today's paper, but Tim wanted something for next week, and a longer piece for his Centenary issue. So I collected my camera and trotted over to the library to take the photos I'd forgotten to take last night.

Tim had sent me on a photography course in Riverton when he gave me the job. I took to it like a duck to water. Something about being on the other side of the lens suited me; it meant I could legitimately hide from the world.

I brandished my equipment at Nola.

'The dress?' she queried. 'Ian told me it was hush-hush until you discovered more about it.'

'I don't suppose you know who it belongs to?' Nola was acquainted with most people in Sweet Wattle Creek. It went with her job.

'Sorry. Mr Scott might though. He has an amazing memory for a man of ninety. Why not ask him?' She smiled in a way that struck fear into my heart. 'He'll be at my next poetry evening. You can talk to him then.'

'Yes, I'll . . . thanks. But Tuesday isn't such a good night for me.'

'Just as well it's on Thursday next week then, isn't it?'

Satisfied, Nola waved me through, and I opened the door into the backroom. Ian looked up from his desk in the corner. Maybe it was my imagination but his eyes seemed to brighten when he saw me.

'I've found out who left the box on your steps,' he said.

'Who?' I was strangely elated he hadn't told Nola first.

'Coffee?' He held up a cup. He was stringing it

out. I could see by the slight tilt at the corner of his mouth that he was enjoying making me wait. But his coffee was so much better than mine that I wasn't about to refuse the offer.

'Okay, thanks.'

I waited as he poured a cup and tried not to tap my foot with impatience. After I had taken a sip he handed me a torn piece of paper with a name on it.

'*Mrs Davies, Morwenstow,*' I read. Did I know her? The name didn't ring any bells, although I was aware Morwenstow was one of the older properties out beyond The Grand. I told him as much.

'Yes, I know. I even have directions.' He looked pleased with himself. 'Mrs Davies is elderly, so she got her nephew to drop the dress into town for her. He mixed up the library and the *Herald*. He runs the farm now, more or less, and she does the cooking for him. She's a widow with no children of her own.'

'You've spoken to her?' I felt betrayed, as if he should have waited. Did I really think the dress was my property? In a way I did, because I'd been the first to find it, but more likely I just wanted to be the one to solve the mystery.

Perhaps he sensed my disappointment because he shot me a look. 'Ah, no, not yet. I thought I'd drive out to see her. I want her okay on letting Miriam do some work on the dress. And anything she can tell me would be helpful at this stage. I need a provenance for it. Well, I don't need it, really, although Miriam would see it differently, but I'd like to hear the story of how the dress came to be in the family, who wore it, etcetera etcetera.'

'Oh yes, you must find out everything you can.' My adrenaline was kicking in. 'Do you think Belle and Charlie might still be around? We could ...' I was going to say 'return it to them' but then I realised it was more than likely both or one of them was dead.

'Mrs Davies should be able to answer those questions,' he said, and then his next words were exactly what I hoped he'd say. 'Would you like to come with me, Sophie?'

I nodded, knowing I was grinning at him. My face felt flushed, but maybe that was the coffee.

He drained his mug. I couldn't do that, it was too hot, but I took another gulp and then put it down. We started for the door in step. It was ridiculous really, but we were like children heading for a Christmas party.

He opened the door for me. 'I rang Miriam last night. Or tried to. She's in London for some conference or other.'

'London. When will she be back?'

'Next week. Until the expert returns I'll just have to do my best,' he added with a trace of irony that made me smile. I liked him more when he displayed such human frailties. I pondered if he and Miriam had been together long, and whether they had children. But no, how could they? Miriam in London, Ian here. No children and no pets either. It sounded lonely in the McKinnon household.

'I wonder if Mrs Davies' name is Belle,' I said, as we made our way across the park. The sun was already hot and the weather forecast had promised a stinker.

He sighed. 'I can't help thinking it won't be that easy. Will we take my car? It's right here.'

There was a time when I would never have gone off alone in someone's car. I'd be suspicious and cautious in the extreme. But people in the country didn't feel like that, and despite my reasons to be vigilant I had found myself gradually settling into country ways.

Ian's car was a dusty station wagon that didn't look like it had been cleaned, ever. There was a book on the front passenger seat and he picked it up and slid it into the glove compartment.

'You live over that way,' I said, as I pulled on my seatbelt. 'Opposite the old Grand, I mean.'

'Yes.'

'I usually run there.'

'Yes. I saw you outside the other evening. You were wearing shorts.' He gave me a look up and down and then he actually blushed.

I might have made a joke about the shorts, but his blush threw me off kilter. What was that about? I didn't know whether to be insulted or amused or embarrassed. In the end I folded my arms over my baggy t-shirt and didn't say anything. Instead, I turned away and stared out of the window. Ian seemed to be busy starting the engine, his ears still pink, and then he pulled out and sped up as we left town. Neither of us spoke for a while.

The earth looked dry and parched, and the leaves on the gum trees hung down as if they were trying to escape the bright sunshine. A group of sheep clustered around the tree trunks in the shade watched us indifferently as we passed.

I took a breath, putting away the shorts comment for now. I would consider it, and his obvious discomfort, later on.

'So. The Davies farm . . .?'

He seemed relieved I'd broken the silence. 'Morwenstow. That's what it's called. I believe they named it after a place in England. I've heard it means swampy and wet.' He gave me a quick sideways glance, and I recognised the gleam in his eyes—it meant he was enjoying the absurdity. 'I think they could've done a bit better than that, don't you?'

'Hot-as-buggery, maybe?'

His lips twitched in response.

Our silence became more companionable and in due course he slowed down. 'This must be it,' he said, and turned off the road and down a long driveway that ended in a gate through the wire fence. I could see a paddock in front of the house with some horses in it and large trees shielding the building itself. He got out and opened the gate without asking me to do it, before setting off again. I would have opened it if he'd asked, but the fact he didn't made me think he was keen to get back into my good books.

Morwenstow was a sprawling, verandahed farmhouse, the sort I'd seen many times before. This one looked so old it seemed to have settled into the landscape. There was a vegetable garden to the side—the tomato leaves wilting in the sun—and some hardy shrubs at the front. When we got out of the car a border collie ran towards us, wriggling its tail with joy, and dropped down at Ian's feet.

He bent to pat the animal. 'Obviously not a guard dog,' he said to me, with that amused glint back in his eyes.

I smiled. 'No.'

We walked up the steps to the front verandah, which was set with some comfortable-looking cane chairs and a matching table, as well as a vast collection of potted plants. Ian opened a creaky screen door and tried to open the wooden inner one, but it was locked. He knocked and waited, and then knocked again. When still no one answered he went along the verandah and peered in through one of the windows.

'I can see her,' he said, and when he turned to me there was a panicked expression on his face. 'She's lying on the floor. She's not moving.'

My brain kicked into action, as it always does in an emergency. 'The back door is probably open,' I said. 'Otherwise we'll need to break a window.' The dog was barking, as if it knew something was wrong, and I caught hold of its collar.

Ian had set off around the house and a moment later he was letting me into the cool interior of the house. I followed him through to the room where Mrs Davies was lying. She was wearing a floral apron over her summery dress, and I could see her stockings, thick opaque ones. She was slender and old and brittle and I was worried that she was also dead.

'I can feel a pulse.' Ian was bent over. 'Stay here with her while I phone for an ambulance.'

I knelt down in his place. There was a cut on Mrs Davies' forehead, as if she'd fallen and struck herself on something. Probably the table a few feet away. I crawled across to the sofa and found a cushion, embroidered with forget-me-nots, and lifted her head carefully to slide it under. She groaned, stirred, and her eyes fluttered open.

They were watery blue, vague, but then they focused and she was staring up at me. And then she smiled the most beautiful, angelic smile.

'Oh, Belle,' she whispered. 'You've come back.'

CHAPTER 9

BELLE

Sweet Wattle Creek, 1931

*H*OME.

Belle, tired and overwrought, felt as if the ground was moving beneath her feet. Violet had hold of her hands now, squeezing them in sympathy or emotion. Her eyes were a very clear light blue, and Belle couldn't seem to look away.

'I'm sorry I wasn't here for my aunt's funeral,' she heard herself saying, her voice odd and stilted. 'I-I wasn't aware she had died.'

Violet's smile wavered and her eyes narrowed in puzzlement. 'But, Belle,' she blurted out. 'Surely you know Martha wasn't your aunt. She was your mother!'

'I know . . . but she gave me away when I was a baby so I don't remember —'

'You weren't a baby. You were four years old.'

Outside Belle was aware of Frank's boots drawing nearer. 'Generator won't start,' he said in disgust. He frowned when no one answered him, looking sharply from one to the other as if he could read minds. 'What is it?'

Jo pulled a face. 'Mum's just dropped a bombshell. I think.'

Violet had put a hand to her mouth and was staring at Belle with those big blue eyes. For a moment Belle wondered whether it was all an act and Violet had done it on purpose, but then the older woman reached out to her again with such a pained expression that she dismissed her doubts. 'I'm sorry, Belle.'

Belle managed to find her voice. 'I knew Martha was my mother. But since only recently, when my father . . . I mean Henry, he found a birth certificate. *My* birth certificate.'

Jo's eyes widened in astonishment. 'No one told you?'

'I believed my mother was Iris and my father Rory. They never told me. It was rather a shock.'

It was a shock yes, but since Rory's death she'd thought a lot about it and had constructed her own version of events. She was a baby and Martha didn't want her, or Rory did, but whatever the reason she was given away shortly after birth. To hear she wasn't a baby but a four-year-old child threw her creation into chaos. Somehow this seemed much worse. As if after four years Martha had decided she wasn't good enough to keep.

She'd had four years in another life she didn't remember!

Violet was looking even more contrite. 'Oh my dear, I'm so sorry. When Martha told me she had taken you to stay with her brother and his wife, I thought it was just for a little holiday. Everyone did. Rory had lost a child, you see. Poppy, that was her name. Scarlet fever. Very sad. Martha said she was going to offer them her condolences. Then when you didn't come back I tried asking her why but all she'd say was that it was for the best. Eventually she refused to answer me. Martha was very good at keeping secrets.'

'Didn't you ask Mr Ambrose?' Jo demanded.

Violet shook her head in disgust. 'He was a drunkard. I couldn't get any sense out of him.' She turned back to Belle and squeezed her hands again. 'My dear, Martha loved you. If she sent you off to Rory and Iris then she must've had a good reason.'

Belle swallowed. *Poppy.* She remembered her mother's . . . Iris's words as she lay in the hospital bed. Poor Iris. Could Martha really have given her up to replace a dead child? She felt tears stinging her eyes but held them back. There had been enough tears shed recently. Violet Davies was right. Martha must have had her reasons and Belle's life had been a good one up until the past few weeks. She had been very lucky in her parents and her home, and to begin believing she was abandoned and hard done by was ridiculous.

The kerosene lamp flickered in a draft from the open door. It seemed to break whatever spell she was under, and Belle stepped back, making Violet let go of her hands. They had begun to tingle from the other woman's frantic grip.

'This was a hotel, wasn't it?' she said. 'The Grand? My father . . . Rory said his father was a publican.' *I think he was ashamed.* But she didn't say that. She already knew she sounded as if she considered herself a cut above, but a hotel was quite beyond her experience. The truth was she'd never been inside a working man's hotel. Belle had only been to stylish places like the Windsor, or the classy restaurants frequented by the Bartholomews and their friends. The idea of entering one of the smoky public houses set on street corners in St Kilda, or anywhere else, had never occurred to her.

It wasn't her world.

Violet was explaining. 'Martha let the licence go during the war. She still lived here though. This was her home. When she died in June last year it was left empty and travellers moved in.'

Violet exchanged a look with her children, the sort that families do, as if there was more to the story and it had often been discussed between them.

'Was anyone with her when she died?'

Violet forced a smile. 'Don't worry about that now, my dear.'

Another secret. Belle knew she should insist on knowing every last thing about Martha's life and her death, but she was tired. She didn't want to ask more questions, not if she couldn't have the answers, and she was beginning to think there were details Violet was not going to tell her. Not without a struggle anyway.

Jo put the brush and pan carefully on the bench, and at the same time gave Belle a doubtful look. 'You don't really want to stay here tonight, do you, Belle? Come back to Morwenstow with us.'

She wavered. She could do that, couldn't she?

She could go back with them to what was probably a very nice bed and in the morning she could catch the train back to Melbourne and Henry and return once more to a comfortable life. She could do that, but if she did then she would never know the whole truth. Questions would remain unanswered, and she'd spend the rest of her life wondering.

'Thank you but I want to stay,' she said firmly, as if her answer had never been in doubt. 'This is all very new to me and I'm still coming to terms with it. I think staying will help. Thank you so much for tidying up and . . . and cleaning. I hope you didn't go to too much trouble, Mrs Davies . . . Miss Davies . . .'

Frank cleared his throat and Jo smiled without humour. Violet was the one to answer her, lying through her teeth, Belle thought wryly. 'Of course it was no trouble, my dear. Now, we haven't been able to prepare all the rooms, but the bedroom that used to be Martha's has fresh sheets and is nice. It's at the top of the stairs on the right. The tank still has some water in it, and if you turn on the tap there it'll run through. And there's food in the larder, tea and milk, so you'll have plenty to keep you going. We'll drop in to see you in the morning. Oh!' Again that hand over the mouth. 'I forgot. Stan has an appointment with Dr Campbell.'

'My father is an invalid,' Jo explained. 'He was gassed in the war.' She and Frank exchanged another of those glances, and Belle could see they were deciding which of them would draw the short straw. 'I'll come by,' Jo said when her brother didn't appear to be about to offer.

Belle wanted to tell them not to bother but that would be rude after all they'd done. She was a stranger and it was only because of Martha that they were here at all. Anyway, she'd be gone soon enough.

'Thank you,' she said, knowing it sounded awkward. 'Thank you for everything.'

The awkwardness amongst them increased and she was glad when they began to move towards the door. 'Oh,' Violet turned just as they were about to close it. 'I forgot to tell you, Aneas Thomas has all of Martha's personal papers. He'll be able to explain anything you want to know.'

Aneas Thomas, she remembered, was Martha's solicitor. 'I'll see him tomorrow, then.'

'We should go,' Jo said, taking her mother's arm in a firm grip. 'Belle will be all right now, won't you? I really think she wants to be alone, Mum.'

Violet murmured, 'Of course,' her blue eyes still anxious. And then finally they were gone, their voices fading in the yard and the gate creaking shut. Their car started up but a moment later someone was jogging back to the door.

Frank handed her the suitcase she'd left in his cart. 'You'll need this,' he said.

'Yes. Thank you.'

'Lock the doors. You'll be quite safe,' he said, with that intent look that made her so uncomfortable. She thought he might say more, but he only nodded and retreated once again into the darkness. This time she heard the car moving away followed by the *clip clop* of horses' hooves, until there was nothing but complete silence.

Belle stood with the suitcase in her hand and told herself it was good to be alone. Alone in the hotel that had been her mother's and Rory's when they were children. The hotel she had been born in? Perhaps. Certainly she had lived here for four years of her life. She must have run through the rooms and laughed and cried. Martha and Nathan Ambrose had been here, they had been her parents for those first four years of her life, and then they had taken her to Melbourne and handed her over to Rory and Iris, and never come back.

Belle picked up the lamp in her other hand and opened the door from the kitchen into the remainder of the building. There was a space here, almost like a vestibule, with another door to her left, and a staircase rising to a landing in front of her. She took the left-hand door and found herself in another room. It was full: furniture and ornaments and other items she couldn't recognise in the half-dark. There were jumbled piles in corners and against the walls, reaching upwards and outwards, almost to where she was standing.

Belle decided it was probably better to do further exploring in daylight.

Violet had said that Martha's room was at the top of the stairs, on the right. The bare staircase creaked under her shoes. As she reached the landing and turned to mount the final flight, the shadows fled before her lamp and above her she could see a passage with closed doors on either side. And at the far end there was one other door.

Unexpectedly Belle was cold. It was a clamminess that seemed to come from within, despite the captured heat inside the building. She couldn't move, and stood anchored to the spot. She found that her eyes were fixed on the door at the very end of the passage. It had a small brass knob and she felt as if it might move, turn, and something come out. Something she didn't remember but which terrified her.

What she was feeling was primal. A sensation without reason. But at least it was brief.

The fear or terror or whatever it had been was already draining out of her. Her head ached. A memory? Or simply being overwrought and over-tired? She turned to Martha's bedroom and with trembling fingers twisted the porcelain knob and pushed the door open.

The lamp light showed it to be a large room with pale-coloured walls and two sash windows. The bed was one of those old-fashioned high ones, and covered in a quilt made of green-and-pink-patterned squares. Belle didn't know what she had been expecting, but this felt peaceful and pleasant. She set the lamp aside and pushed herself up so she was sitting on the edge of the mattress. Her feet didn't touch the wooden planks of the floor.

She looked about her. There were about half a dozen small framed paintings on the walls. Landscapes, she thought, although it was difficult to see. A heavy chest of drawers was against one wall, with a wardrobe, and a Victorian dressing table with a mirror in a barleycorn frame. A candle sat on the dressing table, ready to be lit. The fireplace was filled with pine cones in a basket and there was a colourful rag rug on the floor.

Were these all Martha's belongings or had Violet brought them with her? What had The Grand been like when Martha died? From the piles of rubbish she'd seen in the room downstairs Belle had a sinking feeling that things had been bad. She would ask Jo tomorrow. Jo seemed the sort to tell the truth rather than spare her feelings.

She began to unpack her few belongings, hanging up the spare blouse in the wardrobe, and placing her shoes beneath it. Her brush and comb she set on the dressing table, with her soap, toothbrush and dental paste, Ponds cleansing cream, and her few items of makeup. Her underwear she slipped into a drawer.

The others were all empty. There was nothing left here of her mother, of Martha. Not even a stoppered bottle which had once held perfume.

Her pyjamas felt comfortingly familiar and the scent clinging to them reminded her of Annat Street. She breathed in deeply and wished she was home. And then she reminded herself that she had no home. Although that wasn't quite true, was it? She had The Grand.

Belle thought about brushing the dust out of her hair and then wondered whether she could be bothered going back downstairs and getting something to eat. Violet had promised there was food. But now it was just too much effort to leave the bedroom, and the thought of seeing that door again made her queasy.

There was a basin and jug with cold water in it. She poured the water and splashed it over her face, eyeing the Ponds cleansing cream and deciding against it. She was too tired.

What was Henry doing? Was he thinking of her? More likely he was out dining with his important client, putting on a good show. Belle moved restlessly. Thinking of Henry wasn't as comforting as she'd hoped and instead her thoughts turned once more to the mystery of Martha and Nathan Ambrose.

Why had they given her up? If she had been meant as a replacement for Poppy then why hadn't they visited? It was almost as if all communications had been cut between brother and sister, not something you'd expected after such an act of kindness. If that was indeed what it was.

The lamp flickered and Belle turned it out and went to the window. It had been opened for the breeze and she left it that way. The night sky was clear and starry, and it seemed different. Wider and brighter and quite beautiful. Belle found she was spellbound as she leaned over the sill, looking up.

Why hadn't Rory spoken of The Grand? Was he really so ashamed of his past?

So many questions. Belle knew they would have to wait until the morning when she spoke with Aneas Thomas. And for that she needed a good night's sleep.

Belle opened her eyes. She felt disorientated. It was still dark and it took a little while for her vision to adjust. The air had cooled in the room and she had been deeply asleep, but something had woken her.

An image of the door at the end of the passage, the one with the brass handle, came immediately to mind. As if it had been waiting to spring on her.

'Don't be ridiculous,' she told herself sharply. Her voice seemed very loud and she was about to get up and light the candle when a flickering glow came through the uncurtained window.

A light. It happened again and then seemed to shift away, jerkily, as if someone was walking and carrying a lantern at the same time.

She remembered Frank's talk of travellers and the constable seeing them off. Had they come back? Perhaps, she thought, they were out there somewhere in the dark, trying to get inside. As a woman alone she was vulnerable.

Carefully, she climbed out of the bed and tiptoed over to the window. Her toes curled on the bare floorboards as she concentrated on the view beneath her.

This bedroom faced the side of the hotel away from the road, and there were paddocks stretching towards a distant line of trees. It wasn't as dark as she'd thought because of the stars, but the mysterious light seemed to have gone. And yet . . . she had the strangest sensation that someone was out in the darkness, watching her.

Shivering, she wrapped her arms about herself. She felt no desire to go outside, alone, and hunt down whoever it was. The Grand enclosed her. It was hers, she was home, and somehow she felt ridiculously safe. Tomorrow would be soon enough to face whatever surprises and revelations awaited her beyond its strong walls.

CHAPTER 10

SOPHIE

Sweet Wattle Creek, 1986

THE AMBULANCE HAD arrived from Riverton. We'd made Mrs Davies comfortable and tried to reassure her that help was on its way, but after calling me 'Belle' she'd lapsed back into unconsciousness. Josh, her nephew, had turned up just after the medicos, looking wild-eyed with worry.

I let Ian do the explaining. I was feeling a bit shaky myself as I sat down on the front steps of the farmhouse. The border collie snuggled up against me—he was in a similar state to Josh— and I was happy to pet him and watch from a distance. I had an association with ambulances I didn't really want to relive just now.

Mrs Davies was loaded into the back of the vehicle, and when it drove away, Josh followed after it in his ute. Ian watched them go before he came over and sat down beside me.

'You okay?' he asked, and he looked at me as if he really wanted to know and wasn't just being polite.

I wasn't used to that, and it took me a few seconds to answer. I didn't intend mentioning what Mrs Davies had said. I still wasn't quite sure I'd heard her correctly, or that was what I was telling myself. Really, I knew I had. It just seemed so odd that I wanted to mull over it for a while, and try to sort it out for myself.

'Yep, I'm okay. What about you? Did they say she was going to be all right or . . .?'

'They didn't say much.' He stared towards the road, where the dust was still drifting from the departing vehicles. 'Josh asked if we'd look after Smithy.' The look he gave me this time made me think he expected an argument.

'Smithy?' I was imagining some ageing gentleman, bedridden, in a back room.

'Smithy,' he said, and slid his hand under the collie's muzzle and lifted it up so we were eye to eye. 'This is Smithy. He's Mrs Davies's pride and joy. Named after Charles Kingsford Smith, the aviator. Mrs Davies saw the man himself when she was a young woman and was rather smitten.'

'Oh.'

'Smithy's not a working dog and Josh is worried he might pine away here on his own, but I think he's *more* worried about what his aunt will do to him if anything happens to Smithy.'

'Oh. And you couldn't refuse?'

He pulled a face. 'It seemed churlish to say no in the circumstances. Would you have refused?'

'Of course not.' I sighed.

It was tranquil out here. A big pepper tree protected the building from the full force of the sun, its feathery leaves stirring faintly whenever there was the whisper of a breeze. There wasn't much livestock that I could see, apart from the horses, and they stood in the shade, too, tails swishing. If the Davies's family business had been reduced to an old lady and her nephew, I could understand why it was so quiet.

'Come on, then,' Ian said, getting to his feet. Smithy followed him and didn't seem too concerned about jumping into the back of the car, although he did pause to give me the sort of look that seemed to say: 'Are you coming?'

As I walked from the house and the shade of the tree, the heat felt stifling. We needed a storm to cool things down, but by the look of the eye-watering blue sky there wasn't much chance of rain.

Ian's car didn't seem to have a functioning air conditioner, so I half opened Smithy's window—not far enough for him to jump out—and then my own. Ian waited for me to get settled and then he started up the station wagon. This time I got out to open the gate, without being asked, and he smiled at me when I climbed back in. That was nice. I hoped Miriam appreciated him, I thought, as we drove back in the direction of Sweet Wattle Creek.

'So much for our detective work,' Ian said, raising his voice above the noise from the open windows. 'We still don't know the story of the wedding dress.'

'We can ask her later. When she's recovered.' I didn't like to mention that she may not.

'Do you mind if I drop Smithy off with you at the *Herald*?' He glanced at me to gauge my reaction. 'I don't think Nola would like it if I took him into the library with me.'

'She might. What do you think, Smithy? Can you sort books for Nola?'

Ian snorted a laugh.

'Ian, I have a very small backyard,' I said, wishing I could say no. 'And a very large cat.'

Ian didn't seem to consider those excuses good enough. 'I'll come and collect him later,' he said. 'Or maybe Josh'll take him back to Morwenstow.'

I peeped over to the back seat, where Smithy was lying. He lifted his head, his doggy eyes miserable, as if he knew we were discussing him.

'Oh, all right. If it's only for a little while. I don't think my landlord would approve if I had him for too long.'

Tim was my landlord and he wouldn't mind, but I wasn't going to encourage either Ian or Smithy.

'Thanks, Sophie. I'm sorry to dump the dog on you, but . . .'

'Neither of us could say no.' I tucked my hair behind my ears, aware of my t-shirt sticking to my sweaty skin. The breeze through the window was warm, but it was better than nothing. 'Can you take me and Smithy home? I'll ring Tim and let him know what's happened.'

'I'm sorry to mess up your day,' he said with an anxious look.

'You haven't messed up my day,' I assured him. 'It wasn't your fault it went wrong. Poor Mrs Davies. And poor you, Smithy,' I added over the seat. 'Perhaps Josh knows about the dress?' I said hopefully, turning back to Ian. 'Did you ask him?'

'No, it didn't seem the right time. I'll ask him when I ring later on to see how his aunt is doing.'

Once we reached town I directed Ian to my house and he pulled up outside. When I opened the back door of the car, Smithy crept out and sat, tail moving tentatively, looking from me to Ian. I knelt down.

'It's all right, boy. This is just temporary. You'll be fine if you stay away from the cat. He'd tear you to shreds.'

Despite my warning, Smithy seemed to perk up at the mention of a cat and he followed us inside the house quite cheerfully.

Ian led the dog through the big glass windows that opened onto the small concrete patio and the rectangle of lawn. I'd put some potted herbs out there, but they didn't look very happy. After a year I still wasn't used to the dry heat of Sweet Wattle Creek. I'd grown up in the tropics, to humidity and lush vegetation, and sometimes the parched brown land was depressing.

I found a water bowl and some old blankets for a bed and took them out onto the patio. Ian was giving Smithy a pat and a talking-to, so I left them to it and put the kettle on.

I have a theory that people who are kind to animals are usually good people. It isn't always foolproof but very nearly. Walter had no time for animals. I should have known what sort of person he was the first time he said it, but by then I was in too deep.

The kettle had boiled by the time Ian joined

me in the kitchen. He'd rolled up his shirtsleeves today—a small concession to the heat—but he didn't seem to feel it like I did.

'I'll have to get back to the library,' he said. 'There are things I need to sort out—you'd be amazed how many donations I get every day. And then I want to set up some more displays in the hall. Nola told me the committee's planning a surprise visit.'

'Sounds daunting. Just as well she's on your side. Although I'm sure they'll be happy with what you've done.'

'Thanks. They want their money's worth. I understand that.'

'Coffee?' I asked. 'I only have instant.'

'Is there any other kind?'

While I was making it, he wandered through the arched doorway into the lounge and peered at the framed prints on my wall. They didn't mean anything, they were just random objects d'art. I'd left all my belongings behind me. But there was one small print of a flowering flame tree, its red flowers brilliant against a cloudless blue sky. I'd had one just like that outside my house in Brisbane, and somehow when I saw this for sale in an op shop in Riverton I just couldn't resist.

'I like this,' he said.

'Yes, it's nice, isn't it? So, apart from the Centenary Exhibition . . . what else is the committee arranging? Sorry, I should know. Tim's always telling me.'

He turned to look at me and for a moment I thought my swift change of subject had given me away, but an instant later he smiled and it seemed as though I'd got away with it.

'A ball with everyone in fancy dress and a Back to Sweet Wattle Creek at the primary school for all the former students. There'll be posters and pamphlets to hand out to the shops. I think the committee's also paying for a few radio advertisements, and one for television in the last week before the big weekend. And of course we have the *Herald*'s invaluable publicity.'

'Ah. I'll get on to that. Pity about the dress, but I think I need to know the whole story before I can put it together. Perhaps I'll take a photo of you on that ladder in the hall and do a bit about you and Miriam.'

He set down his cup carefully and then looked at me. 'You say that as though Miriam and I are an item.'

Did my mouth fall open? 'Aren't you? You said "your partner" so I just assumed . . . '

'That I was being precious about calling her my girlfriend?' He gave that wry half-smile and I noticed his ears were pink, which meant he was embarrassed again. 'She's my business partner. Nothing more. Well, she's also a friend. We've known each other for eons.'

'Right. Sorry.' I fiddled with my own cup, the coffee half drunk. 'Not that it's any of my business, of course.'

He didn't answer.

'Eh, so you're living next to The Grand. Not exactly the view I'd want from my front window.'

'I suppose not. It has quite a history, you know.

The Grand. It may pay you to read up on it. Might make a good story for the *Herald*. I'm planning a special corner for it at the exhibition. The Bartholomews owned it, one of the original settler families. In fact, they were here before Sweet Wattle Creek.'

I made the right noises but I wasn't really listening. I was still trying to work out why he'd been so adamant about Miriam not being his girlfriend, and why he thought it should matter to me. Did it matter to me? Why did I have this light, fluttery feeling going on inside?

He finished his last gulp of coffee. 'That was good but I'd better go. Thanks for your help with Mrs Davies and Smithy. I never meant to involve you in any of that.'

'There's nothing to thank me for, and it really wasn't your fault. You'll let me know how Mrs Davies is?'

He stared at me as if there was more to say but he couldn't remember what it was. Finally he just nodded and turned to leave. I heard his car start up and drive away, but I didn't move. Not for a long time.

I arrived back at the *Herald* after lunch, and Tim met me at the door of my office. He'd been bemused when I rang him earlier and told him what had happened, and he still didn't seem to be ticking any boxes.

'And this was the Mrs Davies who sent the parcel? The wedding dress, you said?'

'It belonged to someone called Belle, who married Charlie.'

He shook his head. 'Sorry. Doesn't ring any bells in my sleep-deprived mind.'

I looked at him hopefully. 'Would *you* like to look after Mrs Davies's border collie?'

Tim stared and then he began to laugh. 'No! Here, I took some phone calls for you, told them you'd get back to them.'

'Right. Thanks. Do you know much about The Grand? Ian thinks that would make a good story.'

'Ian, huh?' He chuckled.

'You're being childish.'

Tim had already moved on. 'Hmm. The Grand. We probably do have some stories from the old days when my grandfather ran the *Herald*. Bill would've written one about the fire, that's for certain. I can search the archives when I have a spare minute.'

Which meant never. 'I'll do it.' I didn't mind. I liked searching through the *Herald* archives. They were a treasure-trove of information.

When Tim had gone I returned the phone calls and completed some work on sporting events that had happened or were due to happen. The local football team was on the verge of folding after another poor showing in the finals, but it had been limping on for years. My ideas for the Centenary edition of the *Herald* were coming along nicely, although I still needed to find out who Belle and Charlie were, and who the dress had belonged to, but I was confident that would come. I just hoped Ian wouldn't find out before I did.

Idly, I wondered how he was getting along with the visit of the committee to the hall. Were they impressed? I couldn't imagine they wouldn't be but you never knew. I was tempted to go over on the pretence of taking that photograph of him on the ladder, just so that I could eavesdrop. But no, I'd spent enough time with Ian McKinnon for one day. He might start to get the wrong idea.

Actually, I was worried he already had.

I turned my thoughts to old Mrs Davies lying on the floor, looking up at me and calling me 'Belle'. I had fair hair, so perhaps Belle did, too. And blue eyes? Or was the old lady affected by her head injury and simply seeing things that weren't there? But she must know Belle. Her name was on the box containing the wedding dress, so Mrs Davies had to know her from somewhere, and surely you didn't give your wedding dress to a total stranger?

Thinking of Mrs Davies reminded me of Smithy. I glanced at my watch. Dillon would be home from school soon. I'd left him a note on the kitchen bench so Smithy wouldn't be a complete surprise to him, but I needed to see to the dog's needs. In other words, I had to get food.

'I'm heading home,' I told Ellie. She nodded, ear still glued to the telephone, and waggled her fingers. Her nails were painted blood red today. Brad had already gone but he'd had an early start. Tim's small staff were a dedicated bunch.

Leaving the search through the archives for

another day, I set off for the general store. Word of
Mrs Davies seemed to have got about. There was
a cluster of three women around the dairy fridge,
shaking their heads and looking concerned. I
found myself listening to them as I hesitated over
vintage or cheddar.

'I knew *old* Mrs Davies,' said one of them. 'The
mother. Violet, she was. A dear soul. Heart of
gold.'

I'd noticed before that once someone died
their reputation suddenly assumed saintlike pro-
portions, no matter how awful they might have
been in life. But perhaps I was cynical.

'She had her crosses to bear,' murmured the
second woman. 'Her husband was gassed in the
First World War, you know. Mustard gas. He was
never right after that. Couldn't do any of the
work on the farm.'

'Plenty never came back at all,' muttered the
third woman, not to be outdone in the bad-news
stakes.

I decided this was my chance. I didn't know
any of them very well, only to nod and smile at
and talk about the weather. But they knew who
I was, I was sure. People in small towns were like
elephants when it came to social history, and it
was possible one of these three knew about Belle
and Charlie.

'Excuse me,' I said, giving them my best smile. 'I
couldn't help but overhear. I was going to interview Mrs Davies before she took ill. She has a
dress that she's given to the Centenary Exhibition.'

They turned to eye me in surprise and a little suspicion. 'You're from the *Herald*.'

'Yes, I am. The dress Mrs Davies gave to the exhibition was a wedding dress and we think . . . *I* think it might have belonged to Belle, who was going to marry Charlie.'

Glances were exchanged. 'Charlie? No, I don't think so. Nothing to do with Mrs Davies, dear. Sorry.' Their mouths closed and it was clear nothing more was going to be said, even if they did know the answers to my questions.

I thanked them and went off to buy the dog food.

When I got home Dillon was sitting on the sofa watching cartoons, and Smithy was at his feet. BC was sitting high up on the bookshelf, glaring down at the scene with contempt.

'Where did the dog come from, Mum?' Dillon asked as soon as I was through the door. He took the bag from me and put it on the counter, taking out a tin for Smithy. 'He's hungry. I gave him a biscuit but I don't think that'd be good for his teeth. Christy said he needs proper food.'

'Christy?'

Did he blush? 'She was over for a little while. Homework.' He shrugged as if that was all there was to it. I knew Dillon was a good boy, but he was still sorting through what had happened a year ago. I didn't want him embroiled in a relationship at fourteen.

Smithy was wagging his tail enthusiastically as Dillon opened the tin and put out the dog food on one of my best plates. We both watched, smiling, as the dog wolfed it down. It was only when BC let out a raucous meow that we remembered he also had to be fed.

My son did that, too, petting the cat and placing his food far away from Smithy. I remembered my thoughts of earlier, that those who were kind to animals were generally good people. Well, if that was the case then my son had to be one of the best.

CHAPTER 11

BELLE

Sweet Wattle Creek, 1931

WITH AN EFFORT, Belle swung her legs over the side of the mattress. She'd forgotten how high it was and only just saved herself from serious hurt as she landed on the floor. Limping across to the window in her ecru satin pyjamas, she took in a view of horses standing in dry brown paddocks, tails already swishing in the heat, and then a line of trees beyond which there was a trail of smoke. She tried to make out whether it was coming from a chimney or a distant bushfire, but the sky was so blue it made her eyes ache.

No sign of her visitor of last night, but now that it was morning it seemed entirely possible she had imagined the moving light. And the watching eyes.

She leaned forward, resting her elbows on the sill, and tried to picture Martha standing here at her bedroom window, thinking of the day ahead. Perhaps thinking of her daughter far away. Belle squeezed shut her eyes, sending herself back into the past, trying to remember. A bird shrieked and the scent of gumtrees and dust made her nose twitch. She squeezed her eyes tighter but no matter how hard she tried nothing happened. If the memories were there they weren't eager to make an appearance, not yet anyway.

She may never understand what had driven Martha to give up her daughter. The reason may not even have been a complicated one. Maybe it was as simple as Martha, busy having a hotel to run, finding the effort of looking after a child just too much trouble, and seeing an opportunity to rid herself of the problem. Had she been unwanted from the day she was born?

That was a painful thought, and yet it was entirely possible. Many children were unwanted. She'd been lucky that Rory and Iris had loved her and given her such a comfortable life. And yet . . . she didn't feel as if that was the reason. The very act of giving a child to such a couple showed a level of caring. And there was more, she knew it. The knowledge throbbed away like an aching tooth and she wanted, *needed*, to know.

The sun was getting higher. She must clean her teeth and wash her face, and then she would examine the food left by the Davies women and decide what she wanted for breakfast. Her stomach rumbled and she realised how hungry she was. She was halfway down the stairs when the clammy feeling came over her.

She stood, frozen. The need to look back, over her shoulder, was so urgent she could no longer resist, even though she wanted to. Reluctantly, she turned and her gaze fastened on the closed door at the end of the passage. Her heart gave a heavy thud.

At this angle she could see the small brass knob and it seemed to be turning. Opening. Whatever was behind it was about to step out . . . Her body gave a violent start and just like that the sensations began to dissipate. She tried to hang on to them, to understand, but already they were gone.

'For heaven's sake, Belle,' she scolded aloud, 'pull yourself together.'

She couldn't remember a thing of her early life, and yet she was afraid of a door! Taking a deep breath, and then another, she pushed away her jumbled emotions and continued down to the kitchen.

She was going to see Martha's solicitor this morning. Aneas Thomas. Henry said that he was the man to talk to, and Violet had told her last night he had care of Martha's personal papers. Belle was returning to Melbourne on the afternoon train so she needed to accomplish all her tasks as soon as possible.

Normally that wouldn't be a problem. Belle was someone who was used to getting things done in a timely manner. Unfortunately, it was Sweet Wattle Creek that didn't seem to be in a hurry.

The old adage was true. A full stomach did improve one's outlook on the world. Narrowing her eyes once more against the brilliance of the day, she stepped outside the back door of The

Grand. Hands planted on her hips, Belle surveyed the yard.

Some of the out-buildings looked as if a strong wind would blow them over. She pulled at the rickety door of the old stable building but it had dropped and was now stuck on the paving. Belle needed a couple of good tugs to get it open, and she had to stop once and brush dust off her pencil skirt. She didn't really know what she was looking for, but this had been her home and she wanted to see if there was anything that might jog her memory. A few sticks of broken furniture—bits and pieces that had clearly been put in here, out of the way, and then forgotten. Curtains of cobwebs hung in swathes from the ceiling beams and she backed away with a grimace, wondering if they were occupied.

From the appearance of the place, it had been a long time since anyone had kept horses in here. Which seemed to imply that the horses in the paddocks couldn't belong to Martha.

Next was the garage, whose door opened much more easily. Inside was an object covered in a tarpaulin. She eyed it cautiously before easing off the covering. A motorcycle, the body painted green, with *Triumph* written in white, and attached to it was a sidecar that looked like a large cane basket with a padded seat.

The sight was so unexpected that Belle laughed out loud. Had this been Martha's? She tried to picture her mother speeding around the countryside with herself in the sidecar and couldn't. Besides, it wasn't that old. She remembered particularly because Charlie had had one like it and, after the war, every time she saw a young man riding by it had been a reminder of all she had lost.

Although the motorcycle had been covered, it seemed remarkably clean when everything else was filthy. Almost as if someone had been working on it. She was certain, if she tried to start it, that the engine would fire up.

The motorcycle could be sold. Although, her hand lingered on the shiny body, she wasn't sure who it belonged to, despite it being in her garage. Perhaps someone was storing it here because they believed The Grand to be empty?

She turned around and that was when she saw the makeshift bed. It was tucked in between a pile of crates and the wall, which was why she hadn't seen it when she'd come in. Belle went over to look, noting the stack of neatly folded blankets and the pillow on top. There was something almost military about the precision.

She was still standing there, puzzling, when she heard Jo call out her name.

'How did you sleep?'

That was Jo's first question. In the light of day she looked taller, more slender, her brown hair braided and coiled around her head rather than cut short as Belle had imagined it to be last night.

'Well, thank you,' said Belle, her polite voice firmly in place.

Jo didn't reply but she looked sceptical. She had a basket with her and an armful of what appeared to be towels and various other household necessities. 'We have plenty of eggs and milk. That's the joy of living on a farm, if we're hungry we always have something we can cobble together. Makes us luckier than most at the moment.'

Belle must have looked bemused.

'People without work, without homes, without food,' Jo explained a little impatiently. 'The children at my school, some of them don't have shoes. They haven't eaten. Isn't it like that where you come from?'

'Yes, yes, of course.' Only it wasn't, not in the circles the Bartholomews had moved in. She hadn't been heartless, just blind. With a mental jolt she realised that she would have to think about such things now.

'Mum sent you these. There's a bag of biscuits from the store, too. Not the broken ones.'

'Store?'

'We own the general store. Frank runs it mostly, but we all take our turn. Flo's there some of the time—she's a widow from Riverton—or Mum goes in.'

The Davies were the entrepreneurs of Sweet Wattle Creek, Belle thought, but didn't say it. Jo would think she was being facetious.

'I'm sorry if Mum upset you last night, Belle, but she means well. She was so keen to see that you were properly welcomed home. For Martha's sake.'

'I know, I didn't . . .' She shook her head, trying

to decide how to approach her new acquaintance. Belle preferred to keep a bit of distance between herself and the world. She held back and didn't give of herself willingly. Not since Charlie.

'I didn't quite know what to expect when I arrived. Certainly not so much kindness.'

Jo had been watching her with a frown but now she smiled. 'Let's go,' she said. 'It'll only get hotter.'

Belle hesitated. She hadn't shown Jo the bed or the motorcycle in the garage, and now she didn't know if she should. If it was one of the travellers the constable had meant to move on, then what would happen if his hiding place was discovered? She'd been sorry for the people she'd seen yesterday, walking along the train tracks. A sort of fellow feeling.

'Are you all right?'

Jo was looking at her oddly and Belle forced herself to smile. 'Yes. Sorry. Shall we go?'

The Morris was already hot inside and they wound down the windows. A trickle of perspiration was making its way along the middle of Belle's back and she wriggled to divert it. She smoothed her skirt and felt her stockings sticking to her damp legs. Although she'd left off her jacket, it had seemed important to dress up for the solicitor.

'Your brother said your farm is beyond The Grand,' she said, making conversation.

'Morwenstow? Yes. First the Beauchamp's place and then Morwenstow. The Davies were some of the earliest settlers here in Sweet Wattle Creek.

Not as early as your family, of course.'

Her family.

'The horses in the fields around the house.' Belle could see they'd already reached the out-skirts of town. 'Are they yours?'

'Goodness me, no. The Beauchamps own all the horses. You probably can't see their house for the trees, but it's only a twenty-minute walk from The Grand. Less if you're riding. They have sta-bles and they race. They also own the cinema in Riverton. One of the boys is something to do with talking pictures, down in Melbourne. They consider themselves a cut above the rest of us,' she added with a smile, to take the sting out of it. 'But don't let that worry you. They're newcom-ers. The Bartholomews and the Davies . . . we're Sweet Wattle Creek aristocracy.'

'Considering I've only been here for five min-utes,' Belle spoke wryly and Jo chuckled. It felt nice, comfortable, and Belle wondered whether, if she stayed here longer, Jo might become a friend.

The town centre had a number of verandahed shops and businesses on either side of Main Street. Jo was chatting about the cinema in Riverton.

'They showed Al Jolson in *The Jazz Singer* last Saturday night. Amazing to actually hear people talk on film! The Beauchamps had to get the cin-ema updated especially. Before that they'd only been able to show the silent films. Not that I have anything against them. I loved *Flesh and the Devil*. Don't tell Mum that though.'

Belle had seen *The Jazz Singer* when it came out a couple of years ago. She wasn't rude enough to say it but Jo guessed.

'You'll find we're behind the times out here,' she said, clearly not concerned. 'If you stay long enough you'll be grateful for *any* film, no matter how old. But then you won't be staying, will you?'

'No. I'm going back today. The afternoon train.'

Jo said nothing more. They'd pulled up at the kerb on Main Street and it was time to get out. 'Thank you,' Belle said again. 'You've been very kind to me. I know your mother remembers me from when I was a child but that was such a long time ago. She went to a great deal of trouble for a stranger.'

'Country towns are like that,' Jo replied. Her eyes were amused. 'We'd never let one of our own starve or sleep in grubby sheets. And despite what you think, as Martha's daughter you *are* one of our own.'

'Aneas Thomas has his office just there. You have to go upstairs. If I'm still in town when you've finished I can give you a lift back. I'll be over there so if you see the car then you'll know I'm still around,' and she pointed across the street where there was a small park and the familiar statue of a soldier with his head bowed. A memorial to those lost in the Great War.

Belle climbed out of the car, a new trickle of perspiration following the other one down her spine. She had the distinct sensation that she might begin to melt into a puddle on the footpath.

The solicitor's office was situated above a shop.

From a glance in the window at a display of sad-looking handbags with tarnished metal clasps, she thought it was a second-hand shop, but then she noticed the plaque. 'Cash paid for goods'. A pawnbroker, then.

Belle climbed the stairs, straightening her skirt and smoothing back her fair hair. The air was as still and hot as the inside of an oven. How on earth could anyone work?

The door to the office opened onto a small space where a woman sat at a desk with a Remington typewriter in front of her and a rattly electric fan to her side. She was clacking away on the keys, frowning fiercely down at her work, and with all the noise she didn't notice Belle.

'Excuse me. May I speak to Mr Thomas?'

Her head came up with a start and she stopped typing. Her hair was a reddish colour mixed with grey and her eyes, under heavy unplucked brows, were a washed-out blue.

'Oh! You did give me a fright. Yes, he's in. Who shall I say?' Her face was flushed as she got clumsily to her feet and Belle could see her floral blouse had large damp circles under the arms.

'Miss Belle Bartholomew. My aunt . . . that is, Martha Ambrose, left me her hotel.'

Now the woman's eyes narrowed. 'Oh my goodness. Oh yes. I'll go and let him know you're here, Miss Bartholomew.'

She vanished through an inner door, and although Belle couldn't hear what the woman was saying, she could pick up her agitated tone of voice. It was upsetting really, Belle thought, that her personal life was being discussed by people she didn't even know. This, she suspected, was the uncomfortable reality of life in a small town.

The woman reappeared, her stare avid, and she held the door open for Belle. But Mr Thomas had followed her out and came to shake hands. He was a tall, gangly man with a circle of grey hair around a bald dome of a head. He was wearing a jacket with shiny elbows and his shirt cuffs had been darned. Belle couldn't help but wonder how good a solicitor he was if he couldn't afford to buy new clothes. Henry wouldn't be seen dead in something so shabby. But then she reminded herself that it could simply be the hard times.

'Miss Bartholomew!' He seemed genuinely pleased to see her and his pale eyes shone with warmth. There was an undercurrent of excitement about him, as if he had been looking forward to this meeting. 'Lyn and I went to meet your train yesterday, but when it was so late we didn't know if you were coming. I'm afraid the train service has become very unreliable.'

'I'm sorry to have put you out. I didn't realise.'

'Never mind, you aren't to blame. I believe Frank Davies stepped in.'

He showed her into the office and offered her a chair. 'The weather has been trying the past week,' he said with understatement. She noticed his gaze taking her in. Martha had been his client for many years, and he was bound to be curious. Did he see a resemblance? Did she look like her mother?

A moment later his secretary brought them tea

and some jam drops. The woman was smiling a tight, forced smile, and when he didn't acknowledge her, she tapped her finger on his shoulder. He gave her a startled look. 'Oh, I'm sorry. This is my sister, Miss Bartholomew. Lyn Thomas.'

'Miss Bartholomew, eh, Ambrose, so nice to meet you. I don't remember you as a child, I'm afraid, and I don't suppose you remember much about Sweet Wattle Creek, do you?'

'Not a thing.'

Lyn was clearly dying to prolong the conversation but her brother wasn't having it. He gave a meaningful nod at the door and, with a frown at him, she turned and left them alone.

Aneas Thomas waited until he'd stirred a teaspoon of sugar into his dark brew and then got down to business.

'I'm sure you know I handled Martha's affairs while she was alive, and I'm her executor now that she's deceased. I was rather surprised when the letter I wrote to her brother wasn't answered. I expected Rory to come back to Sweet Wattle Creek. Although he wasn't the beneficiary of his sister's will, one would think . . . his sister dying . . . that he would want to attend her funeral.'

His look was curious and Belle did her best to explain the inexplicable.

'He didn't tell me she'd died. I'm sorry. I only found out after . . . after Rory himself was gone. But of course our solicitor, Henry Collier, will have told you about all of that.'

'He mentioned there were business problems at the time that prevented Mr Bartholomew from travelling.' His expression was frank and sincere and also, Belle decided, kind. She felt herself relax a little. Possibly Martha had relied upon Aneas Thomas for more than legal representation. Perhaps he had been her friend.

He sipped his tea and set down the cup carefully, turning it so that it was perfectly placed. 'The long and short of it, Miss Bartholomew, is that Martha left you all of her worldly goods.'

Such as they were. A hotel in the middle of nowhere and a Triumph motorcycle. But was there more? A surprise stash that would help her save the house in St Kilda at the last moment?

'Can you explain what "her worldly goods" consist of, Mr Thomas?'

'Of course. Although,' he gave her another of his keen looks, 'if you're hoping for a windfall, I'm afraid there's very little in the way of financial benefit. The Grand hasn't been a functioning hotel in a very long time. Mrs Ambrose was advised to sell but she refused. I doubt anyone would buy it in the present financial climate.'

Belle was smoothing her white gloves, removing the creases from each finger with care, as if flawless gloves would help her through this difficult time. Or was it that she just didn't want Mr Thomas to see the panic in her eyes.

'She left no money?'

He didn't seem to mind her bluntness—in fact he smiled, and was blunt himself. 'Very little money. There are a number of bonds but with the stock market crash and the current financial situation, I wouldn't imagine you'll be able to cash them in. If you could sell the property . . . but as I said, I doubt anyone around here would be keen on buying.'

Belle sat very still. She had come to Sweet Wattle Creek only to find a circumstance that was eerily similar to the one back in St Kilda. But at least Henry could sell the St Kilda house. What was she meant to do with The Grand? Let it slide further into decay?

'I don't understand why she would want to keep it. It must've been a millstone around her neck.'

'Oh I can answer that,' he said. 'Martha wanted to keep it so that she had something to leave. She hoped . . . I know she always hoped that you would come home. I can only think that was the reason.' He smiled. 'You're very like her, you know. Not in appearance, although you have something of her in your face, but in the way you ask questions. As if you expect an answer straightaway. That's pure Martha. She was always trying to hurry us up.'

Belle felt tears sting her eyes and looked away, her voice dropping. 'I don't understand why she gave me away. It seems quite bizarre to discover at my age that my parents aren't my parents.'

Aneas shuffled his papers, possibly embarrassed by her emotion or his inability to explain his client's actions. 'I'm afraid I don't know the answer to that question, Miss Bartholomew. Martha was a private person. Her friend, Violet Davies, might've been in her confidence. Or Michael.'

The name seemed to resonate. Did it mean

something to her? Belle wasn't sure. She was tired and emotional and she might be imagining things.

'Michael?'

'Michael Maxwell.'

'I thought my father's name was Nathan Ambrose?'

'Yes. Nathan Ambrose died in 1915.' Again that hesitation followed by the apologetic smile. 'To be honest, Miss Bartholomew—and I think like Martha you prefer me to be honest with you—Nathan was an alcoholic. He lived at The Grand but their marriage had become a formality only.'

Her father was a drunk. 'Poor Martha.'

'Yes.'

'And Michael Maxwell. Who is he?'

'His parents were residents of Sweet Wattle Creek but they perished in a fire when he was still a boy. Martha was very fond of him. He stayed with her at The Grand, and helped with the running of the place. He was a pilot. Went off to fight in the war but afterwards he came back. The Grand was no longer a working hotel by then—Martha had given up the licence when Nathan died—but he helped her with the upkeep. Unfortunately, he was away when she passed on. I did hear a rumour that he was back in town, but I haven't seen him myself, nor had a chance to speak to him.'

It sounded intriguing and slightly worrying.

'But . . . I would've thought, in the circumstances, she would've left her property to this Michael Maxwell.' It sounded to Belle as if

Michael had been more of a son to Martha than she had been a daughter.

Aneas hesitated and then he sighed. 'Once again I'm being candid, Miss Bartholomew. She *did* leave The Grand to Michael originally, but she changed her will not long before she died.'

'Oh.'

He cleared his throat. 'In regard to Michael . . . I should warn you . . .'

A tap on the door interrupted him. Lyn stuck her head in. 'More tea?' she asked brightly.

'No, not for me,' Aneas replied a little rudely, Belle thought.

'Nor me, thank you, Miss Thomas.'

Lyn widened her eyes. 'Oh no, it's *Mrs* Thomas,' she said. 'Aneas calls me his sister but I am in actual fact his sister-in-law. I was his brother, Alister's wife.'

The clarification seemed so important to her that Belle felt like apologising, but as she opened her mouth to do so, Lyn turned to Aneas.

'Are you nearly done? I'm sure Miss Bartholomew must have other errands to do, and she wouldn't want to miss the afternoon train.'

'Yes, of course. Nearly done, Lyn.'

The door closed again.

'Which reminds me . . .' Aneas stood up and went to a safe behind him, unlocked it and took out a brown Gladstone bag, which he then set by Belle's chair.

'Mrs Ambrose left this with me for safe-keeping. It contains all her personal papers, everything that she wished to preserve. I'm sure you'll want

to take it with you. Of course when you're finished, if there's anything you want to ask, I'd be
more than happy to attempt to answer your questions.'

Except, as he'd already intimated, Martha kept
her private affairs to herself.

Belle reached for the bag. The leather was old
and battered, and it was heavy. She hoped Jo was
still here, because carrying the bag all the way
back to The Grand would be a feat of endurance
she wasn't sure she could manage.

Abruptly the room felt even more stifling, and
when she stood up black spots danced in front of
her eyes and she wondered whether she might
faint. She took a deep breath and then another,
until things steadied.

'Again, if you need my assistance, Miss Bartholomew, please feel free to call.'

'Thank you. I will.' With an effort, she followed
him out of the office.

Lyn was standing by her desk. 'I hope you have
a pleasant journey, Miss Bartholomew,' she said,
but she sounded stilted and insincere. 'I think
you're doing the right thing going home to Melbourne. Really, you wouldn't enjoy staying here
in Sweet Wattle Creek. You don't belong.'

Belle knew then with absolute certainty that,
if Aneas had been her mother's friend, then Lyn
Thomas was not.

CHAPTER 12

SOPHIE

Sweet Wattle Creek, 1986

I DIDN'T USUALLY GO in to work on Saturday but I did today. This morning I'd barely opened my eyes before I was already thinking about the *Herald* archives and what tantalising treasures they might hold. Because I couldn't write about the wedding dress, not yet, it seemed sensible to begin planning another piece, and ever since The Grand had been mentioned I'd been chewing it over. Yes, it was now an old burnt-out ruin on the edge of town, but once it had been an important building, and there must be a great deal of history attached to it.

Ian McKinnon was doing a display on The Grand in the RSL Hall and he might be able to help me to . . .

Hang on! I stopped dead with my key in the lock. Where had that thought come from? Why should I need Ian to help me? Was I only doing this because he'd mentioned The Grand and I wanted to spend more time with him?

I searched my conscience, but finally concluded that wasn't it. I was genuinely caught up in the history of The Grand and the dress and the whole Centenary thing. I was good at detecting and now I had the chance to put my skills to use. I missed my job in Brisbane. I missed being me. I was still coming to terms with Sophie Matheson and this was a way of merging the two me's together, the new and the old.

Satisfied with the results of my soul searching, I opened the door and turned on some lights. Tim had said he was taking the family into Riverton today for shopping, Brad was playing footie and Ellie was up at the river with her boyfriend. Anyway, they didn't work weekends unless asked. I didn't expect to be interrupted. As for Ian, I hadn't seen him since he left Smithy with me. He hadn't dropped in as he'd said he would and the border collie was still in our backyard, much to Dillon's delight. My son had promised he'd take the dog for a walk this morning and maybe throw a ball around for him.

Smithy and Dillon seemed to have become best friends in a very short space of time. Much to Black Cat's displeasure. The cat had spent the night on my bed instead of Dillon's, and out of the blue I was getting lots of purring and loving looks from those usually baleful yellow eyes.

Before I started my search I wanted to make some phone calls about the dress. I'd asked Ellie to think of the names of elderly people who might remember something about Charlie and Belle.

'The CWA,' she'd said instantly. 'If you want to know anything about anything, Soph, they're the first place you go to. My gran belongs to the association, and you should hear the gossip she brings home!'

That made me smile now as I unfolded her list of names and numbers. The Country Women's Association started in Victoria in 1928, so surely someone must remember Belle if she lived here. I picked up the telephone. On the off chance, I tried Nola's Mr Scott first, hoping to escape the Thursday poetry reading, but he wasn't answering. Most of the others were less helpful than I'd expected, but maybe they genuinely didn't remember and I just had a suspicious mind. It was a long time ago, after all, and people had their own concerns.

'Sophie!' Mrs Green, Ellie's Gran, seemed happy to chat. 'My granddaughter is a clever girl, isn't she? Working for a newspaper.'

Eventually I got around to my question.

'Belle? The only Belle I knew was . . . no. I'm sure I don't remember her. Or Charlie. There was Charlie Sutcliffe, but he was a boy when he joined up in the Second World War so it can't be him. Oh dear, it's all so long ago. Best forgotten.'

'What do you mean "best forgotten"? What is best forgotten, Mrs Green?'

'Goodness me, Sophie, how you do pick one up. I didn't mean anything. Now tell me, is Tim going to charge extra for his Centenary edition of the *Herald*?'

No doubt he was, but I wasn't getting into an argument. I made some vague answer and ended the call. So much for the elephantine memories of the elders of the town.

The *Herald* archives were stored downstairs in the basement. It was actually an old cellar. Bill Shaw had kept his treasures upstairs, wherever he could find space for them, and by the time Tim took over it looked like a hoarder's paradise. There was barely room to move. Tim had paid for work to be done on the cellar, to make sure it was waterproof and damp-proof, and now all the old issues were down there in numerical order.

I opened the cellar door and flicked on the rows of fluorescent lights. The air always felt chilly down here and today I didn't mind. Compared to the heat already gathering outside it was pure heaven.

I was planning to search for mention of The Grand, but as I set down my bag, it occurred to me that Belle and Charlie might be waiting to be found in the First World War issues. It was a long shot, but the dress *was* from that era, according to Ian. So what if they were married? Here in Sweet Wattle Creek? Just maybe there'd be a long paragraph about Charlie and Belle tying the knot. Surely it was worth a try? I told myself I'd go through each newspaper, each wedding column, and it shouldn't take me too long. I wouldn't be distracted by anything else, no way. I was on a mission to find Belle and Charlie.

I'd heard that some of the city newspapers were transferring their older issues to microfilm, which saved space and made it much easier to look up items of interest. The *Sweet Wattle Creek Herald* wasn't quite that modern. I was going to be heaving around piles of musty paper, and turning pages of faded and sometimes smudged copy to find the item I was looking for.

There was a long table and a wooden chair, so I loaded the newspapers I thought might be relevant onto a trolley—Tim had bought it second-hand from the Riverton hospital—and trundled them over.

It wasn't long before I realised this was going to take a lot more time than I'd optimistically imagined. Nor was it as simple. Wedding columns were all very well, but I soon noticed that sometimes a wedding was mentioned elsewhere in the text. Especially if the couple was of importance in the town hierarchy, or there was a story to tell. And Bill Shaw certainly loved to tell a story.

By lunchtime I was deep into 1917, I had a headache, and I hadn't found either Belle or Charlie. I had discovered, however, that The Grand was owned by a Mrs Ambrose, who had given up the licence about the same time her husband had died—not in the war but here at home, in Sweet Wattle Creek.

Mr Nathan Ambrose of The Grand Hotel, after a lingering illness, who leaves his widow, Martha, to mourn his passing.

I also found lists of the men in the district who had gone off to war and been in killed in action, or were missing or sick. Bill Shaw liked to include names of relatives and friends, even if they didn't live here. I suppose people came to him with their distressing news and expected him to publish it. There were one or two men called Charles but nothing about a wife or fiancée with the first name Belle, and, well, they just didn't seem right for *my* Charlie.

My progress through the war years got slower and slower. Story after story caught my attention and I couldn't seem to skip anything. For instance, I found a request from the Red Cross for items urgently needed—hand-knitted scarves, hand-knitted bedsocks, hand-knitted mittens, and something called 'hussifs', which for the life of me I couldn't fathom. And there was a concert held for the returned servicemen, which was—in Bill Shaw's words—*much appreciated by our brave boys.*

In October 1917 he wrote a piece on one of the many fundraising events, with the money going to the war effort. This was at Morwenstow, the home of Mr and Mrs Stanley Davies:

As most readers would know, Mr Stanley Davies has joined up to fight the Hun with his elder son, Edmond (Ted). The two are currently somewhere on the Western Front, no doubt displaying the sort of courage for which men of this district are renowned. Here at home, and not to be outdone, Mrs Violet Davies is hosting a Salvation Army dance at Morwenstow, where she will be raising funds for our Australian Army hospitals. A donation will be gratefully accepted from those who wish to attend. Sweet Wattle Creek has fond memories of Mrs Davies's previous efforts and no doubt she will find herself once more having the pleasure of the company of most of the town.

This Mrs Davies of Morwenstow wasn't the same Mrs Davies who Ian and I had found unconscious. It couldn't be. It must be Violet's daughter-in-law, or perhaps even some other relative. A niece?

I set aside Mrs Davies of Morwenstow and picked up the next newspaper. One more, I thought, and then I'd go back upstairs for some coffee and a bite to eat. Just then my gaze slid down the Killed in Action, Missing and Injured section, and stopped with a jolt.

Killed in Action—Lieutenant Alister Thomas, AIF, husband of Mrs Lyn Thomas, brother of Aneas Thomas, of Sweet Wattle Creek.

Killed in Action—Private Edmond (Ted) Davies, AIF, son of Mr and Mrs Stanley Davies of Morwenstow, Sweet Wattle Creek.

Missing—Private Michael Maxwell, Australian Flying Corps, son of the late Mr and Mrs Cyrus Maxwell of Sweet Wattle Creek.

Ted Davies, who had joined up with his father to fight the Hun, was dead. I felt as if I'd known him personally, and while I knew it was silly, I couldn't help the sense of sadness. Violet's son was dead and her husband was still fighting. I wondered whether she had enjoyed the Salvation Army dance and I hoped she had. I hoped she'd had a wonderful time, because I doubted she'd be enjoying herself much a week later when she received the news about her son.

'Enough.' I closed the newspaper and loaded it onto the trolley with the others, and then wheeled them back to the rows of steel shelving.

Upstairs it felt twice as hot after the frigid air of the basement. I made myself one of my tepid coffees, found a couple of Monte Carlo biscuits, and sat down to read over the notes I'd made.

No mention of the couple I was looking for, which was frustrating, and yet I did feel as if I had learned rather a lot about Sweet Wattle Creek during those years of devastating war. And I knew more about Morwenstow and the Davies and their loss, and that family was surely linked with the dress and my search. Belle must come into it somewhere, if I kept searching.

Restlessly, I got up and went over to the window, the one that faced the street and looked across to the library. Nola had closed up on the stroke of twelve, as she always did, but I recognised the car still sitting out the front.

Just for a moment I felt a little tremor inside, which was worrying, until I told myself it was because I wanted to talk to Ian about the dress and the Centenary and the Davies of Morwenstow. I had to tell someone, and he was the logical choice. Besides, he might have been in touch with Josh by now and know the whole story.

Really, I told myself, it would be remiss of me not to go over there right now and ask him.

He seemed pleased to see me, which did my ego a lot of good but at the same time made my stomach clench with anxiety. I reminded myself that I used to have male friends, men I was comfortable with and could share a joke with, and I needed to get myself back to that place. The before–Walter place.

'I was over the road and saw your car,' I explained, just in case he imagined I was stalking him. 'Did you talk with Mrs Davies's nephew? With Josh?'

'Yes, I did.' He led the way into his room, knocking against some books on top of a free-standing shelf. He tried to catch them but several slipped through his grasp and fell to the floor. 'Sorry I didn't get back to you. Things have been hectic.'

While I waited for him to pick them up, I noticed that Belle's wedding dress was gone from the table and there was other memorabilia in its place. Bundles of old letters and a box of old-fashioned preserving jars and a handmade patchwork quilt. There was also a large white board set up against the wall, with an enlarged photograph of a young man wearing a uniform on it.

'So what did Josh say?' I prompted, as he finished returning the books to their place.

'No luck. He doesn't know a Charlie or Belle. Honestly, I think he's too worried about his aunt to give it much thought at the moment. Coffee?'

I nodded. My own effort had barely made a dent in my headache. I went over to the photograph and peered at the soldier's face. Dark hair and eyes, and a bit of a smile. A nice face, I thought. He had a badge with wings sewn onto the front of his uniform. A pilot then, one of the early ones.

'A bit of a mystery man,' Ian said, with a nod at my friend. 'Not exactly famous himself, but he had plenty of brushes with others who were.

Charles Kingsford Smith for one.'

'Smithy? He keeps popping up. This chap didn't die like Kingsford Smith, did he?' The aviator had gone down in 1935, while attempting a new record from Britain to Australia, his body never recovered.

'No. Well, I don't know. I'm still trying to find out.'

He handed me my coffee.

'Miriam rang,' he went on with a quick glance, as if the mention of her name might throw me into fits. I was still slightly embarrassed at my assumption they were a couple, but I told myself I needn't be. It was an honest mistake. 'I told her about the Eileen Nicholson dress. She was really thrilled. I thought she might jump on the next plane home.' He chuckled.

'So does she think it's genuine?'

'She's being cautious, but when I gave her the details, and told her about the initials on the tag, I'm sure I heard her start to hyperventilate.'

Funny man.

'She wants to see it when she gets back, so I said we'd bring it down to Melbourne.'

We?

He hurried on before I could speak. 'Did you want to come? I had the impression you were keen to get the scoop. Scoop? That's the right word, isn't it?'

He looked nervous, as if he thought he'd said too much, or maybe it was just the way I was staring at him.

I pulled myself together. Did I want to go? I

did. I wanted to be there when Miriam saw the dress and I wanted to record every word she said. Nothing could stop me solving this mystery, not even going to Melbourne with Ian.

'I'll have to sort something out with Dillon,' I said coolly, after I'd accepted his invitation, 'but it should be all right. He loves Smithy the dog by the way. He always wanted a dog but Wal . . . eh, we couldn't have one.'

Oh, God I wasn't cool after all. I was gabbling. I'd almost said Walter. What was wrong with me? But Ian didn't appear to have noticed.

'Don't worry. Mrs Davies won't be home for a while and Josh doesn't seem to care about Smithy, so if your son wants to hold on to him for now I'm sure it'll be okay.'

I turned to the bundle of letters so he wouldn't see how rattled I was. 'What do you have here?'

'They're from the First World War. Nola found them in storage. There's all sorts in there but the biggest bundle was written by one Lyn Thomas, who seemed to know everything that happened in Sweet Wattle Creek. The town sticky beak, in other words. A gem for historians.'

'I'll bet.' I told him about the old newspapers I'd been looking through and what I'd found. He grew quite fervent.

'I might need to take a visit to your archives myself,' he murmured, and I swear he was hyper-ventilating, too.

'Knock yourself out. I'm sure Tim won't mind. He's very proud of his grandfather and the *Herald*. It's been owned and run by the Shaw family since it started, you know. He plans to pass it on to his own children.'

'Another story to go up in the RSL Hall. Thank you. I'm starting to wonder if I shouldn't have asked for bigger premises.'

There was something endearing about his enthusiasm. Hastily, I picked up the letter on top of the stack and began to read aloud.

'Dear Alister, We are both well. I hope you received the socks I knitted. I have heard it is cold in France and thought they might be useful.'

I turned over the envelope. *Lieutenant Alister Thomas.* I had seen that name before. I scratched around in my bag for my notebook and opened it at the most recent page.

'Lieutenant Alister Thomas was one of the soldiers named as killed in action in the *Herald* edition for the 20th of October 1917.'

The date on the letter was earlier than the death notice, but I couldn't help but ponder if, when the letter arrived, Alister was already dead.

'Yes,' Ian said, when I explained my thoughts. 'The letters would have been sent back to his family with his personal possessions.'

'So who was Lyn?'

'Look at the bottom of the page.'

I read. 'Your loving wife, Lyn.' Gloomily I stared down at the faded ink. 'Are there any letters from Alister to her?'

'A couple. They'll make a poignant addition to the exhibition. And there might be something in them about Charlie and Belle. If they were here at the time then you can be sure Lyn Thomas would've known about them.'

'Do you think so?' I stared longingly down at the letters, my fingers itching.

'Here, you take them and have a read.' He packed up the letters and put them into a shoe-box and handed it to me.

'Thanks.' I was ridiculously touched.

'My pleasure.' His ears had gone just that little bit pink.

'Oh, I meant to ask. I found a word in a list from the Red Cross, among the things that were needed by the soldiers in the trenches. Knitted socks and so on, but there was also something called "hussifs". Do you know what they were?'

'A hussif was a sewing kit. Needles and thread, spare buttons and things like that. The soldiers used them to repair their clothing.'

I couldn't help my smile. 'You really do know everything, don't you?'

His ears got even pinker.

'Not everything. Ah, Josh was going to drop in Smithy's bed and bowls. I can bring them over, if you like.'

He was treading cautiously and I didn't blame him. I must be giving off some very mixed sig-nals. But I was convinced we could be friends, if we weren't already. So I looked up with a friendly smile and said, 'Sure.'

It was only when I got outside, the box clutched to my middle, that I acknowledged how scary this was for me. I had made some bad choices in my life. I was still living with them. And the last thing I wanted was to screw up again. When you're someone who makes mistakes when it comes to men, then it's hard to trust yourself with even the most innocent interactions. I liked Ian McKinnon, I really did, but history had taught me I was a bad judge of character. Not to be trusted.

I couldn't allow myself to make a wrong turn. Not just for my own sake, but most of all for Dillon's.

CHAPTER 13

BELLE

Sweet Wattle Creek, 1931

ON THE STREET it was surely even hotter than before, but Belle was grateful that at least she was out of Aneas Thomas's stuffy office. The shadows seemed to have contracted. As if the heat was sending them into retreat, to hide along the shopfronts.

She'd heard the two of them arguing as she left, Aneas and Lyn, their voices hushed and angry. She should have asked Lyn what she meant but she was feeling faint and all she'd wanted to do was escape. Now it was too late to find out what Martha had done to make Lyn disapprove of her so. Another mystery she might never solve.

She shifted the heavy Gladstone bag from one hand to the other. In the next building along from the pawnbroker, a man had come out to sit on his front steps and survey the streetscape. His sleeves were rolled up his forearms and his receding hair was the colour of snow.

'You look like you could do with a sit-down,' he said, eyes curious in his craggy face. 'Do you want to join me?' and he gestured at the stairs.

The thought of sinking down on the cold stone was very tempting, but probably not quite proper in the circumstances. 'No, thank you. I'm meeting someone.'

The man cocked his eyebrow. He got up and went inside, but before she knew it he was back, strolling towards her. He was holding something and Belle saw that it was a parasol with an orange tassel around the edge.

'Take this,' he said. 'Give you some shade while you wait. Damned hot to be out in the sun today.'

She didn't want to take it, but he was pressing it at her, and she noticed his fingers were ink-stained. 'I can't possibly . . .'

'Go on. It's a gift,' he said. 'For Martha's daughter. That's who you are, aren't you? You're Belle?' He stepped closer, taking advantage of her frozen silence. 'You don't remember me but I recognise you.'

'How can you recognise me?' Belle asked, feeling her heart clogging up her throat. 'Do I look like Martha? Or Nathan?'

He angled his head. 'No. Martha was dark. So was Nathan. You're unique, Belle. I always said so.'

But how could she be unique? She must resemble someone, surely? The memory of the black ink obscuring her father's name was making her wonder if there was something here she was missing.

'Now you're frowning because you didn't hear what you wanted to hear.' He grinned, the lines in his face deepening. 'That's pure Martha, that is.'

Her frown intensified. 'My father . . . Nathan.

What was he like? Everyone speaks of Martha but no one mentions him.' *Except to say he was a drunk.*

'He came along at the right time for Martha. She was struggling to keep The Grand open and he had some money.'

'So not a love match?' Belle couldn't help the cynical note in her voice.

'He was older than her. He arrived in town and the first person he set eyes on was Martha. She always said that if it hadn't been for Nathan Ambrose she would've lost it all. Rory wasn't interested in coming back, so it was her alone with the weight of the place on her shoulders. Nathan stepped in when she needed him the most and she never forgot that.'

He was looking at her in a curious way, as if he was making calculations or comparisons in his head, as if he was thinking things he wasn't about to speak aloud. He made Belle uncomfortable and she edged away.

'Martha's famous Gladstone bag,' he said, nodding at the object hanging heavily from Belle's hand. 'Aneas had it locked in his safe, I understand. All of Martha's secrets, and let me tell you, she had a few.' He waited, as if wanting her to confirm it, but Belle forced a smile and said nothing. He smiled back, in a way that seemed to know much more than it revealed. 'I'd better get back to work. Can't stand here gossiping.' He waved a hand and turned and walked back to his building, disappearing inside.

Belle stood holding the parasol in one hand

and her mother's bag in the other. Across the street in the park was Jo's Morris, resting under the shade of a tree. Belle felt a surge of relief at the thought of Jo's friendly face. Securing the bag in both hands, and the unwanted parasol under her arm, she set off.

It was dismaying, being known in a place where she knew no one. Belle told herself the man probably hadn't meant to seem threatening, he was likely thinking he was being kind, but she wished he hadn't waylaid her like that. Maybe she could give the parasol to some passing stranger, except that everyone but her had more sense than to be wandering about in the heat of the day.

Jo wasn't with the car. Uncertain, Belle looked around her, but there was no sign of the slender figure. There was nothing to do but wait. She strolled over to the memorial and, shading her eyes, began to read the names carved into the stone faces of the column.

A few of the soldiers were from the Boer War, but by far most of them had died in the Great War. Every family in Sweet Wattle Creek had doubtlessly lost someone. It was the same in towns all over the country, where boys and men had gone off on a big adventure and had never come home again.

One of the names was familiar and she read it aloud. 'Davies, Edmond. Private.'

Frank Davies was most likely too young to have fought so this could be an elder brother. She remembered that the father, Stanley, had been gassed in the war and was an invalid, so he must be still alive.

Her legs were wobbly. Belle sat down on a bench placed near the base of the monument. Cicadas hummed in the trees that ran in a crooked line behind her. There must be a stream down there somewhere, because she could hear the vague trickle of water. Was this the creek that gave the town its name? It was all very restful and Belle's eyes began to close.

She hadn't slept much last night—there'd been that mysterious light outside. Now she couldn't seem to stay awake and her head nodded, sending her into a half-dream state.

Someone was holding her hand. She tried to wake, to open her eyes, but she couldn't manage it. In her dream the touch was gentle. 'It's dangerous down near the creek, Belle,' a voice was saying. 'There are deeper pools well over *your* head. Hold my hand and I'll keep you safe.'

She looked up. The boy was taller than her, older, and he had brown hair and serious brown eyes that turned warm and smiley when she met them.

'Come on,' he said, giving her hand a little tug. 'Let's go home now, and I'll pour you a big, big glass of lemonade.'

It sounded heavenly. She'd just set off with him, skipping by his side, when the other voice intruded.

'Wake up. Wake up!'

Belle opened her eyes wide. Two faces were peering down at her, their expressions ranging from concern to laughter.

'Are you all right?' The concerned girl appeared to be about fifteen, slim, with hollow cheeks and big brown eyes. Her chestnut-coloured hair was fastened up under a grubby scarf.

'She was dreaming. In the middle of the day.' The other girl, the amused one, was about ten, her hair also chestnut but curly, hanging in ringlets about her pretty face. Her big brown eyes were a replica of the other girl's. They were obviously sisters.

'You shouldn't go near the creek,' Belle said, not thinking, still in her dream.

The two girls glanced at each other and giggled.

'*That* creek do you mean?' The younger girl pointed behind her, towards the trees. 'There's not enough water in that to drown a . . . a mouse!'

Her sister gave her a frown. 'Don't exaggerate, Gwen. There are deeper pools, remember? Michael told us not to go near them because they're dangerous.'

The boy in her dream had said that. Belle tried to gather her thoughts but they seemed to be in bits.

The two girls were conferring, heads close together. Yes, they were definitely sisters.

'What are your names?' she asked, thinking Jo might know them.

'Gwen and Tilly,' the younger one blurted out before her sister shushed her angrily. 'Why not tell her? She's all right. She looks like a film star.'

'You're so silly, Gwen. If she was a film star she wouldn't be here in Sweet Wattle Creek, would she?' Tilly stepped away, suddenly serious, tugging at Gwen's hand. 'We have to go back now,' she said, her eyes watchful.

'Back where?' Belle stood up.

'If the copper sees us we'll be in trouble,' Gwen explained, ignoring Tilly's angry hiss, and looking much younger than her years. 'You won't tell will you?'

Belle understood then that they were travellers, and almost certainly two of the travellers who had already been moved on. Only clearly they hadn't moved on. Were young, vulnerable girls like this really on the track? Shouldn't they be with their parents? She'd stepped outside her own limited experience and it made her realise again how naive she was.

'I won't tell,' she promised.

Gwen's eyes slid to the parasol and she smiled hopefully. 'Do you want that? It's so pretty.'

Belle held it out and the girl darted forward and snatched it from her hand. The last Belle saw of it was the orange tassel vanishing into the vegetation.

Jo's call made her turn. The other woman was striding towards the memorial, a string shopping bag in one hand. 'It *is* hot, isn't it?' She was smiling.

'Yes. Too hot to walk. I'm glad you're still here.'

Jo waved a dismissive hand. She looked at the Gladstone bag. 'Aneas give you that?'

'Yes. It was Martha's.' Belle pointed across the street. 'There was a man over there. He seemed to know who I was. White hair and ink on his fingers.'

Jo turned back. 'You mean Mr Shaw? He owns the newspaper, the *Sweet Wattle Creek Herald*. He knows everyone.'

That explained the ink, and the impression he gave of being the keeper of the town's secrets.

They walked towards the Morris. 'Are you still going back on the afternoon train?' Jo asked, checking her wristwatch.

'Yes. I mean, no. I don't know.' She felt confused, disorientated. The dream had done that, and the two girls. Who was Michael who knew about the dangerous pools in the creek? Surely it couldn't be Michael Maxwell, who should have been the owner of The Grand. And what of Mr Shaw and his hints and curious stare? And then there had been Aneas and Lyn Thomas arguing as she'd left the office ... Belle's eyes were heavy and her head ached.

As they walked towards the motor car, Jo spoke easily about her life, and Belle struggled to take in her words and respond. She was engaged to be married to an Englishman who taught at a girl's school in Melbourne and who was some distant relation of the Davies. It meant they didn't see as much of each other as they'd have liked, but at least they were able to save towards their wedding and the life they hoped one day to have. 'There's little enough work with the way things are so when you find a job it's best to hang on to it.'

'Are there many travellers passing through Sweet Wattle Creek?' Belle asked when silence fell again. 'I don't think I knew before ... I thought I understood what was happening in the world but really I don't.'

Jo considered the question. 'Yes, there seem to be more of them arriving all the time. Most of them come from the shantytowns in the city that the government has set up for the unemployed and the homeless. The men I can understand, but when I see whole families on the road, yes it is distressing. Frank says they steal his sheep. He says Constable Nash has to move them on or we'd be overrun. I don't know. If everyone moves them on where can they go?'

'Well, The Grand has plenty of rooms,' Belle said.

Jo stared with a mixture of doubt and amusement. 'Do you mean that? Would you run it as a lodging house?'

Her dizziness was making her silly. 'Why not? A lodging house and soup kitchen for strays and travellers.'

Belle could feel laughter, slightly hysterical laughter, rising up inside her, and when Jo started to giggle she joined in. There were tears on her cheeks by the time she stopped but Jo didn't seem bothered.

'I'm sorry,' Jo said. 'It just sounded so funny. I won't tell Frank. He'd be appalled.'

Belle climbed into the car and they moved away from the park, along Main Street.

'How did Martha die?' she asked, feeling the air against her face through the open window as Jo sped up. At least it was moving and it was air, even if it was warm.

Jo gave Belle a quick scan. 'Don't you know?'

'No. Why?' Was this another mystery?

'You need to understand,' Jo said carefully. 'Martha went a little bit strange in the last months. She changed. Not noticeably at first but gradually, until she was, well, strange. Physically she was still strong for her age, but mentally,' and she shook her head to finish the sentence. 'She drove her friends away. She didn't want help, she said, so we left her alone. My mother hoped she would get better, or at least come to her if she was in difficulty. Unfortunately that didn't happen. When Frank found her she'd been dead for —'

Abruptly she stopped, aware of the heavy silence, and Belle's horrified stare.

'I'm sorry.' She bit her lip. 'This is awful. Your father passing away—I mean Rory—and then . . . You must be feeling overwhelmed.'

'Yes. I do. I am.' She swallowed, forcing the shock away.

Jo went on, her voice soothing, as if words could make a barrier between Belle and what she let slip about Martha's death. 'My mother remembers Rory,' she said. 'She says he had the darkest eyes, just like Martha. Soulful, she called them. And he was quite wild. My father remembers him as well. They were friends. They used to be real larrikins.'

'Your father isn't well . . . ?'

'No. He was gassed at Ypres and he's never been the same. Ted, my brother, was killed a week later. Ted didn't tell anyone he was joining up, and by the time my parents found out what he'd done it was too late and he was on his way to France. My father joined up and followed him, to look out for him. I don't think Dad ever forgave himself for coming home alive without Ted.'

Jo stopped the car, drew a deep breath and forced a smile. 'So you see it's all up to Frank and me now. He runs Morwenstow and the store, and I do what I can to help Mum.'

Belle saw they were right outside The Grand. She could ignore what Jo had said before about Martha, pretend she hadn't heard, but she felt an urgent need to bring this one skeleton at least out into the light.

'You said Martha had been dead for some time when Frank found her. Where did he find her?'

Jo sighed. 'You don't give up, do you? I'm not sure where he found her. Not in her bedroom, I know that, or we'd never have put you in there. I'm sorry I said anything. You didn't need to know that, Belle.'

'I did need to know. She was my mother and I think I have hidden my head in the sand quite long enough.'

'But you didn't hide your head in the sand! You were in ignorance of the facts and that was hardly your fault.'

Blissful ignorance, Belle nearly added.

'If you really have to know the grisly details . . . But you're leaving this afternoon, aren't you?' Jo gave her a careful look.

'Yes. That is, I thought I was. But there are so many questions and I'm not sure if I'll get the answers if I leave now.'

Jo nodded, though she looked dubious. 'Look, if you change your mind . . . I'll ask Frank to drop in. Give you a lift.'

'Oh, please, don't bother him.'

'No, it's no bother. If you want to leave he can take you to the station. If not . . . well, you can tell him so. And if you want to know about Martha, ask him.'

Belle said nothing. What could she say? She wasn't sure herself what she should do. No doubt she was being a nuisance and Henry would be worried. She supposed she should have asked to phone him from Aneas Thomas's office but it had all been so peculiar. She pushed her hair back off her forehead, feeling the damp stickiness.

Jo was watching her. 'It's the heat,' she said kindly. 'You're not used to it. Go and lie down for a while and then decide. Do you want me to come inside with you?'

Belle shook her head. She preferred to be alone.

'Thank you for everything,' she said. How many times had she thanked Jo? And yet she meant it.

Jo smiled. '*Au revoir*, then.'

Dust followed the Morris as it drove away, and Belle stood watching it. She felt as if she was at a crossroads. The past was St Kilda and Rory's death, and the future? It was Henry, of course it was, how could it be otherwise?

She turned and looked up at The Grand. The Bartholomew family home. Rory's and Martha's childhood had been spent here, but when Rory had gone off to make his life in Melbourne, Martha had stayed.

All of Martha's secrets, and let me tell you, she had a few. Bill Shaw had said those words but it was only now that Belle sensed something ominous in them.

Something dangerous.

CHAPTER 14

SOPHIE

Sweet Wattle Creek, 1986

DILLON HAD ARRANGED to go to the movies with some of the boys from his class in Riverton High. This was a new development, making friends, and it was one I wanted to encourage. It had taken time for him to fit in and find his feet—like me, circumstances had knocked him about—so for a while he had struggled. I was glad to see his life was coming together.

There used to be an older cinema in Riverton, but it had closed down and the building was demolished and they'd built this newer model. Hadn't someone famous owned it? Or worked here? I vaguely remembered hearing talk. Something else that might be noteworthy to mention to Ian McKinnon. Usually in towns like ours, there was a local historian, the go-to person for all things about the past. Tim's grandfather had been that man but he'd died about five years ago. He'd finished his definitive history of the area and had hoped to publish it, but from what Tim said it was in a bit of a mess. By the end the old man had slightly lost his marbles. Tim had been working towards getting it into shape but I hadn't seen much work on it recently. Although Tim was doing his best to fill Bill Shaw's sizeable shoes, the new baby had knocked him for six.

With Dillon in the cinema watching the movie—called *Troll*, and I did ask whether it was suitable but he'd just rolled his eyes—I went off and did some shopping. I was stocking up on dog food in particular and it was amazing how many different flavours there were for what basically looked like the same picture on the outside of the can. Still, I felt that Smithy deserved my best efforts, and Dillon had already instructed me not to go for the cheapest option.

'We should really be cooking his meals,' he'd said, with a worried glance at the dog, who'd looked perfectly happy with the current arrangement. 'To be sure he's getting the proper nutrition.'

I'd said, 'Hmm,' which meant he could do it if he wanted to but I didn't have time.

The subject had been dropped.

I'd been on edge last night. Ian had said he'd come by with Smithy's bedding and bowls, and although I'd kept telling myself it was no big deal, I was . . . on edge. He's just a bloke I'm working with, I told myself. A friend? Maybe, although it might be a little soon for that. But he could be a friend. I liked him, there I'd said it, and I thought he liked me. I didn't expect to see him again after the Centenary, and maybe that was a good thing, too. And yet, when he didn't show up and it was time for bed, I was disappointed.

And then I had lain in bed and wondered why he hadn't come over. Was he worried I'd get the wrong idea? Or was he just not that interested? Or was he simply not punctual? I fell asleep still none the wiser but determined not to mention it at all next time we met.

When I woke up this morning and went outside the stuff was on the doorstep. Bedding and bowls, all neatly stacked. So he had come, at some point, and left without a word. I imagined him sneaking along, trying not to give away his presence, setting everything down, and then running for his life. I had to smile at that image though, because Ian being Ian, he would surely have tripped over or dropped something.

So I came up with a new plan. I told myself I'd thank him for coming and bringing Smithy's belongings, but I wouldn't ask questions and I'd pretend not to care.

By the time I was finished at the supermarket it was nearly time for *Troll* to finish, so I waited in the car just down from the cinema. I didn't want to cramp Dillon's style. People were coming and going, families and groups of teenagers, laughing and shoving each other. Nothing much had changed since I was that age, sneaking in to watch some awful movie my parents had forbidden me to see.

I'd been a rebellious child in many ways, or just naive when it came to getting myself into difficult situations. The boy who was Dillon's father had seemed fun and nice, but really he was just a kid like me, out of his depth. When I found out I was pregnant his parents closed ranks around him and I barely saw him again. Not that I wanted to, it was hardly *Love Story*, but it seemed sad that Dillon missed out on a father.

Once pregnant I'd had to leave school, but I was still working towards exams at home, and I didn't do too badly. After Dillon was born I had to juggle caring for him with my education, although my parents helped. They'd forgiven me by then— well perhaps not forgiven so much as accepted the situation. Remembering those days now, I understood they'd done as well as they could. I'd disappointed them, but they'd loved Dillon. Once I was financially able to, I left home with their blessing and rented a flat, and then when Dillon went to school I was able to find full-time work.

It would have been okay. I think I would have done all right. I *was* doing all right. And then Walter came into the picture and everything went very, very wrong.

Dillon was eight and I was running late to pick him up from school. I wasn't looking where I was going and as I stepped out of the lift I ran into a big strong body. Two hands grabbed me to hold me steady and a laughing voice said something like, 'Whoa there, little lady.'

I didn't think I was looking particularly brilliant that day—my hair needed cutting and was curling wildly and my makeup had worn off— but the way that man looked at me. He made me feel like I was one in a million.

He walked with me. He spoke easily. He was a solicitor, he said, and he was way out of my league. There were plenty of them around the court where I worked as a bailiff. Police and legal folk, I knew them to speak to, to work with, but they weren't my friends. I was too busy concentrating on being a good mother to Dillon and bringing in my pay packet every fortnight. And I also loved my job and I didn't want to screw it up. I'd stayed away from men. Well, a couple of one-night stands I'd afterwards regretted, but nothing serious, nothing permanent.

But when Walter asked to meet me for a coffee I found I couldn't say no. And that was when the steel door had slammed shut behind me.

I found out later that he'd been watching me. In his mind he'd already decided that he wanted me, and he was going to have me, and that was what he worked towards. Walter was the master manipulator.

I didn't realise it then of course. That there would be no going back from the moment I said yes. I didn't know that he would see my agreement as some sort of unspoken, unsigned contract that we would be together until the end of the world and he could do just about anything he wanted with me.

Now, when I think back, I did have doubts. And yet still I married him. He was like a drug and I craved him. The good times were so good, I was on a high, but the bad times . . . they were beyond bad.

'Mum.' Dillon tapped on the window and snapped me out of my dark journey into the past. I unlocked the door. I was probably the only person in Riverton who ever locked their door when they were inside the car but I couldn't help it. Hopefully, one day I would not feel the urge to keep that barrier between myself and whatever was outside, but that wasn't the case now.

I could see his friends hovering in the background. 'Did you want to do something with them?' I asked him. 'You don't have to come home with me right this minute.' The words were hard to say because I was always afraid for him, but I knew I had to give him freedom. Being controlled isn't good for anyone, at least Walter had taught me that much.

'Nah, it's all right,' he said, turning to wave before climbing into the car, but I caught his sideways glance at me.

'You know, you don't have to worry.' I was carefully offhand as I started the engine. 'I'm fine. You can go off and be with your friends. You know that, don't you?'

He shrugged a shoulder.

'What was *Troll* about, anyway?'

The movie sounded appalling. I preferred something more amusing, like a romantic comedy. It was nice to see that sort of stuff on the screen, as if every family was like that, as if everyone had a happy ending. It was a good thought.

'Anyway, what is this wedding dress you and the McKinnon guy are trying to find out about?' he asked. 'Christy said something about it belonging to Mrs Davies.'

'Yes, I think it does, but she's sick in hospital and can't tell us. It's a First World War dress, and there has to be a story behind it. There are names written on the box it came in. Charlie and Belle.'

'How do you know they have anything to do with the dress?'

'Well, of course they do!' But even as I said it I knew he was right. He did too.

'What if the names are just some random couple? Maybe it was a pie shop, Charlie and Belle's pies, and someone bought a whole lot of them and then reused the box.'

I gave him a crestfallen look.

'You didn't think of that?' Dillon asked me, trying not to smile in triumph.

'No. Neither did Mr McKinnon, I might add. But I don't think you're right.'

And yet the idea worried at me all the way home.

Once inside, Dillon went off to the backyard to play with Smithy, watched broodingly from the window by Black Cat. But if the cat was glaring then I was smiling as my son cavorted with the dog. It was so good to see Dillon happy. A year ago I rarely saw him laugh and smile, and it was only when we left that I understood how much he had changed from the happy-go-lucky kid he had been. He'd become silent and withdrawn, moody and anxious, his eyes always on me, whether because he needed to know what to do, so he could follow my lead, or he thought I might get hurt. Again.

I'd done the right thing. The only thing I could do. The police had tried their best, I knew that, but they were only as good as the system they were working within. When Walter had ignored the restraining order for the umpteenth time, when the threats he'd issued had become so horrifying I could hardly breathe, I decided I couldn't wait any longer.

Because he would have killed me. Dillon and I both knew that. And the thought that Dillon would have to deal with my death, and I would no longer be around to see him grow up, was what finally had driven me out of the house and into the shadows.

Now at last it seemed as if the shadows were receding. We were safe. We could begin our lives again, here in Sweet Wattle Creek, and if they weren't the lives we'd expected to live, then at least we were in one piece and together.

It was too early to start cooking our evening meal. The shoe box Ian had handed to me was on the table, and I pulled it towards me. The letters were stacked inside, old and faded and some of them stained. I began to paw through the thoughts and hopes of Lyn Thomas, writing to her husband, Alister, on the Western Front.

They were fascinating simply as historical documents, and after all these were people from the town I lived in, seventy years ago. I also found them enthralling because of the mention of names I was beginning to recognise. Ridiculous as it was, they seemed like old friends.

I opened them up, the paper creased and stained, and wondered how many times Alister had read them. What horrific sights these letters must have seen. I began to read paragraphs here and there, skipping through Lyn Thomas's one-sided conversations with Lieutenant Alister Thomas.

I slipped some sweet wattle flowers into your envelope. The bushes are flowering all along the creek at the moment, covered in creamy flowers, and the parrots are there from dawn till dusk. You must miss the sights and smells of home, Alister my dear, but chin up, this war must end soon and you'll come home.

Aneas is over at Martha Ambrose's again, offering her legal advice, he says, but you know he always had a soft spot for her. Perhaps they'll get married, what do you think? Would you like to have Martha as your sister-in-law? With Mr Ambrose gone she's given up the licence at The Grand. It's just too much for her, with Michael away. I'm so glad you are safe, Alister.

Aneas tells me that Martha Ambrose is worried about Michael Maxwell. She hasn't heard from him and thinks he is missing. You know what 'Missing' means. I don't know if you have met up with him over there, Alister. He's in the Flying Corps and as you know those poor fellows never last long. She's aged terribly. I don't think you'd recognise her if you saw her now.

Mr Shaw asked after you, and Violet Davies. I've been knitting new mittens and will send them with some other bits and pieces soon. Fruit cake, also, with plenty of brandy to keep it from spoiling. I'm sure the Temperance ladies will forgive my use of alcohol in the circumstances. Where are you? I do so want to find you on my map of France and Belgium.

And then one from Alister, written in May 1917.

Dear Lyn, Your letters keep my spirits up. I know you want to know where I am. I'd tell you but we're not allowed and even if I did they'd blank it out. As you know it's in case my letter falls into enemy hands, although I can't imagine what they would find in it to help them win the war.

Tell Aneas not to work too hard. I can picture him sitting up late with his candle burning. I'm well and I try to keep myself busy. The men look to me and I can't let them see me down in the dumps. I have the wattle flowers you sent me safe in my pocket. I take them out and I can smell home. I've passed them among the men and it brings a smile to their faces. The boys from the bush, anyway.

There were more letters from Lyn. Unopened, many of them, because Alister was already dead and they were returned with the rest of his personal effects.

There were letters other than the Thomases' in the shoebox. I pulled out two more and a single sheet of torn paper. These letters were not nearly as well preserved, but I could make out some of the words. Enough to make sense of them.

. . . lost another two men today. We're all down in the dumps but it's no use thinking too much about the future . . . come home and see you. It's all rain and mud at the moment and I miss the sun and Sweet Wattle Creek. I think, when I get back, I'll never leave again!

. . . Heard Alister Thomas was killed. He was a hero, Martha. Who would have thought, him being such a mild bloke? But then this place changes people. Lyn will be inconsolable. You know how she doted on him. Thanks for the . . . shared them around and everyone said . . . best they'd ever tasted . . . Michael.

Michael and Martha.

I re-read the mention of The Grand in Lyn's letter. So Martha Ambrose was the licensee during that period, a widow with a son or relative called Michael Maxwell. Or was Michael simply someone she was fond of? Clearly they were close, I could tell from the tone of the damaged letters. The name Michael sounded familiar but I was tired and I couldn't remember why.

It was disappointing that I had found no references to Charlie or Belle. The Davies did figure though, with a couple of mentions of Violet and her war effort, which seemed to be phenomenal. Like one of those school-committee mums I remembered from Dillon's early days, who could whip up a sponge cake in five minutes flat and then guilt everyone into running a fundraising stall.

I also recalled reading in the archives that Violet Davies's husband, Stanley, was away fighting with his son, Edmond, and I knew that Edmond did not come home either. Two locals lost would have sent Sweet Wattle Creek into a long period of grieving, and there must have been many more bereavements. I'd heard or read somewhere that the people involved in that war never recovered. They didn't talk about their experiences. They were told to go home and forget about them and certainly not to burden their wives or families with the horror of their encounters. So they were kept locked up inside.

I'd forgotten the single sheet of paper but now I picked it up and straightened it out. The letter had been ripped in two and crumpled and there were stains on it that I could almost believe were blood. Had the soldier kept this letter inside his uniform, close to his heart?

. . . I miss you. I wish it did not have to be this way. I love you and always will. At night I dream that you come to me, just as you used to, across the yard and up the stairs and into my arms, with your hair full of starlight. You made me forget all we had lost. Now I am so alone. Do you think when this war is over we can be together? My love, I am so tired of pretending . . .

My heart ached as I read. I knew this wasn't written by Lyn or Alister, nor Michael because the hand was different. A woman, I thought, pouring out her heart to a man who was fighting on the other side of the world. Had he come home to her? I really hoped so.

When Dillon came in I put the letters down and we began to prepare the evening meal. Chilli con carne and rice. While we worked I spoke to him about the letters and he seemed engrossed.

'Why don't you have a look on the War Memorial in the park?' he said. 'There're names on that. I'm sure I've seen those ones.'

'What? You mean Michael Maxwell?'

'Hmm, not sure. Definitely the Alister Thomas one though. He was a hero. We learned about him last term.'

'What did he do?'

'Saved his wounded comrades from the German machine guns. This was at Bullecourt. They called it the Blood Tub. Cool.'

'I'm glad you're enjoying your lessons.'

He didn't seem to notice the sarcasm and I was

glad, because I was sorry as soon as I said it.

'Are there any Thomases or Maxwells still in Sweet Wattle Creek?'

'Don't think so. No one on the bus to school I know of, anyway. There're a few new kids from that housing estate out past The Grand but I don't think any of them are called Thomas or Maxwell.'

Black Cat was winding his way around Dillon's ankles and he reached down to pet him. The cat, usually so standoffish, was now everyone's best friend.

The knock on the door startled me and for a moment Dillon and I froze. But of course it was all right, everything was all right now. We were safe and a knock on the door was just that.

I went to answer it, opening it a crack to see who was out there. The heat of the evening gusted in, fighting with my old air conditioner.

'Sophie?'

It was Ian, his hair rumpled, his shirt limp, looking slightly wide-eyed and crazy.

'Ian? What is it?' I threw the door wide. I was worried now.

He opened his mouth and the words seemed to burst out of him. 'Sophie, I know who Charlie and Belle are!'

Behind me I heard Dillon snort a laugh and knew what he was thinking. The pie shop. But he was wrong. Ian was far too happy and animated to have reached another dead-end.

'Come inside,' I invited him, 'and tell us all about it.'

CHAPTER 15

BELLE

Sweet Wattle Creek, 1931

THERE WAS BARELY a breath of air. A small bird sat on the fence, a willie wagtail, wriggling about with more energy than seemed natural. She tried to imagine The Grand as a once busy hotel, with customers laughing and gossiping, glasses clinking and clouds of tobacco billowing.

In the bar at the front, where the door to the street was stuck fast, she could still sense the past very strongly. Almost as if at any moment someone might march in and demand a beer. But there was also a musty scent, a disused sort of smell, and it was obvious no one had been served here for many years.

Martha had lived here alone, scrimping and saving to keep this place. Was that sensible of her? It seemed to lack foresight, and Martha did not sound like a woman who took wild flights of fancy. But, as Belle knew all too well, decisions were not always made for logical reasons. The Grand was the Bartholomew family home.

Belle looked at the brown Gladstone bag she'd

placed on the table while she'd made herself a cup of tea. The answers to all her questions could be waiting inside. *Martha's secrets.* Carrying the cup and saucer in one hand and the heavy bag in the other, she made her way up the stairs.

The small door at the end of the passage seemed to loom up with each step she climbed, but she refused to look at it. Eyes down, she turned and went into Martha's bedroom, and closed the door.

Her heart was beating quickly and she took a breath and then another. Silly. Ridiculous. And unnerving when she didn't have a clue what she was frightened of or why.

The air in here was close and warm, but Belle knew it was worse outside. In heat like this the thing to do was to keep the windows closed and draw the curtains. Once that was done, Belle put the bag on the bed and climbed up beside it onto the green-and-pink quilt. She struggled with the stiff locks for some time before eventually mastering them, and with a smile of triumph she pulled apart the two sides of the bag and peered into its mouth.

There was a fragrance. Sweet and faded. Belle tried to think what it was but the name eluded her. An old scent, she thought. One that might have been fashionable last century.

The next thing she noticed was that the contents were jumbled untidily together. It was as if everything had been hastily thrown inside the bag at the last moment.

Had Martha been in a hurry for some reason?

She tried to put herself in her mother's shoes,

the bag open, hands shaking, reaching into a drawer and pulling out her treasured items, pushing them inside. Perhaps in this very room. Perhaps looking over her shoulder.

But surely that wouldn't have happened? There was no reason for Martha to be afraid. Unless her mind was deteriorating, as Jo said, and she was imagining herself in danger. She should question Violet about it. As Martha's best friend, she'd know or at least could make a guess as to what was in the mind of Martha Bartholomew.

But then Belle remembered that she wasn't staying. She was planning to catch the train back to Melbourne this afternoon.

Impatient with herself, aware once more of the breathless warmth of the bedroom, she rifled through some of the loose papers, not knowing what she was looking for or what she might find. Further inside the bag, her fingers came in contact with some thicker type of material. She held it up and saw that it was a page torn out of a sketch pad. She had often seen Iris with something similar at Sorrento, sitting with her hat shading her face and her pencil busy.

This was a drawing. A cathedral, the walls broken and in ruin, rising to a dark and cloud-filled sky. It looked like a preliminary sketch, the sort of thing an artist might do before he put the finished work onto a canvas. Belle recognised it as Reims Cathedral, which was bombed during the war.

Could Martha have had such a talent? No one had mentioned it and Belle certainly hadn't inherited it. She looked more closely at the paper but there was no name for the artist, and no initials.

Setting the sketch aside, Belle returned to the contents of the bag. She found documents to do with The Grand—she must show them to Henry—and some bond certificates which, according to Aneas, weren't worth a bean. Two old books that looked as if they were falling apart. She read the titles aloud: '*The Tale of Peter Rabbit. Alice's Adventures in Wonderland.*'

Belle carefully turned the pages. Had Martha read these books to her, as she sat quietly listening? She couldn't remember and it seemed preposterous, but suddenly she longed to recall those intimate moments. She may have had a splendid childhood with Rory and Iris, but it made no difference to her feelings right now. Martha giving her away had left a space inside Belle; something was missing, and she wanted it back.

Setting aside the books, she began once more to rummage inside the bag, searching for she knew not what. There was a brooch, the yellow stones dull in their old-fashioned setting, and a photograph from last century, a couple stiffly posed, looking important. Her grandparents? That just left a few scraps of paper.

The first one she pulled out was a ticket for the train to Melbourne dated 1904. The second was a note with the address, Michael Maxwell c/- AFC Headquarters, Altona Bay. *Hope you are well, will write more when I get a chance, training going well. Michael.* And the third was a folded letter in handwriting she recognised only too well. It was old and creased and faded, but she had no trouble reading the contents.

12 December 1910,

Dear Sister, I received your letter with news of your intention to visit Belle at Christmas, and I beg you to reconsider. I know I have put you off before, and you understood then that learning the truth from you would cause her distress. Worse, taking her away with you, uprooting her from the only life she has known, could be extremely upsetting for her. I understand there are matters you want to discuss with her, and she will have to know the truth of her birth, one day, but she is so young. She doesn't know who you are and if you abruptly reappeared in her life she would be frightened.

You brought her to us because she was in danger. I remember well the birth certificate you showed me and how you said it had been pushed under your door. Even if Belle is no longer under physical threat, and you cannot be sure of that, emotionally she would be faced with a situation that would be very painful. She thinks we are her parents. How will you explain to her that you are her mother and her father is a man she has never heard of, a man you claim to love and yet we have never met? In short, she is the product of an adulterous affair!

If you cannot see what is best for Belle, then I must be selfish and ask you to think of us. We love her and cannot imagine our lives without her. Iris has been weeping ever since she read your letter and I cannot bear to see her distress. Don't do it, Martha, I beg of you.

Your loving brother, Rory.

Belle set it down. She picked it up again, very

carefully, as if she might have been mistaken, and then sat and stared at the pages in her hand. Tears began to fill her eyes and roll down her cheeks. This was her father, the only father she had ever known, and he loved her. He was begging to keep her.

The words 'the product of an adulterous affair', barely registered at first, and even when they did she could hardly take them in. She'd believed she was Martha and Nathan Ambrose's daughter and now here was this new and bewildering revelation. Belle didn't know how to begin to grapple with it. She tried to think clearly, to list what she knew about herself in a no-nonsense and practical manner.

Her mother had given her away at four years old. No one knew why, not really. She had refused to tell anyone why. And she had never gone to collect Belle and bring her home. This letter showed that she'd wanted to, though. She'd asked Rory to let her come and see Belle at Christmas, and he had said no. And Belle admitted, reading this letter, that she was glad he had.

Her headache was worse. She should stop this now and wait until she got home, where she could consider matters at a distance and more rationally. Where she could ask Henry's advice . . .

She laughed a little wildly, imagining Henry's face as he read the letter. He'd want her to burn it and certainly he'd never want her to speak of it to their 'friends'.

Wiping her face, Belle had reached out to close the bag when she noticed the photograph. It was resting hard against the leather interior and when she tried to slide it out it appeared to be stuck. When it came free, the cardboard backing tore slightly away. Belle held it up. The pose was similar to the likeness she owned of Charlie, before he went off to war, only this was another man, and although it was sepia-tinted she thought he was dark-haired, with creases at the corners of his dark eyes as if he was trying not to smile. He wore an army uniform with an Australian Flying Corps badge.

'Hello, Michael,' Belle said with what felt like relief. 'It is you, isn't it?'

Aneas Thomas had said Michael was back in Sweet Wattle Creek. If she could find him, question him . . . He had lived with Martha here at The Grand. Surely he would know the truth about the man who was her father?

But Belle was going home this afternoon.

She set the photograph aside and flopped back on the bed and closed her eyes. She needed to think, but she was so tired, and the heat wasn't helping. Perhaps if she just rested for a while she would feel energetic enough to get herself organised for the return trip. Yes, that was it, Belle told herself, she'd just have a little rest . . .

She woke to the sound of loud knocking.

Disorientated, she sat up on the bed. Her head was heavy and her mind thick. The air in here felt like treacle and she struggled to the floor. The knocking came again and this time she heard Frank Davies calling up to her.

She'd left the outside door wide open. She'd felt safe here inside The Grand, but after reading the letter in Martha's bag she wondered if she'd been misguided. Perhaps even naive and foolish. The people of Sweet Wattle Creek were possibly not as friendly and harmless as she'd imagined.

'Miss Bartholomew?' Why was Frank Davies here?

'Just a minute,' she called back, not wanting him to come looking for her.

She was struggling to slip her shoes on when a glance in the mirror showed her hair sticking up wildly in all directions. There was a red mark on her cheek, too, where she'd slept with her hand underneath her face. And then her eyes went wide as she realised.

The train! Frank had come to take her to the train.

She swung around, seeing her open, unpacked case, and the papers spilling across the bed from Martha's bag. And her clothes, perspiration marks under her arms and her skirt wrinkled. Her heart sank. She couldn't travel like this. Could she ask Frank to wait while she got ready? But as she hurried out to the stairs, Belle doubted she was going anywhere. Not today. And she didn't know whether to be disappointed, or relieved.

Frank was waiting on the landing halfway down the stairs, leaning against the banisters. He was wearing his work trousers, his shirtsleeves rolled up, and his hat in his hand. She noticed he'd combed his hair and used Brylcreem to slick it back, making him look older.

'I'm sorry,' she began in an anxious voice. 'I fell asleep. The heat . . .'

'Jo said you weren't feeling tiptop.'

She looked down at herself. 'Not looking it, either.'

'I wouldn't say that.'

She considered if he was flirting with her, but Frank didn't seem the flirting type. 'Is it too late? For the train, I mean?'

'I should think so.' But he didn't sound bothered, as if it didn't matter to him that she was wasting his time.

'Oh. I suppose it'll have to be tomorrow.'

'Sunday. No trains tomorrow. You're stuck here for now.'

She was still at the top of the stairs. Was it her imagination or did his gaze slide past her, towards the door at the end of the passage? The door with the brass knob.

'*You* found Martha, didn't you?' It wasn't what she'd meant to say, but the words slipped out.

'Yes.' He turned and walked away, back down to the kitchen, and slowly she followed him. Clearly he was reluctant to talk, but Belle felt the need to push.

'Mr Davies, how did Martha die?'

He was standing in the doorway to the stable yard and beyond him the sky was as blue as ever. There was a large white cockatoo with a yellow crest sitting on top of the brick wall above the open gate. It took him a little while to answer and when he did she knew he wasn't telling her the truth.

'I don't know. You'd have to ask my mother that. She spoke with the doctor afterwards.'

'Please.'

He shot her a glance and then stepped outside to light a cigarette. She followed him. The cockatoo moved, tilting its head, sulphur crest lifting, as if it was curious about them.

'All right, I'll tell you, but don't blame me if you don't like what you hear.' He blew out the smoke. 'No one had seen her for a week or more. Mum was worried and asked me to call in. When I did there was no answer and I looked around. I found her. She was dead.'

'So she was on her own? What about Michael? Michael Maxwell? Was he here?'

His eyes were so fierce she almost took a step back from him. 'Believe me if I could blame Maxwell for it then I would. There's no love lost between us. But he wasn't here. He'd been gone a few months by then. Taken to the road like those loafers he's so fond of.'

She ignored that comment, sticking to the point for now. 'But I thought . . . Weren't they friends? Michael and Martha.'

'Yes. They must have had some sort of falling out because she changed her will. I don't know what it was about. Again, you'd have to ask my mother.'

Violet, it seemed, was the keeper of all knowledge.

Belle knew she shouldn't, for the sake of her

own peace of mind, but she was going to. The question needed an answer and she couldn't go back to Melbourne without knowing what it was.

'Where did you find her?'

But his answer wasn't what she'd expected. He stared over at the shed by the stables. 'In there,' he said. 'She had the door barricaded shut and I had to force it open.'

Belle felt confused. She'd been so sure he was going to say the room at the end of the passage. The room with the brass knob.

'Was she hiding from someone? It sounds as if she was trying to lock herself in. Or someone else out.'

He didn't answer. Perhaps he didn't know. Or perhaps he did and he was simply not wanting to tell her. She thought about pressing him and then decided not to; for now she'd learned everything she could.

Belle smiled. 'Thank you. And thank you for coming to take me to the station. I'm sorry to have kept you from your work.'

He gave her a sharp look, as if he mistrusted her hasty friendliness. 'I'll tell Mum you're staying a bit longer. She'll want you over for Sunday roast lunch.'

'In this heat?'

'You won't get out of it that easily,' he said, and suddenly his mouth curved into a proper smile. It made him more approachable, that smile, and she felt a ridiculous urge to confide her fears to him, as if Frank was someone she could trust. But like everyone else here he was a stranger and she hastily quashed the impulse.

'Goodbye, Mr Davies.'

His mouth tightened. 'Goodbye, Miss Bartholomew.'

After he had gone, shutting the gate behind him, Belle looked up at the top of the brick wall for the white cockatoo, but it had flown away.

Cleaning had always been Belle's way of dealing with times of crisis. It seemed to clear her mind, or kept things from becoming too overwhelming. She'd finished looking inside the Gladstone bag and there weren't any more clues. Right now she needed to do something functional and organised, so that she could keep her emotions at bay.

So Belle set about cleaning the kitchen. Although Violet had done a good job, the grime hadn't responded to a single effort. The tank outside, whose pipe led into the kitchen, was nearly empty, but Belle had noticed the well in the stable yard. Although the circular brick tunnel smelled musty when she lifted the wooden cover, and the winch and rope were old, they appeared to be in good working order. As if they had been used until recently. When she hauled up a bucket of water and tested it, it tasted sweet if a little brackish. Satisfied, she brought the water in to heat on the stove and then set to work scrubbing the kitchen from top to bottom.

Her arms ached and perspiration dripped from

her, but the hard work was cathartic. When she finally finished, leaning shakily on the table and looking about her, she felt a deep sense of satis-faction. She was just about to begin washing out her clothing so that it could dry for tomorrow, when her eye was caught by something that had fallen down beside the wooden cupboard. A hard edge of card.

Awkwardly, she stuck her fingers into the gap and eased it out. It was a small rectangular pho-tograph taken with a box brownie. Four smiling people were posing in front of a tree—two adults standing with their arms around the two children in front.

Belle recognised two of those faces. Tilly and Gwen, the sisters who had interrupted her day-dream by the war memorial in the park. How on earth had this ended up here? Unless the two girls had been here at The Grand before she arrived? Of course that was it. They were living here before Constable Nash had moved them on.

They were only children. Surely no one could send children off onto the track? But she remem-bered there had been children in the groups she'd seen from the train. Whole families, on the move, desperate for work and shelter and food.

Carefully, she slid the photograph into a drawer for safe-keeping. She didn't expect to see the girls again, but it seemed wrong to throw it away.

Belle woke unexpectedly. There was a light

shining up onto her window. She had been deep asleep, exhausted by all her cleaning. She blinked, uncertain what had woken her. Vaguely she had been aware of a noise. The sound of someone moving about inside the building.

She lay there, unwilling to move, staring at the faint glow as it bobbed across the stained plaster, getting fainter and fainter. Whoever or whatever had been inside the building was now outside, and moving away. The knowledge sent her up out of the bed and hurrying breathlessly down the stairs.

When she reached the bottom she felt a breeze that shouldn't have been there. Spinning around, she couldn't quite believe her eyes. The front door was wide open!

Slowly, cautiously, Belle walked towards it. She could see the stars in the sky and smell the night scents. She peered outside but there was no one there, only the darkness and the quiet. As she pulled the door she saw a key in the lock, all ready to be turned.

That was when she heard it, the faraway sound of someone whistling. It gave her a shiver up her spine, and she rubbed the goosebumps on her arms, standing and listening as it faded into silence. Her good Samaritan, whoever he was, had gone.

CHAPTER 16

SOPHIE

Sweet Wattle Creek, 1986

A<small>S SOON AS</small> Ian stepped inside he was greeted by Smithy, who seemed to think this was his new best friend. Dillon was less friendly, propped against the kitchen bench and shooting us suspicious looks.

'Who are Belle and Charlie, then?' I demanded, unable to contain my anticipation any longer. 'Don't keep me in suspense.'

He looked up from attending to the dog, and smiled. He really did have nice eyes. 'Miriam rang again. Last time I spoke to her I'd mentioned the two names, just in passing, and it didn't occur to her until later. She said she was walking down New Bond Street looking in the shop windows when it clicked and she had to stop herself from jumping up and down. Charlie was the name of Eileen Nicholson's only son.'

I similarly felt like jumping up and down. The dress, Eileen Nicholson, Charlie . . . they were all entwined. I was grinning. I couldn't help it.

'So the dress was made by Eileen for her future daughter-in-law? Belle must be Charlie's wife. It was a present. This story just keeps getting better and better.'

Ian nodded, looking equally manic. 'It's going to be a huge drawcard for the Centenary.'

Dillon was looking at us, clearly puzzled. 'You make it sound like a big deal.'

'It is a big deal!' Ian seemed to be hopping on one leg with elation. 'Eileen Nicholson garments sell for a fortune and we have one. But not just any one. A wedding dress. And not just any wedding dress. One that was a present for her son's wedding, one that meant something very personal to her.'

Dillon shrugged as if he still didn't get it, but I could tell he was acting a part. His cool was slipping as Ian's enthusiasm worked its magic on him.

'What about Charlie?' I interrupted. 'Is he still alive? Or Belle? What about Belle?'

Some of Ian's fervour faded and seeing it, mine did also. 'Charlie died during the First World War.'

That sobered me.

'So how did the dress come to be here? In Sweet Wattle Creek?'

'I don't know,' he admitted. 'And Miriam doesn't have anything on Belle. She's going to check it out when she gets home. Speaking of home, she wants us to meet with her next week.'

'In Melbourne?'

'Yes.'

I looked at Dillon and he raised his eyebrows in the way that usually made me smile. As if he was a disapproving grandfather in a fourteen-year-old boy's body.

'Do you mind?' I asked him. 'You'll have to go to Tim and Maureen's,' I added, knowing he'd enjoy being with Christy, and then felt guilty for using the girl as bait. Especially when I'd already decided I didn't want them getting too close at this young age.

He heaved an exaggerated sigh. 'I suppose so,' he said with resignation. 'What about Smithy?'

'Maybe he can go as well. I'm sure Tim wouldn't mind but I don't know about Maureen. You could take all his stuff with you and keep him quiet. Maybe you could offer to mind the baby for them while they go out for an hour or so?'

'Yeah, I could do that, but you've forgotten something.'

'What?' Frantically, I tried to think what that might be.

'BC. What happens to the cat?'

I threw up my hands.

Dillon only laughed. 'Of course you should go. This sounds cool and you need to find out all you can about Charlie and Belle and what they have to do with Sweet Wattle Creek. It'll make a really good story for the *Herald*, Mum.'

'Yes, I agree,' Ian said, giving my son a look of respect.

'It's a mystery,' Dillon added, serious now, 'and you have to solve it.'

He was right, of course he was, but I was so pleased he saw it that way. Sometimes I forgot he was growing up.

'Want to stay for tea?' Dillon asked Ian, to my surprise. 'We have plenty of con carne, don't we, Mum?'

I wouldn't have asked, not without Dillon's agreement, but the fact that he'd done so off his own bat seemed like a nice thing for him to do. 'More than enough.' Con carne wasn't exactly the right meal for a hot evening like this, but a growing boy like Dillon could only have so much cold meat and salad before he began to protest.

Ian agreed to the offer without hesitation. Possibly he was lonely, I thought, as I helped Dillon serve. Although he was friendly enough, he didn't seem to have made any close friends here. Apart from Nola. And living out near The Grand must be slightly daunting, that burnt-out shell to greet him every morning. Which reminded me . . .

'I read some of those letters from Lyn Thomas to her husband. She mentioned The Grand in them, and Martha Bartholomew as the owner.'

'Ah, yes, the Bartholomews. Early settlers. Intriguing family.' His eyes had a faraway look in them I was beginning to recognise meant he was time travelling.

'Intriguing how?'

'Martha was the licensee of the hotel. There was a son but he left Sweet Wattle Creek before the parents died and Martha took over The Grand. A bit of a hothead. There was trouble with a girl. Anyway, it seems as if Martha was considered the more likely prospect in her parents' estimation.'

'In the letters Lyn talks about Michael Maxwell. And, by the way, there were also a couple of pages in there from Michael himself. And '

'Pilot in the Flying Corps,' Ian interrupted, smiling proudly, as if I were a star pupil and he was impressed by my knowledge.

'Michael was reported missing. Did he ever come back?'

'I got the impression that some people would've been happier if he'd died on the Western Front. But yes, he came back. Injured. Perhaps not the same man who'd left. But so many of them were . . .' He shot me a cagey look. 'I was going to say scarred inside and out but that sounds trite.'

'Although true.'

'Lots of pilots found it difficult to get work after the First World War. There wasn't that much demand, not in the beginning. It took a while for the rest of the country to realise the benefits of flying.'

Smithy gave a soft woof. The dog was sitting beside us, looking hopeful, but even Dillon didn't think chilli would go down well. But I did see him slip him a crumbled corn chip when he thought I wasn't looking. Smithy had certainly landed on his feet.

'You live out near that burnt-out place?' Dillon had clearly been listening, in between eating huge quantities.

'Yes, behind The Grand.'

'It's supposed to be haunted, isn't it?'

'Is it?' Ian looked captivated, as if a ghost was simply something else to be researched. Perhaps it even deserved its own board in the RSL Hall. 'No one told me that when I moved in.'

Dillon rolled his eyes. 'Well they wouldn't, would they? Some of the kids take dares to go there at night.'

I felt my face getting tight and anxious. 'Not you I hope?'

'Nah, that's geek stuff,' was Dillon's scornful retort.

'And who is this ghost supposed to be?' Ian pondered aloud.

'It's a woman.' Dillon said it as if nothing had ever scared him, not even Walter. 'She stands at the window and stares out at you with crazy eyes. And her hair is on fire. She was murdered there a long time ago, but when it burned down her soul was disturbed. At least that's what they say,' he added carefully, in case we thought he knew too much for someone who was as disinterested as he was.

'How did the fire start?' I asked curiously.

Dillon shrugged.

'Overturned lamp. That's what I was told,' Ian said. 'Nineteen thirty something or other.'

'Did everyone get out? Was Martha Bartholomew still there?'

'Now that I don't know.'

Once the meal was finished, Ian said he needed to get back. I walked him to the door and he called out a goodbye to Dillon and Smithy. It had been pleasant, his conversation stimulating, his presence non-threatening. Even Dillon had enjoyed it, though I knew I'd be hard-pressed to get him to admit it.

When Ian had gone I turned to Dillon. 'Do you

really not mind about me going to Melbourne? If you do, you only have to say and I won't.'

He gave me a sideways look. 'I don't mind,' he said. 'I think it's a good story, Mum, and you should write it. Anyway, the food's better at Tim and Maureen's.'

I laughed. I still felt uncomfortable about my decision—I might even change my mind—but for the first time in ages I had a chance to follow a dream. It seemed cowardly not to.

The knock on the door startled us both. Thinking it was Ian again, that he'd forgotten something, I opened it straightaway.

It wasn't Ian, and in that moment between seeing the unfamiliar face and realising how vulnerable I was standing there, I felt my skin begin to crawl. But it was only an instant.

'Josh. Mrs Davies's nephew,' he reminded me. 'Sorry to barge in on you.'

Of course it was Josh. I recognised him now. He looked drawn and tired, but managed to pull a smile out of somewhere. 'You're the lady from the newspaper?'

'Yes. Sophie Matheson. How is your aunt?'

'Still unconscious. I came about the dog.'

Dillon had come up behind me and I caught his worried glance.

'Ah, that's okay. We don't mind looking after him,' I said hurriedly. 'No trouble.'

Smithy had crept closer to Josh to sniff his outstretched hand, but the dog didn't seem overly keen. He'd been happier to see Ian than he was to see Josh.

'He's my aunt's dog really. Not a working dog at all. In fact, he's pretty useless with the sheep—scared of them,' he added with a derisive snort. 'I wouldn't have kept him but my aunt fell in love with him and that was that. I don't think he'll be happy being at Morwenstow without her. If you could keep him for now I'd be grateful.'

'No trouble,' Dillon repeated with emphasis.

I smiled.

Josh caught on and smiled, too. 'I brought his bedding around last night.' He held out a heavy-looking shopping bag. 'Here's some more of his stuff. And some food. He eats like a pig.'

So it wasn't Ian sneaking to our door as I'd thought. I was glad now I'd forgotten to mention it. I took the bag and passed it to Dillon, who led Smithy away into the kitchen. He set the bag on the table and began to sort through it. I saw him toss Smithy a ball, which the dog took possession of like an old friend.

'Do they think your aunt will . . . How long before she recovers?'

He grimaced. 'I'm trying not to be negative, but the truth is they don't hold out great hopes.'

'The wedding dress your aunt gave to the Centenary committee. Do you know anything about it?'

He shrugged. 'She gave me the box to give to them, that's all I know. If she told me I wasn't listening. Sometimes she goes on and I just tune out. Sorry.'

'That's okay. Have you ever heard of anyone in your family called Belle? I think the dress might have belonged to her, and no one seems to know who she is. We've discovered she was engaged to Charlie Nicholson.'

He shook his head. He'd begun to lose interest and I could see he wanted to get home. He probably had a lot to do without me waffling on about a wedding dress and people he'd never heard of. But I had one more request.

'Will you ask your family for me? Someone might know. I'm sure your aunt would want us to have the full story, so that the dress can be displayed properly. I want to write about it, too. Do you think she'd mind?'

'She'd like that,' he said. 'And I'll ask for you. That's about the best I can do.'

I wondered if I could ask myself. And yet it seemed ill-mannered to turn up at someone's sick bed and begin interrogating people. I'd see what Ian thought, maybe he'd have enough front to do it. In fact, I was beginning to think this project had become an obsession for him—or maybe all of his projects did. Maybe there was nothing special about this one. For some reason I didn't want to delve into why that idea made me feel a little depressed.

'Thank you, Josh, that would be very kind. And I hope your aunt starts to recover soon.'

After he'd gone I closed the door and stood for a while, thinking. The letters were still stacked in the box on the sideboard and I knew I should read the rest of them, that there were clues in there, but also more mysteries. But I was tired and a night off sounded like a better idea.

'Wanna watch *The Flying Doctors*?' I asked Dillon.

He looked up from Smithy's treasures. 'Do I have to?'

'Come on, you know you like it, really.'

Dillon heaved a deep sigh and moved towards the sofa, and smiling, I joined him.

CHAPTER 17

BELLE

Sweet Wattle Creek, 1931

JUST AS HE said he would be, Frank Davies was at the door to collect Belle from The Grand and take her off to Morwenstow for Violet's Sunday lunch. After another interrupted night, she'd been slow getting up and dressing, but at least this time she wasn't still in bed when he arrived.

'Tea?' she asked politely. 'I've just made a pot.'

She'd decided she would be very polite to Frank. She hadn't been in her right mind last time they met.

The old brown earthenware pot had been in the cupboard and looked as if it had been a favourite of Martha's. As she poured out the dark brew, she thought about her mother doing the exact same thing every morning as she prepared for the day. The thought was oddly comforting and drew her closer to the enigma of Martha Bartholomew.

Frank was leaning his shoulder against the doorframe and now he glanced around him at the neat kitchen. 'You've done some tidying up.'

Belle nodded. 'I thought I may as well. I can't expect your family to keep looking after me.'

'So you tidied up even though you're not staying?'

There, he was starting to irritate her already. She could feel the tension tightening in her stomach, but she forced herself to speak as if it wasn't.

'Someone will live here, I expect. Eventually.'

She sat down and sipped her tea from the flowered cup she'd also found in the cupboard. After a brief hesitation Frank joined her, pulling out a chair opposite her. He put his hat on the table beside him.

He had dressed more carefully than usual, she thought with what she told herself was cool unconcern. Not his dusty working clothes, but grey trousers with braces and a white shirt ironed and rolled up at the sleeves as a concession to the heat. No tie. That was probably a step too far for Frank.

Had he been to church? She imagined a family like the Davies would be churchgoers. Pillars of the community. Rory had attended church occasionally, though rarely once Iris wasn't there to gently persuade him. Belle was ambivalent about the whole thing. She couldn't help but remember ministers in pulpits around the world, exhorting young men to join up and fight the enemy. To die. And she found she couldn't forgive them or their religion.

But then she remembered the Davies owned the store in town. Maybe he'd been there, writing in the ledgers, marking red crosses against the customers who hadn't settled their accounts.

'So, you *are* planning to sell the place?' Frank

leaned back, searching in his pocket for his cigarettes. She nodded when he held them up, asking silently for her permission.

'Henry wants me to sell it.'

'Henry?'

'My fiancé. My solicitor. He's both.'

He lit his cigarette before he spoke again. 'Family solicitor I gather.'

'Yes. Henry's father was a friend of my father.' She paused, the reminder striking her yet again, that Rory wasn't her father and yet he was the only father she had ever known. 'When Mr Collier the elder died, Henry took over. We've known each other for a long time and it seemed . . . suitable.'

It was a stupid word and she knew it as soon as she said it.

Frank gave a brief laugh. 'Suitable. You make it sound like a business arrangement.'

'Well it isn't a business arrangement.'

She felt flustered and angry. And yet, hadn't she thought of it like that herself? She admitted now, starkly, that Henry had been the compromise between never marrying and finding someone who would not demand too much of her.

Frank was watching her through the smoke, his grey eyes narrowed. His gaze unnerved her and his next words surprised her. 'I thought . . .' His glance now was almost shy. 'It seems a waste to marry someone just because they're suitable.'

She stood up awkwardly. 'I need to fetch something from upstairs before we go. I'm sure you must be in a hurry.'

Frank also stood up, the chair legs grating on the floor. 'Whenever you're ready,' he said, echoing her brisk indifference. 'I'll wait outside.'

Belle was about to turn away when she remembered something. 'The front door. We can use that now.'

She could see by his puzzled frown that the functioning door had nothing to do with him. Before he could ask her any more questions, Belle hurried away to the stairs. She heard him making his way down to the front of the building as she reached her bedroom.

Quickly, she changed into the cotton blouse she'd washed and hung up to dry, and then brushed her hair. There'd been no time to curl it, or to do anything other than arrange it into a pale cap about her head. She applied a thin coat of lipstick and a dab of powder and collected her purse. A look in the mirror showed her a woman with wide blue eyes beneath thinly plucked brows who was pale and tired and certainly not looking her best. Automatically, she reached up to touch the scar on her forehead.

Frank was waiting outside.

'The door,' he said, nodding back at it. 'Where did you find the key?'

'Some kind Samaritan found it,' she spoke airily.

If she told him the truth she knew he was the sort of man who would insist she move out of The Grand, and she didn't want to move out and she didn't want to argue with him again. Last night had been strangely like a dream but she hadn't felt threatened. Whoever had returned the key meant her no harm, she was certain.

'I haven't been invited to Sunday lunch for a long time,' she went on quickly, changing the subject. 'When my parents . . .' She stopped, annoyed with herself. 'Well, we used to go out quite often. Rory liked a slap-up meal.'

Frank opened the door of the Morris and waited while she settled herself inside. The day was already hot. Hardly the weather for a roast lunch, but Belle supposed people in Sweet Wattle Creek were used to the summer heat and continued about their lives whatever the temperature.

'Rory was a friend of my parents when they were all young,' Frank said, as he started the car. 'I've heard plenty of stories about him and Martha. He fell out of the old pepper tree at Morwenstow and they thought he'd broken his back. When they all rushed over he just lay on the ground and laughed up at them. Sounds like he was a bit of a tear-away.'

Belle smiled. 'He wasn't afraid of anything.'

Except failure. Except ruin.

Her smile faded and she looked out of the window at the passing scenery. They were on an unsealed road and the post and rail fences were strung out beside it. A house stood among some trees off to the left, and she remembered Jo saying it was the Beauchamp's place. Morwenstow was further on.

'I saw your brother's name on the war memorial in the park.'

Frank nodded. 'I was eleven years old when Ted died in the war. I had all sorts of things I planned to tell him when he came home. He was my big brother. A bit of a hero, I suppose. When Ted was born Dad said the farm was for him, and when I was born, I was going to have the store. Jo, well, she was the girl so she was going to get married and leave.' He gave a wry smile. 'You can imagine what Jo said about that.'

'I can.'

'I knew there were others who went to war and who weren't coming back but Ted seemed so indestructible. So I'd been saving things up until he came home and then . . . he didn't. Knowing I'd never be able to tell him any of those stories . . . It was a difficult thing to come to terms with and it took me a long time to accept he was gone for good. I kept looking up at the door and expecting him to walk through.'

She recognised his pain in the rigidity of his shoulders and the clench of his jaw.

'Where did your brother die?'

'In France. He was on his way to a field hospital. He'd been in some sort of scrap—we never really got to the bottom of it. He needed a dressing on his cheek. He never got there. The truck was shelled and they found it burnt out. Ted was still inside.' His mouth tightened. 'The other passenger survived.'

'But your father came back?'

He glanced at her and some of the strain left his face. 'Yes. He's never been the same since Ypres, but at least he's alive. If Mum had lost them both . . . she's a strong woman, but I'm not sure she could've survived that.'

'And she has you and Jo.'

'Yes, she does.' He gave his half-smile and his eyes searched hers. 'Are you trying to cheer me up, Belle?'

'I don't know. Perhaps I'm trying to cheer myself up.'

The noise of the car engine gave them an excuse for silence, but Belle thought it was a more comfortable one. He'd been a young boy when his brother had died and his father had come back too ill to work, so most of the burden must have fallen to him. He'd have grown up quickly and it explained his quiet authority and his seriousness.

Her thoughts turned back to Henry. She hadn't phoned him as she'd promised. That should bother her . . . why didn't that bother her?

Belle pushed back a damp curl, lifting her face to the warm breeze coming through her window. Right now she was feeling strangely removed from Henry and the St Kilda house. Shock and grief, she supposed. It would pass. That was what people said, wasn't it?

It will pass.

Belle had gone through the contents of the Gladstone bag, and although she'd learned the uncomfortable truth about her birth and her father, she wasn't sure it had helped her get any closer to the essence of the woman who was Martha.

Henry would tell her to forget all this nonsense and come home. Deep down she suspected that she hadn't rung him because she wasn't ready to give up.

'Here we are.' Frank turned off the road and down a long driveway. 'This is Morwenstow.'

Belle could see a windmill. Frank explained they had bores on their property, and the water was drawn up into troughs for the stock. 'We're luckier than some,' he said. 'In drought we don't have to cart the water in.'

Ahead of them a gate stood open and beyond that was the house, with a verandah all around it, and mature trees seeming to embrace the building with their shade. Frank pulled up, and got out, coming around to open the car door for her.

The screened door at the front opened with a bang and Violet came hurrying out.

'Belle!'

She descended the stairs a little stiffly, and Belle had barely got out of the car when she was being hugged as if Violet hadn't seen her for a year. She heard Frank murmuring something about 'Let the poor girl go', but Violet took no notice of him. Anyway, Belle wasn't sure if she wanted to be let go. It felt so nice.

When she pulled away Violet's smile was so warm that Belle couldn't help but smile back.

'Martha would be so glad you've come home!'

Belle's heart sank. She put a hand up to her mouth, but it was trembling, and then their faces blurred and to her dismay she knew that she was going to cry.

Turning away, she tried to shield her reaction, but Violet was already reaching out and making concerned noises and Belle was filled with the sort of excruciating embarrassment she always felt when her emotions overwhelmed her. She gave a shaky laugh.

'I'm so sorry. I can't imagine what you must think of me.'

Violet tucked a hand in her arm and began to lead her inside. 'This heat is enough to make anyone a bit weepy,' she said briskly. 'Here, come and sit down in the cool.'

The room Violet led her to was at the side of the house, with a view over the encircling verandah and the big pepper tree beyond. Belle wondered if that was the one Rory had fallen out of, all those years ago.

The air in here was so much cooler, and before long Violet returned and presented her with a glass of cold water. 'Drink this and you'll feel better.'

Belle drank it.

'You mustn't let yourself dry out,' Violet went on. 'In this weather you could become extremely ill very fast. It's deceptive, the heat. One minute you're all right and the next you're not.'

'I'm sorry for being such a nuisance.'

Violet smiled. 'Belle, please don't say that. You're not a nuisance.'

'I've been looking through Martha's things,' Belle said quietly. 'Trying to . . . understand, I suppose. Why she sent me away and what she thought. I want to be close to her, but I can't. She's a stranger.'

'That's a shame, dear,' Violet said. 'If you want to ask me anything about her, I'll do my best to answer your questions.'

Violet's eyes were shrewd. This was Belle's chance. They were alone and Violet was willing. Belle took a deep breath.

'My father . . . I don't think it *was* Nathan Ambrose.'

Violet gave her a sharp look. 'What makes you say that?'

Belle didn't want to mention the letter, but she didn't have to, because Violet spoke again without waiting for an answer.

'Martha kept things to herself. I remember, once, coming to visit and there were voices upstairs. Your voice, Belle, and a man who wasn't Nathan. Martha wouldn't let me in. She was pleasant about it but firm. I thought then that there was something . . . And Nathan was never the love of her life, but someone was. Someone put a glow in her cheeks and made her smile. I'm sure of it.'

'And you think this was my father?'

Violet smiled sadly. 'Martha married Nathan to save The Grand. I don't know why she didn't marry your father, perhaps they hadn't met then, or perhaps he couldn't marry her. I'm sorry I can't answer your question properly but I think you're right. You're not Nathan's daughter. Good heavens, you don't look the slightest bit like him.'

Belle nodded, refusing to cry again. 'So you have no idea at all? Sweet Wattle Creek is a small town. He must be someone you know.'

But Violet shook her head once more. 'I did think it might have been Aneas. He was devoted to Martha. But I find it difficult to imagine him actually . . .' She put a hand to her mouth. 'Oh dear, I'm sure you know what I mean, Belle. Besides, if he was your father, I'm quite certain he would've married Martha after Nathan died. Aneas is very keen on doing the right thing.'

'I always thought Lyn would insist he marry *her*.'

Jo had come up without them noticing.

'Josephine Davics!' scolded her mother. 'Lyn Thomas is a very good woman.'

Jo rolled her eyes at Belle. 'Oh, Mum, you know she runs his life. They may as well be married. She won't let him do anything without her say-so.'

'She wasn't always like that,' Violet insisted. 'Alister, her husband, Aneas's brother, died in the war,' she explained to Belle. 'She idolised him. She never really recovered. I don't think she wanted to marry again after Alister.'

Jo remained respectfully silent but Belle could see she wasn't convinced.

Without warning Violet jumped up. 'I'd better see to the meal,' she said. 'Carly will be here in a tick.'

'Carly's coming?' Jo looked at her mother, and something unspoken passed between them. 'Did Frank invite her?'

'I think she invited herself,' Violet said.

Jo sighed. Her glance to Belle was apologetic. 'The girl has a—a thing for my brother. He doesn't encourage her, at least not deliberately, although I think he's flattered. He's a man, after all.'

'She's very pretty,' Violet reminded her.

'She has tickets on herself.'

Violet snorted. She stood up and went to the doorway. 'Frank, are you there?'

There were footsteps and Frank appeared.

'Frank, will you take Belle out into the back garden? Stan's there somewhere pretending to water his tomatoes. You can introduce them. And tell him lunch will be ready very soon.'

Jo was murmuring something to her mother, but whatever it was, Belle couldn't hear. She hesitated but Frank said, 'Come on, we've been dismissed,' and led her down the cool dark hallway and out of the back door.

Behind the house were large water tanks and a garden—plots for vegetables and an orchard of fruit trees. Despite the heat and a few drooping stems and leaves, the area was well tended. They must eat well at Morwenstow, Belle thought. Probably much better than some of the other residents of the town and definitely better than the travellers passing through. There wasn't a vegetable garden at Annat Street, Rory had not been one for growing anything, and Iris had preferred flowers. A few stems of mint in a tub by the backdoor at The Grand made Belle think Martha might have tried out her green thumb, but nothing as lavish as this.

Then it occurred to her that the tub may have belonged to the travellers and not Martha, and she turned to Frank.

'Do you know who was living in The Grand before I came? The people who were moved on?'

Frank was lighting a cigarette. He gave her one

of his sharp and disapproving looks, signalling that their earlier intimacy was now to be forgotten.

'Travellers. Seemed to be someone different there every time I looked. Why? They haven't been back, have they?'

Belle shook her head. 'No, they haven't been back. I was just curious.'

She'd been going to ask him about the two girls but she decided not to. Frank was not sympathetic to travellers and she didn't want to inadvertently give away the fact that the sisters were still here.

'What you said before, about a good Samaritan finding the key to the door.' Those grey eyes were fixed on her now with an intensity that made it difficult to look away. 'You need to be careful, Belle. If it's Michael Maxwell, and I think it probably is, then he's trouble.'

'He was Martha's friend.' She sounded curt and tried to remedy it. 'I'm sure he would never do anything to harm Martha's daughter. Aren't you letting your dislike for him colour your judgement?'

He made a sound of dismissal. 'He *was* Martha's friend, but it doesn't mean he was good for her. For anyone, come to think of it.'

'And you know better?' His certainty about Michael Maxwell's character was making her angry.

'Yes,' he said.

'How? How can you know that?'

'Belle, will you listen to me. You're a stranger here. I don't want you to be hurt.'

'I don't need your advice or your concern,

thank you. I can look after myself.'

'Look after yourself?' His disbelieving laugh was like a red rag to a bull. Seeing the flare of anger in her face, he reached out to her, perhaps to shake some sense into her—Frank would be the sort, she told herself—just as someone coughed from among a row of wilting plants.

A man was coming towards them. He was an older version of Frank, a bit stooped, and his face looked grey and drawn with illness. His breathing sounded raspy and he coughed again just as he reached them, his pale eyes sliding over Belle in a manner she wasn't sure she appreciated.

'Put out the smoke, son. You know they catch in my throat. Time you gave 'em up, I reckon.' His voice was barely more than a whisper.

Frank still looked unhappy, but he was trying hard to hide it as he crushed the cigarette beneath his heel. He introduced them. 'Dad, this is Miss Bartholomew.'

'Belle,' she insisted, and held out her hand to the older man.

He took her hand in dry fingers. 'Stan Davies. So you're Belle Bartholomew? Violet can talk of nothing else,' he grumbled, but his expression belied his tone. Clearly Violet was the apple of his eye.

'Lunch is nearly ready.' Frank was watching his father closely, as if he was used to summing up whether this was a good day or a bad one. Stan was one of the 'Whispering Men' she had heard about. Men who had been gassed but were still alive, with lungs that would gradually erode, and as they lost their ability to get enough air they lost their voices, too.

'One of Violet's special roasts,' Stan was saying with a breathless laugh. 'We have to thank you, Belle. We don't get them that often nowadays. Depression's put paid to them. This is a very frugal household.'

He stopped walking and rested against a trellis, taking shallow breaths. Frank also stopped, showing no impatience with his father's disability. 'So you're Martha's daughter,' Stan said again. 'Well, well,' he murmured softly, cryptically. 'Who'd have thought?'

'Frank!'

The woman's high-pitched call startled them. She came down off the verandah, dark hair bobbed and her blue summer dress fluttering around her shapely legs. She reached Frank in a breathless rush, grasping hold of his arm and smiling up at him. Belle wanted to look away— the girl's heart was in her face.

'Carly.' Frank's smile seemed forced. He looked at Belle. 'This is Miss Bartholomew.'

'Oh, of course.' Carly's own smile faded slightly, but she held out her hand and Belle responded. The girl was young, perhaps younger than her years. 'Carly Beauchamp. I'm Frank's neighbour.'

'And we have a slap-up lunch waiting for us inside,' Stan reminded them, a twinkle in his eye. 'I know how fond you are of Violet's roasts, Carly.'

'Very!' the girl responded, her eyes on Frank.

Frank was still looking at Belle, but Belle turned away, distancing herself from the byplay, wanting nothing to do with it. She was relieved when, just at that moment, Jo put her head out of the door to let them know lunch was indeed ready.

CHAPTER 18

SOPHIE

Sweet Wattle Creek, 1986

TIM LOOKED EVEN more exhausted than usual. He sat slumped over his coffee, staring at his computer screen. Evidently the new baby still hadn't started sleeping. I wondered how Maureen was coping, no sleep at night and running her cafe during the day. I felt sorry for them, I really did, but apart from the occasional baby-sitting stint I couldn't do much to mend matters in the short term.

Dillon had been a good baby. Despite all the upheaval and recriminations he'd caused, he'd slept like an angel. Definitely not the sort of baby from hell Tim and Maureen were dealing with.

'Need a hand there?' I asked quietly when I could tell Tim hadn't even noticed me standing beside him.

His head jerked and he opened a bleary eye. 'Oh, it's you.'

'Yes. I work here. Remember? Do you need help with anything? I've finished the story on the sheep duffers. Nice big head photo to go with it.'

'Of the duffers?'

'No, of a sheep. They didn't catch the blokes who did it.'

'Oh yeah.' He straightened up, took a mouthful of coffee and pulled a face. 'I've been looking at Grandpa's 'Recollections'. That was what he called them. They're handwritten and I've started to put them onto the computer for the Centenary. I visualised a book in the days when I could still think about anything but a good night's sleep.'

'Things will get better, Tim.'

'But will I live that long?' He gave me a hopeful look. 'If you're finished, maybe you can do some of the transcribing for me?'

The computer was a new addition to our office, and Tim had been training us to use it. He'd persuaded Maureen he needed one, and although the Commodore 64 wasn't that expensive as computers go—certainly not the high end of the market machine he would have liked to have had—it was still a bit more than most struggling businessmen could afford. He'd heard that in the newspapers of Fleet Street, computers were already moving in. Right now his new toy was for personal use, but Tim said that one day even our *Herald* would be run by them. No more typewriters.

Brad was more interested in the games he could play, and when Tim wasn't around we'd all had some fun. But mostly we used the word processing option and saved the information to floppy discs which we loaded into the special disc drive. Tim gave Brad a talking to, telling him that this was not a toy but part of our working machinery.

But late one night I happened to see Tim playing *Paradroid*, music turned up loud, thumping the desk with glee every time he destroyed one of the killer droids. I crept away and left him to it.

As well as a chance to use the computer, I had been hoping to have a look at the famous Bill Shaw 'Recollections', so I was quick to say yes, of course I'd like to help. Tim smiled. 'I might just go and have a lie-down. Wake me if anything important happens.'

I doubted it would—this was hardly the *Washington Post*—but I agreed, and watched him stagger off to the lumpy old sofa against the back wall. I took his seat, settled the big box keyboard in front of me, and began scrolling up to see what was written on the screen. Within moments I was engrossed.

Summer 1931. The travellers come and go. Mostly they go when Constable Nash 'moves them on', as he calls it. Which generally means he refuses to stamp their cards so they can't get the Susso they're entitled to. They can starve or move on. Or steal. I've heard they've been out to some of the farms helping themselves. That's what young Tilly tells me.

I like Tilly. I have forty years on her, but I can't help but smile when she comes into the Herald offices. A ray of sunshine, that's Tilly.

She's living at the old Grand hotel with Martha's daughter. The constable moved her and her sister on, but they came back and now they're staying, or so they say. I hope they do. Tilly is a great help with the newspaper. She's quick and she has a way with her stories that make them quite gripping. I do have to edit them, especially when they get too lurid. I told her she should be a writer of melodramas, but she just looks at me as if she doesn't believe a thing like that is possible. I think it is. I think she could be a novelist and a damned good one. But time will tell, I suppose.

Martha's daughter has been in to see me. She's an interesting character. I think she was checking up, to make sure Tilly is in safe hands, but she ended up staying for a cuppa and a piece of Lyn Thomas's delicious fruit cake. Michael has mentioned her but I hadn't met her until now. She's a lot like Martha, I think. She doesn't know the whole truth, but not many people do.

It was fascinating, in a cryptic sort of way. I mulled over who Tilly was, and Martha's daughter, both of them living at The Grand. And the fact they were living there at all meant it was yet to be destroyed by fire, of course.

I scrolled backwards but most of the recollections were like this. I thought Tim might have to arrange some sort of directory at the front of the book, with all the names and who they were. His grandfather certainly seemed to have an opinion on everything and everyone.

I searched for the First World War years, still hoping for a mention of the elusive Belle and Charlie.

Spring 1917. I've never seen a family more distraught. Ted Davies is dead, killed on the Western Front, and his father is in a hospital somewhere in England. Violet and her two youngest walk about as if they don't know where they are and care less. Ted joined up first and then his father went to look after him, but it doesn't seem to have been a particularly good plan.

I remember Violet as a young girl. She was quite stunning. I used to think it was Rory Bartholomew she would marry. They were as thick as thieves at one time. I think that was why Rory and Stan fell out. Over Violet. And then Rory left.

I would've liked to have known the full story, but one never does. I can remember seeing them kissing once behind the church hall. As lovely as Violet was, I admit my interest always lay with Martha. We had some lengthy conversations about what we would do when we were older. Of course it was all rot. Martha never went travelling by camel through strange Eastern countries and I never went to New York to be a famous journalist.

Martha is at The Grand, making the best of it with her drunkard of a husband, and I am here, at the Herald. I think I do a good job. People tell me they look forward to reading my newspaper. It may not have quite the circulation of the city papers, but it is read by most people here in Sweet Wattle Creek.

Life never quite turned out the way you expected it to. I knew that, but it still made me sad to think Bill Shaw and Martha Bartholomew had such aspirations and never saw them realised.

With a sigh I got down to work, and spent a good hour typing Bill Shaw's cramped writing onto the computer. Tim got up after that, looking worse than before if that was possible, but he had an appointment Ellie had arranged for a series of advertisements in the *Herald* that he couldn't put off. Money was money after all.

I was restless. Dillon had homework and was busy working at the kitchen table, Smithy sprawled at his side, while Black Cat had placed his fluffy rump on the pile of textbooks, ensuring he was not ignored. Every time Dillon had to pick up a book he had to move the cat, but as soon as he did BC returned and sat neatly on the next book in the pile.

I couldn't decide whether I'd go for a jog. Running helped to centre my emotions and clear my mind, and it made me strong. And the stronger I was, the less likely Walter could take me by surprise.

Yes, I still imagined him knocking on our door one night. Despite telling myself it would never happen, I was still preparing for the moment.

Instead, I picked up the pages I'd photocopied from Bill Shaw's 'Recollections'. These were the ones I hadn't had time to read in the office or copy onto the computer and they looked worthy of note.

1919—Michael is back and Martha can't keep the smile off her face. I remember when he was a kid, always bringing home injured animals for Martha to feed. She told him no more but when he couldn't turn away from some wounded cat or bird—I remember he even had a pet snake at one point—she'd throw up her hands and give in. And here he is, back again.

He's had a rough time of it and I don't expect it'll get much better now he's home. I've always had a soft spot for Martha. There's something so genuine about her, and although Violet Davies is very kind and generous, I've never warmed to her. Perhaps I'm just a cynical old man.

Everyone rallied around Violet when Ted died and Stanley had a dose of the mustard gas. Somehow I doubt they'll do the same with Martha. Small towns like Sweet Wattle Creek have their hierarchy, and the Davies are at the top. Everyone stands by them, everyone likes them, everyone believes in them. Martha and Michael are at the lower end because they don't fit in. Martha has never agreed with anyone in her life for the sake of making friends. That's what I like about her, I suppose. She took on Michael despite the rumblings of the town and she has stuck by him.

I wonder if she knows what really happened on the night Michael's parents died?

CHAPTER 19

BELLE

Sweet Wattle Creek, 1931

THE HEAT MADE the paddocks and fences of Morwenstow quiver, as Jo Davies drove Belle back to town. It had been an interesting few hours. The Davies family were friendly and generous, and it wasn't their fault Belle was pre-occupied with her own concerns. She'd tried to put those concerns aside, but she was aware of the exchanged glances between Violet and her daughter whenever she'd drifted out of the conversation. Stan had eaten slowly but steadily, clearly enjoying the meal, and Frank had nodded now and again in response to Carly's stream of chatter.

'Have you been to our cinema in Riverton yet?' Carly had broken one of Belle's drifting spells. 'My brother is making a talking picture in Melbourne. He's going to show it up here when it's finished. It's called *The Girl from Prahran*. He thought that was an attention-grabbing title because Prahran is an Aboriginal word.'

'Is it about Aboriginal Australians?'

'I don't think so,' she said dismissively. 'He just

liked the name. You're from Melbourne, aren't you?' The girl didn't seem to know whether to be impressed or envious.

'Yes. Our house is . . . was in St Kilda. I have to sell.'

'That's sad.'

'Yes. Henry has his own house in Camberwell. We can live there when we're married.' Belle tried to sound bright, aware of the listening ears all around her.

'You're engaged, then?' Carly seemed pleased to hear it. And her smile became more genuine. 'Congratulations.'

Belle wondered whether congratulations were in order, in the circumstances, but it seemed churlish to remind Carly that her father had just killed himself and she'd lost her home and her mother was someone else.

'How are the stock in the bottom paddock?' Stan interrupted, taking a long drink of water from the glass in front of him. 'Enough feed?'

'I was going to check on them this afternoon,' Frank replied. 'After I take Belle back.'

'I can take Belle back,' Jo interjected. 'You and Dad go and have a look. Take Carly with you.'

'I'd like that,' Carly said, before anyone could answer. 'I never get to go out with the sheep at our place.'

The impression was she was cosseted and pro-tected from such mundane matters.

'Well . . .' Frank turned to look at Belle. She tried to read his expression but couldn't decide whether he wanted her to insist he returned her to The Grand, or he was just glad Carly had spared him the journey.

'You have your work to do, and Carly wants to see the sheep,' she reminded him with a polite smile.

Carly tucked her hand possessively into his elbow. 'I need to learn,' she said seriously.

It was too much for Jo, who rolled her eyes, but Carly was so busy gazing at Frank that she didn't notice. As if he was John Gilbert to her Greta Garbo.

'I'll drive you to the train tomorrow,' he said, in a voice that brooked no argument, although Belle was sorely tempted. She'd had enough of Frank; he unsettled her.

Shortly after lunch was finished, he and his father and Carly went off together and the atmosphere seemed to lighten.

Belle wanted to help Violet and Jo clear the table and do the dishes, but they were insistent. She was a guest. Instead, they made tea and sat in the shade on the verandah, catching what breeze there was. Flies buzzed and the chickens set free in the garden clucked to each other, while the distant bleating of sheep drifted towards them. It was the countryside as she had rarely experienced it, and felt very peaceful.

Belle tried to imagine living here and just briefly it seemed almost desirable, but an instant later she realised how impossible and impractical that would be. Henry could not move to Sweet Wattle Creek! Nor would he want to. Their future was already planned, set out like one of his legal documents, with every eventuality covered.

She felt restless and confused. Violet was talking but she didn't hear what she was saying, and it was only when a silence fell that she understood they were waiting for her reply.

'I missed that,' she said apologetically.

'You're mulling over what I told you,' Violet gave a wise nod of her head.

'Yes.' She wasn't about to tell Violet the truth. 'Thank you for answering my questions. And thank you for a wonderful lunch. But perhaps I should get back now.'

'My dear, it was my pleasure.'

Standing on the verandah as Jo went to fetch the car, Belle took Violet's hands. 'I'll say goodbye. I don't know if I'll see you again.'

Violet squeezed her fingers. 'I think you will see me again, my dear. I really believe you will. Everything happens for a reason, you know.'

The car hit a pot hole as they rattled along the dusty road, bringing Belle back to the here and now.

'I've been shopping for my wedding dress,' Jo said. 'Mum wanted to make it, but I thought it'd be nice to have a real shop-bought dress.'

Belle thought of her own wedding dress, tucked away and never worn. 'Have you found one?'

Jo shook her head. 'No. Not yet. I'd better hurry, hadn't I? We're getting married in May. Perhaps you could help me, although if you're catching the train tomorrow . . . ?' Jo lifted an eyebrow as if she was as dubious as her mother as to the certainty of Belle's plans.

Belle knew she must go home. No wonder she'd been feeling anxious. The more time she spent here in Sweet Wattle Creek the harder it had been to focus on what mattered. On her future instead of her past. She was beginning to think The Grand had cast a spell on her and was preventing her from leaving.

'I need to get back.'

There, she sounded more like herself now. And it was a relief because earlier she'd been very unlike herself.

Last night, before the nocturnal visitor had woken her, she had been dreaming of Charlie. They were dancing together, waltzing to 'Destiny', and she could feel his arms about her, smell the scent of his skin, and he was alive again.

Since his death she'd shut herself down, and it was only now she was beginning to admit that. It was time for her to wake up out of this long dream. At least coming back here had shown her that, even if she hadn't quite solved the mystery of Martha.

They didn't speak until Jo pulled up outside The Grand. 'I'll remind Frank to come by tomorrow to take you to the station,' she said. 'If that's what you want?'

'He must be sick and tired of me changing my mind.'

Jo lifted her sweaty palms from the wheel and thoughtfully wiped them on her skirt. 'Let me tell you something about Frank,' she said. 'He's a catch.' She laughed with a hint of scorn, but Belle could see that despite their differences she was really rather proud of her brother. 'He's good-looking but he's too busy working to pay any attention to girls. Carly is the first one that's latched onto him as if she's serious. Not that I think she is, let's face it, she's never going to settle down here in Sweet Wattle Creek.'

'She seemed keen. She couldn't keep her hands off him.'

Jo laughed. 'She's young and she talks about Hollywood stars as if they're real people. She asked him the other day what he thought of Randolph Hearst and that starlet he's been going out with, and he said, "Are they from over Riverton way?"'

Belle echoed her laughter.

'Ted was the hero in our family. Before he went away to the war, he said to Frank, "Look after Mum and Dad and Jo and Morwenstow, little mate."' She swallowed, the memory bringing her to tears. 'Frank promised he would, and he has. He's run things and he looked after Dad when he came back, more dead than alive, and he's worked all the hours under the sun to keep Morwenstow going, as well as the store. I reckon he'll still be here when he's fifty, working himself to death because it's what he thinks Ted would've wanted him to do.'

'Carly won't let that happen, not if he marries her.'

'She'd be gone in a month—run off with someone else—and he'd still be here. Imagine what that would do to him?'

Belle could imagine quite easily because it

was what she had done when Charlie died. He'd withdraw into himself even further and work even harder. Suddenly, Jo reached out and gave her a brief hug. 'Goodbye, Belle.'

'Goodbye, Jo.'

When she waved Jo off, Belle turned to the front door. She had the key and smiled as it turned sweetly in the lock, the door opening easily and quietly. The cool, musty smell of the old building reached out to her. She stood breathing it in. Despite what she had told Jo, The Grand still held a powerful attraction for her. Already it was winding its arms around her once more, trying to persuade her to change her mind and stay.

The footstep brought her eyes wide open. She held her breath.

There was a whisper and then the rattle of something in the kitchen. The drawer? Belle recognised the sound even after this short an acquaintance. Just for a heartbeat she pictured her mother, returned from the dead, making herself a pot of tea. But of course it wasn't Martha.

Carefully, she began to make her way towards the sounds.

'I know I left it here. Somewhere.' It was Gwen. More rattling followed by the slam of the cupboard door.

'Well you'll just have to find it.' This was Tilly.

'Look, there's some bread. And jam. We could take it with us,' Gwen said hopefully. 'I'm hungry.'

'We don't steal. Put it down.'

'But, Tilly, it'll just go to waste. You wouldn't want that, would you? You're always going on about not wasting *anything*.'

Belle decided she had heard enough and stepped through the doorway. They spun around, their eyes huge, their faces filled with guilt. The door out to the yard was wide open, although Belle remembered locking it. They must have a key. Outside was an old pram with various bits of cloth and a pair of old shoes nestling in the seat.

'Tilly? Gwen? What are you doing here?'

'We thought you wouldn't mind,' Gwen said breathlessly. Her brown eyes were wider than ever and she bit her lip as if to stop it trembling. It was a good performance, but Belle had the impression the girl had learned such tricks to get herself out of trouble before. Perhaps she could star in one of Carly's brother's talking pictures.

As if she was aware the act wasn't working, Tilly put a hand on Gwen's shoulder to stop her.

'We weren't going to take anything,' she said. 'We'd been out looking for things to sell, and we decided to stop by. We thought you'd be gone by now. We overheard someone saying you were catching the train.'

'And even if we did take some jam, we were only going to borrow it,' added Gwen.

Belle laughed.

'Well, not *borrow*. But if you were gone you wouldn't be needing it anymore, would you? Michael said he didn't mind us living here, and it's his house, really. Or it should be,' Gwen finished on a defiant note.

Michael the pilot. Michael, who was Martha's friend. Michael, who Frank had warned her about.

'Where is Michael?' she asked.

'He had to see someone about some work,' Tilly said, not taking her eyes off Belle.

'For him?'

'No,' Gwen looked up, scornful. 'Michael has a job. He flies aeroplanes. This one's for Tilly.' She'd made herself comfortable at the table and was busy sawing through the half loaf of bread.

Tilly explained. 'He was going to ask about me getting a job at the newspaper. Because I'm good at that sort of thing.'

'Making up stories, you mean?' Belle couldn't hide her amusement. 'I think your sister has more of an aptitude for that.'

'Tilly can spell though and I can't.' Gwen was busy tucking into a thick slice of bread, with some of Violet's fig jam ladled on top. Delicately she licked her fingers, which looked decidedly grubby.

She should tell them to go. This was yet another complication she didn't need. She was going home to Melbourne tomorrow.

'Where are your parents?'

'Gone,' Tilly replied. She tucked a strand of straight chestnut hair behind her ear. She had a way of looking up under her eyelashes that spoke of shyness, although her voice was assured enough. 'Dad lost his job in the factory in Melbourne and then we couldn't afford to stay in the house in Fitzroy. We took to the track for a while, until Dad found work in Sydney, on the railway. Mum wouldn't go though, and she said we couldn't either, and then she ran off with Bluey. He's a tinker.'

'A tinker!' Belle thought it was another story and almost laughed, but their faces were so woebegone she knew it must be true. 'Why did she do that?'

'We were with a mob of other travellers on the road. That was where she met him. He had a big smile and white teeth. She said he made her feel young again. When we got here, to Sweet Wattle Creek, she just up and left us.'

'Abandoned you?' Belle sounded angry but she couldn't help it. She was angry.

'Not abandoned,' Tilly spoke hastily, defending the woman despite what she'd done. 'Not like you mean. You have to understand about Mum. She had high hopes, but then she married Dad and had us and . . . sometimes she says she thinks she's drowning.'

Belle wasn't convinced.

'And we had a place to live in—we'd built some shanties by the creek with cardboard and hessian bags and corrugated iron—and it seemed all right. Everyone was happy. Michael came to talk to us and he wanted to help. I s'pose she thought we'd be all right if she went off. But not long afterwards we got moved on. Constable Nash and some of the other men came and smashed up our shanties. We thought about building them again but it didn't seem worth it. The others decided to head off back on the track, but Gwen and me, we didn't want to go. Then Michael came back and said we could stay at The Grand. He said it was his place and we didn't know any different. Everything was all right, until you said you were coming here. The constable came and moved us out again and we've been living down near the creek ever since. Waiting for you to go home.'

Gwen came to stand by her sister, leaning into her side so that they were joined together. 'Did you know there're mosquitoes down there,' she said accusingly. 'And leeches. I hate leeches.'

Tilly gave her sister a sympathetic glance. 'They make you screech nearly as loud as Nellie.'

'No one can screech as loud as Nellie.'

'Nellie?' Belle asked curiously. 'Is she looking after you?'

They grinned at each other. 'Nellie's a cockatoo. Don't you know that? Michael said you knew. He said Nellie belonged to Martha and you loved her. But I suppose that was a long time ago.' Clearly Michael's word was law.

Nellie. Did she remember? Was it Nellie who had visited her and sat on the brick wall? But the girls were looking at her expectantly and there was no time to be distracted.

She felt sorry for them, and she was indignant that the people of Sweet Wattle Creek—all except for Michael—thought it was perfectly acceptable to chase two young girls out of their town.

'Do you want some tea? I'm parched. And there's cake. That is if you haven't found it already.'

They agreed to the tea and cake, although their eyes held a look that told her they had been disappointed too many times to take what she said at face value.

But slowly, as she set about making the tea and cutting the cake, they began to settle in. She removed the photograph she'd found from the drawer and Tilly took it, gazing down at the faces without a word, before tucking it into her sleeve. 'Thank you,' she murmured, as if there was a lump in her throat. After that they didn't say much but neither did Belle—she was busy thinking. By the time they had finished their afternoon tea, she knew she wasn't going to send them back to hide by the creek with the leeches. When they stood up, edging towards the door, murmuring about having to go now, Belle made her decision.

'You can stay.'

They stopped and stared at her, silent, hoping, and yet obviously waiting for their expectations to be dashed.

'But are you staying as well?' Tilly asked dubiously. 'Only when he knows, the constable will move us on again, like before.'

'No, he won't. I won't let him.'

The sisters exchanged a look.

'I don't know what state the other bedrooms are in,' Belle said, getting to her feet as if there was nothing wrong with having two strays share her house. She turned towards the stairs and was relieved to hear them follow, though they crept after her almost as if they were afraid she was playing a game with them. As if at any moment she would turn around and point to the door and demand they leave.

Tilly and Gwen were homeless and alone, and she felt a kinship with them. It was simple. The differences between their circumstances might be vast, but an aching heart was an aching heart.

'We'll need to do some cleaning,' Belle declared as she opened the door to the bedroom next to hers. She frowned. The curtains were filthy and there was dust layered on the furniture, with a veil of cobwebs across the ceiling. The bed was intact, but the mattress would need beating and the bedding washing.

'What about here?' Gwen had darted behind her and before Belle could protest she'd flung open the door at the end of the passage. The door with the small brass handle.

'No!' Belle couldn't help the strangled shout. She froze on the spot, almost expecting a monster to leap out.

In the silence Gwen shot her a frightened look. 'What?' she whispered. 'There's nothing in here but mess. See?'

Slowly, forcing herself to take each step, Belle came up to the girl and peered past her. Gwen was right. There were bags of old clothing in here and boxes of rubbish. It was all perfectly innocent. Certainly no monsters.

Do you know, I wish you'd hit your head so hard that you'd die. That's what I wish.

The words were as clear as a bell inside her mind, disorientating her. She tried to get them back, replay them, but they were gone.

'It's too small for us anyway,' Gwen was saying. 'A baby's room.'

'Shut the door.'

Belle didn't mean to sound so sharp but she

couldn't help it. Harmless the room may appear, but there was something hammering inside her, a fear without name or explanation. Her head ached now and she put a hand up to her scar, running her fingers over the tiny raised line.

Gwen did as she was told and stepped back to where Tilly was hovering protectively behind her sister. The older girl had violet shadows under her eyes and she was very thin. Her clothes were wrinkled and grubby, and they both looked as if they needed a good scrub. No matter what Michael might say, Belle was sure Tilly would never get a job looking like that.

Belle took a breath and then another. It was no use trying to explain to them something she did not understand herself, so she didn't try. 'I think this room will do for now, once we've cleaned it.'

'Can we really stay with you?' Tilly asked her, as if she was only just beginning to believe it might be true. 'Are you sure?'

'Of course I'm sure.'

'And you're not leaving?'

As Violet had said, everything happens for a reason, even if Belle wasn't entirely sure what that reason was. And if there was a sigh of relief deep inside her, a sense that she was doing the right thing, then she refused to examine it.

'No, I'm not leaving. I'm staying right here.'

The Grand was quiet, almost tranquil. Any wrestling with her heart and mind and soul had already been done, her decision made, so there was no point in thinking about it anymore. Tomorrow she must contact Henry and ask him to send her clothing at least. She couldn't keep wearing the same skirt and blouse any longer. Besides, she had to tell him what had happened, to make him understand.

He wouldn't. He'd want her back, he'd be angry and confused and she didn't blame him. But she couldn't leave, she knew that now, and she'd been deceiving herself thinking she could.

Belle needed to know the truth, and the arrival of Tilly and Gwen had forced her to face that. She would stay as long as it took, and afterwards, whatever happened, she would make certain the two sisters were safe.

The girls had fallen asleep almost as soon as their heads hit their pillows. It had taken them till dusk to get the bedroom clean and comfortable, and they were all exhausted. After that Belle had heated water for the sisters to bathe in, though they could barely keep their eyes open, but she'd insisted. *What is the point of putting a dirty body into clean sheets?* she'd said, and then thought how silly that sounded. How many times had they lain down in recent times without the benefit of washing?

Afterwards, Belle had stayed up, waiting.

She wanted to see Michael. She wanted to speak to him. When he didn't appear and it grew later and later, and she couldn't wait any longer, Belle also went to bed.

The Gladstone bag sat on the floor by the window. The sketch of Reims Cathedral was secured in the gap between the mirror and the wooden surround on the dressing table, and it was usually the last thing she looked at every night.

Her eyes started to close and it was an effort to blow out her candle. The darkness wasn't complete because the moon was out and shining through her window. She hadn't drawn the curtains, she preferred to see the sky, and with her window open she could hear night sounds. No rattle of trams, no voices of people passing, no hum of a motor car. Night time here in Sweet Wattle Creek was like being cocooned in tranquillity.

Belle was in the place between sleep and dreams when she heard the sound of the gate opening. In an instant the noise brought her up off the bed and to the window. There was nothing she could see outside, no glow of a lantern, no sound apart from the owl in the trees. But after a moment she heard sounds from downstairs. Inside the house.

She supposed she should have been afraid. Instead she felt tense with anticipation. She slipped on her robe and went to the door, opening it quietly and going to the head of the stairs.

Yes, there was a light coming from the kitchen. The waver of a candle spilling out of the open doorway. Slowly, and as silently as she could, Belle crept close.

He was standing at the stove with his back to her. She saw he had filled the kettle and was in the process of lighting the fire to boil the water. The big earthenware pot was on the table and a mug, ready for his tea. And the cake, which she had left covered, was now cut into two huge slices.

Belle realised she could hear the soft sound of him whistling, more like a breathy sound between his teeth, as he bent to set the fire. He was wearing dark trousers and a light-coloured shirt, but both were well worn and darned. His hair was dark and long enough to brush his collar at the back, and there was something tied about his head with tapes. She could see the knots at the back, and the dull glint of metal.

'Hello, Michael.' She sounded as if her heart was in her throat.

He went very still and then he straightened in one abrupt movement. He was compact and wiry, and it occurred to her that he might be dangerous—so many people had warned her about him that she should be frightened. And yet she wasn't.

Not even when he turned to her and she saw that half of his face was covered by a mask made of grey, unpainted metal, making it appear smooth and blank. She could see the gleam of his eye through the hole fashioned in it.

She wasn't shocked. She'd seen masks like this before, worn by men who had been damaged in the war and whose faces needed to be covered up for the sake of the sensibilities of others. Or because they simply wanted to hide their imperfections behind a replica of who they used to be.

Now the man with half a face smiled with half of his mouth. His eyes were brown and bright with intelligence and something that seemed like expectation.

'Hello, Belle,' Michael said.

CHAPTER 20

SOPHIE

Sweet Wattle Creek, 1986

IAN'S EYES LIT up as he followed me down into the basement of the *Herald* building. I wasn't surprised. I knew he'd be eager when he saw all the old newspapers stacked in year-dated rows, their pages full of stories just waiting to be rediscovered.

He'd come over with a request for Tim to run an appeal for information about the wedding dress.

'Josh,' who was Mrs Davies's nephew, 'got back to me. The old lady is still under sedation, but he asked some of the relatives who came to visit and no one knew anything about it. I just thought, on the off-chance that someone in the district knows something, we should put the word out there.'

I hadn't had any luck either and it seemed like a good idea. Tim was willing and asked me to write the story. He had another sheep duffing/ rustling interview to deal with. Whoever was stealing the stock hadn't been caught yet and the police were coming under pressure. Pressure from Tim, that is. He had an appointment with the police sergeant in Riverton, and sensing the mood he was in from lack of sleep, I just hoped *he* wasn't arrested.

I admitted to myself that I'd been avoiding Ian. The other night, when we'd all sat down to dinner, it had seemed so very . . . well, *nice*. I'd caught myself smiling afterwards for no apparent reason. That had thrown me. So I'd taken a hard look at myself and finally admitted Ian was the sort of man I might have let myself fall in love with, not perhaps in the days when I was still young and silly, but as an older and wiser Sophie, yep he was perfect. However, the thought of my heart being open and vulnerable to any man, no matter how *nice*, frightened me.

Walter had done that. He'd taken away my naiveté and my trust in other human beings. Walter was like a dark storm cloud hanging over me and my son, a warning of what might happen if I made another mistake.

Ian wasn't Walter. Instinctively I knew that. Ian was another kind of man altogether. But I also knew that I must resist this emotional tug towards him, no matter how difficult. I couldn't afford to trust my own instincts and I had no right to put Dillon in jeopardy, and no right to risk everything we had just begun to rebuild by a selfish and hasty action.

Women could live without the companionship of men. Women could live without the sort of hearts-and-flowers love portrayed in books and on television. Some of them through choice and some of them because the right opportunity had never presented itself. So why shouldn't I live a solitary life?

But it wasn't just having a man in my life that I missed. Sometimes I longed to be the sort of woman I used to be, open and warm, not watching my every action, my every move. I'd lost her when Walter moved in, and then when we ran . . . . I'd had to close down that person, hide her deep beneath the layers of lies and subterfuge. Like a spy in a Cold War movie, deep undercover.

There were times when I just wished I could press rewind, and go back to the time before, but of course I couldn't. What was done was done and I had to move forward.

All of this was going through my mind as Ian and I drafted the piece he wanted us to run in the newspaper. He didn't seem to be in a hurry to go. Afterwards, I felt obliged to offer him a cup of my appalling coffee and then watch his face with amusement as he tried to be polite and gulp it down.

He replaced the mug gently on my desk. 'You were talking about the newspaper archives downstairs,' he said, and gave me a hopeful glance. 'I wouldn't mind having a quick look, if you have the time?'

I laughed. 'Now the truth is out! That's the real reason you came over, isn't it? Come and see my archives!'

To my dismay it sounded rather flirtatious— another way of asking someone to come and see their etchings—and Ian noticed. In fact, he seemed keen to join in.

'You've caught me out,' he said with a broad wink. 'Nothing I like more than seeing a pretty woman's archives.'

I froze. The silence between us grew awkward. He looked at me sideways, clearly confused by my mixed signals. He cleared his throat. 'If it's okay I'd love to take a peek at Tim's grandfather's treasures,' he said evenly. 'I promise I won't be any trouble,' he added, raising an eyebrow.

I should have said no, I was busy, but my mouth twitched. I held the smile back but he saw the softening in my expression and stood up eagerly.

I sighed. 'Follow me,' I said with a hint of resignation, but I was afraid I had already given myself away. Some Cold War spy I'd make.

Downstairs in the chill of the basement, he darted back and forth between the shelves, making the sort of noises a hungry person makes when confronted by an all-you-eat-for-a-dollar buffet. He was itching to get started but still he glanced at me, silently asking my permission.

'Go ahead. Just be careful,' I warned, as he lunged forward, and then told myself how silly it was to say such a thing. He was trained to be careful. That wasn't the reason for my reluctance at all, but I couldn't tell him the truth. That it was me who needed to be careful.

Ian reached for a stack of First World War issues and didn't bother to answer, or perhaps he'd forgotten I was there. I noticed he wasn't flipping through them as I'd hoped, searching for the names Charlie Nicholson and Belle. He was reading every word with rapt attention. At that rate he'd never get anywhere, but I understood his absorption.

I was probably almost as bad. History was fascinating, or so I'd discovered. Not the dry and dusty stuff I remembered from school where we were forced to learn about the British Empire and the Norman Conquest. This was Australian history, Sweet Wattle Creek history, and very close to home.

Ian had his head down, murmuring to himself. I had to smile, although I made sure he didn't see me, and then I set off on my own search of the metal shelves. Last night I'd been thinking about The Grand and the fire, and that was what I was looking for as I pulled out a stack of 1930s newspapers. I needed to find a headline. I was sure Bill Shaw would have made the most of the destruction of such a local landmark, in his usual powerful and somewhat flamboyant prose.

The Depression was big news. There were numerous stories on the rising unemployment and suffering throughout the district, as well as further afield. Suicides were up, Bill informed me. I read about the road works in Riverton which had been created expressly to give employment to those without jobs. I'd meant to skim over the stories, but before I knew it I was deep in the middle of a long column Bill had written about a group of homeless unemployed people. 'Travellers' they were colloquially known as.

Evidently, they had come to Sweet Wattle Creek in search for work, and made their home by the creek. It sounded like quite a shantytown, with huts built of items they'd scavenged. Two by four, sheets of plywood, rusted iron, cardboard ... anything and everything was put to use.

Unfortunately their efforts were in vain. Constable Nash moved them on after a month and told them not to come back. Although most of the town seemed to be in favour of this— there were stories of pilfering and theft—Bill was less inclined to believe the answers were quite so black and white.

Times are tough. Times are hard. We all know this. People tend to turn in on themselves and horde their essentials. And yet surely in such times we should be pulling together, as we did during the war? We need to show some compassion for those on the outside of our communities, not drive them away.

Tilly was a traveller and now she is a reporter for our very own Herald newspaper. A girl of seventeen, abandoned and in dire circumstances, she has blossomed under the care of Miss Bartholomew of The Grand. Tilly and her sister have been taken in by Miss Bartholomew, despite strenuous objections from some of the townsfolk of Sweet Wattle Creek. In my opinion we can learn a great deal from such heartfelt actions.

I rubbed my eyes—the print was small and smudged—but I knew I'd heard the name 'Tilly' before. It wasn't that common. Tilly from The Grand, and Miss Bartholomew. And then I remembered. When I'd been transcribing Bill Shaw's 'Recollections', I'd read about Martha's daughter and Tilly, the girl who was forty years Bill's junior, the girl he found so delightful.

I turned the newspaper pages, hoping to discover more on Tilly, but instead I found a story by her. And then another. They started as small pieces, local interest stuff, but grew into more important stories as the months went by. Did Tim know the girl? Was she still around when he was a child, visiting the *Herald* offices with his grandfather, and watching the presses rumble out the next edition? If Bill was that fond of her then it was likely he'd heard talk of her and knew what had happened to her.

Here was another brilliant idea for one of Ian's storyboards. I was just about to call out to him, to explain it to him, when my eye was caught by the very thing I'd been looking for.

The Grand Gone!

The headline blazed up at me, just as I'd expected. Bill Shaw had taken up the whole front page, and it occurred to me, with a chill, that Tilly might have been inside the building when the fire took hold. She might even have perished.

I must have made a noise because Ian said, 'What's up?'

I looked up at him. 'The fire. At The Grand. I've found the reference.'

He came over to me, standing so close I could feel his body heat and smell his subtle aftershave. Something inside me responded but I ignored it, deliberately focusing on Bill's words and reading aloud.

'*Last Tuesday one of Sweet Wattle Creek's most historic buildings was destroyed. By the time the fire was noticed it had a firm hold on the old hotel, and there was nothing anybody could do but stand and watch.*

'Combined with the tragedy of last May, this seems unnecessarily cruel. We must hope the fire was accidental and not deliberately set. Miss Bartholomew's plans to set up a house for travellers, where they could rest and be helped and perhaps find employment, must now be put on hold.

'The Grand Hotel was built by Miss Bartholomew's grandparents in 1886 and run by Mrs Ambrose, formerly Miss Martha Bartholomew, until it was closed to patrons in 1915. Mrs Ambrose continued to live there, making it her home, until she died last year. Since then her daughter, Miss Belle Bartholomew, has been in residence.'

My voice wobbled and I think I gave a shriek.

'Is that . . .' Ian was staring.

'Yes! That's her! That's the connection with Sweet Wattle Creek, Ian. Belle Bartholomew owned The Grand. Charlie and Belle.'

'She was here all along,' he murmured, eyes wide.

'Yes, yes, hidden in plain sight!'

We were face to face, only inches apart. I felt my mouth smiling.

'Belle Bartholomew,' he said. 'You sweetheart.'

And then he kissed me.

CHAPTER 21

BELLE

Sweet Wattle Creek, 1931

HELLO, BELLE.

The buzzing in her head grew louder. She reached out to grasp a chair back, to steady herself. 'Michael? It *is* Michael, isn't it?'

His smile grew broader, at least the half she could see of it. The other half, obscured by the mask, remained perfectly characterless. 'You know me, Belle. You *do* remember. I knew you would. I told Martha you wouldn't forget.'

She'd seen masks with faces painted on them, the features artistically rendered in enamel, and amazingly lifelike. This wasn't one of those. Michael's mask was made out of blank, galvanised metal, and only his eye, peering at her through the hole cut into it, was alive.

There'd been a man once, in Annat Street, outside the house. He'd been staring, but Rory had gone out to move him on and when he'd come back, he'd tapped a finger to his head. 'Damaged,' he'd said.

'I don't remember,' she said now. 'At least, I don't think I do.'

His smile faded, and she saw disappointment, quickly replaced by determination. 'You think you don't but you do.'

'Michael . . .'

'Are Tilly and Gwen here? I saw their pram outside. I can't imagine you'd send them away. Not you, Belle.'

Did he know her so well, then? How could he, when she did not know him at all. How could he think so well of her without knowing her? And all she had to judge him by was what other people had told her and that was a confusing jumble of good and bad.

'They're asleep upstairs,' she admitted at last.

'They're good girls. They've had a rough time.'

'Tilly said their father is working on the railways in Sydney and their mother ran away with a tinker called Bluey.'

'That's about it,' he said, beginning to make the tea, and she saw him add a cup for her. It was the flowered cup she'd begun to think of as her own. Belle sat down, her legs suddenly too shaky to hold her up, and wondered whether this was just a dream and she'd wake up soon.

'Tilly said you were keeping an eye on them.'

'Off and on. I try to help the travellers, especially the vulnerable ones. You'd be surprised who's on the road these days. Most of them can look after themselves and some of them take to the life like ducks to water, but Tilly and Gwen . . . well they're just kids really. Tilly's seventeen, although she doesn't look it, and Gwen's nearly ten. They've had to toughen up in a short space of time.'

He came towards her with the tea, and at the edge of his mask, below his chin, she saw the bumpy scarring that must cover the entire right side of his face.

'I told Martha you'd come back to Sweet Wattle Creek one day,' he said with a note of satisfaction, and set down the cup in front of her.

'I didn't know about Martha, that she was my mother. Not until Rory died . . .'

He shot her a quick look of sympathy. 'I heard about Rory. I'm sorry, Belle.'

She nodded, and waited a beat until the lump in her throat was small enough before she could go on. 'Rory didn't tell me about Martha. No one did.'

He'd sat down opposite her in the candlelight. 'She said once it was for your own good.'

'My own good?' Belle asked, frowning. 'What did she mean by that?'

'I think she meant it was her way of keeping you safe.'

She immediately thought of the letter Rory had written, and then the door with the small brass knob. There was something wrong, she knew it, but as she opened her mouth to tell him she looked up. He was watching her, keeping very still, as if he expected her to vanish. Or perhaps it was more like a cat about to pounce.

'What is it?' he asked. 'What have you remembered?'

She shook her head. Michael seemed to think they were old friends, but she didn't know him and it might not be a good idea to confide too much.

He reached for some cake but stared down at it without eating. 'Don't take this the wrong way, Belle. I'm glad you came back. But why did you? Why now?'

Belle wrapped her hands around her cup, needing the warmth. 'I wanted to see The Grand.'

'And now you have?'

Something in his tone stirred the guilt inside her. 'Michael, I'm sorry. Martha should have left it to you. I don't know why she didn't . . .'

It was an invitation for him to explain, but he didn't take it.

'She had her reasons. So, you've come to inspect your inheritance, is that it?'

'In a way. Henry . . . my solicitor, he wants me to put it up for sale. Rory lost everything and it's my only asset,' she added bluntly. 'I intended to stay one night, but . . . I can't seem to leave.'

Michael chuckled at the admission and sipped his tea.

'You lived here with Martha,' she said.

'Since I was fourteen. My parents died in a fire and she took me in.' He set down the cup, and she saw there were also scars on his right hand, disappearing under the cuff of his sleeve. 'I sat in this kitchen shell-shocked and she fussed around me. I suppose I hoped she'd let me stay but I wasn't sure. I'd overheard Violet Davies telling her to send me away to the boy's home in Riverton.' He shifted in his chair as if he was uncomfortable. 'She didn't, though. I owe her more than I can ever repay, Belle.'

He sounded honest and sincere, and she had no reason to doubt him, but she didn't understand why Violet had said such a thing. Violet did not seem like a woman without a heart, the very opposite in fact.

He sipped his tea again, and Belle noticed how adept he was at drinking from the side of his mouth not covered by the mask.

'Your face. What happened?' she blurted out, and then wondered if he would answer her. She wouldn't blame him if he didn't—he must get the question asked all the time—but if there was to be trust between them then she wanted to know.

'Burns,' he said frankly. 'A shell landed behind the lines, right on top of the truck I was riding in. I was unconscious for a while, and I couldn't hear a thing, but then I came to and there was a fire. I had a broken leg but I managed to drag myself out of the worst of it. The others with me were killed, so I was lucky I could crawl. My right half copped the brunt of it. They did what they could in the field hospital and I was shipped back to England. Some of the poor beggars in that place . . . I started to see how bloody lucky I was. At least my face is still there, if a bit . . . melted.'

He was watching her, probably waiting for her to say how sorry she was, or ask for details to assuage her morbid curiosity. Belle did neither.

'You're a pilot?'

'Yes. I get work here and there. Been all over the country. I flew freight in Western Australia for a few months, until the company folded. Work is scarce. There are a lot of pilots who flew in the war, and now they're all trying to find a way to keep doing what they love.' His laughter had a bitter edge. 'Because of this,' and he touched his mask, 'I'm always having to prove I'm better than them. I don't mind. I *am* better. Well, better than most of 'em at least.'

The silence drew out between them.

'Did you get my letters?' he asked.

Her expression must have told him the answer even before she spoke. 'You wrote to me?'

'After you left I wrote every week for a time. The teacher at school helped me with spelling. And then I wrote every month. I gave the letters to Martha to post to you. She promised she would, and that her brother would read them to you, but . . . You never wrote back so I stopped. Martha said you must be busy but I thought you'd just forgotten me. We were friends when we were little, you and me. It was a long time ago,' he added with a shrug, but she could see he wanted her to remember.

Rory and Iris must have intercepted his letters, or Martha never sent them. It was pointless to speculate, but she thought that if she could have read Michael's letters then she would have known all these secrets long ago. But perhaps that was the whole point of keeping them from her?

'Anyway.' Michael shrugged. 'I always hoped you'd come back one day. You belong here, Belle.'

She took an uncertain breath. 'When Martha died . . . Frank said he found her in one of the outbuildings. That she'd been dead for a week.'

Belle didn't mean to sound accusing, but something in her voice seemed to sting him. His head came up and she was aware of the tension.

'She told me to go,' he said. 'I could've stayed but she said, "No, you go, this is your chance." Do you think I haven't wanted to change what I did ever since? If I'd been here then she might not have died. Or at least, not like that, frightened, alone, with all kinds of stuff pushed up against the door to keep someone out.'

A tingle of shock ran beneath her skin. 'Who do you think she was trying to keep out?'

He shook his head. 'I don't know. She was a very private woman.'

'I've heard that from other people. And that she was losing her mind. Was that it? Was Martha imagining that someone wanted to hurt her?'

Michael made a scoffing sound. 'She was as sane as you and me. She was frightened of someone, I know that, but I don't know who or why.'

Belle didn't know how to answer but luckily he didn't seem to expect her to. He stared down at his tea, the frown deep between his brows, and muttered, 'I'm sorry I left her alone. I wouldn't have gone. But I suppose she knew that. She wanted me to go so she kept shtum.'

Michael felt guilty enough without Belle adding to it. She decided it was time to change the subject. 'Where did you go? When you went away, I mean.'

He sighed and then rubbed the back of his neck, as though it ached. 'There was an air show in Adelaide. I got some work flying stunts. Loops, dives. The customers love to scream and swoon. The closer you go to killing yourself the better.'

Belle could imagine it. Michael, with his half-masked face, would be like a creature from another planet to many of the people who paid to see him play the daredevil. She smiled. 'Are you still flying stunts?'

'Off and on. I pick up work where I can. I know a few people. I'm hoping someone'll take me on full-time. Now I don't have to worry something might happen to Tilly and Gwen, and you're here.'

He cared about the two girls. He had taken their plight to heart. This didn't sound like a man to fear. And then she registered his last three words.

'Michael, I don't know if I'll stay, and if I do, I don't know for how long.'

He stared at her for a moment, directly at her, and whatever he saw seemed to reassure him. 'You'll stay,' he said. 'You're home now.'

'Am I?' Belle looked down into her cup of cooling tea. She was tired and it had been a very big day and she thought she might start to cry. As if realising she wanted him to go, Michael got up.

'Tell Tilly she has the job at the *Herald*. Bill Shaw doesn't know it yet, but she's the best bloody reporter he's ever met.'

He didn't wait for an answer. She watched as he went to the door, scooping up the slices of fruit cake before he left. He'd reached the door before she spoke.

'Michael . . . do you know . . . who was the witch?'

He stopped, and turned back with a frown. 'The witch? Like a fairytale, do you mean?'

Was he really as puzzled as his tone implied? Belle couldn't tell, she didn't know him well enough. 'I don't know. Just something . . . I thought it might be a memory.'

'Sorry, Belle. I don't know any witch. Perhaps it's a dream?'

'Yes, perhaps it is.'

He nodded goodnight at her and then he was gone.

She heard the cricket stop its chirruping in the pot of mint outside the door. Stop and then start up again. The night air was cooler than it had been and when she followed him to the door and looked out, she could see a few drops of rain falling to the earth, giving off a sweet, dusty smell. She thought that this had been one of the strangest evenings of her life.

Michael hadn't seemed concerned that Martha had left The Grand to her and not him. She'd expected anger, resentment, at least some hint of bitterness. Instead, he'd looked at her as if he'd been waiting for her to come back and now that she was here . . . nothing else mattered. Was he such a saint? Or was it just that she hadn't even begun to understand what went on behind his masked face?

As she'd expected, he slipped in through the half-open garage door and closed it behind him, and a second later a glow of lamp light flickered through the dusty window. The bed was his, and probably the Triumph, too.

Belle closed the door and, with resolution, locked it.

CHAPTER 22

SOPHIE

Sweet Wattle Creek, 1986

IT WASN'T A long kiss. There were no tongues involved. Just lips pressed to lips, the rasp of whiskers against my cheek from Ian's ever-present five-o'clock shadow, and the sensation of warm male skin against mine.

Shock had held me frozen, but only briefly. Desire poured through me, hot and urgent, as if my libido had been waiting to make its feelings known on this whole celibacy issue. I reached for him too late, just as he moved away.

He was embarrassed. He shuffled about and looked at me, gave a half-laugh, and said, 'Sorry. Bad timing. Put it down to over-excitement.'

I tucked my hair behind my ear and found that my hands were shaking. 'No. I . . . That's okay. I just . . . There's something . . .' I was gabbling, or blathering, as my Scottish grandmother used to say. I had taken her name after we left Brisbane, and now I was turning into her as well.

'Let's forget it.' He put a hand to his heart. 'I promise to rein in my enthusiasm and not to do it again.' But there was a sparkle in his eyes I couldn't help responding to. I took a deep breath.

'It was nice, but yes, I . . . Ian, I'm not looking for that kind of relationship. I'm sorry if I let you think I was. Things are complicated right now.'

'Me neither. And honestly, I don't know what I was thinking.'

But I was sure that wasn't entirely true. He knew what he was thinking because I was thinking it, too. But I let the subject lapse and we both turned back to the newspaper as if we had made a silent pact. Back to business.

'So is this Belle? *The* Belle?' he asked, although he didn't wait for an answer. 'Miriam should know more by now. She's a research fiend. You're still coming with me down to Melbourne on Monday?'

Was it so soon? Today was Thursday. But of course I knew it was Monday, and I had arranged for Dillon to go to Tim's. He was thrilled about it, especially as Smithy could also go, but not BC. The cat would probably turn green overnight with jealousy.

As if he was worried I was going to refuse, that I might think he was planning some big seduction in a plush hotel, Ian went on, sounding endearingly earnest. 'Miriam said she'd put us up. I mean not "us" as in . . . She has a sofa I'll use and you can have the spare room.'

'Hmm?'

'They're not close. The sofa and the spare room. That is, they are, but I wouldn't . . . You know . . .'

I was enjoying his discomfort, I must admit. I'd never known a man quite as clumsy and socially inept as Ian, and yet at the same time so smart and funny and . . . well. It was time to put him out of his misery. 'That'll be fine, Ian. I'm looking forward to it. And now we can tell Miriam what we've discovered about Belle.'

He'd been watching me, probably wondering what on earth he had got himself into, but now he smiled. 'Good.' He cleared his throat, as if drawing a line under the whole uncomfortable matter, and turned back to the newspaper headline.

'This fire,' I began, once more back to business. 'Do you think it was deliberate? Did they burn down her house because she was helping the unemployed on the roads? It all sounds a bit . . . hillbilly.'

'The townspeople probably felt threatened by strangers arriving. Colloquially they were called 'travellers' and they took to the road because it gave them a certain freedom to be away from the cities and the camps set up for the unemployed. As long as they walked fifty miles they were entitled to use their coupons at the local police station to get food. They were supposed to keep walking, but I can imagine some of them saw Sweet Wattle Creek as an opportunity to settle for a while, set up their own camp maybe.'

'And the locals didn't like it.'

'Well, it was the Depression. Some of them barely had enough to eat and clothe themselves as it was, and then to have to give up their food and jobs to people they didn't even know. I can imagine it would breed resentment. It still does today.'

'So, when Belle took some of them in it stirred things up. Perhaps even enough for someone to take the law into their own hands?'

'It could've happened like that.'

I was beginning to understand small towns after a year of living here. They were generous and open-hearted, yes, and if one of their own was in need, they couldn't do enough to help. But if that person wasn't one of their own? And if giving to a stranger meant someone they'd known all their lives went without? I was in no doubt that things could have turned very nasty.

I glanced at the article again and put my finger on the word 'tragedy'. 'What happened before the fire? I've been thinking about the woman Dillon says is supposed to haunt The Grand. Could this "tragedy" be something to do with her?' I didn't mean to drop my voice but I couldn't seem to help it. 'Was she really murdered?'

'You make it sound like something out of *Ghostbusters*,' he said, smiling, before his expression grew serious. 'Sophie, I don't know any of the answers, not yet. I keep meaning to try to find out but I haven't had time to scratch myself. The committee want their money's worth and I can't blame them. There was a book written about The Grand in the fifties, I think. It's out of print and I can't get hold of a copy, but I'll keep trying. Even Nola's stumped. Maybe I can find one when we go down to Melbourne.'

That sounded cosy. My mind shied away from the image of Ian and I together in his car, getting to know each other.

'I go for a run some evenings,' I said, forcing my thoughts to behave themselves. 'Out to The Grand. Well, you know I do. It really is quite creepy in the twilight. I can easily imagine people believing it's haunted.'

'You should try waking up to it every morning.'

I laughed. I couldn't help it. He had a way of saying something in a deadpan voice that tickled my sense of humour. And the laughter released some of the tension I'd been feeling, relaxing me, so I was able to return to normal. Or as normal as I could be standing next to Ian after he'd just kissed me.

'Okay, well we should look back through the newspapers. There'll be something.'

I had begun to turn the pages, searching for another lurid headline from Bill Shaw. Unfortunately it was not to be. Not today, at least.

'Soph? You down there?'

Tim was back.

'Yep, I'm here!' I called up to him.

'Oh good.' I could hear the relief in his voice. 'That sergeant at Riverton threatened to arrest me, can you believe it? Will you type this up for me? I'm going over to Maureen's for a coffee and a vanilla slice. I think I deserve it.'

Ian and I avoided each other's eyes as we climbed the stairs back to the office. It looked like our search would have to be postponed, at least for now, but perhaps that was a good thing. Too much of Ian was bad for me.

Later, I was sitting staring at the typewriter in

my office, when there was a blinding flash from the doorway. Tim grinned at my startled face, lowering the camera. 'I need new photos for our press cards,' he explained.

'Oh thanks,' I managed to mumble. 'You could have warned me.'

'You always have an excuse. Anyone would think you didn't like having your photo taken.'

Well that was true. I didn't. But not for the reasons he was thinking. I tried to look on the bright side. I was pretty sure Tim's surprise shot would be appalling enough to fool all those who knew me, so even if one of them did see it outside the safety of Sweet Wattle Creek it would be okay.

The Thursday poetry evening had finally arrived. I found myself clomping up the steps of Nola's house in my black sandals, black slacks and pastel-pink blouse. I'd dressed up a little, not sure what to expect, but apart from Nola in a brightly coloured floral dress, no one else had bothered. She'd set out half a dozen chairs in a semicircle, and on a side table placed biscuits, a jug of soft drink and cups for tea and coffee.

'Mr Scott?' I asked her anxiously when I couldn't spot him. There seemed to be a mixture of young and old.

'He's running late,' she said, then smiled brightly at her guests and clapped her hands. 'Hello, everyone! So nice to see you all here tonight. Who will start? Darren, I believe you've been working on a piece you want to share? Sing out anyone if you have a question for Darren!'

It was a long evening. Nola seemed to have gathered together an odd group of misfits. The poetry was okay, even the amateur efforts, but I wasn't in the mood and time dragged. Halfway through I was ready to make my excuses and leave, and that was when Mr Scott finally turned up. He arrived with Ellie's grandmother, Mrs Green, and they settled down on Nola's sofa. Mr Scott was wearing an old suit, rusty black, and a hat he must have bought to go with it. In contrast Mrs Green had the same up-to-the-minute fashion sense as her granddaughter. I hadn't thought of the CWA as trendsetters, but she was sporting a tan midi skirt, a cream crocheted top and her grey hair had a jaunty little flip to it on one side.

When it came time for us to eat our biscuits and drink our tea, I made my way over to them.

'Sophie.' Mrs Green smiled. 'Nola said you might come. Have you written a poem or are you reading someone else's?'

'Neither, I'm afraid. I wanted a word with Mr Scott and Nola said he'd be here.' I turned to him before I could be further distracted. 'Mr Scott, would you mind if I picked your brains for a moment?'

He was holding his cup, and his hand was shaking so badly I was afraid he was going to drop it. Mrs Green clicked her tongue and took it from him. 'You'll have to speak up,' she said helpfully. 'He's quite deaf.'

I did speak up. And up. The rest of the gathering were shooting me looks and I felt sorry for them, and Mr Scott. But now I'd started I felt I had to go on with it. What if he knew about Belle? What if I missed this opportunity?

'Nell?' he shouted at me. 'I don't know any Nell.'

'Belle!' Mrs Green shouted back helpfully.

'She was engaged to Charlie Nicholson. Her wedding dress is going to be in the Centenary Exhibition. Did you know her, Mr Scott? I've been told you have a good knowledge of the town's history.'

'I've lived in this district for eighty-seven years,' he informed me. 'Man and boy. My father was a farmer and I worked for him until I was old enough to get married, and then I worked for myself. When my wife died and I retired I moved into town. Mrs Green and I have an arrangement.' He gave her an adoring look. 'She looks after me. We have chicken chow mein from the Chinese takeaway together every Saturday night. I've never had it so good.'

It was useless. I went over to Nola and thanked her but explained I really had to get back. 'He's mostly deaf,' she said. 'Didn't you know?' I thought she might have told me but there didn't seem much point making an issue of it. 'We'd love to see you again. Next time we'll be exploring Henry Lawson,' she called out, as I made my escape.

Friday came and went, and then the weekend seemed to drag by. I had plenty to do, but for some reason I kept looking at the clock. Well, it wasn't 'some' reason. I knew the reason. I wanted to get down to Melbourne and meet Miriam and hear what she had found out about Charlie and Belle.

I had a photograph of the wedding dress stuck to the fridge door with a magnet. The dress might be somewhat the worse for wear, but it had once been beautiful. A dress to die for. I tried to imagine Belle in it, walking down the aisle. Silly, I know, especially when I didn't even know what Belle looked like, and when I was fully aware there hadn't been a happy ending. But I was as eager as ever to know the whole story, and the sooner the better.

At least that was what I was telling myself. The truth was more complicated.

I kept reminding myself that Ian McKinnon was like the travellers in Bill Shaw's newspaper article. He was passing through. Once the Centenary was over, he would be gone, onto his next job. I doubted I would ever see him again, and in fact I would make certain I didn't. I'd done it before, stepped back from someone who wanted to get too cosy with me, given them the cold shoulder. People usually got the message. But whenever I thought of doing that to Ian something inside me raised its voice in protest.

Then on Sunday morning I got a call that damped down all my anticipation/anxiety at the coming trip to Melbourne.

'Miss Matheson? It's Josh here. Mrs Davies's nephew.'

His sombre tones warned me this wasn't going to be a casual chat and I was right.

'My aunt has taken a turn for the worse. They've transferred her down to Melbourne, but it isn't looking good.'

I remembered with a mixture of sadness and regret the woman I had knelt beside that hot day at Morwenstow, the expression of joy on her face when she'd called me Belle.

There was also the matter of Smithy.

'Please don't worry about Smithy,' I assured him. 'My son loves that dog. It's our pleasure to look after him. Maybe, when you have a spare minute, we might talk about adopting him permanently. If that's all right with you, of course.'

'Yes. It's fine. Thank you.' He sounded relieved. I imagined he had plenty on his plate without worrying about his aunt's failed sheep dog. 'She hasn't regained consciousness,' he went on after a moment. 'I suppose if it happens . . . well, it'll be a peaceful way to go. I know she misses my uncle.'

'I'm so sorry,' I said. 'What was your uncle's name?' I was thinking of the obituary I might soon be writing for the *Herald*.

'Ernest Davies. Although they all called him Pom, on account of him being one.'

'I thought the Davies were some of the original settlers in Sweet Wattle Creek?'

'They were. They are. My aunt was one of those Davies, but Uncle Pom was a ring-in. I think that's how they got together, both having the same name. Seems they got to talking and the next thing they were engaged.' He laughed softly at the memory.

'What was your aunt's first name, Josh? For the newspaper.'

'It was Josephine. Jo, they all called her. She was the teacher here at Sweet Wattle Creek. Pom was a teacher too, before they settled down at Morwenstow.'

I jotted it down on a piece of paper. It was always good to have some facts.

'My dad was supposed to have Morwenstow,' he went on. 'Frank Davies. But in the end he didn't want it. That's why Jo and Pom took it on. And then they didn't have any children, so that's where I came in. I've always loved the land, Morwenstow in particular.'

I was glad to hear the old place would go on with Josh at the helm. Once again I expressed my condolences before we said goodbye. He would get any further news to me as soon as he knew them himself.

I was still sitting, staring at nothing, when Dillon walked in with Christy in his wake. Smithy trotted after them, a battered-looking ball in his mouth.

'I've just heard some sad news,' I began, lowering my voice, as if Smithy could understand me. The dog was staring at me, so maybe he could sense something. I reached down and gave him a pat and he dropped the ball at my feet. 'Sorry, mate, but your mother isn't going to be coming home.'

'She's died?' Dillon cut to the point.

'Nope, but it's not looking great.'

'But . . . What about Smithy?'

I swear he went pale at the thought of losing his newfound friend.

'We could hide him out at our place,' Christy jumped in. 'We can say he ran off. No one would know, Dillon.'

I eyed her with amusement and a growing respect. Blonde and blue-eyed and pretty, Christy seemed to be the epitome of Miss Popular at Riverton High. I'd often wondered why she hung around with Dillon when she could have her pick of the boys. For me, Dillon was obviously number one, but for a fourteen-year-old girl like Christy? Dillon wasn't into partying or drinking, and he preferred to stay home with his mother rather than sneak out on a Saturday night. I'd heard what some of the local lads got up to and it made me shudder, and I was relieved that Dillon wasn't part of that crowd.

And now, here Christy was, willing to turn outlaw for the sake of Dillon and his dog. That impressed me. Still, before they started making plans, I needed to reassure them.

'It's all right. Josh says we can keep Smithy. There,' and I looked down into those doggy eyes, 'you're now officially one of the family.'

Dillon put his arms around the dog. 'Really?' he said. 'Smithy, did you hear that? Cool.'

Christy flicked Dillon a look, her blue eyes dancing. 'Smithy Matheson,' she said behind him. 'Sounds good.'

Dillon looked up at me, and I tried to keep my face bland, but I knew we were both thinking the same thing. Smithy wasn't a Matheson, not really, and neither were we.

Christy made a movement. She was staring at me and I saw something in her expression, just for a second, before she turned away. 'You promised to play Super Mario with me,' she said, her voice a study in indifference. 'And this time I'm going to win.'

He got up, arguing that there was no way that was going to happen, and followed her into the lounge.

Maybe I'd been mistaken. Probably. I hoped I was, because if not then Christy knew. If not the whole truth, then she knew something. And if Christy knew, then who else did?

CHAPTER 23

BELLE

Sweet Wattle Creek, 1931

THREE MORE DAYS had gone by and Belle no longer pretended she had any intention of going back to Melbourne.

Tilly and Gwen would be living with her, and that gave her an excuse to stay in Sweet Wattle Creek. They seemed to have settled into their lives already, and Belle was once more in the familiar position of looking after others. Perhaps that was why she'd felt strangely adrift, because she'd had no one but herself to care for. When Frank Davies had come to take her to the station Michael had met him at the gate and said she wasn't leaving. Belle had been upstairs and she'd heard their voices raised, but she was too much of a coward to come down. Anyway, a short while later Frank was gone.

She'd have to explain the situation to Henry when she rang him from Aneas Thomas's office, which she meant to do this morning. While she'd been oscillating between going and staying she hadn't felt she could telephone him, there'd been no point, but now . . . Well it couldn't be put off any longer.

Michael arrived at the door as they sat down at the table to eat breakfast. He had Nellie, the big white cockatoo, on his shoulder. The two sisters began to chatter to him, eager to share everything. Meanwhile, Belle eyed the bird with interest. Nellie turned her head to peer back at her through flat black eyes, and then the yellow crest lifted, as if in greeting, and the bird gave an ear-splitting screech.

Gwen squealed. 'She knows you!'

Belle thought this unlikely. 'When did Martha first get her?'

'Not long before she got you,' Michael said with dry humour, making the girls giggle. 'Although I don't know what age Nellie was when Martha took her on. They can live to a great age, you know, and she wasn't a chick. Martha said she just arrived one day in February. It was stinking hot that year. Birds were falling out of the sky. Nellie was at the end of her tether and Martha gave her water and kept her cool, until she was stronger. She took her outside then and let her go, except Nellie didn't want to go. She hung around the yard, and eventually got so tame that Martha could walk around with her on her shoulder.'

Belle tried to imagine it, and for a moment she could. The image was sharp and clear. But was it a memory or just something her mind had constructed out of the facts she'd just been fed?

'I saw her one day, not long after I arrived. She was sitting on the wall.'

'After Martha died she disappeared. That's what

I was told, anyway. Bill Shaw tried to find her but there was no sign. I think she got a fright and it's taken a while for her to get up the courage to come back.'

Whoever had been with Martha the day she died had frightened Nellie away, that's what he meant. But Belle didn't want to go into it in front of the two girls. Besides, Tilly was going to work today, and there wasn't time. Belle had altered a dress that Tilly said she'd found on the road, but which Belle suspected she'd stolen off somebody's clothesline. She just hoped it wasn't someone who might be visiting the *Herald*'s offices anytime soon.

She'd listened to Michael telling the girls yesterday evening about his stay in Perth, flying for a mail service, and how he'd had to sneak out of his hotel without paying late at night when the business went belly-up. Tilly and Gwen had laughed, clearly admiring his audacity. Just as they admired his stories of flying through sand storms and thunder storms with nothing but his wrist watch to navigate by.

He was like a wonderful big brother, kind and amusing and full of exciting stories. They were under Michael's spell and she supposed so was she, a little.

Yesterday she had come into the kitchen and caught them whispering together. Gwen had been giggling, and she put her hands over her mouth when she saw Belle, as if to hold in words she didn't want Belle to hear. A secret. Belle pretended not to notice, telling herself it was simply high spirits, but she wondered what it was that made the three of them as thick as thieves. The truth was she was sick and tired of secrets.

'We'd better go, Tilly. You don't want to be late on your first day,' Michael said now. 'Bill's a fiend for punctuality.'

'Don't you want some breakfast?' Belle asked him.

He looked neat, his face and hands clean, his mask in place, but he was too thin. Belle could see the jut of his shoulder bones beneath the faded shirt, and the bones in his wrists, which looked almost delicate. Michael might have been through a great deal, survived the trauma of the war, and all the surgery that came afterwards, but he still looked far from robust.

He glanced at the table and then reached for a piece of toast and jam. 'This'll do,' he said. 'I need to get the Triumph out.'

She'd discovered that just as she'd thought, the motorbike was his. 'My pride and joy,' he'd admitted to her, eyes twinkling. Now he said, 'Do you want a lift into town?'

'Me, me!' Gwen was quick to jump in and Belle noted the jealous look in her direction.

In the end, Michael took Tilly in the sidecar and Gwen perched at the back, her arms clutched around his waist. Michael had given Belle an apologetic look over his shoulder as they roared off down Main Street, and left her staring at the bicycle propped against the wall of the stables. Michael had hauled it out from under some of the rubbish and cleaned it up and pumped up the tyres, but she could see there was a leak in one of them and it was flat again. Besides, she wasn't sure she trusted herself on it, not without some practice.

So she set off in her Oxford brogues, her hat firmly in place. At least it was cooler today, and a shower of rain overnight had settled the dust. It was actually pleasant to be walking.

Once Belle reached the town centre, she noted Michael's Triumph parked outside the *Herald* office, before she headed towards the stairs to the solicitor's. As she climbed she could hear Lyn Thomas's typewriter clacking away busily.

The woman looked up as soon as Belle came into the room. 'Miss Bartholomew!' The frown lines on her forehead deepened. Her eyebrows were thick and quite fierce, unlike the current fashion of plucking them into thin lines, or else removing them altogether and drawing them in.

'Mrs Thomas. I hoped I could —'

'I thought we'd see you before now. Unfortunately Aneas is out. He had to go over to Riverton to see a client.' She was pretending to be upset on Belle's behalf, but there was a glint of satisfaction in her pale eyes.

Belle forced a smile. 'Never mind. I didn't actually come to see your, eh, brother. I hoped I might use your telephone, Mrs Thomas? I need to speak with Henry Collier. My solicitor.' And then, feeling as if she was denying him his rightful position in her life, added, 'My fiancé.'

Lyn stared up at her, considering and Belle wondered what she was thinking. Perhaps she was just making up her mind whether to allow her precious telephone to be used by someone she disliked.

'I'd be happy to pay for the call,' Belle added, shifting her weight from one foot to the other. Her shoes, though fashionable and expensive, were made for their appearance rather than practical walking. She suspected she had the beginnings of a blister.

'I'm sure that won't be necessary,' Lyn said at last. Her decision made, she rose and moved towards her brother-in-law's office. Her clothing was outmoded, the waist of her dress brushing her hips in the style of some years ago, but it suited her. Lyn was tall and lean, with an almost tomboyish quality, and she would have made a stylish twenties flapper. 'You'll be more private in here,' she said, opening the door, the words not quite a question.

Belle followed her. 'Thank you. It shouldn't take long.'

Lyn hesitated as she was about to close the door to the office, her gaze frank and curious. 'I suppose you'll be leaving soon?' she said.

Belle considered whether or not to satisfy her curiosity. It must be done at some point, and she would need to discuss the matter of The Grand with Aneas. She'd told Michael she didn't know how long she was staying, but something about Lyn's manner made her want to displease her. 'No, I won't be leaving after all, Mrs Thomas,' she said and reached for the telephone, ignoring Lyn's startled face as the door finally closed.

She was quickly put through to Henry's office, but was told he wasn't there. Belle knew she should feel disappointed but she wasn't. The questions Henry would ask her would be difficult and uncomfortable, and she was glad to put them off until another day.

She gave her instructions to his secretary, asking that Henry arrange that her all clothing and various personal bits were sent up to Sweet Wattle Creek.

'But, Miss Bartholomew, what on earth are you going to do on your own in such an out-of-the-way place?' The woman dropped her voice as if they were discussing a bereavement. 'Mr Collier will be most upset. Perhaps you should come back and speak to him. Before you make any rash decisions.'

Rash decisions? As if this decision hadn't been tearing at her for days and days now! Belle stopped herself from telling the woman to mind her own business.

'No need.' She kept her tone deliberately light. 'I'll ring again soon and explain. You will tell him about the clothes?'

'Yes, of course I will.' She sounded put out that her efficiency should be called into question.

'Thank you. I must go. The telephone is needed.'

It was a relief to hang up. She was a coward, she supposed. Not physically, but when it came to confrontations and emotional storms she found herself wishing she could avoid them. At some point she would have to speak to Henry. He deserved her to explain. She knew she was going to hurt him, and she felt guilty about that. It wasn't his fault she had decided the life he was offering her was not the one she wanted. She had agreed to marry him all those years ago, and he had taken her at her word. He had a right to be disappointed.

But coming here to Sweet Wattle Creek had given her distance. She didn't know yet what the future held for her, but Belle knew now, very clearly, that marrying him had only ever been a sort of retreat from Charlie and her grief. She'd been seeking sanctuary for a long time, hiding herself away, and perhaps that was understandable. She hadn't wanted to be hurt again. She hadn't wanted to be forced to feel again because loving someone was too painful. But Rory had died and the house in Annat Street was gone, and she was still here, still alive, and somehow it seemed even more cowardly to continue to hide.

If Charlie were here he'd tell her to go out and live her life. Take risks. Fight for what she wanted. The old Belle, the girl she once was, would tell her that as well. The girl who had been buried inside her, all these years.

The girl she was determined to be again.

Deep in her own thoughts, Belle hadn't been aware of the voices outside the office, but now they became apparent. Lyn and someone else. A man's low murmur. Perhaps it was Aneas? There was no help for it, she'd have to go out there and face them with a smile, although at the moment she felt anything but convivial.

The scene she opened the door on was a cosy

one. Frank was leaning against Lyn's desk, arms folded, his hat beside him, and Lyn was looking up at him with a twinkle in her eyes that could almost be called flirtatious. It all changed when Belle appeared. Lyn's expression turned sour and Frank straightened with surprise.

'Belle?' he said with a puzzled glance at Lyn. 'I didn't know you were here.'

'I was using the telephone to call Henry,' she said, also turning to Lyn, who was ostentatiously busying herself with the papers beside her Remington. 'Mrs Thomas kindly allowed it.'

'I came by the other day but . . . Well Maxwell said you were staying on. Is that right?' he said, watching her. Was that regret she saw in his face? Or relief?

Lyn spoke before she had a chance to. 'She is, Frank. Isn't that so, Miss Bartholomew?'

Belle knew her irritation must be showing. Not that Lyn cared, she was too busy enjoying herself. What a meddler. Had she always been like this? Belle was already aware she'd disliked Martha, and now she was transferring those feelings to Martha's daughter.

Frank's gaze narrowed suspiciously. 'I saw Michael Maxwell's motorbike outside the *Herald*,' he said, and she could see him putting two and two together and making five.

Her decisions were none of his business and she resented having to explain herself and yet if she didn't it would look as if she had something to hide.

Belle lifted her chin. 'I am staying, Frank. I've

decided I can't leave yet. And now I have some
visitors and they need my help. Tilly and Gwen.
Michael has found Tilly a job at the *Herald*, that's
why his motorbike is outside. They're young girls,
alone and . . . and friendless, and they need someone to look after them.'

'Travellers, you mean?' Lyn spoke with pretended amazement. 'Miss Bartholomew, we don't
want travellers here.'

'Why should you be the one to look after
them?' Frank spoke over her. 'Has Maxwell talked
you into this?'

'No one has talked me into this. The girls need
help and if I can help them, why shouldn't I?
What else do I have to do? My father . . . Rory is
dead, our house is sold. All I have is The Grand.
Isn't that so, Mrs Thomas?'

Lyn pretended to inspect the paper in her typewriter. 'I'm sure I don't know.'

'I thought you were engaged to be married,'
Frank said, stepping closer. 'Have you broken it
off? Or has Henry? This is all Maxwell's doing, I
know it.'

But Belle had had enough. 'I don't think that is
any of your business,' she said softly, and headed
towards the door.

Of course he followed her.

'I'll tell Aneas you dropped in, Frank,' Lyn called
after him, but he didn't seem to hear her.

Belle could feel him close behind her as she
hurried down the stairs, ignoring the pain in her
heel where the blister rubbed against her shoe.
At the bottom she turned to face him. He nearly

bumped into her and she held up a hand to his chest to stop him.

'Frank, this is ridiculous.'

'Ridiculous,' he repeated. 'Why, because I'm trying to help you?'

'Are you?' she retorted, looking up at him as he stood on the step above. 'Or is it that you're angry with Michael?'

He seemed to be trying to calm himself down. She took a step back, but he simply followed her out of the stairwell and onto the footpath.

'You're a stranger here, Belle. You think you understand but you don't.'

'Then explain to me how you could turn your backs on two young girls? Constable Nash sent them off on the track, despite it not being safe for them. They were sensible enough to stay and hide at The Grand, but when I was about to arrive they were discovered and moved on again. Where were they supposed to go? They've been camping down near the creek. Frightened. They only came back to The Grand because they thought I'd gone.'

She was angry. There was a tremble in her voice. She wanted him to explain himself to her, to give her back her good opinion of him and his family.

Frank sighed and tightened his grip on her hand. 'Come into the store and we'll talk there,' he said.

She didn't want to go with him. She shook her head.

'Please,' he said, his grey eyes intent. 'I want to talk to you and I can't do it here.'

Belle sighed. He'd been kind to her, it was true, and besides, she wanted to hear what he had to say about Michael. So she followed him past Bill Shaw's *Herald* and on to the General Store.

Flo, the woman the Davies employed, was standing in front of the neatly arranged shelves of tins and bottles and jars and other packaged products. When she saw Frank and Belle, she opened her mouth, but Frank jerked his head towards the back, and she vanished with a swish of her apron.

Inside the store was cool and dim, with long narrow windows high up on the walls, and the linoleum floor worn and cracked. It smelt of root vegetables and the bunch of herbs in a jug of water on the counter. Belle knew there were hoppers of sugar, flour and oatmeal under the counter because she'd bought some. A set of cast-iron frying pans rested against the wall, and enamel mugs hung from hooks above, and while some of the items for sale looked like clutter, it was an organised clutter.

'So you're staying?' Frank said, and reluctantly she turned her wandering attention back to him.

'Yes, I am. I know you probably want to see the back of me. How many times have you come to take me to the train, and how many times have I changed my mind?'

He frowned. '*I'm* not your enemy, Belle. And I don't know these girls you mentioned. I didn't single them out. Constable Nash moved on a whole mob of them because they were stealing. I lost some lambs. And not just me.'

'Maybe they were hungry,' Belle retorted. She

was disenchanted with him and he saw it.

'Maybe they were. Times like these, we tend to stick together. I understand you feel sorry for these people, but why don't they stay in the shantytowns the government has provided for them? Why do they come here, expecting handouts? If we opened our homes to all of them we'd have nothing and neither would they.'

'I'm not saying you should open up your homes, Frank. I understand that you can't. But it seems heartless to push them away. I suppose I'm ignorant of the facts. I admit until recently I didn't think much about such matters. I was cocooned in my nice house in St Kilda.'

'You could go back to St Kilda. That's probably the sensible thing to do.'

'Then I'm not being very sensible, am I?'

'Belle.' He was closer and she thought for an uncomfortable moment he meant to put his arms around her. Or would that be too nice? She was sure Frank could be nice when he wanted to be.

But before he could do anything, he looked up, past her, and the expression on his face hardened into something almost like hatred.

Belle spun around. Michael was standing a few yards away, his hands jammed into his pockets, and in the dim light of the store his face looked almost whole. Until he moved and she saw the dull glint of the metal mask.

'Maxwell.' Frank sounded cold, the blaze of emotion she had seen a moment ago shut down.

Michael let his gaze settle on Belle's face and the hard line of his mouth softened. 'Tilly's set up at the *Herald*, and Gwen's helping Bill Shaw with some typesetting. At least, that's what she says. I think she just feels left out. I'll come back and collect her in an hour or so. I was going to offer you a ride home, if you're ready?'

Belle went towards him, barely glancing over her shoulder as she said goodbye. She hadn't realised how relieved she was to see him until he spoke.

Frank came and stood outside the General Store, his arms folded, a look of disapproval on his face, as she climbed into the basket sidecar of Michael's Triumph.

He started the motorbike with a hiccupping rattle of the engine. The sound made him frown. 'Needs some work,' he said above the noise. Then, with a slight nod of his head towards the other man, he turned the bike around and headed for home.

Belle gritted her teeth and hung on. The road was rough and the sidecar less than luxurious. She felt the wind in her hair, tangling her carefully brushed locks, and her eyes were stinging. The thought of riding along like this had held some appeal—until she tried it. Belle laughed at her own lack of daring.

'What?' Michael was looking at her, his mask vibrating with the engine.

She didn't want to tell him what she'd been thinking. It seemed ungrateful to make fun of his pride and joy. But Michael thought he knew already.

'Are you remembering the look on Frank's face

when we drove off? It was a picture.' He grinned. 'Wish I could have it framed.'

Belle shook her head. 'No, that's . . . Frank is . . . well, he's been kind. All of the Davies have.'

He fixed her with a stare before turning back to the road. 'Kind, eh?'

What was this ill-feeling between them?

'Michael, why don't you like each other? You and Frank?'

He stared ahead. 'Not just Frank. The whole Davies family.'

'But why?'

He didn't want to tell her, she could see that. 'Frank has never got over the fact that his big brother Ted was my best friend,' he began reluctantly. 'Frank thought Ted was the sun and the moon. He used to follow after us like a lost dog. Didn't matter how many times Ted told him to clear off, there he'd be, a few yards behind. In the end Ted would run and hide. We could hear him calling. He couldn't blame his brother for it, could he? Ted was his hero. So he blamed me.'

'Poor Frank.' She said it before she could stop herself and then wished she hadn't. If Michael had sought to make Frank sound foolish, then he'd succeeded. And yet that wasn't a reason to still hate someone after all these years, surely? There must be more to the story.

'We're nearly home,' Michael said with another look.

The wind was in her face and her bones were rattling from the shuddering of the motorbike. At this rate she'd be in pieces before they got there.

'Good,' she said with heartfelt sincerity.

He glanced at her again and this time he smiled.

CHAPTER 24

SOPHIE

Melbourne, 1986

THE JOURNEY HAD been uneventful, until we hit the outskirts of Melbourne. As we approached the city the traffic grew heavier and progress slower. Ian seemed to have a cavalier attitude to driving and frequently took his eyes off the road. I supposed he was just used to it and I wasn't, but I wished he'd concentrate. Other than that he was good company and there was no awkwardness.

The kiss had been nothing. I knew it was an impulse thing because I'd felt like kissing him, too. It was just that he had done it first. The thrill of the chase and then to find Belle at last . . . We'd been a little crazy down there in the cellar.

Tim hadn't helped with his raised eyebrows and smirk when we'd both emerged from the archives. *That* had been embarrassing. When I dropped off Dillon's things this morning I'd expected him to say something clichéd, like 'Don't do anything I wouldn't do', but he made do with a little smile he'd shared with Maureen.

They'd been discussing us, evidently, and it

made me upset and angry. I'd opened my mouth to explain, to protest, but stopped myself. I would only make things worse and them more suspicious. Ignore them, I told myself firmly, and it would all go away.

Ian told me that Miriam worked from her home in St Kilda, an apartment that took up half of an old two-storey mansion in Annat Street. He explained that when Miriam had discovered the place was used by Eileen Nicholson during the Depression years, she couldn't resist putting down a deposit.

'It was Eileen Nicholson's home?'

'Not at first. She had a shop in Collins Street. The Paris end of Melbourne,' he added with a lift of his eyebrows. 'But Eileen was losing money and in an effort to keep her business afloat, she sold everything and moved into rooms in Annat Street. I'm not sure who the house belonged to originally, before it was sold and broken up for lodgings. In the thirties many of the big St Kilda mansions of the Victorian and Edwardian era were turned into rooming houses. People moved into St Kilda from the inner city, looking for cheap accommodation, while the original owners moved to the suburbs to get away from the riffraff.'

'She was desperate to hang on, then,' I murmured. 'Do you know what happened to her? In the end?'

'She died. In 1939. In her bed.'

'Oh.' Uneasily, I eyed the large truck Ian was passing. 'She went out with a whimper then, not a bang.'

'In a puff of satin and velveteen.'

I rolled my eyes at him.

The wedding dress was carefully packed into its box and was lying on the back seat of the car. Eileen had put her heart and soul into that dress, and then her son had been killed in the trenches. Was that what she thought about as she lay dying in Annat Street? Charlie and Belle. The wedding that never was.

Perhaps that was a good title for my story. The Wedding That Never Was! It sounded like something by Bill Shaw. I'd discovered I quite admired his flamboyant way with words.

The city was humming but we weaved our way through—Ian seemed to know exactly where he was going. 'We're making good time,' he said at one point, taking a corner with the sort of speed I found petrifying. Was I such a country girl these days? And why was I nervous? Ian seemed more than capable.

You need to trust him, I told myself. That was it, of course. I'd grown out of the habit of trusting anyone else. Walter had done that and I knew I couldn't let him control my life anymore, even from a distance. I forced myself to sit up straight and look about me at the rows of terrace houses and corner pubs as if I wasn't on a white-knuckle ride.

'This is Fitzroy Street,' Ian informed me. 'Where the brothels were in the days of Squizzy Taylor.'

'God, you really do know everything!'

His mouth twitched but all he said was, 'Nearly

there.'

A short time later we were on the famous St Kilda Esplanade, with its lines of palm trees making it seem as if we were in California rather than southern Australia. On one side of the Esplanade was the bay sparkling in the sunshine, while the sandy beach was dotted with sunbathers who didn't have to be working on this fine Monday morning.

Ian had already told me that St Kilda had grown increasingly seedy in the years approaching the Depression. The red-light district was situated here, as well as the crime and gangsters it attracted. Life and rooms were to be had cheap. But still there had been a strong local community at the core of the ebb and flow of outcasts, drug users and prostitutes who drifted through. East St Kilda was where the Jewish community had been for many years and remained so, a separate entity. About twenty years ago, St Kilda had begun to shift away from the squalor that had engulfed it, and had become a place known for bohemians and artists, musicians and entertainers, and for people who were vibrant and a little bit different.

'I'd stop so we could have a walk, but Miriam will be waiting,' Ian said with a smile, seeing my interest. 'Maybe we can do that later.'

He turned off down a side street. Large houses hemmed us in, some of the remnants of St Kilda's boom years, most of them turned into flats and apartments. A moment later he pulled up outside one of them, a fence shielding the rambling garden, and iron lace work decorating the upper and lower verandahs on the two-storey facade.

The door opened as we approached.

'Ian.' Miriam kissed his cheek. She was small and delicate-looking, with a cloud of fair hair and pale-blue eyes, more of a Tinkerbelle than a grown woman. Her energy seemed to be boundless—she fairly crackled with it.

'Hello, Sophie,' she said, smiling at me, her eyes fixed on mine. I mused over what Ian had told her about me. This was a woman who did not miss much, but hopefully she'd be distracted enough by the dress not to ask too many questions.

'Come upstairs,' she said. 'I have my work room up there. I want to see this wedding dress. You can't imagine how much I've been looking forward to getting my hands on it!'

When it was laid out on her table I thought for a terrible moment she might be let down. To me the dress looked very shabby. I'd forgotten how time had taken the shine out of it, and just because I loved it for the story behind it didn't mean she would.

Miriam stared fixedly at the faded cloth and then reached out one finger and gently stroked the velvet band at the waist. Then she looked up at us with a brilliant smile. After that she was all movement and action. She snatched up a professional-looking magnifying glass and turned back to inspect the Eileen Nicholson tag sewn into the bodice. 'Oh yes,' she murmured with deep satisfaction. 'And you say the box had "Charlie" written on the cover?'

Ian produced it for her and she inspected that,

too. Then she went to a glass-fronted case in the corner and took out a book. She brought it back to us and opened it at the place she had marked.

'Charlie,' she declared, with the expression of a magician pulling a rabbit out of a hat.

My first thought was that he was so young. It was one of those wartime photographs, with Charlie in his uniform, looking gravely at the camera, a flop of hair over his brow. I thought maybe his eyes had a twinkle in them and wondered how he could be happy when he was going to die in such deplorable conditions.

But then the young men hadn't known that, or if they did they hadn't believed it would ever happen to them.

'And Belle?' Ian asked, staring intently at the photo.

Miriam sighed. 'No sign of her.'

Ian and I exchanged a glance and we probably looked as smug as Miriam. 'What?' she demanded. 'What is it?'

Ian explained how we had come across Belle's name in Sweet Wattle Creek. 'Of course that doesn't mean it's our Belle,' he admitted when Miriam didn't respond. 'But it seems a possibility we need to follow up.'

'Well there must be something in the Melbourne newspapers. You can go to the State Library and look them up. Do you have time?' Her gaze slid to me. 'While you're here, I mean. Ian said you didn't have to get back until tomorrow.'

'We'll have to fit it in,' I said in my brisk voice.

'I'm writing a story for the *Herald*. Any details I can find would help to fill it out. I want to know exactly who Belle was, her background, how they met, what happened to her after Charlie died. I want her to be a real person, and him, too. That sort of thing,' I ended a bit lamely, aware of their rapt attention.

'Sounds like it could be a book not an article,' Miriam replied thoughtfully. 'Have you thought about writing a book, Sophie?'

My heart did a funny little jump. I had, of course I had, I just hadn't dared to admit it, even to myself. But I would love to write a book. And then my spirits dived again as I remembered who I was. A book would mean publicity and photographs of me. Whoever heard of a writer without a face and a profile? The publisher would insist on it. And once I was out there, in full view, I would no longer be safe from Walter.

'I-I'm not sure,' I stammered, but I was sure they'd noticed my fluctuating emotions and were probably wondering what on earth was wrong with me. 'The article first, then we'll see,' I said, back to brisk.

Miriam turned again to the dress. She began humming to herself and then she looked up at me with a smile. 'Sorry. It helps me to concentrate. We both do it,' she added with a nod at Ian. 'How about Ian takes you down to the kitchen and you can have a coffee and something to eat? Before you head out on your quest.'

We'd been dismissed. Ian grinned at me as he led the way. 'She'll do a good job,' he said, as if he felt he had to reassure me. 'The Victoria and Albert Museum in London tried to headhunt her once, but she thought she'd get homesick.'

Downstairs the kitchen was small but functional, and I sat down and watched as Ian busied himself about it. He knew where to get coffee and milk and sugar, and he was also clued in on the biscuit tin.

'Hmm,' he said, looking inside with satisfaction. 'How about we have some of these and then head over to the library? We can have lunch somewhere when we're ready. Unless you're hungry now?'

I wasn't. I was too keyed up to be hungry. My stomach was churning.

It was strange, when I thought about it, that something like this should make me so excited and enthralled. Two names, two people from long ago, and I was on their trail like a hound dog through the woods.

But Ian was the same. I could see it in his eyes. We made a good pair.

If only . . .

The library was porticoed and grand but I wasn't interested in the architecture, nor in the statue of Sir Redmond Barry looking down upon us from his plinth as we climbed the steps. Although he was here because of his involvement in the building of the library, he was a lot more famous for hanging Ned Kelly. Inside, the ceiling of the Reading Room rose far above, and there was a muted hum of people and movement as I waited for Ian to arrange to have the newspapers we'd requested brought out to us.

'They're currently being transferred to micro-film,' he murmured. 'Unfortunately, they haven't reached the 1917 editions yet. We'll have to look through the originals.'

We settled ourselves at a table and I took out my notebook and made some notes about St Kilda, observations, what Ian and Miriam had told me, and generally the sort of stuff that might be useful for the article. *Or the book.* The thought whispered through my brain, but I pushed it firmly away.

Restlessly, Ian got up and went to check the indexes. I saw him murmuring to one of the staff, before he came back glum-faced. 'That book written about Sweet Wattle Creek in the 1950s? I thought while we were here I'd look it up.'

'And do they have it?'

'They should, but someone borrowed it and didn't bring it back. It happens all the time, evidently.'

Half an hour later the trolley came out, loaded with bound copies of newspapers. They were heavy and unwieldy, but I didn't mind. Microfilm was all very well, but this felt like the real deal. We were turning the pages back through history and at any moment we might find what we were looking for. However, it was time-consuming and we didn't have a great deal of that.

Ian sneezed, and gave me an apologetic look.

'Dust,' he said. 'I have an allergy.'

'How can someone in your profession be allergic to dust?' I retorted, keeping my voice down. This place seemed to demand respect and I hadn't heard anyone laugh. It was rather like a church, with the high ceiling and hushed tones, only the rustle of pages and the scratch of pencils to disturb the solemnity.

Miriam's own research into Eileen Nicholson had given us a probable date for the wedding, and we had Charlie's First World War photo. We knew when he'd died. Ian heaved the first bound volume up onto the table and opened it halfway. A check of the dates and we saw we were at the end of the war, the Armistice, so he turned back chunks of pages until we found ourselves in 1917.

And then we began to search in earnest, Ian on one page and me on the other, so we covered both sides of the newspaper.

Australian Steamships were offering passage from Melbourne to Cooktown in quick time. Someone else was selling the best pianos in Australia for the cheapest prices, and there was the offer of a reward for a lost dog. Nothing much had changed from today, it seemed, despite the distance in years. Everyone was still trying to get the fastest and the best at the cheapest prices, and people still loved their pets and wanted them back.

I made the breakthrough, under a section headed, 'Gleanings from the Suburbs'.

Charles Nicholson, the son of well-known Collins Street couturier Eileen Nicholson, wishes to announce his engagement to Belle Bartholomew, daughter of builder and entrepreneur Mr Rory Bartholomew. The amalgamation of two more unlikely dynasties could not have been imagined, but we hear the couple is well matched. Charlie is the only child of Mrs Nicholson, a widow, whose husband, William, died not long after their son was born. Belle is the only child of Rory and Iris Bartholomew of St Kilda.

I read it over again and felt my initial exhilaration begin to turn to alarm. Ian was looking at me with a frown and I knew he was thinking the same thing. Our Belle Bartholomew was from Sweet Wattle Creek and she was Martha Bartholomew Ambrose's daughter. Who the hell were Rory and Iris?

'We need the birth certificate,' he said quietly. 'That should clarify things. Unless there are two Belle Bartholomews? Perhaps the name was traditional in the family? I'm assuming Rory and Martha are related.'

Well that made sense. 'Brother and sister maybe?'

We stared at each other as if willing the information to magically materialise before us. It didn't, but something magical did happen. One of the librarians appeared at our side, giving Ian an inquiring smile.

'Did you find what you were looking for?' she asked him.

Ian made the most of the moment, or perhaps he was just the sort of man who could twist a certain type of woman around his little finger without even trying. He glanced at the name pin on her chest—Hailey. He called her by her name, and I stood and marvelled as he explained the problem, pointing at the engagement notice, and giving her his half-smile.

I wanted to laugh, or to scowl. Did I have that spellbound expression on my face when Ian was talking to me? I didn't think so. And to be fair, perhaps he wasn't aware of the effect he was having. In fact, now that I thought about it, I decided that no, he didn't. Ian was being himself, a little shy, tentative, clumsy and endearing. God, what hope did the poor woman have?

'There was a weekly newspaper printed around that time. It covered inner suburbs like St Kilda, South Melbourne, Prahan,' Hailey said earnestly. 'It may have more on the Bartholomew family than the big dailies. In fact, Rory Bartholomew rings a bell . . .'

She was off like a terrier, leaving us to sit down and wait. I was starting to get hungry, but I wasn't going to suggest leaving, not until we knew what Hailey had to tell us.

Soon Hailey came back with a handful of photocopied sheets of paper. She looked apologetic. 'Sorry,' she said, 'but I can't bring you the newspaper itself. It's undergoing repairs. But I managed to copy the bits I thought might help.'

Ian took them, head bent over the smudged print, instantly engaged. Hailey looked at him and then at me. Her eyes sparkled. 'Historians,' she said, only half joking, 'you could be on fire and they wouldn't notice, not until the smoke got in their eyes.'

'Even then . . .'

With a soft laugh she left. Ian was still reading. After a few lines he said, 'What?' and looked up. I reached over and plucked the page from his hands.

The first thing that struck me was the banner. A Bill Shaw headline if ever I saw one.

Builder was unhinged.

I felt my mouth twitch but a moment later all urge to smile had gone.

January 1931: Rory Bartholomew, 60 years, the owner of Bart Homes, has taken his own life. The company was rumoured to have been in monetary difficulty for some time, however there was no suggestion that Mr Bartholomew intended to do something so drastic. The suicide was committed at a New Year's Eve party at his home in St Kilda, in the midst of the celebrations. Police say Mr Bartholomew used a pistol he had owned since the war to extinguish his life. The death has come as a shock to all concerned, and is yet another symptom of the current financial situation. His wife, Iris, passed away five years previously after a tragic motor accident, and he leaves a daughter, Miss Belle Bartholomew, aged 30 years.

'What do you think?' I whispered. My hands were sweaty and I wiped them on my jeans. Ian looked slightly shaky himself, but he began to read the next sheet, and I leant in close so that I could do the same.

This one was dated earlier, on 12 March 1926.

Miss Belle Bartholomew has announced her engagement to Henry Collier. Belle is the daughter of Rory and the late Iris Bartholomew, while Henry is a solicitor with the firm Collier and Son. The wedding date is yet to be set.

'So it *is* a different Belle Bartholomew,' I said in disgust. 'Our Belle didn't marry Henry Collier. She ended up at The Grand.'

'Yes, but the Belle who was Rory's daughter wasn't married in 1931when he died. Perhaps they called it off? And if the house was sold, she might have moved to The Grand.'

'What, she decided to leave it all behind her and head out to the sticks?'

He shook his head in frustration. Just then my stomach gave an audible growl. He looked down at it, then up at me, and grinned. 'We'll get something to eat,' he said, 'while we consider our next move.'

We ended up in a cafe tucked away downstairs in a basement, around the corner from Swanston Street. It was crowded when we arrived, but the other patrons soon thinned out as they returned to work, and we were left with a table large enough to spread out the sheets of paper and re-read them as we ate our toasted sandwiches.

I could see the people hurrying past on the street above, one woman in strappy sandals with a tight denim mini-skirt, another in a brightly coloured, flowing maxi. A man wearing acid-wash jeans and a pair of Doc Martens, followed by another in full punk gear with an orange mohawk.

A tram rumbled and squealed on its tracks and

cars roared alongside. I could smell the fumes from here. The whole thing seemed an assault on my senses, which was a bit of a shock for me, who'd been a city girl for most of her life. I'd expected to enjoy being back among the crowds and here I was longing for Sweet Wattle Creek, with its slower pace and quiet streets.

Sad, really. It seemed I had changed. Was there no going back? For the first time it occurred to me that even if the opportunity came up to return to Brisbane and the job I had loved, I may not want to.

Ian interrupted my thoughts with a rundown of his own.

'It sounds as if the business was in trouble. Rory commits suicide. They've lost everything. Belle's left on her own. Maybe Henry Collier didn't want to marry her when he found out. She packs up and heads off to Sweet Wattle Creek, to her aunt's hotel.'

'Yes, but that doesn't explain why Martha was Belle's mother. Unless she really was Belle's mother,' I added, sipping my milky coffee, 'and Rory was her adopted father.'

He stirred his own coffee. 'So it's Births Deaths and Marriages next, and we'll see what we can find out. I think you should be taking notes,' and he glanced down at the writing pad I'd been scribbling on all morning. 'For your book.'

I gave him a narrow-eyed look but he only grinned.

'Really, I think it's a great idea,' he said. 'There're enough twists and turns so far to make a ripper of a book. Hell, why stop at a book. A film!'

My heart was thumping. I looked away so he wouldn't see the expression in my eyes. Because I was roiling with emotion. It was so unfair! Something like this, an opportunity of a lifetime, just fallen into my lap, and I couldn't do it. Because of Walter. Because if he saw my face he would find me. And Dillon.

I blinked, and realised Ian was watching me with a curious expression. He cleared his throat and I thought for a horrified moment that he was going to ask me questions, but he seemed to change his mind and picked up the menu instead.

'Pudding?' he inquired. 'They have banana split.'

'Aren't you looking in the children's section?' I asked, trying to hide my relief with sarcasm.

'I am a child at heart.'

I doubted that, but I said yes. It was years since I'd had a banana split, and when the long glass dishes arrived, overflowing with calories, my mouth began to water.

We tucked in. The syrup ran down our chins and I found myself joining in his laughter. It was actually a lot of fun. I just wished things could have been more clear-cut. I just wished I didn't have to worry about Walter.

CHAPTER 25

BELLE

Sweet Wattle Creek, 1931

IT HAD TAKEN a month. A whole month for the large crate of Belle's personal things to arrive on the train. Which made her think Henry hadn't wanted anything to do with her request. But she was too excited to think about Henry now. It was like Christmas again, when she was a child and Rory and Iris had spoiled her with pretty dresses and expensive toys.

For a whole month she'd made do. The contents of her small suitcase, the one she'd brought with her, had only lasted so long. She'd had to make over some of the musty old garments she'd found among Martha's clutter. Her mother had plenty of clothes after all, it was just that Violet and Jo had removed them from her bedroom and placed them in a wardrobe in another room. The first thing Belle lifted out was a fox fur which promptly fell to pieces. But there were other things the moths and silver fish had not feasted on, dresses and skirts and blouses from decades ago, which could be cut up and restitched for herself and the two girls.

She'd even found a beautiful roll of exotic-looking cloth that Martha must have kept for some special occasion and never used. It was a relief not to have to go begging from neighbours—always assuming they would help—or go to the pawnbroker. Every time she thought of stepping through that door she could hear Iris's voice in her head: 'Belle, it's better to go without than to lower your standards.'

There'd been a number of travellers passing through. Somehow they'd heard of The Grand and stopped by, and Belle did what she could to feed them and let them rest. One or two had stayed longer than a few days, but the others had soon moved on. There was word of a new railway project taking place north of the border, and jobs to be had.

Michael found a live-in position in Riverton for a woman with a young son, but there was nothing to be had in Sweet Wattle Creek. It was obvious to Belle how feelings had cooled towards her, and she'd heard from Tilly via Bill Shaw that Violet Davies had expressed her disapproval. Evidently Belle hadn't lived up to expectations. After welcoming her so heartily they had turned her into an outcast, and she wasn't sure why.

It wasn't like that at The Grand. Michael treated her as if she was an essential part of his plans, and he had lots of plans. He wanted to bring the old place 'back to life', to fill it with people and noise and laughter.

He was lonely, she thought. He missed Martha. Although he found work when he could, they were mainly labouring jobs and he wanted to fly. But flying jobs were hard to come by and required travelling, and he said he didn't want to leave her on her own until she was properly settled in.

Belle had considered herself quite an accomplished cook when she lived in Annat Street. Now she understood how easy it was to call oneself a good cook when one could afford the best ingredients and spend long hours preparing a dish to place on exquisite china. When she first arrived the Davies had supplied her with eggs and milk and butter. That had stopped, and she had learned to make do, spending her remaining money wisely and being grateful for the young lads who came to her door to sell her rabbits they'd trapped.

And she was proud of her efforts. In a very short time she'd taught herself to make tasty and inexpensive meals. She'd turned it into a game. Every evening when they sat down to eat, she gave her three companions the name of the dish in French, as if they were eating in a fancy Paris restaurant. The laughter on their faces was worth the effort.

Last night it had been 'Le Grande lapin avec des pommes'. Michael had laughed and said, 'I can't say I ever had the privilege of eating this when I was over there.'

'What is *pommes*?' Gwen giggled.

'Apples, silly,' Tilly retorted. 'Can't you taste them?'

'What did you eat in France?' Gwen asked.

So Michael went off on one of his fanciful tales, but as usual he ended up talking about flying. He'd held them spellbound with a story about Charles Kingsford Smith and Charles Ulm, flying through deplorable conditions as they made their way across the Pacific on their record-breaking flight. Belle remembered it—the newspapers had been full of it—but hearing Michael tell it was far more thrilling. She felt like she was really there in the cockpit of the Southern Cross, while the plane was rocked and buffeted by thunder storms.

Belle had tried hard to remember Michael from her first four years here at The Grand, but although sometimes she thought there was a ghost of a memory, it was nothing she could fully form. She imagined herself, rather like Gwen although younger of course, sitting wide-eyed and amazed, drawn in by Michael's charisma.

'Will you take us up in an aeroplane one day?' Gwen asked. 'I want to loop the loop, Michael!'

'Perhaps I will. Remember how I was just telling you about Charlies Kingsford Smith?' he said with a grin. 'Well I heard on the grapevine that he's coming to Riverton. He's been barnstorming around the country with some of his mates, getting the money together to start another enterprise. I'll ask him if I can join them, and then I'll take you up, Gwen.'

'Do you really think you'll get work with them?' Belle asked softly, while Gwen jumped up and down.

'I don't know.' His cockiness faltered. 'If I did get a job barnstorming then I could be gone for months. I'd miss you.' His gaze slid away as if the words had slipped out before he could stop them, and added, 'All of you.'

Tilly had been listening. 'This is your home and we're your family. We'll still be here when you get back, Michael.'

Belle felt a sense of pride. The girl was more confident since she'd started working for Bill Shaw, and she had such a kind heart. What she'd said was true, they were a family. An odd jumble of people brought together by mutual necessity.

'What was your family like, Michael?' Belle asked him. He didn't speak much about his past, and never about his life before Martha, and she was curious. 'Your parents, I mean.'

The half of his mouth she could see twisted. 'My father was the sort of man who'd use his strap first and ask questions later. My mother let him.'

It was a shock to hear the words and the bitterness beneath them, but before she could find an answer he disarmed her by coming around to her chair and slipping an arm about her shoulders and giving her a kiss on the cheek. She felt the brush of his mask a moment before he leaned back to grin down at her. It was the action of a friend, she told herself, and she didn't feel uncomfortable at all, because she felt the same way about him.

'I don't think of them as my family though,' he said. 'I think of Martha, and you, and Tilly and Gwen. Tilly's right you know, Belle. We're a family and we should stick together.'

'Through thick and thin!' Gwen was shouting again.

Belle laughed until she cried, watching them cavorting about the kitchen.

Later, when she went upstairs, her belongings were waiting for her. Everything inside the crate had been neatly packed and folded. The cream dress with geometric design she'd been given for her twenty-first birthday, the tweed coat she enjoyed snuggling up in during the winter months, skirts that fit snugly, and blouses in pretty fabrics. Just because Belle had lived at home all her life didn't mean she didn't go out and want to look nice when she did so. Also packed inside was the cocktail frock she'd worn the night Rory had shot himself. There was a note tucked inside.

Belle, I mended this for you. It seemed a shame to throw it away when you looked so pretty in it. Henry tells me you are going to settle in Sweet Wattle Creek— what a darling name! I'm thrilled to hear it. He isn't happy with you but I think you're being very adventurous and very brave. Please write and let me know how you are going when you have time. All my love, Eileen Nicholson.

P.S. I'm sending the wedding dress. Think of it as a good-luck wish from dear Charlie. Who knows, it may come in useful!

Charlie's mother had even packed her hair-setting lotion. She pulled at her fair locks with a grimace. Her hair had grown so much and was no longer the neat cap she liked to arrange in sophisticated curls. If she let it go she would have to braid it and she hadn't had a braid since the war. The modern looks of the 1920s had given her an excuse to bob her hair and it had been short ever since.

Belle lifted the lid of the box with the wedding dress in it, and touched the ivory cloth with gentle fingers. A good-luck wish? Well, perhaps. It might be nothing but satin and lace and velvet, but it was so much more. Each stitch was imbued with memories and dreams.

She couldn't bear to wear it, but neither did she feel she could give it away. With a sigh, she'd slipped it into the bottom of her wardrobe and closed the door.

Belle felt elegant in her blue button-through dress, with the V-neck and white belt. The knocking on the door had brought her downstairs before she could put the scissors to her hair, and perhaps it was just as well, because she wasn't at all sure she could do a competent job of cutting off the untidy strands. Maybe it would be better to wait until Tilly came home.

Constable Nash was waiting for her, and he didn't waste any time letting her know there had been a complaint.

'A complaint about the travellers?' Michael asked her when he came home. He was sweaty and dirty from his latest job of mucking out the Riverton saleyards, and she followed him over to the water tank.

'He said there was some "concern" that we

were setting up a camp for the unemployed, and there were proper places for people like that.'

She was still upset. She'd explained to the constable as politely as she could that they had merely given food to some people who had stopped on their way to somewhere else. As for Tilly and Gwen, they were lodging with her until their parents returned for them. It didn't seem to matter to him that Tilly was working at the *Herald* and Gwen had started school. Jo—friendly and businesslike—had brought books and the sort of confidence a child needs before taking a step in a new and frightening direction. Belle had the awful feeling that if she'd given the constable the word he would have happily taken the girls into custody and moved them on.

Michael must have been angry, too. He was always very careful around her, but now he took hold of his shirt and stripped it off over his head in front of her. For a moment she stared at his lean muscled chest and shoulders, the concave of his stomach and the line of dark hair running down beneath the waistband of his trousers.

Then he cursed and hastily dragged his shirt back on, struggling to cover himself. Belle couldn't help him, she couldn't move. There'd been some scarring, red and raised marks on his hip and along his upper arm, but other than that his skin was clear and smooth and undamaged.

She'd thought the burns would be all over him, that that was why he was always cautious around her. She questioned if he believed himself more disfigured than he was and that she would be disgusted if he so much as dared to roll up his sleeves.

'Belle, I'm sorry,' he was saying. The mask had caught on the collar of the shirt and tilted, and she could see some of the disfigurement beneath it. Suddenly she wanted to know for herself what he was hiding.

'Do you think . . . would you mind if I took off your mask?' she asked tentatively.

He looked shocked. 'Belle . . . my wounds . . . I didn't get to the field hospital soon enough. There was infection and they couldn't put me back together, not the way they wanted to.'

'I understand that . . .'

'In the hospital in England they removed all the mirrors from the walls. No one could see what they looked like, not until they let us. The operations were so painful . . . they wanted to do more for me but I'd had enough. I chose the mask.'

'Michael, please let me see.'

She was sure he was going to say no. He didn't speak for a while, then at last he said, 'All right, but don't blame me if you lose your appetite.' He was trying to make a bad joke out of it, although neither of them was smiling.

He stood stiffly as she went behind him and untied the laces. She could feel his tension and her own hands were shaking, and there was a split second when she asked herself if she was doing the right thing. Did she really want to know? And yet she knew that to Michael his face was a constant source of distress and she needed to see for herself how bad it really was.

Finally, the mask came off and he caught it in his hands. Belle stepped around him.

It was bad. She wanted to look away, but she had asked for this so she made herself stand and look. And after the first shock she knew that she wasn't going to faint or scream or run away. He was right when he said his face had melted, because that was what it looked like. Unnaturally smooth sections where the skin grafts had taken, and places of rough bumps and ridges of scarring.

She reached out to touch him but he jerked away. 'Belle,' he said, and he sounded as if he was strangled. His mouth on this side had no lips and his eye had no lashes, and the lid looked as if it had been re-constructed. Strangely his ear was almost unmarked.

'Let me,' she said, her voice tight in her throat, and reached out again.

He closed his eyes and she brushed his skin with her fingertips. Her heart was beating fast and her legs were wobbly but she persisted, stroking his cheek and his jaw, gently touching his eyelid. He gave a shudder.

'I'm sorry, did I hurt you? Michael?'

He shook his head and it was then she realised he was shaking.

'Michael,' she said, upset that she had upset him. 'I didn't mean . . . I don't mind . . .'

He turned away, fumbling with the mask, and when he turned again it was back in place. 'Now you know,' he said, his voice hard and flat, though he couldn't quite meet her eyes. 'Sometimes I wonder if I would've been better off dead, but then I remember some of the other men I saw in the hospital and I know I should be grateful. I am grateful. I don't like to be pitied, Belle.'

Is that what he thought she was doing? 'Of course not. Michael . . .'

But he didn't want to talk about it anymore.

'I need to wash,' he said.

With a jerky nod of her head, Belle went inside and left him to it. With the door closed behind her, she allowed herself to shed tears, for Michael and the man he had been and the man he now was. But only a few. She didn't want him to see that she had been crying. She didn't pity him, not in the way he imagined, but how could she explain that to him?

Belle had been cleaning and sorting, finishing one room and moving on to the next. She put aside those objects she thought might be useful, or she could sell, but so much of what she found was of no use to anyone but the moths. Martha seemed to have had an aversion to throwing anything away.

Even the room with the small brass knob came under her attention. The fear she had felt that first time had faded. She was able to open the door without the sickening lurch she remembered, but there was still an unpleasant thump of her heart and a clamminess to her skin.

She could see now that the room was being used as a storage area, but the contents seemed to come from two time periods. The later stuff, bags and boxes packed just inside the door, were more or less rubbish. Behind that was what looked like a cot and a rocking horse, but it was hard to see in the gloom. The curtains across the single sash window were thin and rotting, but they still did their job.

Belle dragged some of the bags and boxes away, giving herself room to get inside, and then she climbed across the top of a precariously placed table until she reached the window. One good wrench and the rotting fabric fell away.

She was looking down into the stable yard, but it wasn't the view she was used to. There was an enclosed private area, at the back of the stable and the garage, with the small shed, the one Martha's body had been found in.

Briefly, that sinister sensation stirred at the back of her mind, like the rustling of old dry leaves. She knew there had been someone down there.

The witch?

'*Let her go!*' It was a man's voice, and then a woman, screaming.

Shaking, not knowing if she wanted to see it or not, Belle half closed her eyes and willed the memory to form. She was trying so hard to send herself back into the mind of the child she'd been that she felt dizzy. But it didn't work. Whatever had been hovering at the edges of memory was going.

Until the next time.

Stanley Davies was dead. Tilly had brought the news home from Bill Shaw this evening. Belle hadn't known Stan very well, but she was sorry to hear of his passing and grieved for the family. Belle glanced outside where the light was still bright, although the shadows were stretching out towards evening. 'I should go and see them,' she said.

Michael had been fencing, working for a farmer south of the town. Since the day she'd asked him to take off his mask, he'd been even more cautious around her. She'd caught him watching her sometimes, when he thought she didn't notice. Did he think she'd been disgusted? Shocked? Certainly she'd been shocked, but it had soon passed. She wasn't sorry she knew the extent of his scarring, but his awkwardness was catching. They seemed to have lost some of their easy camaraderie and she was sorry for it.

'All right,' he said now. 'I'll take you.'

Belle wasn't certain that was a good idea, but she didn't know how to refuse him. She decided if Frank was there they would only stay a moment, not long enough for any unpleasantness between him and Michael.

He started up his motorbike and waited while she climbed on behind him, wrapping her arms around his waist.

The Triumph hummed, he gave the bike a rev and they started off, out of the gate and down the lane to the road that led to Morwenstow. They didn't speak on the way, it was difficult with the noise anyway and Belle was happy enough not to. When they reached Morwenstow they went up the driveway to the gate, which was open. At the front of the house there were quite a few cars parked and some horses tethered to the railing.

People had come from far and wide to offer their sympathy. Of course they had, Stanley was well known and liked in the district. All the Davies were.

Michael stopped the motorbike just inside the gate and put his foot down to steady them. 'Do you want me to come with you?' he said.

Belle climbed off, brushed down her skirt and smoothed her hair out of her eyes, giving herself time to find an excuse.

'I didn't think so,' he answered for her. 'Go on, then. I'll wait here.'

There didn't seem much point in trying to sooth his feelings, and after a hesitation, Belle set off. She had barely reached the top step and the verandah when the screen door opened and Jo stepped out.

She must have heard them coming and she looked pale and drawn—grief had drained her of her usual good humour.

'I'm so sorry,' Belle said, feeling her own throat close up, and reached out to give Jo a hug.

But the other woman stood stiff and unresponsive in her grasp, and when Belle stepped back she saw that Jo was staring over at the gate, where Michael sat on his motorbike. Her mouth tightened to a thin white line.

'What is he doing here?' she said in a voice that was almost savage.

Belle turned, as if to make sure it was Michael they were talking about. She knew the Davies didn't like him, but what she was seeing in Jo's eyes was more like hatred.

'Michael brought me here,' she said, not knowing what else to say.

Jo swallowed and turned her gaze back to Belle. 'You won't like me saying this, Belle, but I have to. People are talking about you and Michael. Both of you living in the same house. It's a . . . a well-worn topic, if you want to know. I'm surprised you haven't noticed.'

Of course she'd noticed. The cool stares and the whispers behind her back. She tried for a reasonable tone. 'Jo, really, there's nothing to it. Michael sleeps in the garage with his motorcycle. Tilly and Gwen and I sleep in the house.'

'So he's a lodger, is he?' She sounded as if she wasn't sure whether to believe it or not.

'Well, he pays something every week, when he can. Jo, Michael and I are friends,' she went on when Jo didn't respond. 'You know Martha was almost like a mother to him. So that makes us almost like, well, brother and sister.'

Brother and sister, a voice mocked in her head. Had she felt like his sister when he'd stood there, half-naked in front of her? But Jo didn't need to know that.

Jo was nodding slowly, watching her face. 'All right,' she said. 'But there are things *you* don't understand.' She hesitated, chewing her lip, and then she seemed to make a decision. 'All right. I'm going to tell you. You should know. Dad is gone now and he didn't want it talked about. He said rumours could destroy people's lives and he wasn't going to be responsible for that.'

'What rumours?' Belle said.

'When Dad was in the hospital in France and Ted had been killed, he heard a story from some of the blokes in the same company as Ted. They said that Michael was with him, Ted, I mean. When he died. Michael was with Ted when he died, and Michael had lived. And some of these blokes said that Michael could have saved him and he didn't.'

Belle was shocked. She immediately wanted to deny it, to say that Michael wouldn't do that, and besides he'd been too badly injured to save anyone but himself. She'd seen his face for herself, and he'd said he'd had to drag himself away from the flames with a broken leg. How could he save Ted in those circumstances?

'There's more,' Jo went on. Voices drifted out from the house, and then the sound of a woman, sobbing. Jo swallowed, and taking Belle's arm, drew her further around the verandah. She dropped her voice to a murmur. 'They'd been fighting. Michael and Ted. Ted had a gash on his cheek and had to go to the dressing station, and Michael was in the front of the truck, he was going to the lock-up. He'd started it. There were witnesses. If Ted died then there was no one to give evidence, was there? So it was in Michael's best interests that Ted die.'

Belle shook her head. 'That can't be right.' Then, at the angry stare the other woman gave her, 'I mean, perhaps it is, but there must be more to it. Michael wouldn't let someone die just to save himself a couple of days in prison!'

The voices were coming closer and Jo glanced over her shoulder. 'Take him away from here,' she hissed urgently. She looked on the verge of breaking down. 'He's done enough damage. I don't want Frank to see him. I don't want Michael killing both my brothers.'

'All done,' Michael said matter-of-factly, as Belle climbed back onto the bike.

She was shaken and knew she looked emotional, but she told herself he couldn't know it wasn't Stanley's death that was affecting her. There was a speculative look in his eyes before he turned away to start the motorbike.

Once again she was grateful for the noise that made it difficult to speak and then thought what a coward she was. She didn't believe Michael was capable of hurting Ted, did she? Of leaving him to die when he could have saved him?

Jo had been so angry, and yet stories got mangled over time, changing as they were passed from person to person. Michael had become more important to her than she'd realised, a good friend. She didn't want to think badly of him, and yet Jo was her friend, too.

Belle wasn't aware he'd turned down a dirt track until he came to a halt, and then she saw they weren't at The Grand but somewhere near a horse paddock. The silence after the noisy motorbike seemed unearthly. The evening was on the verge of night and even the birds had gone to bed.

'Right,' Michael was facing her. 'Tell me what she said.'

CHAPTER 26

SOPHIE

Melbourne, 1986

AFTER OUR VISIT to the Registrar General, and then a stop-off at the council offices in St Kilda, where we were handed a wad of photocopied pages from business directories and post-office-address listings in regard to Rory Bartholomew and Bart Homes, we made our weary way back to Annat Street. There wasn't time to go out for dinner, and besides, Miriam had cooked and she was eager to hear our news.

She widened her eyes at the newspaper accounts we'd found at the State Library, and bit her lip when we presented her with the birth certificate which showed Belle was indeed Martha's daughter, and her father was one Nathan Ambrose. She was a highly appreciative audience.

'No death certificate we could find,' Ian said. 'So she either changed her name, moved elsewhere or she's still alive.'

A couple of glasses of Jacob's Creek sauvignon blanc, and we were deep into theories about what could have happened. The fire at The Grand hadn't occurred long after Belle went to live there, and Miriam thought Belle herself had set the fire, for the insurance. Ian pointed out that there was probably no insurance to claim, not during the Depression, and after all, The Grand wasn't a functioning hotel by then.

'If she burned down her home then she'd have nowhere to live!'

Miriam waved a dismissive hand. 'She might have acted on impulse.'

'It's a creepy place, really,' I said. 'The Grand, I mean. It's a shambles now, all blackened from the fire. No one has pulled it down or rebuilt it. I go jogging over there,' I added to Miriam, who was looking at me curiously. 'I see it all the time. Actually, at night, it's creepy.'

'She does go jogging,' Ian said. 'You should see her neon-pink shorts.'

I felt my face flame, but Miriam's eyes were alight with laughter. She leaned towards me, a trifle unsteadily. 'I'd hit him if I were you,' she said softly.

'My shorts are perfectly respectable,' I retorted, annoyed when they both went off into gales of laughter.

'Sorry,' Ian managed at last, and then sobered when he saw my expression. 'I didn't mean . . . I'm being silly. Miriam will tell you I'm often silly.'

'Very often,' Miriam agreed, wiping her eyes. 'But he's also kind and generous and clever. Oh, and did I leave out good-looking?'

Now *I* laughed, at seeing Ian so self-conscious. 'I used to think that one day we'd discover we were madly in love with each other and get married,' Miriam went on thoughtfully, 'but time passed and we never did. We're friends, and I sometimes think friends are harder to find and keep than lovers.'

She was very frank, but I liked it. I liked her. And if there was a tiny sigh of relief deep inside me, to know that Ian and she weren't an item and never had been, then I kept that to myself.

'Did you know that actress who has all of Eileen Nicholson's clothes is in town at the moment?'

'Is she?' Ian perked up.

Miriam looked cross. 'Gwendolyn South, that's her name. I've never met her. I might strangle her if I did. No, a joke. I'm sure Gwendolyn has saved many of Eileen's pieces that might otherwise have been thrown away or lost. In a way she's done us a good turn. I just wish she wasn't quite so greedy when it comes to collecting.'

'So why do you think she's fixated on Eileen Nicholson?' Ian asked, reaching for a dry biscuit and cheese. Miriam had offered to bring out the fondue set but we'd both groaned. She'd cooked an amazing meal, but cheese fondue would have been overkill.

'Well that's the thing. There *was* some connection. Somewhere. She gave an interview years ago and said as a child she knew Eileen and then when she was older, and richer, she had a chance to buy one of her pieces and it went from there.'

It sounded intriguing. *As a child*? Did that mean Gwendolyn had met Eileen in passing or was it a deeper relationship? Did she fit somewhere into this large patchwork quilt we seemed to be creating between us? I imagined a little square of cloth, or perhaps a star, with the name Gwendolyn South on it.

I said as much aloud and was pleased when they smiled in appreciation. 'I like that,' Miriam murmured, and then yawned. 'God, I'm tired.'

'Could we talk to her?' I asked. Suddenly I felt as if Gwendolyn might be the key to everything.

They looked at me and then Miriam gave a decisive nod of her fair head and her eyes lit up. 'Yes. Yes! She's doing some television show over at Channel Nine. She was retired, but evidently they talked her out of it. Probably offered her a shedload of money. I think her last movie was a bit of a flop, hence the retirement. Perhaps you could ask them if she'll see you? If you mention the wedding dress she'll be drooling at the mouth to get her hands on it.'

'Hmm, what a picture you paint,' Ian said, reaching for the bottle. 'It sounds too good to be true, but if she can help fill out the story, why not?'

'How about I ring up and ask?' Miriam said, holding out her glass for a refill. 'I can explain I'm working on restoring the dress for the upcoming Centenary at Sweet Wattle Creek, and we're expecting quite a bit of publicity. Even if dear Gwen doesn't jump at that then I'm sure Channel Nine will.'

'Why do you think you have greater kudos than me?' Ian replied with a lift of his eyebrow. 'A man of my standing.'

Miriam snorted. 'You? You're my minion, Ian, face it.'

I waved a hand at them and said I was going to bed. They were still at it as I closed the door. I could see they enjoyed their silly banter—like the bickering between a brother and sister. As long as I didn't have to listen to them.

Strains of music drifted from one of the houses further along the street —it sounded like The Bangles' 'Manic Monday', which seemed appropriate. I flopped down on the bed and tried to gather my thoughts.

I'd rung Dillon earlier and he'd sounded fine, in fact if anything he was impatient to get back to the board game they were playing. Tim and Maureen had gone to the pub, he'd said, for their one hour of freedom from the Baby from Hell. Of course the BFH had fallen asleep as soon as they'd closed the door, but Dillon was equally sure that as soon as they walked back through said door BFH would wake up.

'Christy has some spare ear plugs she's leant me,' he'd said drolly, when I asked him how he expected to sleep.

It was good to hear him sound so normal and happy. And I was relieved my going away was not bothering him very much—there had been a time when he wouldn't have let me out of his sight.

'How's it going with the wedding dress?' he'd asked, probably to stop me questioning him further.

'All right. We've found out a few things. I'm

even thinking it might be enough for a book.'

Silence. I wished I hadn't said it. I'd told myself I'd meant it as a joke, but Dillon must have heard the wistfulness in my voice and he must see, as I did, just how impossible it was.

'Or maybe not,' I'd added lamely with a laugh, to show I didn't care.

Dillon had cleared his throat. 'We can't hide away forever, Mum.'

I'd realised then that he knew exactly how I was feeling and I'd been foolish to think I could conceal those feelings from him.

'Dillon . . .'

'We shouldn't have to. You should write a book if you want to. You really should.'

And then what? Wait for Walter to come knocking on our door?

'Thank you, Dillon, but . . . I'll think about it. You know, I probably won't have time anyway. You know how hard Tim works me.'

'Maybe Tim could write it,' he'd said.

That had brought me to my feet. I didn't want Tim to write it. The book was mine. But I'd swallowed my words, not wanting to prolong this conversation, and said goodbye and I'd see him tomorrow.

I was tired, but I didn't sleep very well. Too much going on in my mind, and, when I finally started to drift off, a little voice reminded me that Ian was just a few steps away. I turned over and told myself to behave. The strains of Roberta Flack's 'First Time Ever I Saw Your Face' came through my window, and with a snort of disgust,

I finally drifted off.

Miriam had rung Channel Nine by the time we were up and drinking our coffee. They would get back to her, she said, but she thought they'd sounded interested because they'd taken down all the details. She'd tried Gwendolyn South's publicist also, but had only got an answering machine.

'What are you two up to today?' she added, peering brightly over the rim of her cup. She seemed to have suffered no ill-effects from the wine last night, unlike Ian, who looked decidedly seedy.

'Sophie wants to walk along the Esplanade,' Ian said now, sitting up straighter and making an effort. 'And I thought we'd visit Eileen Nicholson's old shop in Collins Street. It's still there, isn't it?'

'Yes. I have the address here somewhere. She used to live above it, but then the Depression affected her business and she came here instead, to Annat Street.'

The name was unusual. It occurred to me that there might be something about Annat Street in the papers we'd picked up yesterday from the council offices. I hadn't had time to look through them yet, but I unfolded them from my bag and began flipping through the pages, only half listening as Ian and Miriam discussed their plans for the day.

'I'll photograph the dress,' she was saying,

'and then make some decisions. I take it you're not planning to have it hermetically sealed in a museum somewhere? You want to be able to show it. Perhaps even for some of Mrs Davies's family to wear it?'

'Well we didn't ask, but I assume they want to keep it.'

'Then we'll go down the restoration path and not the conservation one. I might need to sew on some new materials, and replace any of the old disintegrating bits. I'll clean it up first, and see what I can save. I'll probably have to reinforce the lining and shorten the train. Well,' she added, with a smile, 'you don't need to know all that.'

I was fascinated by what Miriam was saying, but then my eye caught a name on the post-office directory for 1910. I tried not to shriek, but my voice must have been rather high with excitement, because they both winced.

'Annat Street! This is where the Bartholomews lived.' I looked about me as if I expected Rory to materialise beside the fridge.

'Let me see.' Ian perused the entry and his eyebrows rose. 'It's the same number. Could the house numbers have changed over the years?'

Miriam snatched the paper from his hand. 'They could, but I know this one hasn't. Good heavens! It *is* this house.' Now she was looking about her, too, as if seeing her surroundings with entirely new eyes.

'Do you have the title for the house?' Ian demanded, rubbing a hand over his chin. His whiskers rasped—he hadn't shaved.

'It's with the solicitor,' Miriam replied. 'I'll ring.' And she got up and went out to the phone in the other room.

Ian looked at the clock and jumped up. 'We'd better get moving or we won't have enough time to do everything.'

'Ian . . . Would you rather I got the train home? You can stay and do what you have to do.'

'No, I need to get back as well or the committee will sack me. They're slave drivers, Sophie,' he added, leaning down towards me.

'You can't blame them if they want their money's worth,' I said, trying not to laugh.

'Humph.' He gave me another look. 'How did you sleep?' he asked.

'Very well, thank you,' I lied. 'You?'

'Miriam's couch is a bit hard, but I think I drank a bit much to care. I always forget she can drink anyone under the table and wake up fresh as a daisy the next morning. We're not all so fortunate.'

This time I did laugh, and he gave a reluctant smile.

'I'll be all right,' he said, more to convince himself than me. 'The coffee will kick in soon.'

'You and Miriam are good friends,' I said, and then was appalled to realise how wistful I'd sounded. Like an orphan peeping in through the window at a happy family sitting around their Christmas dinner.

'Most of the time,' he said, but he was watching my face.

He was going to ask questions, I knew it, and

was immensely grateful when Miriam came back
into the room, her face alight with news.

'This house wasn't Rory's, it was his wife's
parents who owned it originally. They left it to
Iris, and then Rory inherited the house when
she died. There was a large mortgage and the
house was sold during the Depression and turned
into lodgings. Maybe it was just serendipity that
Eileen Nicholson came here when her business
was in trouble, or else she chose a place that was
familiar.'

'It was their family home,' I said, not knowing
whether to be glad of this new piece of information or sad for Belle, who had lost her home
when her father died. 'Belle must've had no
choice but to go to her aunt . . . her mother, in
Sweet Wattle Creek. The Grand, at least. She must
have felt pretty awful about that.'

I didn't know Belle, of course I didn't, but our
circumstances were similar in a way. I, too, had
left all I'd known behind me after a catastrophic
event, and had to make a new life for myself
among strangers. I thought I knew a little of the
emotional trauma Belle must have been through.

'And then The Grand burned down a few
months later,' Ian finished the story. 'We need to
find out what happened next, don't we? Does
Belle have any descendants? Charlie Nicholson died so she didn't marry him, but she was
engaged to this Henry Collier. Did he go with
her to Sweet Wattle Creek?'

'I don't think so. If Belle had descendants then
why give her wedding dress to Jo Davies?'

'A new start?' Ian suggested. He looked at the clock on the wall again. 'We don't have time to find out anything else today. Not if you still want to go over to the Nicholson shop in Collins Street.'

He was right. Frustrating as it was, we couldn't do any more today. Still, I reminded myself, we had the archives in the cellar at the *Herald*, and Bill Shaw's 'Recollections', as well as various other resources in Sweet Wattle Creek. And we also had the residents. Although they seemed to have selective amnesia where Belle Bartholomew was concerned.

Had she done something of which the good folk of Sweet Wattle Creek disapproved? Was that why she wasn't remembered? Or had she died in the fire at The Grand and was now only evoked as a ghost with flaming hair?

We took a tram into the city and walked down Collins Street. The trees were green and leafy, despite the heat and the traffic. Ian pointed out some of the landmarks, and grumbled about the ones lost to wreckers in the fifties and sixties, to make way for modernisation.

'Eileen Nicholson's shop wasn't one of those unlucky ones. Here it is.'

We stood and stared at the gleaming windows of what was now an upmarket patisserie. The cakes arranged on velvet-draped stands made my mouth water, but Ian was still looking a lit-

tle green. I closed my eyes and tried to imagine
Eileen's clothing there instead, and her name
printed in classy letters on the board above.

I had remembered to bring my camera with
me, and took some photographs. One of them
had Ian in it, leaning against the wall, staring
across Collins Street and looking pensive. I felt a
bit sneaky taking it, but it was such a good shot I
couldn't resist.

'Come on,' he said, interrupting my thoughts.

He held out his hand and nodded towards the
door. 'We'll ask if we can have a look upstairs at
her working space. She also lived up there, you
know, in the last few months before she sold the
place.'

'Oh.' Tentatively I gave him my hand, and he
gave it a squeeze, as if he thought I might be in
need of some encouragement, before he opened
the door and set the bell pinging.

I don't know if they would have let me upstairs
if I'd been alone, but as usual Ian worked his
magic, and soon we were climbing the narrow creaky stairs up to the second floor. This
was where Eileen had overseen her creations, I
thought, with the light from the windows falling over her work surfaces and her employees, all
sewing industriously. And then, at the end, just
herself, working long into the night. Or was I
being too romantic?

But this was where she'd supervised the making
of the wedding dress for her son and Belle. Even
if she didn't set all the stitches herself, I was certain she had personally put the finishing touches

to it. The velvet train and the machine-made lace, the pearls and the diamantes. And maybe it was here she had wept for what would never be, when Charlie died on the Western Front.

I took some more photographs. Moody shots of the room and the light slanting across the polished floor. They'd be brilliant for the newspaper article. And the book. That is, if there ever was a book.

Downstairs, Ian bought me a rich, chocolate-coated pastry and himself a cup of tea. It was a long time since anyone had done anything like that for me, and even while I complained it would make me fat, I was moved.

'You mean those shorts could get tighter?' he demanded, widening his eyes comically.

I had to laugh then. I felt light-headed and giddy, like a girl without a teenage son and a violent husband, like a girl with her life in front of her. And it was terrifying and wonderful, all at the same time.

CHAPTER 27

BELLE

Sweet Wattle Creek, 1931

BELLE LOOKED INTO Michael's stony face. 'Jo seems to think you had something to do with her brother, Ted's death.'

There, she'd said it. She'd told him the truth. Belle stood before him, while the last of the light died around them, waiting for the truth in return.

Michael turned away, walked a few steps, before facing her again.

'Christ,' he whispered. 'I knew someone had been spreading stories at the time, but I was shipped out to the hospital in Blighty and I had more things to worry about than stupid lies.'

'She said you and Ted had a fight and you were going to be locked up.'

He shook his head.

'So you didn't fight?' She wanted him to say no, but she already knew he was going to say yes. There was something in the way he wouldn't look at her, the way he was staring over the paddocks.

'We used to be friends, Ted and me. I told you that. We fell out. When we saw each other again at Ypres it just seemed to blow out of nowhere. He started swinging at me and I fought back, and next thing he was on the ground, bleeding, and I was under arrest.'

'But the truck . . . the shell . . .?'

'They were using the truck as an ambulance. Usually, it was two stretcher bearers walking or a horse and cart, but we were lucky this day. There was an ambulance. Ted wasn't badly hurt, but when we'd been fighting he'd fallen against a spike and cut himself. His cheek needed bandaging and I was on a charge. I was sitting up with the driver and he was in the back because they wanted us separated. The shell hit the back of the truck. We were in a crater when I woke up. The driver was dead beside me and I began to crawl out. Before I got more than a few feet the fire started. If I didn't turn around and save Ted, then it was because I was lucky to save myself and anyway . . . he was dead. He had to be. No one could've survived back there.'

'Why don't the Davies know this?'

'They do. They should. If old Stan had believed the stories he would've taken his 303 and shot me right between the eyes. It's Violet. She's never liked me, not since Martha took me in. I told you how I overheard her telling Martha I should go into the boy's home.'

'Michael, I don't think you did anything wrong. I'm not saying that. Jo was so upset and I . . . I suppose I wondered what the truth was.' Michael was generous and kind, and she couldn't accept he was capable of something so despicable.

'So you believe me?'

'Yes, of course I believe you,' she said, and there was relief in saying it.

He looked at her a moment more and then he nodded. He took a deep breath and let it out in a crack of laughter.

'What was the fight about?' she asked.

He pretended to fiddle with his mask. 'I don't know. Nothing probably. Men used to go a bit crazy when they got some leave. Fighting eased the tension when you knew that you'd be heading back to the trenches the following day or the one after.'

'What did you fall out over when you were boys?'

That crack of laughter again. 'I can't remember that either,' he said, but he sounded resigned. He didn't expect her to believe him but he wasn't going to do anything about it.

'Michael, please.'

'Ted's gone and I won't besmirch his reputation now.'

'What about your reputation?'

But he shook his head and she knew he'd made up his mind. He got back onto the motorbike and she reluctantly slid on behind him.

Gwen's homework was spread out on the table and Tilly was frowning over a story she was writing for the *Herald*. Belle was sewing, altering one of her blouses to fit Tilly's slender form, wishing

Eileen Nicholson was here to transform ordinary fabric into something amazing. Belle's skills were basic at best, but she was getting better.

Michael had been watching her. She could feel his gaze as he sat by the door, removing the laces from his leather work boots so that he could clean them. He had an old cloth and some dubbin by his feet, all ready to go.

Since their conversation on the way back from Morwenstow, they'd said little to each other. He wanted her to believe him and she was trying, but there were things he wasn't telling her and it was unfair of him to expect her to brush them aside. Belle, with her practical nature, needed to hear all of the story before she made her decision.

She fiddled with her needle and thread, wanting to make everything all right again, but it wasn't. Only Michael could do that and he wasn't going to.

'I thought I'd head up north tomorrow,' his voice came out of the silence. He'd picked up one of the boots and was rubbing the concoction of oil, tallow and wax into the old leather.

The girls looked up and so did Belle.

'I'm hoping to catch up with Smithy. He's going to be in Hay before the weekend, and if I can see him then I think I'll have more chance of getting some work. It'll mean being away for a few weeks. Probably.'

'But you'll be flying,' Tilly said. 'That's the main thing, Michael.'

He gave her a smile. 'And I'll be making a bit of money, too. Gwen eats so much we can't keep up with her.'

Gwen protested, loudly.

'I'll give you a few pounds before I go,' Michael said, speaking to Belle, although he was looking down at the cloth, smoothing the dubbin into the old leather with a touch that was almost tender. 'There're some travellers down by the creek. Saw them yesterday. They're all right down there, don't let them try to tell you otherwise. They can stay until I get back and then we'll see.'

Belle wondered what she would do if they arrived en masse, demanding beds and food.

'Belle?'

'We'll be okay, Michael.' She looked into his face, making herself sound positive, nodding her head for added emphasis. 'Don't worry about us. You go and find your friends. I want you to do that. I do.'

'If you need me —'

'We'll send Nellie with a message tied to her foot!' Gwen shouted and dissolved into laughter.

When it came to the girls' bedtime, Michael packed up and said goodnight and that he'd see them before he left in the morning. Belle sat watching a moth dancing with death around the lantern. Michael had fixed the generator but they couldn't afford the fuel to run it.

It hadn't taken her long to go back to being the frightened, insecure Belle, she thought with a mixture of frustration and despair. She'd come to Sweet Wattle Creek to restore her confidence, to find the girl she was before Charlie had died, and now here she was, afraid because Michael was leaving her for a few weeks.

He'd been so good, worked so hard, he deserved to go and do what he loved. She would never ask him to stay just because she was feeling a little delicate.

'You're being ridiculous, Belle,' she told herself furiously as she stood up and lit a candle. She blew out the lantern and then carried her sewing up the stairs to her bedroom, giving the door with the brass handle a glare in passing.

She would show Michael how well she could manage. Obviously he considered she was a fragile flower, but she wasn't, and she would show him.

The Gladstone bag caught her eye and she went over to it. Apart from the moody sketch of Reims Cathedral she'd tucked into the frame of the dressing table, everything else was still inside, and she soon found the photograph of Michael in his Flying Corps uniform, the wings badge prominent on his chest.

She was so used to seeing him in his mask that the image of his face without it seemed unfamiliar. A stranger. She stepped closer to the candle and studied it. He hadn't been handsome, not like Frank or Charlie, but he had a nice face. Good-natured, as if he was on the verge of laughing at the camera, and full of a zest for life.

He'd told her how ironic he found it that he should have been injured in a motor vehicle, instead of how he'd expected to be, in his aeroplane. Pilots and observers often did not survive long over the battlefields of France, not once the enemy learned how useful their observations and maps were to those in charge of the war, in the planning of their campaigns.

She turned the photograph over, feeling the torn backing against her hand, and tried to flatten it down. It was only then that she realised that there was something pushed into the gap, a thin, single sheet of folded paper. Gently she eased it out.

It was a document, or the smudged copy of one.

I, Martha Ambrose, agree to the following . . .'

Belle bent her head closer, her lips moving as she read, her disbelief growing.

I will not see nor contact my daughter, Belle Ambrose, from this day forward. I give her over completely to my brother, Rory Bartholomew, for the rest of her life. In return, Rory Bartholomew will sponsor Michael Maxwell, paying all costs so that he can learn to fly, and he will make all efforts to enable him to join the Australian Flying Corps. Dated 12 April 1911.

Martha had signed neatly at the bottom, followed by Rory, his writing full of flamboyant curls and whirls.

Belle refolded the page and sat on her bed, staring at the window and seeing her own face reflected in the glass. She wanted to feel hurt and betrayed, but she couldn't. She understood. Martha had agreed so that Michael could have a life and a career, doing the thing he loved most. She probably thought Belle was lost to her anyway, so why not use her daughter to the benefit of her adopted son.

It made perfect sense, it did, and she was not upset. Well, not too upset. But then something occurred to her.

Why had Martha changed her will? Why had she left The Grand to Belle?

There was a flicker of light inside the garage. Belle didn't think she would have dared to knock on the door if it had been completely dark. But Michael was awake and tomorrow he would be gone. She needed to see him, to ask him. Surely if anyone knew Martha's mind then it was Michael?

The door opened a crack. He was still wearing his mask but he was barefoot, his shirt half unbuttoned, his trousers hastily pulled on.

'Belle.' He sounded startled, as if she was a ghost, but she knew it was because he didn't want her here with him alone. He was always so careful of her, and part of the reason was her reputation. He must hear the gossip just as she did, and know what people thought and said.

'I have something to show you,' she said, and she heard the suppressed emotion in her voice. 'Can I come in?'

He sighed, ran a hand through his hair, and then stepped back. Belle slid in through the half-open door, noticing the bed made up, the lamp on the floor beside it, and the book lying open to the page he'd been reading.

There was nowhere to sit and he didn't offer her the bed, but stood, watching her, waiting.

'I found this,' she said, and held out the folded paper.

He was still looking at her face. 'What is it?'

'Read it, Michael.' Reluctantly, he took it from her and unfolded it. She thought he might be as surprised as her, but she could tell he'd seen it before, or at least heard about it. 'You knew,' she said, and sounded accusing despite herself.

'Martha told me,' he admitted. 'Belle, I'm sorry, I never asked her to do that. She only told me later, years later.'

He sounded upset, and she realised he thought she must be angry with *him*. Belle shook her head, her smile a little lopsided.

'It's all right. It doesn't matter. If Charlie hadn't died I probably would've lived my life in happy ignorance.' He knew about Charlie, she'd told him not long after he arrived.

'It does matter,' he retorted. 'She gave up her rights to her daughter. Rory shouldn't have asked it of her. Martha told me that he saw it as an opportunity to make sure she never came to find you and tried to take you back.'

There was a poignancy in knowing Rory had loved her so much he would do such a thing. The other side of the coin was Martha, willing to release all rights to her daughter for the sake of this man standing in front of her.

'She did it for you, Michael. I'm glad. I imagine it wasn't easy for you without Rory's help.'

'No. Only the posh boys got to fly. I wasn't at the right school or born to the right parents. Now anyone can pretty much get a pilot's licence if they can pay for it, but it was different then. The gentlemen in the Flying Corps didn't know what to make of me, so I had to prove myself over and over again.'

'But you can get work? You said if you went to find Smithy he'd give you work?'

'Well, we flew together, didn't we. We got through the war and out the other side. He knows me. He'll give me work. I know he'd choose me over some Johnny come lately.'

'Good.' She smiled at him, and abruptly it seemed as if there wasn't enough air in here. She stepped away, meaning to leave, before she remembered the other thing she'd meant to ask him.

'Martha's will,' she began, hurriedly turning back. He'd followed her, though and she bumped into him, so that he put out his hands to steady her. They came to rest lightly on her waist, with barely any weight at all, but still she could feel his warmth through her clothing.

'Her will?' He was watching her mouth.

'Yes. She changed it. She left everything to you and then she changed it.'

He looked up, into her eyes. 'I did that,' he said, and the corner of his mouth curled up as if he was giving her a gift. 'She'd done so much for me and I said I wanted you to have The Grand. I said then you'd have to come home whether Rory wanted you to or not. She liked that. Said it would be a good way to thumb her nose at him from the grave.'

But Rory would have won, she thought. He

hadn't shown her the letter from Aneas Thomas and it was only when he died that she saw it. Perhaps he would never have told her if circumstance hadn't intervened.

Belle reached up and put her hands on his shoulders, as if they were about to dance. 'Did you see Rory? When he was helping you?'

'Sometimes. Never at the house though. He didn't want me there. And after the war, I came and he wouldn't let me inside.'

Her eyes widened. 'You were there? Outside? But I saw you!'

'Did you?' He was very close now. Her hands were linked behind his neck, and she felt the heat of his body against hers as she leaned into him. Gently, she rested her cheek against the undamaged side of his face, feeling the prickle of his unshaven skin, smelling the male scent of him.

It had been so long since she had felt like this. Was it wrong to want to lie down on his bed with him? She'd learned that life didn't wait for everyone. It hadn't waited for her and Charlie. She might not get this chance again if she didn't take it now.

She turned her head and brushed her lips against his. They felt soft and warm, and he began to return her kiss. His mask was in the way and she reached around to untie it, but he caught her hands before she could finish.

'Are you sure?' he asked her, and she could hear all his doubts in his voice.

She nodded. 'Yes, Michael, I'm sure.' Once the mask was gone she kissed him again, and with his lean body against hers and his strong arms holding her, his injury didn't seem to matter a bit.

'Belle,' he groaned as if she'd hurt him, but she knew he wanted her just as much as she wanted him.

'Sshh,' she whispered, and led him towards the bed, bending down to blow out the candle.

CHAPTER 28

SOPHIE

Melbourne, 1986

IAN LED ME off the tram before we got near Annat Street, and we walked along the Esplanade and down onto St Kilda beach. The bay was still sparkling but there were clouds coming in from the sea, and the air had a hushed feeling, as though a storm was coming. Living on the Southern Ocean, with Antarctica beyond the horizon, did not make for boring or predictable weather.

I took off my sandals and Ian removed his shoes, and we walked in the water's edge and then bought a Cornetto from a van parked on the foreshore.

We'd discovered so much. About Belle and her family, about why she left St Kilda and went to Sweet Wattle Creek. About Charlie and the wedding dress, and Eileen Nicholson's life. There was still so much more I wanted to know, but time had caught up to us, and we headed back to Miriam's apartment.

Miriam came down the stairs when she heard us. 'I'll make you something to eat before you go,' she said. 'And I have news. Exciting news!' she assured me, when she saw my doubtful expression. 'Our friend, Gwendolyn, can't see us right now, but she's willing to make the journey north to Sweet Wattle Creek. Her publicist and Channel Nine will be in touch with the details, but it sounds to me as if they're going all out with this. Great publicity for your Centenary, Ian. Couldn't have asked for more, really.'

Ian was grinning. 'Brilliant. Thanks, Miriam.'

I bent to fiddle with the strap of my sandal, so that they couldn't see my face. The news *was* good, very good, I knew that. People would come to see Gwendolyn and hear about the Centenary through her well-oiled publicity machine. Lots of people. Lots of money for the exhibition. I was happy for Ian and the committee. If I had some niggling doubts, it was because I was afraid of losing my nice, safe bolthole.

Photographers and news crews meant there was always the chance Walter might see . . . something. Well, Dillon and I would just have to be very careful. We could do that. And if I was asked to smile and say cheese then I'd pretend to have some sort of rare virus that prevented me from appearing on camera.

The thought made me smile.

'I knew you were happy about it deep down,' Ian said.

I hadn't realised he'd been watching me and probably wondering about my doubtful expression. His eyebrow was raised.

'Of course I am!' I said, and it wasn't all acting.

'Wait until I tell Tim. The *Herald*'s special edition will sell out. He'll be so chuffed. Maybe he'll even give me a pay rise.'

Ian laughed at that, as I'd meant him to, and I thought I'd managed to deflect his thoughts. I hoped so. I really didn't want to have to cold-shoulder him. Once the Centenary came and went, then our friendship could gradually dwindle, and time and distance would do the rest. I didn't want to hurt him, and to be honest, I didn't want not to see him. As it was I'd probably be a mess when he left. Why deny myself the pleasure of his company before I had to?

We ate Miriam's steak and salad, and she promised to have the wedding dress ready before the Centenary.

'Gwendolyn will want to wear it,' she said darkly. 'You wait and see.'

When we said our goodbyes, she gave me a hug and kissed my cheek. 'I'm sure I'll see you again soon, Sophie,' she said with a meaningful look, which I really hoped Ian missed.

I liked her, and I felt as if we could easily be good friends, but I also knew that was something very unlikely to happen. It was best not to imagine a future with Miriam in it—I'd found that dwelling on all the things I couldn't have only left me feeling depressed.

By the time we set off it was early evening and I was tired and looking forward to seeing Dillon. This was the longest time we had been apart for over a year. I'd rung him to explain I'd be later than I'd thought, and he said he'd go home with

Smithy and meet me there. He said he didn't think he could stand another night with the Baby from Hell anyway.

'Even the ear plugs don't work,' he grumbled.

'I'll see you soon.'

'Back to boring,' he said.

'Hmm. Actually, I don't know if I'm a city girl anymore,' I told him, a little uncomfortable with the revelation.

'You've turned into a country hick!' But he was laughing with me, not at me.

The traffic was busy, but we finally reached the outer suburbs just as evening turned to night. Then we were into dark stretches of road with empty country either side, just the occasional gleam of light from a farmhouse. I breathed a sigh of relief. Which made me ask: was it true I no longer wanted to be a city girl?

I couldn't go back. Even though I knew there'd been times over the past year when I wished I could. Go back and alter my decisions, change the course of my life, make everything all right. I'd moved beyond that now. I couldn't go back so what was the point of longing for the past? I was Sophie Matheson from Sweet Wattle Creek, and I had a teenage son called Dillon. That was my life now and I was content with it.

'Are you a city boy, Ian?' I asked aloud, partly to divert my thoughts but also because I wanted to know more about him. Over the past weeks we'd spoken about lots of things but I couldn't remember him opening up about himself.

'Me?' He took a moment to answer, and it

occurred to me that maybe he also had something to hide. But it seemed he was just searching for the right words. 'I was born in the country. By the sea, anyway. Torquay? Bell's Beach?' I nodded to show I understood where he was coming from. The lifestyle down on the Surf Coast was famous.

'I'm imagining you on a surfboard in your Speedos.'

'Board shorts, Sophie. Ripcurl.'

'I stand corrected,' I murmured with a smile.

'My father wasn't well and retired early, and we all went to live like beachcombers. He used to take the dog for a walk along the beach and do a lot of staring out to sea.'

He was talking but there were things he wasn't telling me. For a moment I considered letting it go, keeping the conversation light, but I found I didn't want to do that. 'Why wasn't your father well?' I asked gently.

Ian pulled a face. 'He was in Darwin during the Japanese bombing in 1942. Never got over it. He used to wake up in the night in a sweat, screaming. By the time I came along he couldn't work so we opted out. Early hippies, my mum always called us. She was an artist, quite a good one actually. She used to sell her paintings to the cafes. She'd take us to the local gallery to see the travelling exhibitions.'

His life had certainly been different from mine, but he'd had his ups and downs. Ian knew what it was to be unhappy and to see those around him suffer. Maybe that explained his understanding nature and the kindness I'd observed in him.

'How many brothers and sisters?'

'Two of each. I was the youngest.'

'Wow, five of you.' Did I sound wistful? Maybe I was. As an only child, and *with* an only child, I'd dreamed of being part of a large family. I sometimes thought that if I'd had sisters and brothers, Walter wouldn't have been able to get such a hold on me.

'After I finished school I didn't know what I wanted to do. Mum got me a job in the gallery. It was all right but I knew it wasn't right for me. Although by then I was married.'

'You're married?' I felt something a bit like the Titanic sink inside me.

'I'm divorced,' he corrected me firmly. 'We were children, nineteen, and it was a big mistake, but being nineteen we wouldn't listen. No kids, thank God, at least we weren't that stupid. Not that I don't like kids,' he said hastily, realising how that sounded. 'I do. I just . . . I was too young.'

I understood that at least, although I'd never ever wished Dillon hadn't happened. I forced myself to tone down my smile, to pretend I wasn't very relieved he was no longer married. 'So what next? After the divorce and the gallery?'

'My mother had some contacts. I moved to the city and started working part-time in a high-end antiques shop. Very posh. Not my thing at all. That was when I met Miriam,' he added with a sideways glance to see my reaction.

'So what happened? Hmm, I'm trying to picture you in a place where there are lots of breakables, and I have a feeling it wasn't a good fit.'

He laughed. He seemed very relaxed. 'You're right. She walked in just as I'd knocked over an enamel decorated Anglaise-cased striking French carriage clock.' Obviously he'd told this story a few times, I thought, going by the way he rattled off the words.

'Was it expensive?'

'Yes, it was. Miriam stood there while the owner sacked me. She felt sorry for me and took me out to lunch. We hit it off. She made some suggestions about getting a job I actually enjoyed and we kept in touch, and when she started up the business she thought of me. By then I'd finished my training and had some experience under my belt.'

'And you're happy with what you do?' I asked curiously. 'You don't miss being a beachcomber?'

He flicked me a smile. 'There are times. But if I'm homesick I can always head off for a day at the beach. You ask a lot of questions, Sophie. Can I go next?'

'The journalist in me,' I retorted flippantly. 'Where's your family now?'

'My father died and my mother remarried. My stepfather and I don't get on so well, but she's happy. One of my sisters is still down there, she runs the local craft centre, the other one is on a sailing ship somewhere in the Atlantic. One of my brothers lives in France and doesn't do very much of anything, and the other one is a banker in London.'

'Diverse,' I murmured, impressed. 'Sounds as if

you all have your own ideas of how to live your lives. Nothing boring there, Ian.'

'No, we're not boring.'

I wondered if I would ever meet any of them. I tried to imagine Ian among them, being teased as the youngest, laughing and sharing memories. After a childhood like that, he'd probably had trouble fitting into the real world. Maybe that explained his shyness.

'You think this Gwendolyn thing is a good idea?'

I could see his profile in the faint green light from the dashboard.

'Yeah, I do. It'll certainly ramp up the publicity, and it's free. The committee will love that.'

He chuckled. 'Very true.' He gave me a glance, and I wondered if he was remembering my earlier abstraction.

My voice sounded a little breathless. 'We could do some photographs of her with the dress. Maybe Miriam will relent and let her wear it. What do you think? Tim could publish the photographs and sell them on. World domination for the *Herald*.'

'Hmm, I doubt Miriam's going to let that happen, but yes, it would be great. We need to find out Gwen's story, too. Her connection. I have a feeling that would make lots of people who aren't interested in history sit up and take notice.'

'Yes. The shallow lot.'

He laughed.

I stretched my arms, feeling the seductive movement of the car begin to lull my tired body into sleep. 'There seems to be an awful lot to do, Ian. Will you really be able to get everything ready in time?'

'You forget, I'm used to working under pressure.'

'Like Superman?'

'Batman, thank you very much,' he said, his lips twitching.

'Really? I always preferred Superman. The flying, I suppose. How cool would that be? Batman just has that noisy batmobile.'

The conversation went downhill from there. I gave up fighting my leaden eyelids and dozed for a while. I kept waking up, trying not to let myself fall into a deeper sleep, but it was no use. The movement of the car, the quiet night, and Ian's soft humming did the trick, and I sank into the arms of Morpheus.

The dream arrived with vicious swiftness. Except that it wasn't a dream, it was a memory.

Walter, his fist raised, screaming at me as I cowered in the corner of the kitchen, broken crockery littering the tiled floor. And Dillon, eyes wide and terrified, hiding under the table. I shook my head at him. There was no point in him coming to my rescue, no point in us both being hurt.

I was a grown-up. I could handle it.

The words Walter was saying . . . I always thought that no one would have believed it, if they saw him outside of our home. Foul expletives, the sort of words I had only ever come across in the worst streets in Brisbane. But this was our home. I looked at Dillon and there were tears on his cheeks and I thought: he shouldn't have to hear this. He shouldn't have to see it. And suddenly I knew it was enough.

Despite my crippling fear and because of the person I'd become, the person Walter had turned me into, it was time to step up.

I pushed myself against the wall and used it as support, raising my body inch by inch until I was standing. I was dizzy. He'd thrown me against this same wall a few minutes ago and I'd struck my head. I may even have blacked out for a moment. Now my legs were shaking, but I managed to stop myself from falling.

All this time he was in my face, screaming. The noise washed over me as if I was underwater, no longer making any sense. I reached out with both hands and gave him a shove away from me, as hard as I could.

And I screamed, 'No more!'

My eyes shot open and I moaned. I was breathing quickly and yet couldn't seem to catch my breath. My face was hot and wet with tears, or sweat. I didn't know where I was, and then I felt Ian's hand on my shoulder, anchoring me. He'd stopped the car on the side of the road and he was looking into my face, and in the eerie glow of the dashboard I could see how worried he was.

'Soph? Are you all right? You were yelling. Soph?'

I managed a shaky laugh. I wiped a hand over my cheeks and pushed back my hair from my face. 'A dream,' I said in a husky voice. My throat hurt—I really had been yelling. 'God, how silly. I was being attacked by a monster.'

He looked at me, a frown between his eyes. Did he believe me? I shot him a sideways glance and he caught it. Doubt clouded his face but I wouldn't let him voice it.

'I need to get home to Dillon,' I said in a voice that brooked no argument. 'Ian, can we please go.'

He hesitated but I turned away, staring out of the window. I knew he wanted to ask me what was wrong. Perhaps he thought he had a right to ask. And what would I say? More lies? I could hardly tell him the truth, could I?

I heard the clicking of the indicator and then he turned back onto the road, and I breathed a sigh of relief. But I knew it was not over. He would want to discuss this, if not tonight then tomorrow or the next day. And I couldn't allow it.

I was going to have to push him away, cut my ties with him, apart from the strictly professional ones. I was going to have to hurt him before he could hurt Dillon and myself.

Then why was I the one who was feeling so miserable?

The dark landscape flashed past, the car's headlights picking out a fence here, a gate there, spindly trees and the glowing eyes of a kangaroo. Few cars passed us; we might as well have been the only people alive in all the world.

Finally, I allowed myself to return to my dream. Because that wasn't the end of my story.

I'd stood up to Walter that night in the kitchen, but he'd punched me in the face and broken my nose and blackened both my eyes. Then I'd fallen down and he'd kicked me until I was black and blue and bleeding. He probably would have killed me.

It was only at the hospital that I learned what Dillon had done. There was a heavy cast-iron frypan on the bench. I'd been about to cook our dinner when Walter came in and started his tirade. While Walter was attacking me, Dillon had picked it up and swung it at Walter's head. He'd missed a direct blow—he probably would have killed him if he'd been on target—but he did enough damage to stop him and lay him out cold.

It was Dillon who had rung for the ambulance and then the police, and Dillon who had told them what had happened.

'I'm sorry, Mum,' he said when I regained consciousness, his voice shaking. 'I had to tell them. I'm sorry.'

It is a shocking thing, to listen to your son apologise for saving your life.

'No, Dillon,' I whispered, when I was finally able to. 'I'm the one who's sorry.'

I held his hand tightly while we waited for the police. I told him we would go home and pack our things and find somewhere safe to stay, until Walter was out of our lives. I promised him we would never have to see Walter again. The relief in his eyes made me weep again.

But of course I was fooling myself. Walter wasn't going to leave us alone. He'd chosen me and he couldn't see a future without me in it. The police tried. Walter treated everything they did with contempt. He knew the law better than they did, he said, and I may as well give up now and come back to him.

'You come back,' he said, smiling behind his

dark glasses, 'and come alone. I don't want Dillon with us.'

I'd met him in a cafe, somewhere where there were lots of people, to beg him again to leave us alone. We'd moved half a dozen times since the refuge and he always found us. I'd called the police until they were fed up with me, but it had made no difference.

'Dillon's only a child,' I retorted. 'Do you really think I'd abandon him?'

He just looked at me, and although his eyes were hidden behind the glasses, I knew. If I went back, without Dillon, then he would leave Dillon alone. He'd be safe. It was my life for my son's.

They were frying hamburgers in the kitchen behind us, hamburgers and onions. The smell was making me feel sick and I stood up to leave.

'I'll give you until tomorrow night,' he said, his tone lethal. 'Don't disappoint me.'

That night I spoke to Dillon and explained that it might be best if I did as Walter said, that Dillon could go and live with my parents and have a life. A proper life.

He was horrified. He refused, flat out. He kept refusing no matter how I put it to him. And in the end I saw that Walter's offer was no offer at all, but a death sentence for me whichever way I looked at it. Dillon and I planned long into the night and come morning we knew we had

another twelve hours before Walter came to find us.

We ran.

CHAPTER 29

BELLE

Sweet Wattle Creek, 1931

'BELLE?'
She heard Tilly call as she came down the stairs. Michael had been gone for nearly five weeks now and they were getting used to being here without him. In the mornings Tilly and Gwen either walked into town or rode the bicycle. She'd thought they were about to do just that when she heard them calling her.

Tilly met her in the doorway, her face worried, and Gwen was standing behind her, her brown eyes round with excitement.

'Belle,' she said in what was meant to be a whisper, 'we have guests.'

There was a middle-aged couple by the horse trough. The man's trousers were held up with a piece of rope and he wore a grubby shirt with a collar, and around his neck, incongruously, a tie. The woman was wearing a dress that had faded so much it was difficult to make out the pattern. On her feet were a pair of scuffed lace-up navvy's boots that had had a lot of wear. She had a filthy blanket wrapped around her shoulders, and she was hunched forward and obviously unwell.

'G'day, Missus,' the man said, nodding his head at her shyly. 'Michael said we weren't to trouble you, and we wouldn't have, only Eadie here isn't too flash.'

'Eadie?' Belle's gaze slid over the woman, who had perched herself on the edge of the trough and was whiter than a sheet.

'My wife, Eadie. I'm Mo.' He wiped his hand on his trousers and held it out to her. His hair was grey and straggly, with a matching beard, but his smile was gentle and warm.

'What's wrong with Eadie?' she asked him, after shaking his hand. It might be infectious, and her mind immediately jumped to memories of the Spanish Flu.

'We ate something that didn't agree with poor old Eadie here,' Mo said helpfully. 'Like those mussels we got off the rocks once, down on the beach, remember, old girl? That's all it is. She needs a bed for a night or two and she'll be right as rain.'

Eadie groaned and bit her lip, bending over, with her arms wrapped around her middle.

Tilly edged closer to Belle. 'Michael said we weren't to take anyone in,' she said. 'Not till he gets back.'

Michael had said that, but he hadn't known they'd be confronted with a possible crisis. How could she send them away when Eadie could hardly walk? She needed a bed and rest, and Mo—her nose twitched—could do with a good wash.

'There's no one else with you?' she said in her firmest voice.

'No one,' Mo began, just as Eadie opened the blanket and a fluffy little dog peered out. 'This is Bucket,' she said in a scratchy voice. 'We found him in one, out in the Mallee, near Chinkapook.'

'Bastards were trying to drown him,' Mo said angrily, then remembered himself and apologised for his language.

Gwen took one look at the little dog and melted. A moment later Belle was showing them inside.

'I knew you'd help,' Mo said, an arm around his wife. 'Michael said you were one of the good ones, Missus.'

Belle managed a smile, but there were tears in her eyes. Not that she let Mo see them, just in case he was spinning her a yarn and Eadie wasn't sick at all. She didn't want anyone to think she was an easy touch.

She missed Michael. She wanted him back here with her, together, sitting down in the evening and laughing at the names she thought up for their meals, and bringing her tea in the special flowered cup when she came downstairs every morning.

She wanted to hold him and kiss him and be with him, and as the days dragged on she was frightened that something might happen to him and she would never see him again. Could fate be that cruel? But it could, and Belle knew it.

Gwen was hovering outside the door, Bucket in her arms.

'Come on, Gwen,' she said. 'Let's warm up some water so Eadie can wash. She might need a nightdress, too. She can have one of mine. Do you think you can find a nice one? Why don't you go upstairs and have a look?'

Gwen flew up the stairs, still holding the little dog.

'What about school?' Belle called up after her.

There was a suspicious silence. She knew Gwen was bored with school already. She'd made one friend, Jane, the younger Beauchamp girl, and that friendship seemed to consist of Gwen coming home with all sorts of tales of the rich and famous, and being generally dissatisfied with her own lot.

'I'm going to be an actress,' she'd declared once, striking a pose. 'And I'll wear diamonds even to bed.'

'Good luck with that,' Michael had retorted. 'Horribly scratchy things, diamonds.'

Belle knew she should force the issue and take Gwen to school, but it seemed she had other things to worry about right now. 'Waifs and strays,' she muttered.

The sound of Eadie retching broke through her thoughts. 'Missus!' Mo called out, his voice high with panic. Belle set about dealing with this new crisis.

'I'll get the doctor.'

Eadie was no better, if anything she was worse.

Mo had stuck faithfully by her side, but Eadie seemed oblivious to him now, curled up in the bed. Her skin was hot and dry, and Belle was worried.

'Do you think he'd come?' Mo asked anxiously.

'Of course he will,' she replied with more confidence than she was feeling. If she was still in Annat Street she'd have no qualms about sending for a doctor, but here, at The Grand . . . It might be slightly more difficult. But if Belle had learned one thing, it was that people responded to self-assurance.

Belle was getting more proficient at riding the bicycle. She knew she was all right as long as she stuck to the centre of the road, away from the inch-deep dust at the edges, or the sharp spines of the three-corner jacks along the verge.

As she peddled she thought again of Mo and Eadie. As nice as they were—she'd learned Mo was a former salesman from a country town in the west who'd lost his job and then his home, while Eadie had wanted children but was never blessed—she couldn't help but think of the problems ahead.

She needed money. Tilly's meagre wage wouldn't sustain them now that Michael had gone. Her thoughts strayed to the crate of her belongings, and she knew with a sigh that she would have to begin to sell them. Not all at once, but a piece here and there, just enough to get by.

There were sure to be more strays turning up to The Grand. And when they asked if they could stay she would say yes. Of course she would, how could she not? The Grand had taken her in when she'd needed shelter and it seemed unfair to deny that same shelter to others.

Doctor Campbell might be a gruff Scotsman, but he was no match for Belle, who adopted a manner that suggested she expected to be obeyed in this matter and wasn't going to take no for an answer.

'I don't usually take on travellers as patients,' the man said, white beetle brows lowering over his eyes.

'I'm sure you'll make an exception in this case,' Belle said pleasantly.

He stared at her a bit longer and then gave a reluctant smile. 'Very well, then. I'll see your woman at the end of my rounds. Will you be there?'

'Yes. That is, I hope so. I have another errand to run.'

He gave her a stern look. 'It would be best if you were, Miss Bartholomew.' From which she gathered he may choose not to examine Eadie if she wasn't.

While she was in town, Belle thought she'd visit the General Store. Gwen had developed a liking for Golden Syrup, or Cocky's Delight, as it was popularly known, and they needed another tin. She wheeled her bike to the door and propped it up just outside.

Inside the General Store it was as cool and dim as ever. She noticed among the clutter that there was a sign offering reconditioned tea-leaves for those who could not afford the real thing.

These were actually used tea-leaves that someone had had the foresight to dry out while they still retained some flavour. Belle eyed them, tempted, but then she told herself she hadn't come to that. Not yet.

Looking up, she was expecting to see Flo waiting behind the counter with her ready smile, but instead it was Violet.

She looked thinner, and older. Stanley's death had hit her hard. Rather than feeling the relief of not having to deal with her husband's constant battle with illness, Violet seemed to be missing him terribly. Of course she was. He had come home to her from the war, and she had spent all those years nursing him and keeping him going. It must feel as though it was all in vain.

Belle had gone to the funeral, sitting well back from the family. It had been a sad affair, and there were so many mourners they had spilled out of the door and into the grounds of the church. A very different affair from Rory's funeral. Since then she hadn't seen any of the Davies.

Until today.

'Belle.' Violet's smile was forced, and there was ice in her blue eyes. It was a reminder of how different things had been in the beginning, and Belle wished they could be that way again. She liked Violet, she really did, but she wasn't sure how to mend the situation. In fact, she wasn't even entirely certain what had caused the rift, other than Michael, and if Michael was the problem then apart from reiterating his innocence, she didn't know how to mend that either.

'Frank ordered some cheese from the dairy in Riverton,' Violet had the marble cutting board down and was slicing wedges from a pale, milky wheel. 'Stanley used to love his cheese.'

'Oh, Violet.' Belle took a breath. 'I'm so sorry.'

'He never got over Ted's death, you know. None of us did. If Ted hadn't died like that then I'm sure Stanley would still be with us.'

Stanley had been made ill by mustard gas, not Ted's death, but Belle supposed grief may have played a part. She thought it more likely, though, that Violet was working up to an accusation against Michael and she didn't want to deal with it, not now.

'We all lost people we loved in that war,' she murmured, and waited a beat. 'Violet, could I have a tin of Golden Syrup? I'm sorry to rush, but I need to get back. The doctor will be visiting after his rounds and I have to be there.'

Violet looked up in surprise and with a hint of her old concern. 'Doctor Campbell? Why, what's the matter?'

'There's a woman . . . anyway, she's unwell. She needs the doctor.'

Violet stared at her, and then looked down at the cheese. She cut into the block, slowly. 'Belle, I'm worried about you. When you came back I was so happy and I hoped . . . You remind me so much of Martha and I hoped we could be friends. But then Michael came and now you have those children and a woman who's sick. People don't like it. People talk.' She looked up again, capturing Belle's gaze and holding it. 'Your behaviour isn't helping to endear you to Sweet Wattle Creek.'

'To fit in, do you mean?' Belle tried not to sound hurt or angry. She was aware of how others saw her.

Violet went on. 'Frank says we should give you the benefit of the doubt. Your ways are different to ours, but I say that principles are the same anywhere. Or they should be.' Her mouth tightened with the strength of her belief. 'Martha didn't seem to think the rules applied to her either.'

'Violet,' Belle began, and then didn't know how to go on. Martha was the same? Did she also thumb her nose at convention? Although Belle believed she was simply being compassionate to people who needed help, clearly others saw her actions in a very different light. Maybe if she aligned herself with Constable Nash and went about tearing down shanties and moving people on, then they would all be happy with her?

Violet finished cutting the cheese and began to put it away.

'I'm only helping those less fortune, Violet. I'm sorry if that upsets you. I'm not planning to start my own camp, I assure you.'

'Well, I can see you're different, Belle. I just wish . . . well. I had hoped that you and Frank might . . .' Violet murmured, clearly on her own train of thought. She shook her head. 'But it won't do. You'd only make him miserable and I would never know what you were going to do next. I should've known. I loved Martha, she was my best friend, but she made me so angry sometimes with her waywardness. I never approved of her, not after I knew there was another man who was not her husband. I had Stanley to think of. And then she took in Michael Maxwell. I told her not to, I warned her, but again she wouldn't listen. I don't know why that was. I only ever wanted what was best for her, but Martha always thought she knew best.'

She was rambling but Belle got the gist of it. 'I don't want to quarrel with you. You've been so kind.' She waited a beat. 'Violet, the tin of Golden Syrup . . .?'

Violet didn't respond.

Belle gave up and turned, hurrying through the door. The doctor might be there now, and she had to get back. But there was someone outside and in her hurry she ran straight into them. Her bike went over and Belle with it. Both landed heavily on the footpath. Her elbow struck the hard surface and the pain left her breathless, so for a minute she could barely register what was going on.

'Is she hurt?' Violet's voice sounded anxious, and her big blue eyes were wide as she peered down.

But Belle had had enough of Violet and staggered to her feet. It was Frank she'd run into, of all people, and she pulled away from his helping hand. Shakily, she brushed down her skirt and spoke in a low, angry voice, 'Thank you but I'm perfectly all right.'

Violet and Frank exchanged a glance, but Belle ignored them, bending to lift her bicycle. The wheel was buckled. And there was grease on her skirt. It was one of her better ones, with the pleats, and she brushed at it, wondering if she could wash it out, but only making it worse.

'Blast it!' she whispered.

Violet spoke behind her. 'Let her go,' she said, and there was a note in her voice that told Belle how determined she was not to have her anywhere near her son. 'Frank, let her go.'

'She may be hurt,' Frank retorted.

'I'm not hurt,' Belle said curtly. 'I'm going home.'

'Well you won't be riding on that.' Frank gestured at the damaged wheel. He took the bicycle from her before she could protest and walked away. For the first time she saw the horse standing patiently outside the store, a large bale of straw in the bed of the cart behind it. Frank set the bicycle in the back and held out his hand. 'Come on, then,' he said impatiently. 'Or are you going to walk?'

'Frank.' Violet's voice trembled. 'Please.'

'I'm being a gentleman,' he snapped. 'Isn't that what you and Dad brought me up to be?'

She had no answer to that and Frank reached for Belle's arm, helping her none too gently onto the seat of the cart before climbing up himself. 'I'll be back when I can,' he called over his shoulder to his mother, and shook the reins with a finality Belle had to admire.

Her elbow was aching and she cradled it in her hand. It was just a knock, nothing broken, but as with most bumps to the funny bone it had hurt.

Though not as much as her feelings had been hurt by Violet's words. She looked sideways at Frank, but he was staring ahead under the brim of his hat, his face tense and set.

Belle took a deep breath.

'I should thank you. I didn't mean to be rude.'

'Like my mother, do you mean?' he spoke with resignation. 'Should I apologise for her? What did she say?'

Violet seemed to think that Belle was a bad influence and she didn't want her only surviving son mixed up with her. She could hardly tell him that though.

'Nothing.'

'She isn't herself at the moment. I'm sorry if —'

'You don't have to worry about me.'

'I do worry,' he said. 'Just because you've disregarded my warnings about Michael Maxwell doesn't mean I don't worry about you.'

Belle turned to give him a speculative look. Michael was a touchy subject with the Davies but she wanted to brooch it and this seemed a good time.

'Jo told me that your mother believes Michael let Ted die.'

His eyes narrowed. 'And what do you believe? I suppose he's sworn his innocence to you, has he?'

'I've listened to him, and I believe him. Perhaps Violet has allowed her grief to cloud her judgement.'

He shook his head. 'Do you know what they argued about? What started the fight between them? No,' he said, reading her face, 'I thought not. He couldn't tell you, could he? Because if he did then he'd have to tell you why Ted and he fell out when they were boys.'

Her mouth was dry. She licked her lips, and he watched her do it, avidly. Embarrassed, she turned away. She'd wanted to ask him what he meant but now . . . She sensed Frank's interest in her was more than mere friendly concern—Violet may be right about that—and it seemed important not to encourage him.

'I'll always be grateful to your mother for her help when I first arrived. She was very kind.'

He stared ahead. 'I think she felt she owed it to Martha. She was the last person to see her alive. Evidently, she'd heard that Martha had taken all her personal papers over to Aneas and asked him to put them in his safe. She'd hinted that she didn't trust anyone and my mother wanted to know what it was all about. But when she tried to talk to Martha, they fell out over something. I don't know what it was about but Mum was upset afterwards. When Martha wasn't seen for a week, she got worried and sent me to check on her. That's when I found her dead. Mum's blamed herself ever since. She thinks that if she hadn't left so abruptly Martha would still be alive. Helping you and cleaning up The Grand was her way of making amends, in her own mind anyway. She did it for Martha's sake as much as she did it for yours.'

Belle tried to imagine the two women shout-ing and then Violet following Martha outside, pounding on the door of the shed where she'd barricaded herself inside. It didn't seem to fit, though. They might say bitter words, but they had known each other all their lives, and despite their differences Violet would not have left Martha alone and dying if she'd known her friend was so ill.

They had reached The Grand. Relieved, Belle put a hand on her hat and prepared to jump down to the road. She would say goodbye and thank you, she told herself, and then he would leave.

'Aneas Thomas.'

Was Frank talking about Martha's papers again? On the verge of jumping, Belle turned to him with a puzzled look. 'What about Aneas Thomas?'

Frank tipped his chin and that's when she saw there was a car parked in the shade at the front of the hotel.

'Is that Aneas's car?' she said. 'It isn't the doctor?'

'Doctor?' he said with a sharp glance. 'Are you ill?'

'No, but Eadie is.' As soon as she said it she knew it was going to cause more trouble. Frank would want to know who Eadie was and then he'd tell her what a mistake she was making and then . . . She didn't want to go into it. 'I can't explain now, Frank,' she said hastily, and climbed down. 'I'm very grateful for your help and . . . thank you.'

He wasn't listening to her. He was looking ahead. With an impatient sigh she turned and saw that Aneas must have been waiting for her in the deep shade at the front of the building.

'Miss Bartholomew, there you are!' He sounded

relieved. 'The people inside said you had gone into town and I wasn't quite sure when you'd be back.'

'Hello, Mr Thomas.' She smiled in greeting. She liked Aneas and his presence would help her to send Frank on his way without a squabble.

That's when she saw that Aneas wasn't alone.

There was someone else. Someone in a suit ill-designed for an Indian summer in Sweet Wattle Creek, his face pale and tired from the train journey.

'Hello, Belle,' said Henry. 'I thought if I waited long enough you'd come to your senses. Are you ready to go home yet?'

CHAPTER 30

SOPHIE

Sweet Wattle Creek, 1986

IT SEEMED IMPOSSIBLE that there was only one week to go to the big day—the Centenary of Sweet Wattle Creek.

The anticipation I'd been feeling leading up to the event seemed to have taken a dive. Or maybe it had just dropped down to a faint simmer, like a pot that has gone off the boil. I was tired, and I'd had a cold that had put me in bed for a couple of days. There was so much to do with the *Herald*, and Tim needed me to work longer hours, and . . .

Oh, I had plenty of excuses.

It was true though, that over the past days, there'd been more than enough work at the *Herald* for even the worst of workaholics. With a real-life celebrity coming to boost sales, Tim had pulled out all the stops. As well as the normal day-to-day running of the paper, he'd been working late at night, trying to get Bill Shaw's 'Recollections' ready for publication. As he said, it seemed the perfect time to launch them into the world, and I knew he felt he owed Bill for bequeathing him the business.

I'd reminded him to pass on anything he found about Belle or the wedding dress, but I had my doubts that in his current sleep-deprived state he'd remember.

At least the baby was finally beginning to settle into a routine. Just as well, with Maureen busy too, getting her cafe ready for the influx of tourists. Dillon and I, with help from Christy, had taken on babysitting duties when we could.

My son and Christy seemed to spend a lot of time together doing homework or watching tellie. Dillon said her boyfriend had dumped her and he was standing in until she found another. From the looks I'd caught Christy giving him, I wondered if he really was just a stand-in. Anyway, I had decided I wasn't going to worry.

I was too busy to worry. I'd written the article about the wedding dress, using all we'd found out since the morning the cardboard box appeared on my doorstep. I knew it wasn't the complete story, but we weren't going to discover anything more before deadline.

'This is great!' Tim was very complimentary when he read it. 'You've really tugged my heartstrings. I want to offer it to some of the nationals. What do you say?'

He was grinning. My surprise turned to a sense of pride of a job well done, but a heartbeat later I was in a panic. *What if Walter saw it? What if he came looking for us?* I talked myself down. My name was different. He wouldn't, couldn't know.

'Soph?'

I forced a laugh. 'It's okay. I just . . . thank you, Tim, that would be . . . Do you really think they'll want it?'

His eyebrows rose. 'Want it? Let me see. Young soldier dies on the Western Front and the dress his fiancée was to wear at their wedding, made by a famous couturier, who is also his mother, turns up in a country town, where his fiancée is forced to relocate after her father kills himself during the Depression. Not to mention Miss Gwendolyn South's involvement. I think we're pretty safe they'll want it, Soph.'

I laughed again, properly this time.

'Good publicity for the book,' he added, as he walked away.

I opened my mouth, closed it again. I'd pushed the book idea to the back of my mind. It would never happen, I knew that now. It had only been a fantasy.

Just as Ian had been a fantasy. A very persistent fantasy.

After trying to call me at work, or turning up and being told I was sick—which was true—or I was busy—which was also true but it hadn't stopped me seeing him in the past—I'd hoped he'd get the message. It seemed not.

As I left the *Herald*, still walking on air after Tim's praise, he bailed me up in the street.

'I know what you're doing.' Ian's voice came from behind me. He sounded pissed off and I didn't blame him. I felt as if I'd been wounded, as if my heart had jumped out of its proper place and was flopping about like a landed fish. But

I couldn't dwell on that. So I straightened my shoulders and turned around to face him, telling myself that I had to be cold and heartless, for both our sakes.

Facing him was worse. The fish in my chest gave an almighty shudder. I had to squeeze my hands into fists to stop them reaching up to touch him.

He took a step closer and I swear his aftershave made me dizzy with longing. 'I know what you're doing,' he repeated softly. 'I didn't think you were a coward, Sophie.'

That hurt but I let it go. He didn't understand.

'Do you really believe I would hurt you? I understand there's something . . . someone. I'd be an idiot not to. I didn't say anything, I didn't ask questions, because I hoped there'd come a time when you'd trust me.'

'I don't know what you're talking about,' I said dully, trying not to feel like that spy in a Cold War movie. 'You're wrong, Ian. I just . . . I don't want a relationship. I told you that but you weren't listening.'

His laugh was humourless. 'Fool yourself if you want to,' he said, 'but don't think you can fool me.'

He walked back the way he'd come, and he didn't trip over a single thing, which made my heartache just that much more painful. I took a breath, and then another one, and turned. And very nearly ran into Dillon.

He'd just got off the bus and was still in his uniform, his satchel slung over one shoulder, books dangling precariously. He was watching me, but he looked down as soon as I caught his gaze. Without speaking, we began to walk together towards my office.

I didn't want to talk about it, but I could sense him working up the courage to say his piece. It seemed cruel to cut him short, even when I knew what my answer was going to be.

'Mum, are you sure? He seemed like a nice bloke, you know. He'd probably be okay.' He made an awkward gesture. 'I mean, if you told him about . . .'

'And then what?' I tried to sound calm and knowledgeable, and not like I was about to cry. 'He starts to think we should go after Walter, and not hide. Because hiding is for cowards, right? Or he gets careless and Walter finds out, and then Walter hurts him. And then he hurts you and me.'

Dillon was silent.

'It wouldn't be fair. Ian *is* a nice bloke, and he deserves to find someone without a Walter hanging around their neck. If I'm mean to him now it's going to save us all a lot of heartbreak in the future.'

'If you say so,' he muttered, sounding unconvinced. Maybe a year had been long enough for him to begin to forget what it had been like? Memories blur and fade. That was a good thing, too, as long as he remembered enough not to begin to get complacent. Because Walter was still out there, searching, and I knew it.

I accepted I was grieving for Ian and the relationship we might have had, in an ideal world. He and I together had seemed like a pretty good team as we worked towards our goal. Now, without him, I found I didn't really have the same sense of dedication.

It wasn't until I'd had to break away from him that I'd realised how deeply I'd invested in Ian and the possibilities he represented. I'd thought I was being so careful, so clever, and it was only now I understood how stupidly, how heavily I'd fallen.

'Is this Sophie?'

The voice was familiar, the tone hard, as if I'd done something wrong. At first I struggled to place it. And then I recognised it. Miriam. I put on my business voice, light and upbeat.

'Hi, Miriam. Are you ringing about the wedding dress? I sent you a copy of the article. Thank you so much for the information you supplied. I did a mention for you, and —'

She cut me dead. 'What's going on, Sophie? Ian says you won't talk to him. I don't consider that cool. I'm not often wrong about people and I thought you and he were pretty close, or could be.'

I reminded myself it had taken guts for her to call, even if it was none of her business. 'He had no right to discuss me with you. There are reasons and . . . I'm sorry, Miriam, I can't talk. I can't.' My voice broke and I held my breath, hoping she hadn't noticed.

She had. Or at least she'd noticed something,

because when she spoke again she sounded less aggressive. 'I'm bringing the wedding dress up to Sweet Wattle Creek in the next few days. Can you talk then?'

'It isn't possible, Ian and me. Please don't try to understand, Miriam. I wish I could tell you. I wish . . .'

I hung up, and stared at the wall. That went well, I thought with grim sarcasm. If there was anything designed to draw in a woman like Miriam I had set the trap perfectly. What now? Leave town?

It was an option, but the Centenary was upon us and I couldn't walk out on Tim after all he'd done for me. And why should I run? I would just say 'No', and keep saying it, until they accepted I meant it.

And there was the problem. I felt the shift inside me, the betraying quiver of hope. And I knew then that whatever I was saying on the outside, inside it was a completely different country. Amazing how stupid I could be. How deluded. Because how could everything possibly turn out all right?

It had been a hellish day and I was glad to see home. My legs were aching and I remembered I hadn't been running lately, not since I'd had the cold. I needed to be strong, I knew that, but I seemed to have lost some of my fight. I wanted to curl up into a ball and weep for myself and my lost happiness and all my dreams gone up in smoke.

My misery lifted a little as I reached our gate and I saw Dillon sitting on the front step with Smithy beside him, and Christy leaning against the wall behind him. It looked like a deputation. I even smiled. Like some old Western movie, with the sheriff and his deputy come to make an arrest. Complete with dog.

Smithy bounded up to me and I told him what a fine dog he was, and then he ran back to Dillon and licked his face. Dillon pushed him away, and it was so unlike him that I stopped dead on my way down the path. Christy met my eyes and pulled a face, and it was a warning.

'What is it?' I asked, and the fear in my voice made it tremble.

Dillon reached down and picked up the newspaper that was folded on the step beside him. He held it so tightly that I heard the paper tear, and then he thrust it out to me.

I took it very carefully.

'I'm so sorry, Sophie.' Christy's voice came from far away, chock-full of misery. 'I told Dad not to do it, that you wouldn't like it, but he went ahead anyway.'

I was looking at my face on page four of one of the big national newspapers. It was right beside my story about the wedding dress, about Belle and Charlie. Tim had been true to his word about getting me into the dailies.

'Can you tell ... I mean, does it look like me?' I asked stupidly.

Dillon's expression said it all. The photograph was the one Tim had taken in the office while I was at my desk, catching me by surprise. I'd been positive it would be so bad no one would recognise me, but I'd been wrong. My hair might be dyed blonde instead of brown, but the short cut I'd stuck with as much as possible since I left Brisbane had grown out more than I'd realised, and was beginning to curl in the old way. I'd always loved my curls. I wasn't wearing the closed expression I was used to seeing when I looked in the mirror. The wary look. And my face had begun to fill out again as I regained some lost weight, my cheeks softer and rounder, my lips fuller instead of a hard, straight line. There was no doubting it was me.

I swallowed the fear that was threatening to choke me and shook my head. 'This doesn't mean he'll see it. It doesn't mean he even cares. I'm sure it'll be all right.'

'It's in all the newspapers, Mum. It's in the *Brisbane Courier.*'

Smithy whined and wagged his tail, and even he had a worried expression. I sat down beside Dillon, giving Smithy's ears a pull. I could feel Christy hovering behind me and the fact that she was there, that she knew, was something I didn't want to go into just now. Although I knew I'd have to, and soon, but Christy knowing seemed small fry in the face of this disaster.

'We'll just have to deal with it,' I said firmly, sounding as if I was in complete control. 'If he comes . . . if he threatens us . . . we'll just have to deal with him. We have friends here, Dillon. We're safe here.'

'We thought we were safe in Brisbane but we weren't,' he muttered. His face was tight and angry, and his eyes looked as if he was trying not to cry.

'That was different.'

It sounded lame and he didn't bother to answer.

I sucked in a breath. 'Things are different now, Dillon. What happened before . . . it won't happen again. If he comes then we'll stand up to him.'

'Mum, he's dangerous,' Dillon said, and his voice broke a moment before my heart. 'He'll kill us. He said he would and now he will.'

'You need to call the police,' Christy said, and she was sobbing, her pretty face almost ugly with fear and grief. 'Sophie, you need to call them. Now!'

CHAPTER 31

BELLE

Sweet Wattle Creek, 1931

BELLE MADE TEA. Frank had followed them in, and although she wasn't exactly sure that it was a good idea, she didn't know how to tell him to go in a way that would be both quiet and unobtrusive. Then she decided that he might serve some purpose by staying. His presence would keep Henry at a distance, until they could be alone. Until she could talk to him properly.

And then there was Eadie and the doctor's imminent arrival, and Gwen wagging school. Of all the times for a confrontation, he couldn't have chosen a worse one!

She began to set out plates for the fruit cake Aneas had brought with him. 'Something Lyn thought you might like,' he'd said when he'd handed it over.

Gwen would definitely like this—she was impossible to fill lately. The girl had peeped over the banisters at them but then, clearly not feeling sociable, had vanished again.

Belle thanked Aneas, and told him to pass on her thanks to Lyn. Anything to distract herself from

Henry's silent glowering presence opposite. He didn't belong here at The Grand. He belonged in Melbourne, in Annat Street. In the past.

Guilt had been her companion since she'd made her decision not to marry him. Relief, too. Once she'd chosen her new path she'd felt as if a great weight had been lifted from her. Not because of Henry himself, but because marrying him would be the entirely wrong thing to do. But she couldn't expect him to understand that, and yet she was going to have to try to explain it to him. And soon.

After his words to her outside, Aneas had taken charge, murmuring, 'There'll be time for that later,' and 'Will we go inside?'

'Thank you for sending my things,' she said to Henry as she poured. They had been a month late but now was not the time to quibble, although perhaps he thought she was thinking it. His tone was defensive.

'I've been rather busy.'

'I'm glad. I mean, that you have lots of work.' She hesitated, not wanting to open the subject, and then doing so anyway. 'The house?'

'Sold,' Henry said bluntly. 'The bank took the proceeds.'

She'd known there was only one answer to her question but still it hurt.

'There are papers to sign.' He shot a glance at Frank, as if he wasn't quite sure who he was and what he was doing here, even though Aneas had introduced them. 'I'm staying overnight with Mr Thomas and his sister-in-law. We thought you could come by this evening, and we could talk then. About . . .' He lifted a hand, let it drop. 'Things.'

'Yes. Of course.' She was relieved. Henry would have planned this, he never did anything without a plan, and he wouldn't want to make a scene. Surely he hadn't changed that much?

Aneas reached for a slice of cake and set it on the flowery plate. Frank stirred milk into his tea. There was a glint in his eye that told her he was amused by the situation.

Belle bit her lip. She should be glad someone was getting enjoyment out of this awful state of affairs, but she was too closely involved to feel any herself.

Henry certainly wasn't amused. He sat with his back very straight, his gaze darting around the room. She'd noticed him looking as they'd walked through the building from the front door, and knew he was assessing how much the property was worth. Belle no longer thought of The Grand in terms of pounds and shillings. It was her home. It was a roof over her head. And the heads of Michael, Mo and Eadie, Tilly and Gwen.

'Huhmm,' Aneas cleared his throat. 'Tell me, Frank, how's Violet? Holding up?'

'She's as well as can be expected, Aneas.'

'And Jo?'

'Busy with the school. She has all ages this year, from four to fourteen. She sees it as a challenge. If they learn at least one thing a day then she says she'll be happy.'

The knock at the back door startled them.

'Miss Bartholomew?' Doctor Campbell had one of those naturally loud voices.

'Doctor, thank you for coming.' She got to her feet, just as he stepped from the sunshine into the shadow. Belle saw the surprise on his face when he realised she had guests.

'My goodness, what a gathering. Aneas! Well, well. And Frank. And . . .?'

'Mr Collier,' Belle said, 'from Melbourne.'

'Oh aye.' He shook Henry's hand briefly, before turning back to Belle. 'And my patient?'

'This way.' She led him out of the kitchen and he followed her, the stairs creaking under their combined weight.

'Quite like the old days,' he was saying. 'Men with their feet under the kitchen table and Martha making them tea.'

'You knew my . . . you knew Martha?' But of course he did. What was she thinking? He'd been her doctor, and he had seen her dead body, after Frank had found her.

'Oh aye, verra well. Martha always had her admirers. Not that she thought of them like that. Never seemed to play favourites. But all the same, admirers they were.'

Belle opened her mouth to protest but he caught her eye and winked. 'Nothing wrong with a woman having admirers,' he said with heavy-handed humour. 'She had her enemies. Gossip is a terrible thing,' he went on, growing serious. 'Friends fall out over it. That's what happened with Martha and Violet. They were the best of friends when they were young girls.'

'I know they were friends,' Belle said faintly, wondering where he was going with this.

'Oh yes.' Doctor Campbell seemed keen to enlighten her. 'You see, Violet had a soft spot for Rory. I think she would've married him, but she was engaged to Stanley Davies. Stanley found out and they fought over her. Blood was spilt, as they say. Rory lost and left town, and Violet married the victor. But I think she always dreamed that perhaps she might've had Rory. And who knows, perhaps she would have, if Martha hadn't told Stanley.'

'Why would she do that?' Belle cried. Rory and Violet? Martha whispering in Stanley's ear, causing the fight? She tried to picture Rory and Stan, fists raised, but couldn't. She imagined them rolling on the ground like dogs in the dust, growling and snapping, and now she could. She didn't know what to make of it.

'Rory was a bit of a tearaway. Martha believed he'd ruin Violet's life and then leave her. She knew her brother too well and she was protecting her friend. I take it Rory did settle down eventually?'

'Yes, yes, he and Iris were very happy together.'

Strange to think that if Violet had had her way, Rory would never have left Sweet Wattle Creek. Did Violet think of him, and what might have been? When Stanley came home, sick and an invalid, perhaps she began to doubt whether she had made the right choice. She might think that Martha had spoiled her chance of a happy life.

Was that what their quarrel had been about the day Violet stormed out and Martha died?

They'd reached the bedroom and she opened the door.

The room had a faint odour of vomit and illness, but the basin by the bed was emptied and washed. Mo was dozing in a chair by the bed and Eadie was lying in it, curled up and apparently asleep. Her face looked flushed and hot.

'Well, now.' Doctor Campbell set down his bag. 'Let's have a look at you.'

Mo woke up with a grunt, confused. Eadie opened her eyes and tried to push herself up against the pillows, but it hurt too much and she subsided with a groan.

'She's no better, Belle,' Mo said, rising awkwardly to his feet. 'I've never seen her like this. The pain just won't go away.'

The examination that followed was brief. 'You were right to call on me, Miss Bartholomew,' the doctor said, arching a woolly eyebrow. 'She has appendicitis. It may even have ruptured. We need to get her into hospital as soon as we can. If you'll go and fetch some of those strong gentlemen downstairs, they can help carry her to the car.'

Frank was soon lifting the ailing woman, and, with Mo hurrying behind, bearing her down the stairs and out to the doctor's car. He'd decided it would be quicker than the ambulance, which had to come from Riverton anyway.

Belle managed a word with him before he followed. 'Will she be all right, Doctor?'

'I don't know. She may die.' He saw the consternation in her face, and added, 'I thought you'd want the truth without sugar-coating?'

'Yes, of course.'

He nodded at her approvingly. 'Martha was the same.'

Doctor Campbell was soon on his way, with Eadie and Mo in the back, and Belle stood watching the dust from the departing car. When she returned to the kitchen, Gwen was by the back door, feeding Nellie pieces of cake, and listening to something Frank was saying, as he stood there smoking.

'More tea?' she asked Henry and Aneas. It felt strange to be sitting down, drinking and eating and making conversation when Eadie might die. She wanted to go outside to Gwen and give her a hug and tell her not to worry. Gwen would know the truth though. She'd probably been eavesdropping on the stairs.

'Is it true you've taken on this girl and her sister?' Henry said with a nod towards the yard, his voice lowered but not nearly enough. 'And that woman the doctor took away, and the man as well?' Wearily, she recognised the note of disapproval in his voice.

'That's right.'

'Belle, they're not your concern.'

'Of course they are!' she retorted, exasperated.

But Henry wasn't listening. 'Aneas says that people in Sweet Wattle Creek don't trust these strangers. Travellers, is that right? They don't want them here. You shouldn't be getting involved, Belle. Besides, you have your financial situation to think of. You have no money, Belle. You've rushed into this thing. I know that's difficult for you to understand, you've never had to worry before, but you need to be very economical if you are to survive. Can't you see that I'm here to help you and —'

Aneas was looking uncomfortable. 'Perhaps we can discuss all of this tonight, Henry?'

Henry looked as if he wanted to discuss it now, but that would be impolite and Henry, who prided himself on his good manners, swallowed down his words. 'Very well.' He stood up and moved as if to kiss her cheek, but she stepped away, angry with him and not wanting him to, and there was another awkward moment. At last the two men turned to leave, and she followed them down to the front door and watched them climb into Aneas's car and drive away.

She didn't think Henry looked happy. When she'd decided to break off the engagement she hadn't really thought about him, she admitted to herself. What if he refused to go quietly? Henry was a pragmatic man who hated scenes, but he was still flesh and blood. If he was being unpleasant to her then it was to punish her for hurting him, and she could hardly blame him for that.

She had Michael and he had no one.

The memory of their night together, the warmth of his body next to hers, the low timbre of his voice as he spoke in the darkness, telling her everything and nothing. The ache of possession and the pleasure afterwards.

Yes, she thought, whatever Henry said tonight, she would accept it without argument. She would be chastened and she might even weep—it would not be difficult to cry in the circumstances. It was the least she could do.

She closed the door and turned. Frank was standing behind her.

'Sorry,' he said, and reached out to steady her, taking her arm. The day had been an emotional one and she felt raw. She didn't want to argue with him. She opened her mouth to tell him so, but before she could, he'd pulled her against him, his mouth coming down roughly on hers.

Surprise held her still. In another moment she would have struggled and pushed him away.

'Stop it!'

The voice wasn't hers and yet those were the words she'd been about to say. Belle stumbled back, holding a hand to her mouth, which felt bruised.

Gwen, furious, hands clenched and face red, was yelling, 'Stop it! Belle, you shouldn't be kissing him. You shouldn't. You belong to Michael!'

They all stood there, shocked, but before anyone could speak or move, Gwen spun around and fled.

CHAPTER 32

SOPHIE

Sweet Wattle Creek, 1986

THE SERGEANT WAS waiting for us at Riverton police station. I sat beside Tim in an interview room and answered questions. When I'd first rung the station I had to face a lot of scepticism, but then gradually the tone had changed. They'd left me hanging while they put a call through to Brisbane and the officer who had been my contact there. After that things moved swiftly. By the time we were seated in front of the sergeant, there no longer seemed to be any doubt in his mind that I was who I said I was. And I was telling the truth.

As for what he could do to help me, well, that was another matter. Tim, who wanted immediate action and plenty of it, was clearly frustrated by the slow-moving wheels of protocol. But this was an officer of the old school—cautious and guarded—and he wanted to be sure about everything before he acted. The trouble was, Walter was more your slash-and-burn type of offender, and he wouldn't be ticking off a check list before he arrived.

He could already be here.

'The Brisbane detectives are currently investigating your husband's movements.'

'Ex-husband.'

'They'll get back to me when they know. You can be sure they're . . . *we're* all taking this matter very seriously, Miss Matheson.' He paused and cocked an eyebrow at me. 'You are going by that name?'

'Yes. I think it's less confusing for now.' Besides, I'd grown quite used to it. Sophie Matheson suited me, the new me. I just hoped the Sophie persona was luckier than the previous one.

The sergeant hadn't finished. 'In the meantime, Sophie, I need you to be very careful. I want you to stay among friends. Don't go off on your own. And if something is worrying you, anything, or if you think there might be a problem, don't wait. Ring me straightaway.'

'Of course. Thank you.'

'Shouldn't you put someone on her, to guard her? Or better still, put her into protective custody?' Tim sounded belligerent, but I knew that he and the sergeant didn't get on.

'You've been watching too many cop shows,' the sergeant said with a smirk. 'This isn't New York, Mr Shaw. We don't have a lot of safe houses here. And we don't have anyone spare to follow Miss Matheson around all day. The Centenary in Sweet Wattle Creek is taking all our resources— we've called in extra men as it is. Let's wait until we know where Sophie's ex-husband is before we start to go overboard. For all we know, he could be sunning himself on the Gold Coast.'

Tim was still furious as we left the building. I tried to calm him down, to explain.

'They can't stop him, Tim. They never could. They can try, and they did try, but if Walter is determined then he'll run rings around them. That's why Dillon and I went into hiding.'

He looked at me. I could see the anger and frustration in his face. He was behaving like a typical man, wanting to do something, to fix it, to make it better. I was grateful, but him getting arrested wasn't going to help matters.

'I know,' he sighed, suddenly deflating. 'I know. I'm sorry. This is my fault. I thought I was doing you a favour and instead I was putting your life in jeopardy.'

'*I'm* sorry, Tim. I should've told you. I should've trusted you. Only . . .'

'Only you couldn't,' he finished for me, managing a sort of smile. 'Make a great story for the *Herald*. When it's sorted, I mean,' he added hastily, when he saw the look on my face.

I wanted to hit him, but instead I laughed. 'Or a book? That's two books I'm going to write.'

'Two? Oh, the wedding dress. Have you seen it since it was refurbished? Or whatever it is they do to distressed vintage clothing.'

'No, I haven't seen it.' Or Miriam, although I expected she wouldn't hold back next time we came face to face. 'But she promised to have it up here in time for tomorrow's opening.'

He checked his watch. 'I have to get back. I'm putting the finishing touches to the magazine for tomorrow's edition. Centenary Day at last!'

The old presses at the *Herald* wouldn't be able to handle the sort of state-of-the-art printing Tim was planning, so he had arranged with the printers in Riverton to run off the magazine for him. It was going to cost an arm and a leg, but he believed it would be worth it. He was expecting to still make a profit.

'Thank you for coming with me, Tim.' His presence had meant a great deal to me, despite debating a couple of times whether he might punch the sergeant in the nose. Last time, in Brisbane, I went through the whole thing alone, apart from Dillon, although I'd tried my best to keep him out of the worst of it.

'No problem.' He shot me a sideways look that was an odd mixture of guilt and anticipation. 'Soph, I've asked someone to pick you up and take you back to Sweet Wattle Creek.'

Someone? He nodded across the road and the fish that was my heart, which I'd thought was dead, gave a bit of a flutter. 'Tim . . .'

'Now don't worry. It'll be fine.' Tim gave my arm a firm squeeze and then he was gone.

The three of them were sitting at one of the cafe-style tables in front of the newsagent. Dillon and Christy had ice creams, but Ian had his arms folded and was frowning into space. I wondered what he was thinking, how he was feeling. He hated me, probably. I wouldn't blame him. And yet I didn't want him to hate me, I really didn't.

I took a deep breath and crossed the road.

He looked up and when he saw me he jumped

to his feet.

'Aren't you busy?' I asked him, my voice a little high. 'Tomorrow's show time.'

'Everything's under control,' he assured me, but I noticed his eyes looking me up and down, as if checking for damage. 'Anyway, some things are more important, despite what the Centenary committee says. I think you deserve priority.'

That was nice. I gave him a wobbly smile. Dillon and Christy had given us time alone, which was very sensitive of them, but now they came up. Something nudged my leg and Smithy appeared from under the table. As I bent to ruffle his ears I saw that he had some cream around his muzzle. Did dogs eat ice cream? I wouldn't have thought so, but evidently Smithy didn't know that.

I hadn't said much between seeing the newspaper photograph and calling the police. There'd been the trip into Riverton in Tim's car, and his questions, and his shocked expression. I hadn't had time to talk properly to Dillon or Christy. Obviously, though, they had been discussing matters among themselves, and with Ian.

Now I opened my mouth to explain, to apologise, but he shook his head.

'You don't have to say anything,' he said quietly. 'Not now.'

Tears stung my eyes. I hadn't cried for a long time, and I didn't want to start now. I had a lot to get through and it wasn't the time to cry. Not yet.

'Mum,' Dillon put an arm around me, and Christy followed suit. 'Sorry, Soph,' she murmured. 'I should've told Dad, but I didn't expect him to do something so stupid. I *think* he was trying to be nice,' she added, pulling a face that seemed to be asking my forgiveness.

'It was no one's fault,' I said firmly, hugging them back. 'Or maybe it was Walter's.'

Dillon and Christy exchanged a glance. 'We'll get Smithy some water and take him for a walk in the Botanical Gardens,' my son said with admirable maturity. 'Come and get us when you're ready.' He went to go and then paused, straightening his shoulders as he turned back. 'Mum, you're not angry with me, are you? For telling Christy?'

I shook my head. 'No, love, I'm not angry.'

'I just couldn't hold it in anymore, and it seemed ... sometimes it seemed like a dream, even though I knew it was real, and telling her didn't seem so bad. I know it was. I know I shouldn't have, but —'

'It's fine, Dillon. I think you did the right thing. Whatever happens, well, we'll work it out. I think we can now. We're strong. Aren't we?'

He nodded, but there was a flicker of doubt in his eyes as he left. I didn't blame him. I really hoped Walter was still in Brisbane, oblivious to us and Sweet Wattle Creek, but I had an awful feeling that our luck had finally run out.

Ian took my hand, breaking into my grim thoughts. He was searching my face, probably contemplating if I was going to tell him to go away again, and I managed a smile.

'Sorry,' I said, meeting his eyes. 'I know it doesn't help, but I didn't want you caught up in all of this. It didn't seem fair, when you didn't know the whole story and I couldn't tell you.'

'Sophie, I said I understood and you didn't need to explain anything.'

'Well I do need to. I want to. Better late than never.'

It occurred to me that maybe he was just being kind to me and that he had no intention of taking up where we left off. That was fine, I told myself bravely. I would accept that. I understood completely why someone wouldn't want to get involved with a woman with a violent psychopath for a husband. My own personal Freddy Krueger, except this wasn't a horror fantasy.

Maybe my face showed what I was feeling, because Ian's hand tightened on mine. 'Come for a walk,' he said. 'The Riverton Settlers Museum is open and they make a damn fine coffee.'

I laughed, but my throat had that lump in it again. 'I could do with a coffee,' I said, and let him lead me into the building, once a hotel and now a musty, crowded receptacle for Riverton's past. Only Ian would think this a comforting place for a traumatised person, but in my case he was perfectly right. I did feel calmer. Or maybe that was just because he was with me.

The cafe was empty apart from us, and we sat in an area at the back, in front of a large blown-up photo of a stump-jump plough.

I wanted to tell him, and yet I didn't. It was nice just sitting here with him, knowing he didn't hate me. But I took a deep breath and began, and it was actually quite easy once I'd started. The words spilled out of me, and I imagined this was what had happened to Dillon when he'd told Christy. I felt as if I'd been a prisoner of Walter, even when I thought I'd escaped, but with the telling of the truth I was set free.

When I finished he was quiet. He looked white and he was clenching his hands around his mug, the coffee cold by now. 'Sophie,' he said at last, 'I'm so sorry this has happened to you. Now. When you thought you were safe.'

'I don't know,' I murmured, shaking my head. 'Maybe I was kidding myself thinking we could hide here forever.'

'Do you think . . .' He looked up at me. 'Do you think you'll leave again? Go somewhere else, find a new name?'

I hadn't thought of it, I realised in surprise. Before it would have been the first thing I did, making new plans, getting ready to run and hide, but I hadn't even thought of it.

'No. I think the time for running is over. I don't want to anyway.'

His mouth curled up. 'You're amazing, you know. Sophie, you're the bravest person I know.'

I hadn't expected him to say that, and I certainly wasn't sure I deserved it. All the same, tears slid down my cheeks and this time I didn't try to hold them back. He reached out and pulled me to him and I pressed my face into his neck, where it was warm and smelt of Ian, and I wept for some time.

Afterwards, I tidied myself up in the bathroom and we went down to the gardens. I could see Dillon throwing a ball for Smithy, and Christy laughing and clapping her hands. They looked like any ordinary family. I suppose we did, too, Ian and I. The fact that we weren't was frightening, and I didn't know how I was going to live the rest of my life if something couldn't be done about Walter.

I told myself I wasn't going to think about it. Not now. This moment was for us, and when Ian slipped an arm about my waist and pulled me closer, I snuggled against him.

'At least you can write that book now,' he murmured against my hair.

'Yes. I suppose I can.'

'Miriam brought up the wedding dress this morning,' he said. 'She's staying for the Centenary tomorrow. She seems to think she can persuade you to give me another try. What do you think?'

I leaned back to look at him, a long look that said things I had yet to say. 'I think she might be right.'

CHAPTER 33

BELLE

Sweet Wattle Creek, 1931

AFTER THE SCENE in the hallway, Frank reached for her again and she pushed him away, hard. He stood staring at her as if he didn't want to believe she wouldn't change her mind, even though it must be clear to him that she had no interest in him. He looked angry and upset, but she didn't feel sorry for him. She'd never asked for his attentions. When he left, Belle looked for Gwen but she couldn't find her. She suspected that she was at the Beauchamp house with her friend, Jane, and Belle considered going over there and fetching her home. But on second thoughts it seemed best to leave her be. Surely there was enough turmoil without dragging an unwilling ten-year-old back along the dusty track? Probably screaming all the way, if she knew Gwen.

She did find Bucket, though. The little dog was in Eadie and Mo's room, hiding under the bed, and when Belle had coaxed him out, she carried him down to the kitchen. She found some rabbit stew and ladled it into a dish, and couldn't help smiling as the dog lapped it up.

The memory of that earlier scene made her uncomfortable. Frank grabbing her like that, and Gwen so angry. Belle wasn't sure what she was going to say to Gwen when she did come home. Obviously, the girl had got it into her head that Michael and Belle were going to get married and live happily ever after with the two sisters.

Belle didn't know if that would happen. She hadn't set her heart on anything. At thirty, she felt as if she had more sense than to believe in fairy-tales, and although she thought she might be in love with Michael, she didn't know how he felt, not really. Anyway, there were still questions to be asked and answered before she could believe in happy ever after.

Bucket had finished and was staring up at her, wagging his tail. She sat down and tapped her knee and up he came, turning around and around until he was comfortable, then flopping down with a deep sigh.

Belle stroked the warm little body and knew she had to put Frank out of her mind, and Gwen. And Michael. She must face Henry tonight, and it was only fair she give him her full attention.

Tilly was home early, shadows under her eyes, and her fingers as ink-stained as Bill Shaw's. He worked her hard, but Belle knew how much Tilly enjoyed her job. She was far more serious than her sister, and since she'd been at the *Herald*, she'd grown up a great deal.

Her face lit up when she saw Bucket, and Belle was happy to hand him over, watching while Tilly stroked him and talked nonsense to him.

'Poor Eadie,' she said, when Belle explained what had happened. 'Do you know, I saw some more travellers today. They were sitting in the park, by the creek. I tried not to look at them.' She gave Belle a glance up through her lashes, and it was clear she felt guilty. 'I'm sorry for them, but I don't want them here. Michael's right. We don't know anything about them, do we?'

'I didn't know anything about you either,' Belle reminded her.

Tilly pulled a face, as if that wasn't the same thing at all.

At four o'clock, just as she was about to get ready for her evening with Henry at the Thomases'—Aneas was collecting her at five—Doctor Campbell arrived. He wanted to let her know that Eadie had been operated on soon after she arrived at the hospital and was resting comfortably. In the circumstances the Riverton hospital committee had agreed to accept her as a charity case, and Mo was spending the night in town at a lodging house the doctor had recommended. 'You did the right thing, Miss Bartholomew. Any longer and the woman would've died.'

'That was your doing, Doctor,' Belle said, relieved to hear Eadie would recover.

He turned to go, but there was something she wanted to ask him, so she walked with him to the front door.

'Doctor Campbell, my mother . . . Martha. You saw her, didn't you, after she died?'

He gave her a sideways look and then stopped. 'You want to know about that, do you? Well, there's not much I can say. In my opinion it was her heart. She'd been having fainting spells in the months before, and I'd warned her: no excitement.'

'But she was locked in the shed in the stable yard. She was hiding in there. Could someone have frightened her so much that her heart stopped?'

He frowned, and she thought she'd gone too far. Doctor Campbell might be a gossip, but he was a professional with a reputation to consider.

'I suppose that's possible, but why would they do that? No, I canna say, Miss Bartholomew. I'm a mere doctor. It's a detective you're after there.'

At five o'clock Aneas arrived as promised to collect Belle. It was still warm, the air with a breathless feel. Bucket was stretched out in the kitchen doorway, catching whatever breeze there was. But there was a storm coming, she knew it.

Belle had just had time to quickly splash water onto her face, before she changed into an elegant green summer dress with a high collar and a narrow white belt. It seemed to strike a nice balance between formal and the constraints of the hot weather. A comb through her hair, no time to curl it, and a dash of powder and lipstick on her face.

Her blue eyes stared back at her from the mirror, and she touched the scar with her fingertip, smoothing it back and forth. It seemed she was no closer to solving the mysteries she had come to Sweet Wattle Creek to solve than she'd been the first day she stepped off the train.

But that wasn't true. It was just that the questions had changed, and she was sure that the answers were still out there. Somewhere. And one day she would find them.

The Thomas house was on the far side of town, large and sprawling and full of furnishings that hinted at a family that had once been quite well-to-do. Things had become rather shabby now, though—there was an air of fading grandeur about the place. The smell of food cooking greeted them at the door, and although it was stifling outside, inside the high ceilings and long central throughway made it much cooler.

'Belle,' Lyn said, and if her smile wasn't brimming with warmth at least it was welcoming. She was dressed in a loose cream frock with a starburst pattern, a string of pearls about her throat, and her greying hair was held back with clips. The heat had leached her face of colour and she wasn't wearing any makeup. 'Henry's in the sitting room. I thought perhaps we could have drinks in there. Before we eat.'

'Lyn, I think they want some time alone,' Aneas interjected, his tone unusually testy.

Lyn looked at him in surprise, and with a little hurt.

'I do need to talk to Henry,' Belle agreed. 'If you don't mind, Mrs Thomas?'

'Well of course not.' Lyn waved a hand dramatically. 'Talk all you like. *I* won't interrupt you.'

Aneas looked as if he was fighting the urge to tell his sister-in-law what he really thought, and then he seemed to recover himself. Belle could imagine them sitting at opposite ends of the house, Aneas with a book and Lyn listening to the wireless. It was a strange situation, but she supposed no stranger than hers. This was the world after the war to end all wars, where so many people lived in the past and made do with the present.

He nodded towards a doorway. 'That's the sitting room, Belle. Take your time.'

'Thank you,' she murmured, taking a deep breath before she headed towards it and entered.

Henry was seated on a leather armchair, pretending to read the local newspaper. Or perhaps he *was* reading it, she thought, as she stood watching him. For a brief moment she imagined they had married, and every night she would come into their sitting room and find him thus. She knew then, if she had not known before, that this was not the life or the man she wanted.

'Henry?'

He started. 'Belle!' Setting aside the paper, he stood up.

She came across the room to him and stretched up to kiss his cheek. She'd regretted pulling away earlier and this seemed a good way to show him she was not intending to be stand-offish. For both their sakes they must meet halfway to air their feelings and their grievances. As long as he didn't think she was coming back with him, because she wasn't.

'Henry . . .'

But he cut her off. 'First I want to talk to you about your circumstances.' He looked as if he had worked himself up and was intent on getting this off his chest. 'If you won't listen to sense from anyone else then perhaps you'll listen to it from me. Belle,' he went on with an edge to his voice, 'you've led a sheltered life. You've never had to take care of yourself. Rory was there to protect you, and then I hoped it would be me. You aren't used to people . . . certain types of people. They'll take advantage of you.'

'Henry —'

'No, let me finish. We can still get married. This has been nothing but a hiccup and you can come back with me tomorrow. You can put all of this behind you and we'll never speak of it again.'

Belle sat listening until she could listen no longer. When he began telling her how much she meant to him, she put a stop to it.

'Henry, please listen. I'm not going to marry you. I should never have said I would. It was a mistake, and I accept responsibility for it.'

He stared at her, his frustration evident. 'But why not?' he demanded, dropping his voice, because even in this moment of high emotion he was fearful they'd be overheard, that there might be a scene witnessed by others. 'Make me understand why I'm no longer good enough for you,

Belle!'

Belle sank further down on the chair opposite him. He also sat down, leaning forward to see her face, crowding her so she wanted to push him away.

'Is there someone else?' he demanded when she didn't answer. 'That pilot chap Lyn was talking about. Michael Maxwell?'

She shook her head. 'Henry, you have to accept I made this decision on my own, not because there's anyone else.' Michael was not the reason for breaking off their engagement—she wasn't going to complicate matters by mentioning how she felt about him.

'Then what?' he challenged, and she could see hurt and bewilderment in his eyes.

'I wanted to marry Charlie, so much. But I agreed to wait. It was sensible . . . to wait. And then he died. I . . . I went into myself. I didn't want to face the world. I felt as if there was no point in living, but I had to keep getting up, day after day. My father and mother, they needed me. So I locked Belle away, the Belle I was when Charlie was alive. I put her high on a shelf somewhere and let the dust settle on her, and that was the only way I could go on.

'When I agreed to marry you, Henry, I did it because I knew you would look after me and keep me from having to face a world I was no longer sure I wanted to face. But then my father, then Rory died, and I knew I couldn't be that person anymore. I had to reach up onto the shelf and find myself. I had to be that Belle again. It was painful, but I had to do it. And then, coming to The Grand, I began to see more clearly the person I had become when Charlie died, and I knew it was wrong. I had to be brave enough to live again, even if it hurt.'

'Charlie, always Charlie. I'm beginning to think you prefer a dead man,' he said with derision.

'No. I can't bring Charlie back, and who knows what things would've been like if he'd survived the war. Perhaps . . . perhaps we would've been miserable. No, it isn't because I prefer a dead man to you. This is about me. The person I was and the person I want to be again.'

He didn't seem to understand, or perhaps he didn't want to. Belle sighed. 'You've been a good friend to me and my family. In that way I love you and will always love you, but I can't marry you. I can't be the wife you want.'

He reached down and she saw he had his brief-case there beside his chair. Well, naturally he did. Now he opened it and withdrew some papers. 'You need to sign these,' he said, and retreated into his role of her solicitor. 'They're to do with the house.'

'Of course.' She barely read the pages before setting her signature to them. He took them, giving her a wry look. 'What?'

'I could've put anything in front of you, Belle.'

'I knew you wouldn't. I'm sorry, Henry. Really I am. It'd be simple to push all my doubts away and marry you, but we'd be wretched. I'd end up hating you, and probably leaving you. And I couldn't do that, not to you.'

Henry shook his head as if he didn't believe her, or didn't want to. He began to say something about Annat Street, but she didn't hear. Belle was looking past him at the painting on the wall. It was set in a gold frame and it hung in pride of place above the fireplace. There was an arrangement of flowers beneath it that had the look of a wreath.

But that wasn't what she was looking at. It was the subject matter—Reims Cathedral under a lowering sky, its bombed walls raised like begging arms to the heavens. The sketch from Martha's bag had been almost identical, but this was the finished work.

'What's that?' she said, her voice strange.

Henry frowned and turned to follow her gaze. 'The painting? I think Aneas said it was done by his brother, Alister. Rather good, isn't it? Evidently he was quite an artist. He was killed in the, eh, in the war. Why?'

Belle's lips were trembling. Her mind had become startlingly clear and sharp. Unexpectedly, everything made sense, and after all the shadowy speculation, the truth had a blinding intensity to it that made her want to close her eyes.

'Because,' she said, 'I believe that was painted by my father.'

CHAPTER 34

SOPHIE

Sweet Wattle Creek, 1986

'DA-DAH ... HERE it is!'

Miriam sounded pleased with herself and I thought she had a right to be. The wedding dress was beautiful. Well, to me it always had been, but now it had been brought back to life.

Miriam had cleaned it and replaced the worst of the damaged materials. There was still a bit of wear and tear, but I thought that was okay. It was an old garment and it had history, we didn't want to forget that. The pearls were all neatly sewn back onto the bodice, and the diamantes glistened from the folds of lace. The long train was no longer tatty and grubby, but curved around the dress in a protective circle, its edging of tulle crisp.

I tried to imagine Belle wearing it. Belle, a woman I'd never met or seen, but who I thought I knew.

'Well, what do you think?'

I realised Miriam had been waiting for compliments and I'd been struck dumb. I turned to her and I think the tears in my eyes were compliment enough. She gave me a beaming smile.

They—that is the committee—had decided the wedding dress should be displayed in the library where they could keep a close eye on it. Nola had arranged for a suitable glass case to be brought in, and a mannequin, one of those blank-faced ones, without the strange smile. Miriam had arranged the dress to her satisfaction and now the whole thing was behind the glass, safe from sticky fingers.

'There's something I didn't tell you,' I said, looking at Ian.'When we found Jo Davies unconscious that day at Morwenstow, and you went to phone the ambulance . . . I was sitting beside her and she woke up. Just for a minute. And she called me Belle.'

Ian stared at me.'Did she?'

'It was so strange. I didn't know what to think, and then I suppose I told myself she was probably hallucinating. Do you think Belle might've looked a bit like me? I mean, with blonde hair and blue eyes? Maybe poor Mrs Davies saw a woman bending over her with blonde hair and slipped back into the past.'

'It's possible, I suppose . . .'

'Is she still in hospital in Melbourne?' Miriam asked.

'Yes. As far as I know,' Ian answered her, but he was looking at me.'I'll take some photographs of the dress in case she wakes up.'

'Good idea,' Miriam murmured, and with a glance between the two of us, moved discreetly away.

Ian had already told her about me, about Walter, and about us. She'd given me a big hug when she first saw me. 'I'm sorry I gave you a hard time the other day,' she'd said.

'You didn't know. I'm sorry I didn't tell you what was going on.' I was sorry for a lot of things by then.

'What will you do?' she'd asked.

Of course I told her I'd be all right, that we didn't even know if Walter was still a threat, blah blah, but I think she appreciated I was diverting her from what was probably the truth. That he was still very much a threat and he might already be here in Sweet Wattle Creek.

I was still staring at the wedding dress in its glass case when Ian put his arm around me and gave me a squeeze. 'People are going to love this,' he said, nodding at the display. 'We've had requests for interviews from all over the world. Walter would have to be an idiot to think he could creep in here with all of that going on.'

The trouble with that theory was Walter didn't give a damn about what other people might or might not think. And the more difficult the task the more he would like it. He'd see it as a challenge.

'Sorry.' I rested my cheek against his chest and sighed. It was nice listening to his heart beating. 'I'm not very good company right now. I should go home and check on Dillon and Christy anyway.'

'I'll come with you,' Ian said.

'No, stay here. You have so much to do.'

'I've done everything I need to do. And if I haven't then it's too late now. Miriam,' he called out. 'I'm just going to take Sophie home to check on her son. Will you be okay here?'

Miriam barely looked up from the book she was reading. 'Sure. Fine. See you later.'

He rolled his eyes at me, and led the way out of the library. The weather was still hot, and promised to be the same over the weekend of celebrations. I told myself that at least we didn't have to worry about rain. Tomorrow was the official opening and tomorrow night was the costume ball. After that there would be displays and a parade and stalls. There'd be a special place put aside for children to be entertained, and marquees for those who liked their beer cold. Really, a mind-boggling amount of good things put on by the people of Sweet Wattle Creek.

He reached for my hand and I let him have it, giving him a smile. It was just so wonderful to be able to be open with Ian, not to have to watch my every word and pretend. Despite my anxiety over Walter, there was a definite upside to breaking cover.

Tim arrived at the house at the same time as us. 'I've just come to rope in Dillon and Christy to help me get the special edition of the paper out to the shops,' he said. 'Brad and Ellie are holding the fort. The magazine should be inside each newspaper, but I haven't had time to do it. I seem to have fallen behind.'

He looked exhausted but at least he was smiling.

'It all looks fantastic,' I assured him. 'Do you want me to help?'

He glanced at Ian and then shook his head. 'Nah, you take it easy. You've done your bit. The story about the dress was a huge plus, Soph. And you have to interview Gwendolyn South tomorrow, remember.'

'Can't wait.' I was sincere about that. Meeting and interviewing the actress would be a tremendous experience, and I couldn't wait to hear what she had to say about Eileen Nicholson and Sweet Wattle Creek. I'd done some research on her life, but she seemed very reticent when it came to her early years. I knew the signs of a mystery just waiting to be uncovered.

Dillon and Christy were rounded up. Dillon gave me a hug—he'd been doing that a bit lately. Smithy hadn't been invited but it didn't seem to occur to him that he wouldn't be welcome. He jumped into the car and made himself comfortable on the back seat, which had us all laughing. Just as they were going, Christy called out to me.

'I made you a costume for the ball tomorrow! Wait and see. You'll love it.'

'A costume?' Ian said, when they'd gone.

'Christy's a bit of a creative wiz,' I informed him. 'She does fashion design at school. It's probably very avant-garde.'

'Hmm, maybe I should wear the red braces after all,' he said, making me smile.

Inside, Black Cat was sitting alone and regal on the kitchen bench, pretending he didn't care that Smithy had been allowed to go and he had to stay. I gave him a pat as I put on the electric jug and set out the mugs for coffee. Maureen had sent over some hummingbird cake and since Dillon hadn't eaten it all yet, I got that as well.

Ian was in the other room, and I noticed he was inspecting the picture of the flame tree. He looked over his shoulder as I came up to him. 'I wondered about this. I was looking at it one time I was here and I could tell you didn't want to talk about it. You're very adept at changing the subject, Sophie.'

'Sorry. I've had a lot of practice.'

'So it does mean something to you?'

'The flame tree? Yes. I had one like it outside my house in Newstead. In Brisbane. I was feeling homesick when I bought that.'

'Are you still homesick?' He was watching me, intrigued by my answer and maybe a little tense.

I shook my head. 'Not really. Sometimes, but not so much, no. There are still good memories but the bad seem to outweigh them. Anyway, I feel as if I've moved on.'

And I did. I knew that if I went back and revisited those scenes from my past that I would be disappointed. Nothing is ever quite the same as your memory of it.

Ian smiled and put his arms around my waist. I reciprocated by putting mine around his neck. And it seemed natural to go the next step. The kiss started off lightly but soon became more serious. I felt my heart beating and my body getting that slow, drugged feeling that told me how much I wanted him.

'Ian, come to bed,' I whispered into his neck, and tried to press every inch of myself against him.

He groaned, and I knew he wanted to. I could feel the hard jut of his arousal against me. 'On one condition,' he murmured, bending his head and looking for my mouth again. 'You wear those shorts.'

I smiled against his lips. I didn't intend to wear anything and I'm sure he knew that. I took his hand and led him to the bedroom, and closed the door on BC's curious stare.

Of course afterwards there were doubts, although I tried not to let them in. I wanted to lie in his arms beneath the ceiling fan and enjoy the languid feeling in my body, and the happy throb of all those places that had been missing a man's touch. Ian's touch.

But I couldn't relax for long when Walter might be out there, and if he knew about Ian then he would be a target, too.

He felt me tensing up, and turned onto his side, resting his arm over me and pressing his face into the place between my shoulder and my neck. 'Love you,' he said. 'Loved you from the moment I saw you. Well . . . from the moment you came into the RSL Hall with the wedding dress and smiled at me.'

'I'm glad you clarified that,' I said, feeling my eyes well up.

'Come on, then.' He gave me a little shake. 'When did you realise you loved me?'

'I think I desired your body from the moment you opened the box and looked at the wedding dress and displayed your superior knowledge to me. I've always been turned on by clever men.'

'Really?' He sat up, sexily dishevelled, and looked down at me. He seemed flattered and I contemplated his past and the girl he'd married and the other women he'd probably known and loved, and I opened my mouth to ask him about them and then thought better of it. There would be time for all that. Just now I wanted to enjoy this special moment between us.

He stroked my breast with a fingertip, watching with a smile as I tried to breathe steadily. 'Do I need to think of something clever before you'll do it again?' he asked, trying not to look smug when my soft nipple turned into a tight little bud.

'I think we can dispense with that for now,' I reassured him, and went into his arms.

CHAPTER 35

BELLE

Sweet Wattle Creek, 1931

THE KITCHEN WAS stifling despite the windows and doors being thrown open. It looked as if Lyn had been making gravy in a pan, while the meat sat resting, covered, on the table. Aneas was standing in front of her and she was crying.

Belle had burst into the room full of righteous purpose, determined to have the truth from them, but now she hesitated. Her certainty, which had carried her through Henry's protests and attempts to stop her, faltered.

Aneas looked up, startled. 'Belle!' Lyn, catching sight of her, turned her face away, quickly wiping her eyes and picking up the gravy spoon so she could pretend to fuss with the pan.

'The painting of Reims Cathedral,' Belle said, and she sounded breathless. Emotions were simmering beneath the surface, but she felt in control of them. She wasn't going to start crying and shouting, she wasn't going to begin to scream hysterically, as Henry no doubt thought. This was too important.

'My brother, Alister painted it,' Aneas said evenly. 'He did it when he was on leave from the war. He had some friends in London and they sent his paintings to us after he'd died. There are others . . . he was affected by what he saw, and he said he found the act of painting helpful.'

'Martha has a sketch just like that.'

Aneas stared at her for a moment, but she couldn't read anything in his face apart from surprise, and then he looked at Lyn. She was still stirring the gravy, her back rigid.

'Perhaps he gave it to her?' Aneas said quietly. 'A-a gift.'

'I think he did. He sent it all the way from London. But not as a gift. I think he did it because she meant something to him. Because he was my father.'

Aneas's eyes slid away as if he couldn't meet her gaze any longer, and it was Lyn who answered. 'That's ridiculous!' she spluttered. 'What do you base this . . . this fantasy on? Martha had one of Alister's sketches? Probably half of Sweet Wattle Creek had one of his sketches.'

'It was in her bag, the one Aneas gave to me, the one that held her most precious memories.'

Lyn shrugged one shoulder, her face still turned away. 'I'm sorry, Belle, but I don't believe you.'

'Do you have a photograph of Alister?' Belle asked Aneas. 'I'd like to see him. Even if I'm wrong, surely a photograph would prove it one way or the other?'

'Belle,' Henry warned from behind her but she ignored him.

'Alister was my husband,' Lyn's voice was low and dogged. 'He was mine. You have no claim on him, you or Martha.'

'I'm not going to take him away from you,' Belle protested. 'I just want to know. That's all. I need to know.'

Aneas sighed. 'Very well,' he said, and left the room. Lyn turned sharply, watching him go, and then her gaze slid to Belle and hardened. There was a bitterness in her face that had probably been growing for years. Thirty years.

She seemed to be struggling between her need to speak out, to release all her anger and pain, and her determination to keep her memories shut away. But the opportunity to give vent to all that suppressed emotion was too much for her.

'Yes! Yes, I think he probably is your father. *My* husband. Martha stole him without a backward glance, and the worst of it was, he went with her. He didn't care that he'd broken my heart and ruined everything. She had some hold over him. Something . . .' She waved a hand, searching for the word and then shook her head when she couldn't find it. 'Men found her fascinating. You have it, too. Something base,' she said with a savagery that was as painful as a slap.

'Lyn!' Aneas had returned and his voice was sharp. He looked pale and weary, as if his own emotions were draining the life out of him.

'I found your birth certificate in his drawer,' she said defiantly. 'Why would he have that if you weren't his? I couldn't bear the thought of him taking it out and . . . and gloating over it. Thinking about Martha. So I pushed it under Martha's door.'

'You defaced it,' Belle murmured, shaken. The savagery of the black ink, erasing her father's name, made sense now.

'This is Alister,' Aneas interrupted, and the photograph he handed Belle was of a man in uniform, with two pips on the shoulder straps. He was staring into the camera lens, serious, his hair cropped short, his moustache carefully clipped.

Belle tried to see a resemblance to herself. His eyes looked pale in the black-and-white photo, but his hair was darker, not the unusual white-blonde of her own.

She looked up at Aneas, and knew he could read her disappointment. But he had another photograph in his hand and now he handed that to her.

'Oh.'

This one was of a boy. He was posed in a studio, an unlikely set of snow-capped mountains in the background, and he was half turned to the camera. His hair almost appeared white, and his pale eyes were as round as marbles.

'His hair darkened as he got older,' Aneas said quietly. 'Yours has stayed the same. You do look like him, Belle. I saw it the moment Martha showed you to me. I don't know how many other people saw it, perhaps not many. But Alister was my brother, and I could see the resemblance.'

'I see it, too.' Belle held the photograph tenderly, before passing it back to him.

Aneas smiled down at his brother's young face.

'When Alister joined up to fight I was surprised. He was a gentle soul. But he made us all proud, and ended up a hero. Took out a German machine-gun post and saved his men from certain death. His own life for theirs. Quite remarkable. We're very proud of him, you know, Belle. You should be, too.'

'Were they in love?' she said softly. 'Alister and Martha.'

But Lyn couldn't stand any more. She threw down the spoon, splashing herself with gravy. 'Love! It was an adulterous affair. It destroyed him, you know.' She nodded her head. 'He was never any good for anything after her. I kept expecting her to leave her drunken husband and run off with Alister, but instead she stayed and somehow that was worse. The waiting, the wondering, the lying there at night not knowing if Alister would still be here in the morning. It went on for years! I was glad when he joined up. He was killed at Bullecourt, but he died a hero. At least I have that. I am the wife of a hero and she's nothing.'

She swept her gaze over Belle and there was no doubting her contempt. 'And then there you were. Belle Bartholomew, arrived in town. All tricked out as if we were beneath you. Suddenly, Aneas and-and all the others were looking at you just as they had Martha. Like hungry dogs with a bit of meat.'

'My father . . .'

Lyn raised her hand and for a heartbeat Belle thought she was going to strike her. So did the other two, because they stepped forward. But the rage seemed to drain out of Lyn as quickly as it had come. Her face was working.

'Don't you dare,' she whispered in a voice that trembled and shook. 'Don't you dare say that. He was never yours. Or Martha's. He was a lamb and she was the wolf and she destroyed his life. She destroyed my life. Once she got her hooks into him he was never the same. I tried to stop it. I tried to reason with him. He wouldn't listen. He was *in love*, he said.' She spoke it with venom. 'What did he know of love? Of sacrifice?'

Now Lyn's face was flushed and damp with tears and sweat, her eyes blazing, and her carefully pinned hair had begun to spring loose, tendrils sticking to her forehead and her neck. And just like that Belle recognised her.

'You were the witch!' she cried in astonishment. 'You came to my room at The Grand. You did, didn't you?'

Lyn blinked, startled by the words, and then she gave a harsh laugh. She bit her lip to stop it. Aneas put his hand on her arm to steady her, but she shook him off.

'You did come to my room.' This time it wasn't a question but an accusation, and Belle knew it for the truth. The memory was there, tantalisingly close, and she reached out and finally grasped hold of it.

She was in her room, standing on a chair so that she could look out of the window. She liked to look out and today Mama had opened it up, not knowing about Belle's favourite trick. Sometimes she could see the horses being harnessed or unloaded, and sometimes there were people coming and going. Sometimes Nellie watched her from the brick archway, her sulphur crest standing straight up, like an angry cat's fur.

Today, though, what she saw was quite surprising. Mama was down there, in the little area between the back wall of the house and the outbuildings. She had her arms around Alister Thomas and she was kissing him. Kissing him so hard that Belle thought she might even be hurting him.

She didn't hear the steps behind her, only the hiss of anger. It frightened her and she spun around. Mrs Thomas was behind her, her eyes wild in her white face, and she looked so like the witch in one of Michael's stories that she lost her balance. Mrs Thomas didn't try to help her or save her, she just watched as Belle fell off the chair and struck her head on the windowsill.

It hurt, the pain making Belle feel dizzy, and then everything went dark. But it was only momentary. As soon as she regained consciousness, Belle screamed.

Someone cried out in response, down in the yard, but Belle was too busy struggling to get up, to get away. The witch loomed over her. 'Do you know,' she said, 'I wish you'd hit your head so hard that you'd die. That's what I wish.'

Finally Belle got up. There was something warm running down her face and she knew it was blood. It was dripping onto her white pinafore. She tried to reach the brass door knob, but the witch grabbed her and swung her about, high, so that her feet left the ground.

The window was open and Belle knew that in an instant the witch would toss her out of it and she would be smashed to pieces on the ground below.

Alister was there. She hadn't heard him come in, but

now he took her from the witch, holding her, staring at her face and the blood. Then Mama was there as well, taking Belle from him, holding her so tightly. She heard the sound of Alister's hand on the witch's face. She knew he'd hit her, because Mama loosened her grip and Belle could turn her face, and she saw the bright-red mark on the witch's cheek.

It was a jumble of movement and sound after that. The witch was crying, sobbing as she ran out of the room, and Belle could hear her blundering down the stairs. She wondered if she'd fall and then thought that she might be glad if she did. Then Alister had his arms around Mama and Belle, and it felt so safe.

'They mopped me up,' Belle said now, aloud. 'Cleaned up the blood, and my cut.' She touched the small scar on her forehead. 'I remember him, my father, I remember him saying that I would have to go away, and Martha shaking her head and telling him that she would look after me, but Alister was crying. I remember him crying. And he said, "You know what she's like." And I think that was when I went to live in Annat Street.'

'How can you remember? You can't possibly remember that!' Lyn tried to bluff her way out of it.

'I do remember.' At four years old the memory had been frightening enough to remain, hidden deep, and now in this moment of high drama it had been released.

Alister was her father, she knew that now, but he'd caused pain to those closest to him. Martha, too. Both unhappily married, they had found each other, loved each other, but there had been a terrible cost.

'I think Belle should go home now,' Henry spoke behind her. She'd forgotten he was there. 'I'll drive her, if you would be kind enough to lend me your car, Aneas.'

Aneas hesitated. Lyn had turned her back again and was staring at the stove. 'Yes, very well,' he said, and he sounded very weary. 'I think that would be best. We've all had rather a shock.'

'Thank you for telling me about my father,' Belle said, but Lyn didn't bother to look up, and it was Aneas who nodded. Slowly, like an old man, he followed them as they made their way out.

'Lyn has taken all of this very hard,' he said, and hesitated. He was offering excuses for her and he knew it, but perhaps it had become a habit. 'She loved Alister, but . . . I suppose the worst of it was that they made her believe the affair was over. After you were born he promised her it was finished. When she followed Alister that day, the day you remember, she caught them together. It was overwhelming for her. She had a sort of breakdown.'

Belle shivered, remembering her feet so close to the open window.

'Alister felt responsible. He insisted you be sent away.'

'But you knew who I was?' She searched his face. 'Couldn't you have done something then?'

Aneas turned his face and she sensed that the past did not sit comfortably with him. 'I knew who you were. I suppose I should've said something, done something, but I was content for you to go. I was worried about my brother, and Lyn. It was all so . . . disruptive. I wanted my peace back again, Belle. I'm not a very courageous person. I'm sorry.'

On the way back in the car Belle watched lightning flash over in the west, zigzagging across the sky. No rain yet, but she could smell it in the air. Henry glanced at her as he drove cautiously on the unfamiliar road.

'Are you all right?'

She tried to find an answer. 'I don't know. I think so. At least now I have my answers.'

'I know Lyn is a nasty piece of work, but I can't help feeling sorry for her.'

'No one won, did they? Alister, Martha or Lyn. They were all miserable.'

Henry was silent, and she wondered if her words had struck a chord with him. Perhaps he was beginning to realise that marrying the wrong person could have dreadful consequences.

He cleared his throat. 'Was it worth it? Coming here and stirring up all this scandal? Or do you think you would rather have stayed in Melbourne and never have known?'

Belle was aware of his gaze on her as he drew up outside The Grand. 'I'm glad I came, Henry.'

'What will you do now?'

She turned to face him. 'I don't know. I want to stay on. I have Tilly and Gwen to think of. Whatever you say, Henry, they are my responsibility. And there are others I can help.' And there was Michael, she thought to herself. Her heart ached to have him here now, to have his arms around her.

'You won't be coming back to Melbourne, then,' he said, and it wasn't a question. He looked resigned, as if he'd come to terms with her decision at last.

'No, I won't. I'm sorry, Henry.'

He nodded and dredged up a smile. 'Goodbye, Belle,' he said. 'I wish you well. I really do.'

It was good of him, especially when he considered she was making the worst mistake of her life. Belle smiled at him. 'Goodbye, Henry,' she said, and climbed out of the car.

The storm had finally broken and Belle lay, listening to the rain on the roof. She'd left her window open a few inches, and the smell of damp, clean air filled her room.

Everyone was in bed. She hadn't told Tilly and Gwen what had happened when she got back. She hadn't decided yet whether she would tell anyone about Alister and Martha. As for herself, she was glad to know the truth, but remembering how much they had damaged themselves and those around them made her consider if it would be best to leave their memories to the past.

When she'd come up to bed, she'd stood for a while outside the room with the small brass handle, before opening it and looking inside.

It was just a room. The tremor of fear, the clammy horror that had once held her enthralled was gone now that she knew the truth. It had been a terrifying experience for a four-year-old child, but as an adult she could look at it with fresh eyes. She didn't approve of what Lyn had done, but she could understand.

The knock sounded soft on her bedroom door.

Belle sat up, thinking Gwen was having nightmares or Tilly was looking for Bucket. She slid off the bed and made her way barefoot to the door, just as the knock came again.

'Belle?'

A tingle like an electric current ran through her, making her skin prickle and her heart beat faster. She opened the door a crack, and stared out wide-eyed. 'Michael?'

He was standing in the shadows and it was him, really him.

'Michael,' she whispered, and reached out to take his arm. He was wet, dripping wet, and now she saw that his hair was plastered to his head and his clothes were sodden. 'Michael!'

'Sshh,' he said, almost laughing. 'You'll wake them. I got caught in the rain. The motorbike broke down a mile or two down the road, and I had to walk. I'll have to fetch it in the morning.'

'You're back,' she said stupidly, and wanted to fling herself into his arms and hold him tight. Suddenly she felt shy. She'd been so looking forward to seeing him again and now she was tongue-tied. He was the same man and yet he was different because of what had happened between them.

'I'll be barnstorming at Riverton day after tomorrow,' he told her, and there was quiet pride in his voice. 'Thought I'd come here first and make sure everything's all right.'

'Oh. That's . . . that's wonderful.' She meant it. He was flying, doing what he loved best.

'After Riverton we go on to Melbourne, a few stop-offs on the way. If Smithy wants me, I'll head on over to Adelaide after that. Who knows where else. I got to him at just the right time, Belle. One of the pilots fell ill and he was short a man. He grabbed me with both hands when he saw me walking up to him in Hay. I didn't think he'd let me come home first, before Riverton, but I persuaded him I had to. That was the deal.'

'I'm glad you did.'

She wanted to tell him about Alister, about Martha and Lyn. About Henry. But there would be time tomorrow. Right now she needed to put her arms around him and hold him.

'Will you come in?' she said, watching his face.

He reached out and touched her cheek, his fingers cold from the rain. 'Better not,' he said. 'Don't want to wake the girls. I can wait, Belle. I've waited this long.'

She leaned forward to kiss his lips, and they were cold, too.

'We both have,' she whispered.

The kiss deepened and she thought he'd change his mind and come into her room after all, but then, reluctantly, he drew away.

'Goodnight, Belle,' he whispered.

'Goodnight, Michael.'

He nodded, and left, and she heard him going down the stairs and then the door at the back closed. Belle couldn't contain her smile as she climbed into bed.

CHAPTER 36

SOPHIE

Sweet Wattle Creek, 1986

THE DAY OF the Centenary was finally here. The Shaw household had been on the move from first light, and it was pointless trying to sleep. Tim and Maureen had insisted I stay over with Dillon, although I hadn't slept much, my brain and body seemed to be on high alert. But maybe that was because of Ian.

He and Miriam had asked me over to his house beside The Grand, but I'd felt the need to stay close to my son. I knew he understood, although I almost changed my mind when he gave me a goodbye kiss. But I told myself we would have plenty of time. In fact, I told it to myself so many times I think I was almost convinced.

Then again there was always the bleak possibility that I was going to die at Walter's hand sometime over the next two days.

Something else had happened to give my already fragile emotions a battering. Yesterday Tim had received a call from Brisbane. 'Soph?' He'd had the strangest expression on his face, so I knew it was serious as he handed over the phone.

'Is this . . . Sophie Matheson? I saw your picture in the newspaper and I . . .'

She didn't have to go on. I was already in tears and the next minute so was she. It was my mother and she'd recognised me and tracked down the number for the *Herald*. It wasn't a long conversation but it was a very moving one. We covered a lot of ground. She seemed to think this was all their fault and I had to assure her it wasn't, and then there were apologies for not intervening on her part and not asking for help on mine. 'We miss you both so much,' she'd said, and that set me off again. When we finally finished the conversation, I knew that Walter or no Walter, Dillon and I were going to be seeing my parents in the not-too-distant future.

'Miss South will arrive at ten,' Tim shouted from the kitchen, where it sounded like he was in the midst of organised chaos.

'That's only four hours from now!' Maureen added with a large dose of sarcasm. Clearly things were tense.

'I'll take Dillon with me,' Tim said when I joined them, bleary-eyed. 'He'll be fine. And then he has that school thing after lunch.'

Riverton High was going to perform a historical re-enactment in Main Street as part of the Centenary. Costumes would be worn and speeches made, their drama teacher's bright idea. Very uncool in Dillon's opinion, but at least he would be amongst friends and teachers, so I felt I could leave him without worrying too much while I did my work.

Christy joined us then, and she was carrying what looked like a plastic suit bag. Self-conscious and trying to pretend she wasn't, she laid it carefully on the sofa and began to unzip it.

'Ah, the big moment,' her father said with a chuckle.

'Sshh.' Maureen nudged him with her elbow.

Christy lifted the garment from its wrapping and stepped back. 'Voila!' she said, turning to me with a smile. But I could see she was desperately worried I wasn't going to like it.

She needn't have been. I was speechless, something that tends to happen when I am feeling extreme emotion.

'She spent *hours* making it, Mum,' Dillon hissed urgently in my ear. 'Say something nice.'

'You don't need to tell me that.' I laughed, and there was a hiccup in there, as if I might be about to cry. 'It's amazing, Christy. Really. Just . . . amazing . . .'

The dress was probably a nod towards the 1930s. Elegant, slim-line, it was the colour of the ocean on a sunny day. The buttons at the front were just for show—there was a zipper underneath. She'd also added a little hat with a neat piece of net attached.

I gave her a hug. 'Thank you, thank you,' I said. 'Where did you get the idea for the design?'

She was blushing with pleasure but pretending to be cool. 'Ah, in some of those books Ian's always looking at. I was in the library and I was reading one and saw a dress I liked. He said it was an Eileen Nicholson design, and I remembered the wedding dress and how much you liked it, so I thought I'd try something else of hers.'

'Christy, it really is beautiful. Thank you so much.'

She laughed and rolled her eyes. 'Okay.'

Tim and Maureen were standing behind us looking proud, and then the baby gave a howl and Maureen groaned and went to pick her up.

'You're not really calling her Centenary, are you?' I asked Tim.

'Actually,' he glanced at Maureen for confirmation, 'we thought we might call her Belle. What do you think?'

Of course I thought that was perfect.

Gwendolyn South was immaculate in a yellow-and-orange flower-print dress, and a cream linen jacket with big shoulders. Her hair was that grey-blonde tint older women seemed to go for, and her eyes were very dark. I thought she'd had some work done on her face, but maybe she was just well preserved. She was certainly striking. When we were introduced she held out a beautifully manicured hand with a single diamond ring on her little finger.

'Sophie. How good to meet you. You can't imagine how delighted I am to be back here in Sweet Wattle Creek. I like to think of it as home,' she added with a warm smile.

I murmured a response. Although I didn't know her, there was something in her eyes that led me to believe this wasn't 'home' at all. She was acting. Playing the part of Gwendolyn South, while the real Gwen looked on.

Photographers clicked their cameras. I had dark glasses on and my hair was brushed over one side, and I'd convinced myself that no one would be looking at me. Anyway what did it matter? The cat was well and truly out of the bag.

We did a fast walk through the exhibition in the RSL Memorial Hall, although she did pause briefly at the blown-up photograph of the young airman, and then a stroll around the town. She kept saying, 'Oh yes,' and 'Very nice.' It was a performance and I was beginning to think it unlikely I would hear anything like the truth from her lips—with their carefully applied pale-orange lipstick.

The CWA had a stall in the park and were handing out scones and jam and cream. Mr Scott was seated on a chair with a cup of tea balanced precariously in his hand, and Mrs Green and Ellie waved at us as we went by. They seemed to have gathered quite a crowd. Brad was manning his own stall, stacked high with the centenary edition of the *Herald*. I hoped Tim was paying him overtime.

The Riverton mayor was coming towards us, tricked out in his robes, the gold chain so polished it was almost blinding. Gwen had already met him. He was a big fan, evidently. Perhaps even Gwendolyn South could hear too much about her past glories because without warning she turned to me, clutching my arm so hard it hurt.

'Can we go and see The Grand?' she asked.

That was a surprise, but I was quick to agree and the next thing I knew her chauffeur—courtesy of Channel Nine—was whisking us away in air-conditioned comfort.

I debated whether she expected the old hotel to be the same as she remembered it—and why did she remember it anyway? Had she known someone who lived there? I wanted to ask lots of questions, but now Gwen had gone quiet. She'd shut down and I didn't know how to approach her.

Once we arrived she climbed straight out of the car, wincing at the blast of heat, and began to pick her way towards the blackened remains.

I was watching her, trying not to be obvious about it, but I wanted to know what she was feeling. Honestly, it was hard to know, those sunglasses were enormous. She stood for a long time, staring at what was left of The Grand. A warm breeze stirred the leaves of the trees and the dust at our feet, and she reached up to brush a strand of hair from her face. It was the slight tremble of her hand that gave her away. Despite what she might claim in public, I knew that these weren't happy memories.

Gwen turned to me and forced a smile as she pointed across the fields, where the housing estate was inching forward.

'That's where the Beauchamps had their house,' she said. 'It was Arthur Beauchamp who got me into movies. He was a producer and he always said I was a natural. Jane Beauchamp was my friend, and we kept in touch when I left.'

'And the Davies. Did you know them, Miss South?'

'Of course I knew them. Stanley and Violet. Jo was the school teacher. And Frank, of course.'

I wondered why 'of course', but before I could ask she'd turned back to The Grand with a frown, and said, 'Why have they just left it like that? Like some sort of awful memorial to Belle. It doesn't make sense. They all hated her.'

I'm sure I started. I was so desperate I wanted to grab hold of her and shake her. Force her to tell me everything she knew. But at the same time I was aware that Gwendolyn was someone who needed to be handled gently. I would have to find the right opening, make her feel she could trust me, and only then would she give up what she knew.

'Oh, you mean Belle Bartholomew,' I said evenly, pretending to peer at the building, even lifting my sunglasses for a better look. 'You knew her, then?'

'Of course I knew Belle! My sister, Tilly and I lived here with her.'

Her sister? I tried not to let my mouth fall open. 'Tilly worked at the *Herald* for Bill Shaw, didn't she?'

'Yes, she did. After The Grand . . . well, we went to live for a time in Melbourne. With Eileen Nicholson. She was Belle's friend, and Belle thought it was best while she decided what to do with us.' The words made her smile. 'Then our father came to find us and Frank gave him some work. Or maybe it was Violet's idea, she enjoyed playing the lady bountiful when it suited her, and she probably felt guilty for treating us so badly. I stayed on with Mrs Nicholson, but Tilly missed the *Herald*, so she came back, and then . . . he married her, Frank did. I remember thinking at the time that it was an awful waste. She was such a good journalist. She could have gone anywhere, done anything. Perhaps Frank realised he'd never be able to keep her happy in Sweet Wattle Creek. He took her to London and Jo and Pom took over the farm. They came back, but not to Morwenstow. They seem to be great travellers, Frank and Tilly. Or so I'm told. She wrote a book about The Grand.' She turned to look at me. 'I'm surprised you haven't read it.'

'No, I haven't.' It must have been the book neither Nola nor the State Library could find.

'They probably banned it from Sweet Wattle Creek,' she added, and laughed. 'I can imagine it had some uncomfortable truths in it, knowing Tilly. We lost touch. I haven't heard from her in years.'

She looked away, but I sensed the sadness in her. 'I think I know her son,' I said, trying to keep the elation out of my voice. Gwen knew so much. I was beginning to believe she could answer all my questions.

'Josh? He's a Davies through and through,' Gwen said dismissively. 'Not a creative bone in that boy's body.'

I wanted to scrabble in my purse for my pen

and paper so that I could write everything down, but I thought if she saw me doing that she might clam up.

'And Belle? What happened to Belle?'

Abruptly she went pale and tottered on her wedge sandals. I caught her arm, steadying her, fearing she was going to faint. 'I hate the heat,' she murmured. 'When you're young you don't really notice it, but now I can't abide it. Not any-more.'

'Ian's house is just there,' I said, pointing towards the lane. He'd given me the key in case of emer-gencies. 'Do you need to rest for a moment? I could get you some water?'

It was selfish of me but I didn't want her to get back into her air-conditioned car and drive off. I had a feeling if I let her out of my sight she would vanish and then I'd never know what happened to the people I cared about in this story.

She glanced back at the car and saw that some of her entourage of reporters and television cameras had caught up with us. I could hear the clicking as they recorded this moment for pros-perity and the six-o'clock news.

'Come on, then,' she said with a hint of laugh-ter in her voice. 'I used to wag school, you know. Loathed it. Maybe I haven't changed that much after all.'

CHAPTER 37

BELLE

Sweet Wattle Creek, 1931

'STREWTH.'

Michael shook his head. He'd been staring at Belle, totally engrossed as she told her story, and now that she was finished he couldn't seem to take it in.

He'd brought the Triumph back to The Grand in the early morning, and by the time she got up he was tinkering with the engine out in the stable yard. The rain had stopped and the sun had a softer quality, as if finally admitting summer had ended. Belle stood before him, Nellie on her shoulder—the cockatoo had decided that, as Michael was busy, she was the next best thing.

'I knew there was something Martha was keeping from me,' Michael went on, sounding thoughtful. He looked up at Belle again, and she wondered whether he was trying to see Alister Thomas in her face. 'I remember him. He used to be around here sometimes before you left. I didn't realise. I was only a kid myself. It never occurred to me there was anything between them.'

'They kept it quiet.'

He wiped his greasy hands on a rag and stood up. 'Do you think Lyn had anything to do with Martha hiding herself in the shed? Would she still be holding enough of a grudge after all these years?'

Belle considered it. Lyn had come here when Belle was four and tried to hurt her, and it had frightened Martha and Alister so much they had sent her away. But Belle knew the circumstances of that incident. Lyn had lost control of herself, and although last night she had been angry and upset, Belle thought that usually Lyn kept her emotions carefully in check. Snide remarks and nasty asides were probably more her thing. That didn't mean she might not explode like a volcano that has been rumbling for years, but it seemed unlikely.

'I don't think so. Unless Lyn thought Aneas might decide to marry Martha? But no, Aneas is too wary of Lyn's feelings. He might've dreamed about it, but Aneas dislikes disruption. He admitted that last night. He'd be fully aware of the sort of upheaval he'd unleash on himself if he told Lyn he was going to ask Martha to marry him.'

She nodded at the motorbike. 'Do you think you can fix it in time for tomorrow?' Michael needed to be in Riverton early.

He gave her a smile. 'Don't worry, I'll manage it. Will you come and watch me loop the loop?'

'I wouldn't miss it for the world.'

Belle wasn't sure she wanted to fly that far above solid ground. She wasn't as intrepid as Michael and she was happy to admit it, but perhaps that was a good thing. They balanced each other out.

'There might be a chance for me to buy my own plane, if I can get the money together.' He was crouching down by the bike again, as if the words meant nothing, but Belle heard the edge to his voice. 'It's an old Sopwith. I think I could get it working again, and once it's in the air . . . well, there's a chance I can get some work flying. Nothing big to start with, just a few jobs, here and there.'

'Michael . . .'

'I thought I'd talk to you first.' He looked up at her and she could see the hope and doubt warring in his eyes. 'I'll probably have the money by the time I've finished with the barnstorming. Well, most of it,' he added with a crack of laughter. 'But then there's fuel and repairs and upkeep. Aeroplanes suck up money like rain on the dry earth. It's a risk, that's the thing, Belle. A big risk. But then I'm a risk, too, aren't I?'

Belle could see what he was thinking. That he wasn't the sort of man she might want to spend her life with.

'Missus?'

Mo was peering in the gateway. His face brightened when he saw Michael, and he came loping over. The two men shook hands.

Michael gave her a glance, a wry smile in his eyes. It was frustrating but perhaps it was better this way. She could think about what he'd said and find the right words to reassure him.

'I'll see you later?' he asked quietly.

'Of course.' She was going into town, and then

there was the promise she'd made to go to see Gwen at the school. Belle nodded at Mo and left them to it.

It was her birthday tomorrow.

Not that it mattered, not really, but she'd wanted to tell Michael, to have him hold her and kiss her. Well, it would have to wait until later. The aeroplane as well, and Michael's plans and hopes and dreams.

She wanted him to fly, and if he could make a living from it, then he should. Did he really think she wouldn't want him to do that? It occurred to her that if he needed money, then she could help him, and perhaps by doing so she would be able to show him with more than words how she felt about him.

With a new sense of purpose, Belle made her way upstairs.

The pawnbroker opened the box and stared down at the wedding dress. Belle was tense and anxious but refused to let him see it. She had come here to make the very best deal she could and it was important to show a brave face. The man had listened to her as she explained this was an Eileen Nicholson, a renowned dressmaker from Melbourne, and if he took the trouble he could probably sell it for twice the amount she was asking.

'How do I know you're telling me the truth?' he said.

'Why would I lie?' Belle stared hard at him. 'Mrs Nicholson is my friend. I can ask her to come up here and talk to you herself. In fact, perhaps I should just take the dress somewhere else.'

He knew who Belle was, he'd probably listened to the gossip about her, and therefore he must know she was telling the truth.

'I did hear that the mayor's daughter was getting married soon,' Belle said offhandedly. 'I imagine he'd like something special for her.'

'An Eileen Nicholson,' he murmured.

She had him then and they both knew it. There was some more haggling to do, to get the best price possible, but by the time Belle walked away with the money folded and tucked into her pocket, she knew she had done what she'd set out to do.

Michael would have his money, and she could show him that she supported him completely. That she loved him, absolutely.

There was a corner of her heart that would always be Charlie's, and selling their dress had been painful, but not as painful as she'd expected. Charlie was gone and his mother had wished her well. *Think of it as a good-luck wish from dear Charlie. Who knows, it may come in useful!*

Belle knew she was finally leaving the past behind her, and she felt lighter, less weighed down. She even smiled to herself as she walked towards the Sweet Wattle Creek school.

Gwen had begged her to come. They were having tomorrow off class, she'd said, because of Charles Kingsford Smith coming to Riverton.

But today they were going to be talking about the famous aviator and his historic flight across the Pacific. And there was more.

'We're making an aeroplane! Miss Davies got lots of brown paper from the General Store, and string, and cardboard for the wings. Will you come and see it fly, Belle?'

The school was a small wooden building, set above the ground to protect it from the threat of white ants. And snakes. There was a water tank to one side, and a dunny on the other, and the playground was bare apart from a large pepper tree, its green skirts almost sweeping the dusty ground.

Belle could hear the children's voices, and then Jo's, raised and asking for quiet. She climbed the steps and peeped inside the door.

Jo had the blackboard covered in drawings of aeroplanes, and there was a map of the pacific with coloured markers showing the progress of Smithy and Ulm's 1928 flight from America to Australia. In the middle of the room was the children's pride and joy, a large model of a plane, complete with cardboard wings and thin wooden struts and a teddy bear in the pilot's seat.

Gwen had seen her and now she jumped up, irrepressible as always. 'Belle, Belle, look! We're going to fly our plane. Miss Davies said we can take it up to the top of the *Herald* building, onto the roof, and we're going to let it go.'

Jo looked up, startled. She smiled, but a moment later had caught herself and wiped it from her face. Belle was sorry for that. She'd always liked Jo and she'd hoped that away from Violet, they could be friends again.

'My goodness, that'll be exciting to see,' she said now, with a look at Jo. 'Do you need some help, Miss Davies?'

Jo was going to say no, Belle could see it in her face, and then she seemed to change her mind. She gave a brisk nod, her teacher demeanour firmly back in place.

'Thank you, Miss Bartholomew, I would like your help. I think we're just about finished. What do you think, children? Is it time to make our maiden flight?'

There were plenty of shouts of agreement. By the time they carried the model—which was almost as large as Michael's Triumph—outside, several more parents had arrived. And Frank.

He'd brought his horse and cart, and Belle realised he had been chosen as the lucky man to convey the aeroplane to the *Herald* offices. When he saw her his face brightened, before, like Jo, he shut down any sign of emotion.

It was worse than awkward. Belle was tempted to make her excuses and sneak off, but Gwen was clinging to her. Gwen had seen Frank, too, and was sending him scowling looks. Belle thought that she would stay, just until the aeroplane had flown, and then she'd make her escape. Anyway, she didn't have to speak to Frank, did she? She could keep her distance.

'Come on, children!' Jo was clapping her hands, and she soon had her eager charges under control. They carried the model out to the cart, and Frank helped them secure it, before setting off into town. It was only a ten-minute walk, and Belle trailed along after the children and Jo, ignoring the glances she was getting from the other adults.

Normally she didn't care. She'd grown used to being treated with suspicion. But for some reason today it stung. She didn't deserve this. She hadn't done anything wrong, even if Martha had.

'Gwen says that Michael will be flying tomorrow.' Jo had dropped back to her side, lowering her voice so that they weren't overheard, although the children were making so much noise that seemed unlikely.

Belle couldn't help her smile, and when she looked up she saw Jo watching her. She suspected that Jo saw everything in that moment.

Jo's mouth tightened and then she sighed. 'You know you've broken Frank's heart,' she said, but the animosity was gone from her voice.

'I'm sorry if that's true, although I don't think so. I never gave him any reason to think I wanted his heart.'

'That's not what Mum thinks,' Jo responded after a pause. 'She'll always take Frank's side. Ted was the apple of her eye, but Frank comes a close second.'

'And what about you?' Belle asked curiously.

'Well down in the pecking order.' Jo seemed to be resigned to the fact.

'Anyway, your mother wants me to stay away from Frank, she told me so. She thinks I'm too much like Martha to be trusted with him.' Some of the children began pushing and shoving, and

Jo had to restore order. Belle thought she might walk off and leave her again, but to her surprise she stayed by her side.

She decided this was probably as good a time as any to ask those questions she'd been mulling over. It couldn't hurt to try.

'I know Violet claimed Martha as her oldest and dearest friend, but they had a terrible argument the last time they were together. Their lives had taken very different directions, hadn't they?'

Jo shot her a curious look. 'Well, she was very keen to come over to The Grand and tidy it up for you, Belle. Or have you forgotten that? You should've seen the state it was in when we first arrived.'

'I know. I'm sorry. I didn't mean to sound ungrateful.'

But Jo wasn't finished. 'I'm sorry to say this, but Martha did seem to bring out the worst in people. She was so sure of herself. Mum can be a bit of a prig, I know, but Martha was always right. She liked to cast doubt on other people's actions, but as for her own, they were beyond question. In her eyes anyway.'

This was a new slant to Martha, and one Belle didn't feel entirely uncomfortable with. Had Martha been so self-righteous? It explained why she had told Stanley about Violet's fling with Rory. She wouldn't think of the hurt she might cause Violet and Rory, only that it was the right thing to do. Violet might never have forgotten that, especially when later on Martha had an adulterous affair. And then Martha taking in Michael when Violet advised her not to, and Violet believing Michael had left Ted to die. Yes, Belle could see very well how these events might fester in the heart.

'When they had the argument . . . why didn't Violet go back and see how Martha was? Why did she send Frank? I would have thought, being her best friend, she would have gone herself.'

Jo said nothing, staring ahead.

'Did she know that Martha was already dead? Was that why she didn't go herself? Did she feel as if the argument had caused her heart to stop and it was her fault?'

Now Jo shot her an exasperated look. 'You and Martha! You never let a thing go, do you? No, to answer your question, Martha was fine when Mum left, in fact she ordered Mum from the house, but the quarrel had been a bad one. They'd both said things they shouldn't have and Mum was shattered. I know, I was there when she came home. That's why she sent Frank, because she couldn't face her. And there's something you don't know, Belle. Whether you believe it or not, that's up to you.'

'What don't I know?' Belle spoke with a sense of urgency. 'Please, Jo. Whatever it is, I want you to tell me.'

'All right.' She seemed to set herself, as if this wasn't a pleasant task. 'Martha was good at hiding things. She'd had plenty of practice over the years, and now it was second nature to her. She was losing her memory, Belle. She had dementia. Even Dr Campbell didn't realise how much she'd deteriorated. Some days she struggled to remember how to light the fire and boil the kettle. After so long on her own, and being so fiercely independent, the thought of having to ask others for help must have been devastating for her.'

'Yes,' Belle whispered. 'Oh yes, it would be.'

Jo continued without pausing, as if now she had started she wanted it all out in the open. 'I've heard that people with that illness also begin to suspect others of plotting against them, that they begin to mistrust even their nearest and dearest. Well Martha was like that. Mum said that she thought the town was out to get her, and that was why she'd taken all her precious personal things to Aneas. Evidently she still trusted him. And Michael, she trusted him. In fact, she wanted him safe, and I think that's why she made him go away just when she needed him most. Of course Frank thinks it was all Michael's fault but I don't agree.'

'The mess in the house . . .' Belle's voice trailed away, remembering the rooms full of rubbish, the decline of a place that must once have been spotless. A metaphor for Martha's mind?

'We didn't realise it was quite that bad until we went there to tidy for you. She hid that too, kept the doors closed. All the same, Mum was worried about her. She asked Martha to tell the doctor what was happening, but Martha wouldn't. Martha could be very strong-willed and Mum isn't much of a fighter. That day though, the last day Mum saw her, Martha said things . . . I don't know what, Mum didn't tell me, but I imagine it was about the past. It was an awful business, to fall out like that after being friends for so many years. They'd had disagreements before but never as bad as this. Mum walked out, and she believes that once she'd left, Martha's illness took over. In her confusion she must have thought we . . . someone was coming for her, and she hid herself in that shed. Locked herself in. One of the Beauchamps said they saw Nellie screeching and flying off around that time, as if Martha was driving her away. Perhaps she was trying to save her, I don't know. But I think once she was locked in the shed, her heart gave out. Awful to think of her in there, frightened and alone, believing her friends were coming to hurt her.'

Belle closed her eyes to try to shut out the image but that only made it worse. Jo's version of events fitted the facts perfectly. Martha had followed her own path and that hadn't made her popular with the townspeople, but they hadn't attacked her or hounded her to death. It was her own mind that had turned against her, sending her fleeing from shadows.

Jo drew a shaky breath. 'Now you know. Please don't mention it to Mum. It's over and I want her to forget. She still feels bad that she didn't send Frank sooner, but she was so upset and Martha frightened her. She did nothing wrong, Belle, and she doesn't deserve to suffer any longer.'

'Thank you for explaining it to me,' Belle said. 'And I don't blame your mother any more than I blame Martha. I can see it was just a series of unfortunate events. You do know I'll have to tell Michael?'

Jo shrugged irritably. 'That's up to you.'

'Jo . . .'

'Jane Beauchamp, stop that this instant!'

This time Jo did stride away, once more restoring order to her unruly bunch. Belle didn't follow. A few more steps and they were at the *Herald* offices, and Bill Shaw was standing in the doorway welcoming them, a big grin on his face.

'This is very kind of you, Mr Shaw,' Jo announced, prompting the children.

'Thank you, Mr Shaw,' they dutifully droned.

'My pleasure, children.' Bill Shaw rubbed his hands together. 'Now you'll all be sure to buy a copy of the *Herald* tomorrow, won't you? Tell your parents! You'll all be in it, names mentioned.'

Tilly was peeping over his shoulder, and seeing Belle she smiled.

Inside they went in single file past the presses and up some rickety, wooden stairs. There was a door to the roof, and they stood blinking in the sunlight, as Jo instructed her pupils to keep back from the low brick wall which was the only thing between them and the ground. Frank and another man had manoeuvred the aeroplane model to the edge. Below in the street Belle could see they'd drawn quite a crowd. There was Flo from the General Store, and Aneas and Lyn Thomas had come out of their office entrance. The pawnbroker was there as well, and other faces she knew and recognised.

And then she saw Michael. He'd parked his Triumph outside the store—maybe he'd been looking for her—and now he stood, shading his eyes, looking up. Her heart flipped over, and then began a quick march. She gave Frank a sideways look, hoping he hadn't noticed, telling herself there was nothing to worry about.

But Frank had noticed and he didn't look happy.

'Are we ready?' Jo claimed their attention. 'Look out below!'

The men held the aeroplane carefully, and then, with a great cheer, it was launched into the air.

Belle had been expecting it to crash immediately to earth, but to her surprise it actually flew a short distance, lifting its nose to the sun and rocking slightly from side to side. Most likely a breeze had caught it just at the right moment. But then the inevitable happened. It went into a dive and seconds later crashed into the street below.

A groan went up, but no one seemed overly upset. By the time the children were climbing back down the stairs, they were laughing and jostling again. Bill Shaw was shaking their hands, congratulating them, and Gwen ran over to give Tilly a hug before her friend, Jane dragged her away.

Outside, Michael had come over to inspect the damage, and he looked up with a smile when he saw Gwen and Belle. Jo hesitated, as did some of the children. They knew Michael, they understood about his mask and why he wore it, but they were wary of him. Perhaps their parents had told them to be.

And then Jo seemed to make up her mind. 'This is Mr Maxwell,' she said. 'He's a real pilot in a real aeroplane. You'll see him tomorrow in Riverton.'

And somehow it was all right. Belle caught Jo's glance and knew she'd done this for her. Could they be friends again? She hoped so, she really did.

'Michael, Michael.' Gwen was dancing around him.

'You're no hero, Maxwell.'

It was Frank and Belle hoped that in the clamour no one had heard him, but of course they had, and then he said it again, louder, just to make sure they did.

'Not now, Frank.' Jo tried to catch her brother's arm but he pulled away. He looked angry and upset, and Belle wondered if this was really her fault. Could she have prevented this from happening, somehow? But she didn't think so. Frank and Michael had always been on a collision course, and although her presence may have exacerbated the situation, it would have happened anyway.

Michael was standing, staring back at the other man. Gwen was still holding his hand, but now she was turning her head anxiously from one to the other.

'Come on, children!' Jo shot Frank a warning look and began to herd her flock across the road. She collected Gwen on the way, and they scooped up what was left of the model aeroplane.

'Ted was worth twice of you,' Frank said in a low, furious voice. 'And you left him to die.'

Michael made a jerky movement. He seemed to be trying to decide whether to respond or not, and he must have decided it was better to walk away. He began to do just that.

'Coward!' Frank wasn't ready to let him go and now he came after him.

Michael turned around, taking a step backwards and then another, as Frank came at him. 'I'm not going to fight you, Frank,' he said warily.

'Murdering bloody coward.'

There was a gasp from the people watching on. Belle wanted to step between them, but she was afraid of making it worse. 'Stop them,' she said, looking about her. That's when she knew that everyone apart from her was on Frank's side. Well of course they were! He was the respectable Mr Frank Davies.

Suddenly Belle felt sick. She had to stop this. She'd begun to head towards them when Gwen's voice piped up.

'Michael you have to fight him.'

Gwen was still there, standing on the other side of Main Street, and the look of determination on her face . . . She couldn't be about to say what Belle thought she was. Please, please . . . 'Gwen!' But it was too late.

'You have to fight him because he kissed Belle.'

Michael turned to stare at her, disbelieving or disappointed, she wasn't sure which. This was all so silly. She wanted to tell him so.

'Michael,' she began, and then didn't want to go on in front of all these listening ears and avid faces. 'Michael,' she whispered again, trying to make him understand with that one word that Frank's kiss had meant nothing, that it was him she loved. Because she *did* love him and she wished she'd told him so this morning, instead of waiting until the chance had passed.

But whatever Michael saw in her face only added fuel to his fire. Next moment he'd launched himself at Frank and they were rolling on the ground.

CHAPTER 38

SOPHIE

Sweet Wattle Creek, 1986

GWEN'S ENTOURAGE WERE reluctant to let her go, calling out, asking for her to pose in front of the old hotel. The actress smiled and made promises for later, and then she strolled up the path and we went into the house and closed the door. But once inside all her professional cheerfulness vanished, and she sank down into a chair. She looked pale and drawn, and every one of her sixty-five years.

'I'm sorry,' she said. 'This has been far more exhausting than I expected.'

I fetched her some water. Ian's house was tidy enough, but Miriam was also staying here and her possessions seemed to cover most surfaces. The shelves along the walls were full of books, and there was a lingering aroma of beef and black bean sauce from Chinese takeaway.

Gwen drained the glass. 'That's better,' she said with more energy. 'Now we can talk.'

That was when I finally understood that it wasn't just me who was desperate to delve into the past. Gwen was just as desperate to tell me.

For whatever reason, she wanted to talk, and I was the lucky person chosen to listen.

'The, eh, the wedding dress. Can you tell me about that?'

Gwen was watching my face. She'd taken off her sunglasses so at least now I could see her eyes. 'If you mean Belle's wedding dress, she kept it in her wardrobe at The Grand. Tilly and I tried it on once, or at least Tilly did. It was too big for me. Belle didn't know about that.' She gave a little smile. 'She would've been upset with us if she'd caught us. I thought it was destroyed in the fire, at least I did until I read your article.'

There was a speculative look in her face now, and I wondered if Miriam would be proved right and Gwen would try to get her hands on it.

'You collect Eileen Nicholson, don't you?'

'Yes, I do. Her designs remind me of happier days. Eileen and I got on well together and she encouraged me to follow my heart. I'm grateful to her for that, and grateful to Belle. She was a good person and she tried to do her best for us. People weren't so kind to travellers then.'

'I read about that in Bill Shaw's —'

But Gwen wasn't listening to me. 'Belle took us in. We stayed at The Grand with her. And Michael, of course. You've heard of Michael?' Her gaze slid over my face without really seeing. 'Eadie and Mo came along afterwards, and there were always the odd strays who stayed for a night or two.'

'But not everyone was so sympathetic.'

Gwen pulled a face. 'You have to remember

that country towns have their good and bad sides. Sweet Wattle Creek was a small place and in the Depression the people here had struggles of their own. They didn't want to be burdened with strangers who meant nothing to them.'

'So the fire was deliberate?'

She stared at me. 'Yes,' she said quietly, 'it was.' She held out her glass. 'Do you think I could have some more water?'

I went to get it, telling myself not to panic. She wanted to tell me and she would, she just liked to stretch it out. I could wait. I had time.

'Thank you.' She took a sip. 'The Grand should've been Michael's, really. Martha left it to him, but then she changed her mind and left it to Belle. Michael was hurt in the war, the Great War, of course, but it never seemed to matter to him. There were tensions between him and Frank Davies. His older brother, Ted, died in the war and for some reason Frank thought Michael should have died instead.' Her mouth tilted up in a smile of malicious delight. 'But he got his own back on them.'

When she didn't go on I was forced to ask her why.

'Why? Because Frank was in love with Belle but Belle loved Michael.' She smiled again, as if reliving something in her head, something enjoyable. It was frustrating, but I gritted my teeth and waited.

'On the track life was . . . unpredictable.' Gwen looked up at me and now her smile was gone. 'We'd been so poor, scrounging anything we could, stealing when we had to. I knew I couldn't bear to do that again. I couldn't go back on the track no matter what.'

I had a feeling, that sick sort of excitement you get when you know you're about to hear something awful. 'Miss South ... Gwen. Are you trying to tell me that it was you who started the fire at The Grand?'

She blinked at me and then began to laugh. 'Me?' she spluttered. 'Of course not. It wasn't me. I had nothing to do with the fire. I didn't even like fried bread.'

I blinked. 'Do you know who did start it, then?' I leaned closer, smiling as if I was her best buddy. 'I think you do know. My friend, Miriam, thinks it was Belle herself and she wanted to claim the insurance.'

Gwen snorted. 'Ridiculous. Belle loved The Grand. It was her home. She'd lost everything once already, do you really think she'd want to lose it again? As for Michael ... his parents had died in a fire when he was young. They both had their past tragedies, Belle and Michael.'

'Did she die in the fire? Belle, did she ...?'

Gwen looked at me as if I was stark raving mad. 'No one died in the fire, Sophie. Don't you journalists believe in research?' She shook her head and said firmly, as if she knew for certain, 'No. It was someone in the town who started it. After Frank and Michael had their fight, someone must've decided they wanted us gone. They waited until the next day. Did you know Charles Kingsford Smith was in Riverton? The crowds who came to see him, it was amazing, but he was famous. Real fame, I mean, not the manufactured kind of fame we see these days.'

Someone was knocking on the door. 'Miss South? Miss South?' It was time to go.

Gwen was enjoying herself, and she had taken me along for the ride, but she didn't have a clue who started the fire.

The ball had been opened by a local politician and was now well under way. Nola whirled past me in Ian's arms, her face flushed and ecstatic. For such a clumsy man he was a very good dancer. If only Nola wasn't wearing a hooped skirt that threatened to upset anyone close to her. She waved merrily as she passed. I smiled and waved back.

Ian had his hair slicked back and wore dark, straight-legged trousers, a white shirt and red braces. He looked more like a gambler from the American west than a Sweet Wattle Creek pioneer, but I thought it suited him.

The day had been a huge success. Gwen South had left an hour or so ago, waving and smiling at the crowds. She'd been good value, posing for photographs for all and sundry, and chatting with visitors as if she was their best friend. I didn't have a chance to talk with her again, although I'd seen her closeted with Ian, her hand resting possessively on his arm. By the time I remembered I hadn't asked her what exactly had happened to Belle after the fire, it was too late. Anyway, I wasn't sure she would tell me anything more.

The Grand had burned down fifty-five years ago and no one had died. I'd enjoy discussing the possibilities with Ian, later, when we could be alone. Whenever that might be, with Miriam staying with him, while I was crammed in with the Shaws.

I looked across the room at Dillon and Christy, in a huddle with Tim and Maureen. They seemed to be having a good time, especially as Baby Belle was asleep in her carrier. I'd already admired her pretty bonnet of lace and ribbons.

'You look ravishing.'

Ian had escaped from his duties and come to stand by my side. His gaze slid over me appreciatively and I pinched his arm to stop him. Actually, I was pleased with my dress—Christy's dress. The slim, elegance of it was wonderful and when I danced it swirled around my ankles in a way that made me feel as if I had stepped back in time, into the thirties. It was funny, but it was an era that I always imagined was very sophisticated. Clarke Gable and Joan Crawford, Spencer Tracy and Katharine Hepburn. But of course I'd forgotten the Depression and the lingering tragedy of the Great War, with the loss of millions. It had taken my search into history for Belle and Charlie to give me a clearer view.

'Hey.' Ian slipped an arm about my waist. 'Are you all right? I see you have a guard tonight.' He nodded towards the door and I saw the sergeant from Riverton standing there. He was out of uniform but there was no doubting it was him.

'Have you heard any more about Walter?'

I shook my head. 'Only that they're still looking. I'm not sure that's a good sign, are you? If they haven't found him by now then they probably won't.' Until it's too late.

He gave me a reassuring squeeze in reply. 'Enjoy yourself,' he said. 'Don't let him spoil this for you, Sophie.'

He was right, I knew he was, but it was hard to pretend Walter wasn't there, looming at the back of my mind. 'I take it the committee's happy?' I asked him, changing the subject.

'Ecstatic. They're paying me a bonus.'

I looked at him sceptically.

His smile made my heart flutter, just a bit. 'No, you're right, they're not. But their praise was unstinting.'

'You deserve a bonus, Ian. You've done a wonderful job.'

'Well thank you. I'll expect my name to appear in your book when it's out. "The marvellously clever Ian McKinnon" and "I want to thank Ian, without whom I would never have written this" and such like.'

That made me laugh.

By the time I'd recovered he was serious again. 'So, if Sophie Matheson isn't your real name . . . What is?'

I chewed my lip, deliberating, and then I told him.

He considered it. 'Nice,' he said.

'Dillon wants to be Dillon, he tells me. A new

leaf. Maybe Sophie is my new leaf. It seems to have worked for us so far.'

He smiled. 'What did Gwen South have to say?' he asked after a beat. 'I noticed you were a bit distracted after your interview.'

'She was amazing but she doesn't know who started the fire. She says she does, that it was someone from the town, but . . .' I stopped, struck suddenly by Gwen's definite tone, as if she was working hard to convince me she was right.

'Unless she's trying to lead you away from the real culprit,' Ian suggested, as if he'd just read my mind.

I looked at him in admiration and he laughed.

'What? Have I solved the mystery for you? Come on, you can't stop there. Who?'

But from the corner of my eye I could see Nola bearing down on us. 'Honestly? I haven't a clue but I'll meet you outside in five minutes and we can discuss the possibilities, that should give you long enough to escape.'

'Escape?' he mouthed, just as Nola put a possessive hand on his shoulder. I saw alarm flare in his eyes before he turned with his charming smile.

I watched them twirl off into the crowd. A waltz this time. He really was a rather fine dancer—perhaps it was similar to people who stutter and yet can sing beautifully. No wonder Nola was keen to snaffle him. I told myself I didn't begrudge her. She was welcome to dance with him all night. As long as he came home with me.

The ball was being held in the RSL Hall, among all the displays, although everything fragile had been taken over to the library, or else moved back to a secure position against the walls. There was nowhere else in town that had enough floor space for so many guests, and as it was they had spilled out into the park.

I could see a group of teenagers mucking around, pushing and shoving, the girls shrieking with excitement, and I went in the opposite direction. The area was well lit and I didn't feel any need to be afraid, especially as there was another couple seated on the bench close by. The air was cooler out here after the stuffy hall, and I lifted my face to the stars, the Milky Way spread out above me in a magnificent display.

It was good to be alive.

The knowledge washed over me in a warm, soft wave of feeling. I hadn't felt like this for a long while, and I stood and stared upwards at the stars and smiled. There had been times in my life when I questioned if I'd get through the next minute let alone a year, but I had. I was still here in Sweet Wattle Creek and I was happy.

I was also in love, which seemed a strange state of affairs for someone who had sworn off men. But Ian had crept under my guard, and even while I tried to keep my distance I was longing to get closer to him. Another thing—I was optimistic. I looked into my future and although there were problems ahead—well, big problems actually—I believed I could overcome them and live a life I might actually enjoy.

The touch on my arm took me by surprise. 'Ian?' I said, and went to turn.

'Hello . . . Sophie.'

That voice, I knew it so well.

I tried to get up, to run, but now he had his arm over my shoulder and around my throat, holding me back against him. Where was the other couple who had been here? They must have gone while I was stargazing, but it didn't matter. They wouldn't have been able to save me. I needed to get away . . . As if he'd read my mind he tightened his grip and I could hardly breathe.

'Don't struggle.' His whispered words stirred my hair. 'I'm going to take you somewhere nice and quiet and we're going to get reacquainted. I'm sure you missed me just as much as I missed you.'

I could feel his body against me. I could *smell* him and I felt sick and terrified. This was what it had always been like. He had the power to sap all my strength so that even if I wanted to escape him I couldn't. Like a mechanical toy with the batteries run down, I was helpless.

For a moment I really felt that I couldn't get away. And what was the point in trying? He could do what he wanted to me and I would let him.

But I *had* got away. For a whole year I'd been free and I was strong and he couldn't do this to me again. I told myself I wouldn't let him.

I sagged and whimpered, just like I used to, and he laughed softly in my ear, because this was the woman he knew and he had expected no differently. And then I lifted my heel, the nice sharp stiletto, and brought it down on his instep.

He wasn't anticipating it. He was so sure of

himself, so arrogant, and the point of the stiletto went deep into his foot. He tried to catch his breath but could only manage a strangled moan. I slipped out of his grasp and the shoes and began to run.

I didn't know if he was following me, but I headed towards the hall. There were lights and people and, if I was lucky, help.

That's when I saw Dillon.

He saw me, too, and then he saw Walter. His face looked green in the coloured lights strung up around the eaves, his eyes were black holes. He began to yell, and at the same time to run towards us.

'No,' I moaned.

Walter was watching my son, and I knew if he couldn't have me then he'd have Dillon, and there was no way I could let that happen. My life for his seemed a reasonable exchange, but even so I wasn't going to give myself up lightly. I was going to fight.

I made a sharp turn to the right and headed towards the pepper tree and its long trailing skirts, and beyond that, the creek.

'Come on, come on,' I whispered. 'Follow me . . .'

CHAPTER 39

BELLE

Sweet Wattle Creek, 1931

FOR ONCE CONSTABLE Nash had shown an open mind. He'd let both Frank and Michael off with a warning. Frank, his nose swollen and bleeding, had stalked off alone, while Michael, the eye on his undamaged side red and half closed, had walked silently beside Belle to his motorbike.

They'd only managed to get a few punches in before the constable separated them. He'd been watching from near the pawnbroker's, and was quick to put a stop to the entertainment. Belle had heard a few disappointed murmurs from the crowd, saying they'd been enjoying it and to let them be, but she wasn't one of them.

'Will you be able to fly tomorrow?' she asked quietly.

He gave her an incredulous look. 'This is nothing. I've flown with far worse. Anyway, I have two eyes, at least I have that. I may not be as handsome as Frank, probably not as good a kisser either, but I can fly.'

'Michael, please. It wasn't like that. He kissed me but I didn't kiss him. Anyway,' she gave him a narrow-eyed look, 'I don't think he was trying to knock your block off because of that. There's more to it and I want to know.'

He didn't reply. They'd reached the Triumph, but instead of climbing on it he stopped, breathing hard. 'All right,' he said. 'All right. I'll tell you why Ted and I fell out when we were kids. And why we fought the day before he died in that ambulance. I'll tell you, if you really want to know.'

'Michael . . .'

'Come on.' And he climbed onto the bike, waiting for her to get on behind him. Belle put her arms around his waist.

They took a side road away from The Grand, down a narrow dirt track, where there were willows growing near an old dam. When he stopped and got off the bike he walked over to what had once been a house. She could see the mounds of soil and stone, overgrown with weeds, and an old rose that had somehow survived despite neglect.

Michael was standing with his back to her and tentatively, curiously, she joined him. She wanted to hold his hand, to tell him it was all right and that whatever he had to say would not change how she felt about him. But he was standing so tensely, his shoulders rigid and his jaw set. Whatever story he was about to tell her wasn't going to be a happy one.

'I'm listening,' she offered quietly.

He turned his head towards her and she wouldn't look away from him. She wanted him to see that she was here by his side and she wasn't going anywhere. He almost smiled, but then he resumed his resolute stance, digging his hands into his pockets and setting his feet apart, as if preparing himself for what was to come.

'Ted and I were good friends. I was a bit in awe of him, to tell the truth. He was capable of anything when the mood took him. He was brave, yes, but there were times . . .' He kicked at a small pebble, moving it around. 'He knew I had a tough time at home. My father was a brute. He'd been brought up to be tough and he was doing the same to me. It was his way or the belt, and most times it was the belt. My mother deferred to him. She might've stood up to him when she was younger, I don't know, but by the time I came along he was the boss and that was it.'

As much as she wanted to, Belle tried not to move or make a sound. This was his story and he had to tell it in his own way, in his own time. Later on she would be able to hold him and kiss him and try to take away some of the unhappiness.

'Ted got it into his head that I'd be better off without my parents. He said Martha wanted me, and if they were gone I could live with her. I could fly, something I'd always wanted. It was a dream, and I talked about it all the time. I knew about the Wright brothers and Hargrave, I read everything I could on them. When Ted started saying things like that I agreed, just going along with him, you know, not understanding he really meant it. I was fourteen years old, Belle, and working like a man. I couldn't see a way out, I really couldn't, but I wouldn't have done what Ted did.'

'He set the house on fire,' Belle murmured. 'This house?'

Michael nodded. He looked relieved he hadn't had to say it. 'Yes. They couldn't get out. He swore he didn't lock the doors, but I don't know . . . After that I didn't want anything to do with him. He couldn't understand that. He'd saved me and I wasn't going to be grateful for it.' He bent down and picked up the pebble, holding it in his palm, and Belle saw that it was a marble, the colours faded and warped by time and the weather.

'That's what the fight was about in France. We were tired, scared, and there'd been a lot of casualties that day. Nerves get stretched, tempers flare. He reminded me how ungrateful I was, and that if it wasn't for him I'd never have got to fly. We just got stuck into each other. Then we were in the ambulance, and next thing the shell hit and he was dead. He was already dead when I woke up. I didn't leave him. I wouldn't have done that.'

Belle nodded. She reached out and slowly, giving him time to move away, slipped her hand through his arm. The muscles felt tight and tense, but at her touch he seemed to relax slightly.

'Frank doesn't know, but even if he did he'd never believe anything bad about Ted. Stan might've guessed, and Violet, but she won't ever admit it. She can't. Ted could do no wrong. How could she ever admit to him killing two people in a deliberately lit fire? She's been putting the blame on me all these years.'

'Can't you tell them this wasn't your fault? *I* can tell them.'

He laughed softly. 'Oh, Belle, it's too late for that. The people of Sweet Wattle Creek have been believing for twenty years that I'm a rotten apple. They're not going to change their minds now. Not even if you stand up on the roof of the *Herald* and shout it out. Not that I wouldn't like to see that, mind you.'

She squeezed his arm. 'Michael . . .'

'I know,' he said, pulling a face. 'It goes against the grain to let it go, but we have to. Let it go, Belle.'

They stood together, looking at the debris that had once been Michael's life. Belle leaned her face against his shoulder.

'When Frank kissed me . . .'

'No, don't tell me,' he said quickly. 'I didn't believe it of you. Even when I was hitting him, I didn't believe it. I *was* thinking that he might be a better choice for you, and that made me angry.'

'He's not a better choice for me,' Belle retorted. 'You're my choice. I love you. Don't you know that? You must. I love you and I want to be with you.'

He searched her face, and she knew she was flushed and emotive, but she wanted him to see exactly what she was feeling.

'Good,' he said softly. ''Cause I love you.'

The Riverton showgrounds were awash with

people. Flags were flying and the sun shone down. People had come from everywhere, the outlying districts as well as Riverton and Sweet Wattle Creek. Even as far as the border, if Bill Shaw was to be believed.

The planes were grouped together while their pilots posed for photographs and signed autographs. You could go up for a ride with one of them if you paid ten shillings. Belle shaded her eyes to try to make out Michael among the group standing in their padded flying suits and helmets and goggles.

'Do you think you'll speak with Smithy?' Gwen asked her sister, eyes wide. 'Can I come when you do?'

Tilly was writing a story for the *Herald*, and was very nervous about it. She glanced at Bill now, who had joined them at the edge of the field, where the white fence was a handy place to lean against.

'You'll be fine,' he assured his protégée. 'Go over and have a look at the planes, get a feel for it all, and then I'll come and introduce you.'

Tilly nodded but it was Gwen who took her sister's hand and tugged at her. 'Stop it,' Tilly tried to shake her off, clearly feeling her dignity was being compromised.

Gwen had apologised to Belle and Michael that night after the fight. Michael was inclined to laugh and say she did him a good turn, and that Frank wasn't quite as pretty now. Belle required a promise that it would never happen again. Of course Gwen promised very prettily and sincerely.

'There's Michael!' Gwen shouted and the two girls were off, waving their arms.

Bill, leaning closer to Belle, said, 'Our hero, Charles Kingsford Smith, is rather partial to pretty faces. He's not going to take any notice of an ugly old bloke like me,' he added with a snort of laughter. He gave Belle a look of frank assessment. 'You'd do, though. I reckon he'd be putty in your hands.'

Belle ignored him. Bill Shaw always had that effect on her. She liked to see him, she looked forward to their conversations, and then five minutes later she was wishing him miles away. He seemed adept at getting under her skin.

Tilly and Gwen had reached the aeroplanes now, and Michael came to welcome them and take them through the roped-off area. He went over to have a word with the famous Smithy, and then Tilly was at his side, fumbling out her notebook and pencil. It was Gwen who Michael lifted into the plane.

The aircraft started up, propeller spinning, and then it began to move across the rough ground. Soon it was in the air, and Belle stared upwards, craning her neck as Michael circled the showgrounds.

'Aneas! Lyn!' Bill's greeting brought her gaze down to earth, just as Aneas Thomas, his arm about Lyn, walked quickly by. They didn't look at her, not even a polite nod. Well, what did she expect? They would never acknowledge her and she couldn't really blame them.

'I would've married Martha, you know,' Bill

said. 'If she hadn't taken on old Nathan, and she hadn't fallen for Alister Thomas. Even afterwards, if she'd wanted me. But she didn't. I think she only had enough love in her for one man and that was Alister. And maybe a bit left over for Michael,' he added with a smile, nodding towards the far side of the grounds.

So Bill had known all along. Well of course he had, Bill Shaw knew everything. The drone of the plane was getting louder and Belle saw that Michael was coming in to land. The plane bounced slightly but soon steadied, rolling to a stop.

'How did you go, Tilly?'

'Good, Mr Shaw. He was very nice.' Tilly was back and trying not to blush.

'I thought he might be,' Bill replied.

'Belle, come on.' Tilly had her hand and was leading her away, gently but firmly.

'Come where?' But she knew. Tilly turned and laughed at her. They were wending their way through the crowd towards the aeroplanes.

'It's your birthday,' Michael said, when she was strapped in. Belle asked herself if she was really going to do this. She'd always preferred her feet on the ground. Or perhaps that was the other Belle, the one who had hidden herself away for years. The new Belle might enjoy some thrills and adventure. She tried to smile.

Michael chuckled. 'I promise not to loop the

loop,' he said.

'Oh my goodness,' she breathed, hands clenched on the hand rests in front of her seat.

'Happy birthday, Belle!' Gwen was watching from a safe distance. Tilly waved, smiling.

'How did you know?' Belle asked him, as he slid into the pilot's seat.

'I remember everything about you,' he said, and turned to look at her before sliding on his goggles.

'Michael.' She still had the money to give him. She'd wanted to do it today before he left for Riverton, but there'd been too many people about, and it hadn't seemed right. She tried to get it from her pocket, fumbling at her skirt, but he'd already turned away.

'Ready!' he shouted, and a second later they were moving.

Belle kept her eyes closed for quite some time. It wasn't until they were in the air that she opened them, and then she couldn't seem to close them. Down below was the showgrounds and all the people, so many coloured dots walking and looking back up at her. And then that was behind them and they were flying over paddocks and there were sheep and horses and farms.

The wind was tugging at her hair, and the collar on her blouse had turned inside out. Michael had given her a leather jacket to wear, but it was still chilly up here with the birds.

She could see the creek now, and the line of trees that grew on its banks. There were some buildings in a bend there, and she could see people seated outside, with the smoke of a fire drifting upwards. Travellers, she thought, and wondered if they would arrive at her door before too long.

Eadie was out of the hospital and Mo had taken her back to The Grand to rest. No excitement for her, not today.

'What do you think, then?' Michael had to shout for her to hear him. 'Still think it's better to keep your feet on solid ground?'

'I love it!' she said, the wind whipping at her words. 'I love you!'

'Happy Birthday . . .' He stopped and looked down, and then he turned the plane, making her gasp and cling tighter. 'Look!' he shouted, and he was pointing.

She looked across towards where the town must be, and then further off towards The Grand. And there was smoke. Thick clouds of it belching into the air.

The Grand was on fire.

'I'm going to land.' Michael's words barely made sense to her until she realised the plane was getting lower. He circled, over the paddock with the Beauchamp's horses in it, and at first she thought he was going to land there. And then he was over Main Street and coming down, and she guessed he was going to use the road as an impromptu runway.

A moment later they were down. As soon as they stopped she was tugging at her straps, and then Michael helped her out, lifting her to the ground, and they were running.

The Grand was on fire. Her home. Their home.

She felt tears on her cheeks, but Michael was pulling her along and she didn't have the breath to cry or speak.

'Mo!' Michael was calling as they reached the building. Flames were reaching up above the roof, and the smoke stung her eyes as she tried to see. They ran around to the laneway that led to the gate, and there they were. Faces blackened, Eadie clutching Bucket in her arms, looking like she might faint.

Michael put his arm around her, leading her over to the verge and sitting her down. He looked back at The Grand, as if preparing to go back inside, but Mo grabbed him.

'You can't,' he said, his eyes red and streaming. 'We tried to get upstairs but it was too fierce.'

Belle sank down on the ground beside Eadie, shocked and silent. 'How . . . how did it happen?' she asked.

The pair exchanged a glance. 'I'm sorry, Missus,' Mo said, and a tear ran down his blackened cheek. 'I was cooking Eadie some grub. Got a nice piece of bacon and an egg, and some bread. Fried bread, she loves that. The fat caught fire. The flames went up the wall and then they were in the ceiling, and it was so fast . . .' He swallowed, rubbing his hands over his face.

'I'm so sorry,' Eadie was holding her hand. 'Oh, Belle, I'm so sorry.'

Belle managed to nod her head. She tried to get to her feet but Michael reached out to help her and they stood, his arm around her, and watched while The Grand burned.

'Everything's gone,' Michael murmured.

Of course, she thought, this was more his home than hers. 'But you're here. And me,' she said. 'That's all that matters, isn't it?'

He turned his head and the bleakness left his face. He bent to kiss her on the lips, and it felt like a promise. 'Yes,' he said, 'you and me, that's all that matters.'

CHAPTER 40

SOPHIE

Sweet Wattle Creek, 1986

I HAD ALMOST REACHED the pepper tree now. I looked back, my heart pounding hard in my chest, and I saw that it had worked. Walter was following me. Dillon was safe. But my relief was short-lived because by sacrificing myself I knew I was on my own. Ahead of me were the shadows of the creek, and Walter was already gaining.

I'd been jogging for a reason. Keeping strong. Even in the dress that clung to me too tightly and impeded my stride, I was faster than Walter. He'd never been that big on physical exercise, unless you counted assaulting his wife.

I told myself I could beat him at this, I could get away, I could.

I was in the trees now, the foliage clinging to my clothing and scratching my legs. My stock-inged feet were already bruised. But the creek must be close and perhaps I could hide down there, and . . . That was when the ground sud-denly gave away. I lost my footing. For a moment I thought I'd saved myself, but then I was rolling. I didn't feel the scrapes and knocks of stones and undergrowth. Down the crumbling bank, down into the creek.

It seemed to take ages for me to come to a stop, and then ages for my head to stop spinning. I lay there on my side, and there was solid mud beneath me, dried out over the summer. I just wanted to stay here and catch my breath, assess the damage. I wanted to stay there and I thought: he won't find me. I'm safe here.

But I wasn't. I could already hear him above me, up on the bank I'd just fallen down. Something else I could hear, but further away. The voices of my rescuers.

That gave me hope. They were coming and all I had to do was stay alive until they reached me.

I scrambled to my feet. My legs felt wobbly, and I knew that my knee wasn't working properly. I'd hurt it when I fell and it was only now that the pain was kicking in. I reached down, supporting myself with one hand, and there was a rock there, just large enough to fit into my palm. So I picked it up.

The skin on my legs was stinging where my stockings had torn and I'd been cut and grazed. Christy's beautiful dress was muddied and ripped where it had caught on some branches, and that upset me, despite my precarious position. And then I thought how silly it was to be worrying about a dress when in a heartbeat I could be dead.

I crouched, the rock in my hand, and I tried to listen, tried to hear above the bumping of my heart and the harsh sound of my own breathing. I tried to hold my breath but my head went fuzzy and I had to take a great gulp. It sounded so loud.

'Sophie!' Someone was calling. 'Sophie!' They were closer now, but still too far away.

Walter was here with me. I knew it, sensed it. It was very dark, here in the creek, with the trees leaning over me and the banks rising to blot out any light. But he was here and my skin prickled in awareness.

But I was going to fight him. I wasn't going to go down without hurting him as he had hurt me and Dillon. So I stood, trying to quieten my breathing, listening and waiting.

'Sophie.' His voice was like a whisper on the wind. 'It doesn't matter what you call yourself now. We don't need names, you and I. You're mine . . .'

He was behind me. I turned, slowly, trying not to sob. My knee wouldn't hold me up properly, and I was suffering from shock. And yet I turned to face him.

The voices weren't close anymore, they seemed to have drifted off further down the creek, away from me. We were here alone, he and I, and I knew if I was going to get out of this alive then it was up to me.

'Did you really think I'd let you go?'

His voice had moved around to be behind me again. This time I turned jerkily and my knee hurt so much that I groaned and fell to my knees. And there he was, standing in front of me. A shadow in the darkness.

'You're mine,' he said. 'That was the deal. To have and to hold, till death us do part.'

The strange thing was he believed it. I knew he did. I was his and that was all there was to it. He began to walk forwards and it occurred to me that my being on my knees was actually a good thing. He saw me as no threat. I'd given up and he could do what he liked with me.

Walter had always said when he killed me then it'd be with his bare hands. No blade or gun for him. He'd do it flesh to flesh, and feel my life leave me as he squeezed my throat tighter and tighter.

But to strangle someone you have to get in close to them.

As he bent towards me, his fingers brushing my skin, I swung my arm up and hit him as hard as I could with the rock. I heard something crunch and I felt the jolt of connection right up my arm, and then I dropped the rock and began to scream.

My rescuers weren't as far away as I'd thought. I'd hardly begun to drag myself up the bank on the other side of the creek when hands were reaching for me, pulling me over the brink, and torch lights were shining.

I remember turning my head just as I came up over the edge. The torch beams were illuminating the creek bed and I could see Walter. He was lying on the ground on his back, his arms thrown up, and his face was clearly visible. And there was blood. Lots and lots of blood.

I put my head down on the dusty earth and I thought: he must be dead, I've killed him. And I felt a strange sense of elation and sickness. Because if Walter was dead then all my troubles were over.

And if Walter was dead, maybe they'd just begun.

Someone had scrambled down to him and now they shouted up, 'He's alive!'

That was a bad moment.

And then Ian was there, and he had his face against my hair, and he was saying, 'Ah, Sophie, oh, God, Sophie,' in a voice that sounded choked and very unlike him.

They had a stretcher for me because I couldn't walk. There seemed to be an awful lot of policemen, as if they'd known all along Walter was here. And of course they had.

Later, when I'd been to the hospital and they'd strapped up my knee and treated my cuts and bruises, they sat me down in the police station and told me. They'd been setting a trap, only they hadn't wanted to tell me. They thought I'd give myself away in typical girly fashion.

That made me angry. And then they told me that Walter was in hospital and it didn't look like he'd regain consciousness, or if he did then he wouldn't be able to do much more than lie there.

So perhaps there was a God after all.

★★★

My house looked unfamiliar, and then wonderfully ordinary. This was where I belonged, this was my home. I lifted my head and the air felt cooler—while I'd been going through all the questions and signing statements, there'd been a change in the weather. I stood and let it dry my tears.

'Mum,' Dillon said, sounding as if he was crying. 'It's over.'

I didn't want to disillusion him. Perhaps it was, perhaps it wasn't, but whatever happened from now on we had won. Walter was finished. I told myself I had beaten him once and I could do it again.

Smithy came up and licked my hand and I laughed and manoeuvred my crutches so that I could bend down to hug him. Ian was behind me. 'I had a surprise for you, Sophie. You ran off before I could show you.'

'I think I've had enough surprises,' I told him.

'I promise you'll like this one.'

I sighed. I didn't really want to do anything more than lie on the couch with my two best men and close my eyes, but it seemed I wasn't going to be allowed to do that. And who knew, perhaps it would be something really nice. In fact, I looked up at Ian's worried face, if it was a surprise from him then it had to be.

'Okay, then.'

We were inside now, and Dillon switched on the lights. My head ached. Well, why not, everything else did.

Ian was looking for something in his jacket, and slipped out a photograph. He held it turned away from me, but I'd already seen it was one of those box-brownie type of photos, small and sepia.

'You remember the board I was doing with the airman on it, Michael Maxwell? Well, this turned up. Guess who gave it to me? Gwendolyn South.'

I tried to take it in. 'Stop teasing,' I said, my voice hoarse from all the screaming I'd done.

'Show her, Ian,' Dillon added, leaning back with

his arms folded and trying to be cool, but there was something in his face that told me this was a good surprise and he wanted me to enjoy it.

Ian handed me the photo.

It was a man and a woman, close together, smiling at the camera. Behind them was an aeroplane, and there was some sort of bird sitting on one of the wings, a cockatoo maybe. But I was looking at the couple. The man was the same one as I'd seen before, only he was older and he was wearing a mask over one side of his face. The woman was petite with pale-blonde hair and a lovely smile, and she was nestled against him as if he was . . . well, the love of her life.

'Belle and Michael,' Ian said quietly, almost reverently.

When I had stopped crying, and they'd sat me down and made me a hot tea with lots of sugar, Ian told me the rest.

'Gwen said they went up north, to the Gulf Country. Michael bought a plane and he started a company, flying out to all the stations there, taking them mail and supplies. He did okay, she said. She went up to see them in 1949, and that's when she took this.

'They were out together—sometimes Belle flew with Michael just for the hell of it—and there was a storm. Gwen said they never returned. She said they searched but never found them, and that they're still out there. She likes to think that they're still flying together. Somewhere.'

Ian lay down on top of the bedcovers with me. Dillon said he was cool with that, in the circumstances, as long as he could have Smithy with him. That made us all laugh. Ian gave him a little talk about being a serious chap who had serious feelings for me, and that he was going to be around a lot from now on. Dillon took it well, I thought.

'So are you moving up here with us?' he asked.

'I can work from here as well as anywhere else. There'll still be travelling to do. If that's all right with Sophie, of course. I know it might take some adjustment . . . some give and take.'

They both looked at me as if expecting some profound words of wisdom. 'Cool,' I said.

I slept okay, considering, although I kept thinking I was somewhere in an aeroplane, flying. There was a phone call sometime around seven am, and I reached across and picked it up.

It was Josh Davies.

'My Aunt Jo is awake,' he said, and he sounded pretty happy. 'Don't worry, she doesn't want Smithy back. She was happy to know he has a family who loves him. But I asked her about the wedding dress and she said that she found it in the pawnbroker's in Riverton. The guy had tried to sell it to the mayor for his daughter but she didn't want anything old. He wasn't very happy so he gave it to her for a discounted price. She recognised it, you see. My mother used to talk about that dress, so she'd have known it was Belle's, even if the pawnbroker hadn't told her. I think Aunt Jo liked Belle a lot, but there were reasons she didn't feel she could reach out to her. So she bought the dress. It was her way of being Belle's friend.'

'Make sense?' Ian asked, when I told him.

'Yes, I think so.' I sighed. 'Why do all the best love stories end tragically?'

He blinked at me. 'God, please don't say that. I have no intention of ending tragically, and I certainly don't want you to end at all, not for many, many years to come.'

I was laughing.

'Okay,' I said. 'Come here, then.'

And he did.

ACKNOWLEDGEMENTS

TROVE IS A wonderful online resource, and once again it gave me an insight into how people were thinking and behaving during the various time periods covered by *Sweet Wattle Creek*. There is so much information currently available about the First World War, but one of the books I read was *The Great Silence* by Juliet Nicholson. We seem to look at history as a series of events, each with a beginning and an end, but this book showed me how far the effects of that war spread and how those effects were still being felt many years later. I also reread author Kylie Tennant to get a feel for the Depression years, particularly *The Battlers* and her biography, *Kylie Tennant, A Life* by Jane Grant (National Library of Australia, 2006). The expression 'travellers' is one she uses for the unemployed people who took to the track during these difficult years, and is one I have also used.

When I decided to put a computer into the 1986 part of the book, I didn't realise how cutting edge the technology was at that time. Thank you to the State Library of Victoria, my editor Alex Nahlous and my nephew Matt Bennett for their help. Thanks also to my friend and fellow writer Christine Gardner, who researched a section I was planning to use in the book but later abandoned. Maybe next time!

My mother proved invaluable, recounting her life in country Victoria and her memories of those times, so I hope I have done justice to them. In particular she remembered, as a little girl, going to see Charles Kingsford Smith during one of his barnstorming visits. This book is for her.

Sometimes history has to be tweaked slightly to fit in with the fictional story, and if I have done this, or inadvertently made mistakes, then the fault is mine.

My thanks to Sue Brockhoff and Annabel Blay and all those at Harlequin—I appreciate your support more than I can say. Thank you to Alex Nahlous, my editor, who once again did such a thorough job. To my agent, Selwa Anthony, who supported and encouraged me, and assured me that I really do worry like that over every book I write and it always works out. My husband Robin kept things on an even keel, reminded me to be calm when panic set in and I honestly couldn't do this without him. Finally, throughout the writing of this book, my faithful black cat was by my side, as she has been for many, many books. She passed away in January, holding up her part of the bargain to stay until the book was done, and I miss her. I thought she deserved a spot in the story.

AUTHOR BIO

KAYE DOBBIE HAS been writing profes-
sionally ever since she won the Big River
story contest at the age of eighteen. Her career
has undergone many changes, including writing
Australian historical fiction under the name Lilly
Sommers, to romance written as Sara Bennett
and published in the US and Australia. Her books
have been translated into many languages. She is
currently writing under her 'proper' name, Kaye
Dobbie, and is published by Harlequin Mira in
Australia and Weltbild in Germany. Kaye lives on
the central Victorian goldfiends, where she cre-
ates her stories and spends time with her family
and four important cats.

She writes immersive dual timeline stories
about strong women and family secrets.

Visit her website and sign up to her Newsletter
for the latest.

www.kayedobbie.com
www.facebook.com/KayedobbieAuthor

SWEET WATTLE CREEK
Copyright © 2021 by Kaye Dobbie

2nd Edition
Published by Dobbie Enterprises
ebook 978-0-6489371-6-6
Print 978-0-6489371-7-3

Cover Design and Interior Format